UNDERTOW

Also by Lara Hays

Oceanswept: Book One of the Oceanswept Trilogy

"Intruder in the Brig" (*Oceanswept Chronicles*)

"Stowaway" (*Oceanswept Chronicles*)

UNDERTOW

LARA HAYS

Book Two of the Oceanswept Trilogy

Haze Publishing

ISBN-13: 978-0615934938
ISBN-10: 0615934935

Acknowledgements

To every single person who read this book—thank you!!! It's crazy to think that anyone else could care about this little world in my head, but you've proven that you do. You've made my dreams a reality and I love you for it.

The love and encouragement of a mother is the most powerful force on earth, transcending even death. Thank you, Mom.

Thank you, Jamie, for alpha reads, beta reads, proofreads, and giving legs to my dream. Who said long-distance relationships never work?

Ryan Brijs, I hope you're keeping a tab because I owe you so much.

A sincere thanks to Amber Bare, Jeromy Caballero, Meagan Spaulding, Ashley Stoker, and Tisa Woolf.

Julie, it means a lot to me that you asked to read this in its half-formed state, didn't judge, found the diamond in the rough, and cheered me on.

Melanie Lindsay, you were the first fan I didn't personally know to contact me. Thank you for your support. It's been fun building a friendship with you and I'll always consider you the queen of my fan club.

Justin, you've done so much for your crazy wife—from giving up television to buying dozens of reams of paper in the middle of the night. This book wouldn't exist without you and my heart wouldn't be happy without you. I love you.

----For my mom.

PROLOGUE

I WONDERED WHAT HAUNTED his dreams. What creations of sleep could possibly terrorize my pirate warrior? I sat on the edge of Nicholas's bed in the blackness of midnight, humming softly as my fingers slowly swirled through his hair. I could still feel the dampness of sweat on his scalp.

The sea was tumultuous tonight. The sails were reefed but I could still hear them snapping in the wind a deck above us. The air was heavy and damp and smelled strongly of brine.

Nicholas seemed as restless as the weather. He moaned and writhed.

"Shh," I whispered, stroking his cheek to relax his tense jaw.

He never talked about the nightmares. Even when I asked. Although, once I thought I heard him cry out, "Mama."

I traced the shape of his lips with my fingertips. He finally stilled, his breathing growing deep and steady. I bent over and kissed his cheek, then stood to leave.

His hand reached out and grabbed mine. "Stay with me?" he whispered, sliding to make room on the bed.

I took my place next to him. He buried his face in my hair. And we both slept.

CHAPTER ONE

I STOOD AT THE porthole in my cabin, hypnotized by the undulating waves of the ocean and the rocking motion of the boat. The Caribbean sun burned relentlessly, turning the waves into reflective mirrors. Down in my cabin, there was no breeze to break up the heat. The smell of the ship was strong on days like this—the smell of baking wood and a whiff of mildew. I had never thought much about the smell of wood before, but Nicholas did. He loved wood and whenever his hands touched a plank or a rail, it was with reverence. He talked about the way wood smelled, the way it spoke in creaks, the way it cried sap when it was fresh. I absentmindedly placed my palm on the bulkhead and let my fingers press against the smooth, unyielding wood, willing it to speak to me the way it spoke to him.

A soft rap sounded at my door. "Tessa?"

There were only the two of us on the ship. I smiled over my shoulder, inviting him in.

"There is a ship approaching us."

"Pirates?" I asked, unable to mask the fear in my voice.

Nicholas smiled broadly, his hands slung casually on his hips. "A ship from the British Royal Navy."

My eyes grew wide. "Oh no. Do they think *we're* pirates?"

Nicholas laughed. "I think your father has sailed out to meet you."

"Sailed out to meet me? How? Why?"

He looked at me shyly. "I sent a letter."

Back in Curaçao, when we heard rumors that my father had survived the hurricane that I thought had killed him, Nicholas encouraged me to write a letter and send it ahead of us since we had to wait a couple of weeks for my broken leg to get stronger. I refused to write it, too scared to hope my father was actually alive.

Nicholas looked only slightly contrite at his small act of defiance. "You did?" I eagerly looked out the porthole but saw only the familiar view of endless sea and sky.

"Portside," Nicholas clarified.

I grabbed my cane and took a few shuffling steps with my splinted leg—a souvenir from my last encounter with pirates. Nicholas scooped me into his arms and carried me out to the wide corridor—more of a foyer that spanned the width of the ship—and gently deposited me in front of a porthole that looked out over the other side of the ocean.

A giant, tri-masted ship flying Britain's colors crested on the waves about a half a league away.

Nicholas looked at me anxiously. "Are you excited? It will be no time at all until you see your father again."

I smiled uneasily, still staring at the ship on the horizon.

I felt Nicholas behind me, his arms circling my waist.

"You're nervous," he stated.

"I'm not nervous."

"What is it?"

His lips found a soft spot on the side of my neck.

"This happened so fast," I said truthfully.

A moment later, Nicholas prodded me again. "What is it really?" He turned me towards him, breaking the spell the window had on me.

Nicholas's striking looks still took my breath away. Vibrant grey eyes fringed with black lashes; full lips; tawny skin; thick, dark hair that fell in waves around a chiseled face; a strong chin with a dusting of dark stubble. Everything about him was rugged and untamed. I could hardly believe he found me as irresistible as I found him.

His eyes blazed with concern—he wasn't used to me being unsettled. "Everything has worked out perfectly. Your father is alive. He has come to welcome you home. He can grant me a pardon. I will no longer be a fugitive. Our life together can begin at last. You should be ecstatic."

"I know," I mumbled. I *should* have been ecstatic, but I was far from it. I was eager to be reunited with my father. For the past three months we had both thought the other dead—him, the victim of the hurricane that sank our ship during the crossing from England, and me, claimed and murdered by pirates.

A stray hair fell over my face and tickled my nose—a constant occurrence with my new chin-length style. Still watching me with apprehension, Nicholas brushed the lock behind my ear. Even that little action stoked a horde of unsettling questions.

How would I answer my father when he asked what happened to my hair? Would I tell him that it had been sawed off, handful by handful, by a revenge-crazed pirate captain? When he asked what had happened to me over the past three months, would I tell him that I had been tried and found guilty of witchcraft and murder, ignited a mutiny and barely escaped with my life, then worked as a scullery maid in a bordello? And how, exactly, would I explain the renounced pirate officer who had his arms around me?

I caught Nicholas's hand and pulled it to my face, kissing his palm. "I have become accustomed to my freedom here on the...*Freedom*," I smiled knowing we had named Nicholas's ketch well. "I am not sure how I will adjust back into a world of corsets and crumpets and chaperones."

I took Nicholas's face in my hands and kissed him on his lips. "I will have to learn to do without certain things."

Nicholas let out a full-bodied chortle. "I have certainly corrupted you!"

I blushed but didn't turn my gaze away from his. "Everything is going to change."

"Some things will change," Nicholas conceded softly. "But not everything. Not the way I feel about you."

"I know that."

"Are you afraid of what your father will think?"

"No," I answered quickly. Too quickly. I paused and gathered my thoughts. "The girl I was in England…the girl I became over the past few months…they seem like two different people. Today I have to reconcile them."

Nicholas lifted my chin and pecked me on the nose. "We've been renegades long enough, luv. It's time we let society civilize us a little."

I nodded nervously. "I suppose so."

"There is only one thing I need to do," he said.

I cocked my head. "And what would that be?"

He lifted my chin with his fingertips and, with a crooked smile, ran the tip of his nose along mine. I closed my eyes and tilted my face to his and he pressed his lips to mine. A familiar excitement blossomed in my stomach. I placed my hands on his arms to steady myself, feeling the swell of his biceps under his thin shirt. He cupped the back of my head with a hand and pulled me closer, his kiss growing from tender to fierce in an instant. I met his passion, pressing myself into him. He kissed me again and again, his lips urgent and hungry. I was overwhelmed, lost to an undertow I could not fight.

"Kisses like this will be in short supply for a while." Nicholas gave me a flirtatious smile and kissed the tip of my nose, but the truth of his statement hung heavy between us.

"Let's get our fill, then," I whispered, weaving my fingers into the hair at the nape of his neck and pulling him closer for another kiss.

An earsplitting roar tore through the stillness.

Nicholas stood alert, his eyes sharp as they swept around

the room. "Cannon fire," he stated matter-of-factly. He sprang up the ladder to the main deck. I cursed my broken leg, wishing I could follow.

Through the porthole I saw that the British ship was on us. They had made excellent time. I took up my cane and hobbled to the base of the ladder.

"Nicholas?" I called. "Is everything all right?"

The staccato sound of boots was my only answer. Nicholas was barefoot. Someone else had boarded the ship.

"Hello?" I called. No one answered. "Nicholas? What's happening?" I paused and listened. I heard voices, but could not decipher what they said. More footfalls. "Nicholas?" Still no answer. Fear pooled in my stomach. "Nick!" I called.

Something was wrong.

In a panic, I tried to pull myself up the ladder.

"Down there!" an unfamiliar voice sounded from above. After a scuffle of footsteps, two strange faces looked down at me from the main deck. Startled, I fell off the ladder, my splint catching on the rungs, and landed with a violent thump.

"Are you Miss Monroe?" one asked.

I nodded.

The men jumped down the hatch and crowded over me, peppering me with questions.

"Are you all right?"

"Are there any others?"

"What is the matter with your leg?"

"Are you hurt?"

I closed my eyes and threw up my hands, gesturing for the men to stop their ranting. They quieted immediately.

"Where is my father? Is he here?"

The older of the two sailors stepped forward and helped me to my feet. His face was pocked and lined. He wore a white wig that hid his natural hair color but his eyebrows were flaming orange. "Madam, I am Commander Ephraim Bidlack. This is Lieutenant Johnson." He jerked his head to the dark-haired sailor next to him. "Your father is not here. He is breaking through a pirate siege at Nevis. In fact, he knows nothing of your whereabouts."

"He did not issue the order to find me?"

Commander Bidlack continued his explanation. "When your captor's letter arrived, the admiral was gone. I read it in his stead and ordered instant pursuit. Your father would not have wanted us to waste a day."

My captor?

"Lieutenant? Are there any others?" a voice from the main deck called.

Johnson climbed partway up the ladder so he could talk to someone on the main deck. "No, sir. Just Miss Monroe."

"Is she well?"

"It appears she has an injured leg, but she is stable."

"Can she be moved?"

The man named Johnson peered down at me. "It would be difficult for her to board the other ship."

"Very good," the voice from upstairs said. "We have the pirate in custody and we will take him to the other vessel instead."

I looked frantically at the gentlemen with me. "What does he mean by that? He has the pirate in custody?"

"Don't worry," Johnson comforted, stepping off the ladder. "You are safe now."

"I was safe ten minutes ago," I insisted, my frustration finally exploding. "I demand you tell me what has been done to my escort."

The men exchanged a surprised look.

Commander Bidlack coolly said, "We understand him to be a pirate. He has been arrested."

"Release him! He is not a pirate, he is my rescuer."

Johnson knitted his brows together in confusion. "We received a threatening letter."

"You received no such thing!"

"Do you have the letter, sir?" Johnson asked Bidlack.

Commander Bidlack nodded and retrieved a folded piece of

parchment from his coat. I recognized Nicholas's slanted writing—I'd seen it enough in the log books. I snatched the letter out of Bidlack's knotty fingers.

Dear Sir,

By way of introduction, I am a humble sailor who had the good fortune of meeting your daughter, a certain Miss Tessa Monroe, under circumstances of duress. I write to inform you that she is well. She is presently in my custody in Willemstad, Curaçao, where she is recovering from an injury. As soon as her strength returns, I shall take her aboard my fishing ketch and sail to Basseterre, St. Kitts, to reunite the two of you and discuss further arrangements. I hope this news finds you well. I anxiously await our meeting.

Your Obliged,
N. Holladay

"This letter is not threatening," I hotly chided.

Bidlack pounded the letter with a finger. "This is practically a ransom note."

I quickly reread the letter, then looked back to Bidlack, confused.

Bidlack huffed and scowled.

"The man we apprehended upstairs," Johnson began, "is he not Nicholas Holladay?"

"Yes," I answered tentatively.

"And is he not the same man who is a pirate known by the name Marks?"

I groaned. "He answers to the name Nicholas Holladay. He has acted as my protector for the past twelve weeks and does not deserve to be treated as a criminal."

"Our sources were quite clear. He is the quartermaster of the pirate vessel *Banshee*," snapped Bidlack.

"He is the *former* quartermaster of the *Banshee*. He has

renounced his *former* profession and is, in fact, wanted by that pirate crew for desertion."

"His letter professes custody over you," Johnson said, reading over my shoulder and pointing out the words. "The mention of your injury. Duress. Your return in exchange for further arrangements."

"You've made a lot of assumptions." I quickly folded the letter and returned it to Bidlack. "I am indebted to Mr. Holladay—a man who rescued me *from* pirates and nursed my injuries. He has brought me to St. Kitts at great personal sacrifice. *My father* is indebted to him."

Johnson softened, his warm brown eyes mystified. "All this can be sorted out. For now, he's already aboard the other ship. You'll see him back in St. Kitts."

I huffed dramatically and prayed for a swift wind.

CHAPTER TWO

I ENDURED THREE DAYS with my new shipmates. They worked efficiently and refused my help, so I had nothing to do but sit idly and distract myself with reading from the few books on board. The royal frigate kept speed with us. I watched the ship constantly, but I never saw so much as a glimpse of Nicholas. He was most likely locked in the brig. I hoped that was the extent of his misfortune.

On the third day, a jade-colored triangle broke through the blue of the horizon: the island of St. Kitts—my new home.

The agile ketch made it into port first. As I was unloaded onto the docks, Bidlack and Johnson were looking to hire a carriage when they spotted someone they called "the baron" and arranged for me to ride with him.

I was deposited into a strange carriage like a burdensome bag of cargo. I stared out the window in self-pity, waiting for "the baron" to board his carriage.

This was not the homecoming I imagined. Going to a strange home in a strange carriage with no one to greet me. I finally caught sight of Nicholas. His hands were shackled but he showed no signs of abuse. He was too far away for me to call out to, and my splinted leg prevented me from running to him. I uneasily watched as he was locked in the back of a prison transport.

My escort entered the carriage and took the seat next to me. "Good day, *signorina*," he said with a tip of his hat. His accent was undeniably Italian.

As the carriage began its bumpy journey down the cobblestone streets of Basseterre, the capital of St. Kitts, I stealthily eyed the ebony-haired stranger sitting next to me. He was a young man, perhaps a year or two older than Nicholas, and everything about him was slim. A slim face with a slim, arching nose. Long, slim legs. Gracefully gloved hands with slim fingers. And slim lips that curved into a polite smile. He was fashionably outfitted. Johnson and Bidlack had called him *the baron*. I now knew that it was not a sort of nickname but a bona fide designation of this man's social status.

I was acutely aware of how disastrous I looked: short, boyish hair in complete disarray; rumpled clothing inappropriate for anything but manual labor, and a massive splint on my leg.

After a moment in awkward silence, the baron asked, "I understand I am taking you to the Monroe household?"

I nodded without looking at him.

"I have been working closely with Admiral Monroe. He came here several months ago and has shown great valor in reinforcing the settlement from greedy eyes. I consider him a valuable friend and I am bound to protect his interests. What is the nature of your business with him?"

I issued a soft chuckle, but quickly stifled it. Being so carefree with Nicholas had made me forget my manners.

The man looked at me quizzically.

"I'm sorry, sir," I apologized. "I meant no offense. I was simply amused by the fact that you were introducing me to my own father."

The Italian man's jaw dropped. "But...you're...you can't...*anvédi che robba!*" The baron took a deep breath and stared at me, his eyes large with sincerity. "Is it true? You are the Admiral's lost daughter?"

"Yes," I confirmed, stifling a laugh. "So it is true that he is alive, then? Is he in good health?"

The baron grinned broadly, reveling in the humor of such a situation. "*Sì signorina*, he is alive and well. As well as a father mourning his only child can be."

I nodded knowingly.

"Please forgive me," the baron said, "I have forgotten my manners. My name is Emilio De Luca."

"So pleased to meet you. I am Tessa Monroe."

Lord De Luca took my ungloved hand and breathed a kiss on the back of it. It was so long since I had been treated like a true lady, I had nearly forgotten how to respond. I felt my cheeks turn pink.

"The pleasure is all mine, Miss Monroe. Am I right to assume that your father is unaware of your arrival?"

"That is my understanding. I hear he is at sea."

Lord De Luca nodded in confirmation. "He has had a sort of bloodlust for pirates ever since he thought he lost you."

With his statement, Lord De Luca gestured out the window. I looked out of it and gasped. Seven corpses dangled from a monstrous banyan tree, nooses tied around their necks. I shut my eyes against the gruesome sight but could not erase the images of the bodies swaying in the Caribbean breeze, their clothing more intact than their skin.

"Seven of the Caribbean's most notorious pirates," Lord De Luca explained, a timbre of pride in his voice.

I was suddenly more afraid for Nicholas than I had ever been. I clutched Lord De Luca's wrist. "Do not take me home. I must go to the jail."

He idly took note of my hand gripping his arm. "The jail? Why?"

I released my hold on the baron's arm. I chided myself for being too familiar yet again. Nicholas truly had corrupted me.

I juggled my thoughts quickly, deciding how best to explain

my interest in Nicholas. "I must investigate the well-being of the man who rescued me. He was arrested by some naval officers and he must not have a pirate's fate."

"I am sure there is no reason to fret. He is no pirate, so he will not have a pirate's fate."

I bit my lip.

Lord De Luca's eyes widened.

I hurried to explain. "After the hurricane, I was...rescued...by a pirate ship. An officer named Mr. Holladay deserted his crew and helped me escape. Three weeks ago, he sent word to my father that I was alive and en route to St. Kitts. His commander—a Mr. Bidlack—intercepted the letter and arrested Mr. Holladay on charges of piracy."

"A pirate officer?"

I nodded.

Lord De Luca glanced at the grisly banyan tree. "He faces a pirate's fate indeed."

"Please," I begged. "He has renounced it all. He mutinied against his captain and was nearly killed by his crew. If it wasn't for his protection...well, I cannot even imagine how horrible my fate would have been. I cannot abide the thought of any harm coming to him."

With a decisive nod, Lord De Luca thumped the roof of the carriage with a silver-topped cane and we rattled to a stop. Stepping out of the carriage, Lord De Luca instructed the driver to take us to the fortress immediately.

"Thank you, sir. Your understanding means the world to me. It might save Mr. Holladay's life."

"What can I say? I am Italian—I would do anything for a pretty face."

I awkwardly smoothed my dress. "The sailors I was with at the pier...they called you a baron?"

"A title that means nothing living under the British flag," answered Lord De Luca humbly.

"And what brought you here? Did you not enjoy life in Italy as a baron?"

"You do not hold back, do you?"

My cheeks grew hot. "I apologize. I've been isolated from society for months. I fear I have forgotten my manners."

The glint in his black eyes put me at ease. "I quite like it. Too many people hide behind pretense. Please, promise never to hold back."

I smiled shyly. "I promise."

"Sugarcane," he said simply.

It took me a moment to understand his odd response. "You left your courts to come to the new world and…farm?"

Lord De Luca laughed loudly. "*Sì*. I own a plantation. It's actually one of the largest in the Leeward Islands. Your father is my nearest neighbor."

The carriage slowed. I peered out the window and saw a grey-stoned fort with an ominous gothic gateway towering ahead.

"Welcome to Fort Charles," Lord De Luca said dryly.

The carriage stopped. I opened my door and shifted my weight, carefully planning my exit with my damaged leg.

"Whoa, whoa, whoa, *signorina*!" he exclaimed in his spirited Italian accent. "Wait! I shall help you."

Lord De Luca exited the carriage and rushed around to help me down, his hands gripping my waist to steady me. He eased me onto the rough flagstones.

"Wait here. I will have your friend brought to you. That way you will not have to walk so much."

"Lord De Luca, I am quite capable—"

"Of course you are! Any girl that survives pirates with only a broken leg is capable of anything! However, you will find your friend faster this way, I promise."

He was right, of course. And I was willing to go along with any plan that would bring me to Nicholas sooner. "Yes, my lord," I agreed.

Lord De Luca spoke quietly with the guard. I took the time to appreciate my new surroundings. The fortress strategically overlooked the harbor below, lapis-colored water shimmering in the sunlight. Small hills swelled in the landscape, tropical grasses and tangled jungles coloring them a verdant shade of green. Dusty roads, small towns, and a patchwork of plantations pocked the countryside. However foreign this island was, it was my home now.

I turned my attention back to the baron's conversation. His voice was growing louder, more insistent. "She is Admiral Monroe's daughter and she has the right to an audience with the prisoner."

The guard nodded, "I do not argue that. Their rendezvous can take place within the dungeon."

Lord De Luca tilted his head towards me. "You would ask an injured woman to descend those steps?"

The guard looked at me suspiciously.

Lord De Luca cleared his throat. "Summon the warden."

The guard was instantly contrite. "Please, sir. Is it necessary?"

"I asked you to call for the warden."

The guard backed up a step and cast his eyes downward, his cheeks were reddening. "Yes, m'lord."

The warden appeared a few minutes later and acquiesced to bringing Nicholas to us, so long as there was more security. Four more guards came up the stairs, bayonets ready.

Lord De Luca returned to my side. "Your friend will be escorted to you for a few moments. Shall we?" He offered me his arm. I graciously accepted and leaned heavily on the baron as we entered the fort. Roughly hewn volcanic walls rose around me. Cannons were placed at strategic intervals. Stairs rose and sank around the perimeter of the fort, leading up to parapets and down to unknown dungeons.

Two figures crested from a subterranean staircase—Nicholas, with his hands in iron cuffs, and another armed guard.

The guard tipped his head at me, then looked at Nicholas, "Your visitor."

I stared at Nicholas, desperately wishing we were alone. After a halfhearted inner struggle, I forsook propriety and threw my arms around him. He leaned into my embrace—the most he could do with his hands bound.

"Oh, Nicholas," I breathed into his ear, "this is all a terrible mistake. Have they mistreated you?"

"I'm fine. Are you safe?"

I nodded, looking up into his face. His whiskers had grown in and his eyes were bloodshot.

He inclined his head to Lord De Luca. "Who is your escort?"

I looked at the baron who had remained several paces behind me. "His name is Lord Emilio De Luca. He is a neighbor and friend to my father. He was flagged down at the docks to take me home. I asked him to bring me here instead and he did."

Nicholas nodded at the baron, a gesture of gratitude.

"They arrested you because they thought you were my kidnapper. My father is out to sea. As soon as he returns, he'll right everything and you'll be free again."

He smiled at me, but it was a smile of resignation.

"What?" I asked.

"I hope you are right."

"You know something. What aren't you telling me?" I pressed.

That hopeless smile remained on his lips.

"Now is not the time to start keeping things from me."

He squinted into the sun. "I am to be hanged."

My hand flew to my mouth. "No," I whispered. The sight of the pirates dangling from the branches of the banyan trees filled my mind. The air went out of my lungs and my head felt light. After all Nicholas had done for me, I had brought him to this fate. I thought he'd died once before and it nearly killed me. I could not stand to lose him again. I was nauseous. Trembling. This was my fault. Was this the price of returning to my father? "No, they can't do it."

"Well, they intend to."

"When?" I was unable to keep a tremble out of my voice.

"Monday, at dawn. I am sure they would do it sooner if they could, but tomorrow is the Sabbath. I guess it's not fittin' to execute someone on God's day," he joked.

I searched his face as if it would hold all the answers. "How do we stop it?"

Nicholas smirked, his attitude as cocky and inappropriate as ever. "I'll infiltrate the guards and stage a mutiny."

I didn't laugh.

"Tessa, I'll find a way. Break out somehow."

"You can't. If you break out, you'll be wanted."

Nicholas's brow furrowed, "As the authorities on this island have already issued me a death sentence, I am not sure why that would be a problem."

"No. I meant that my father—when he returns—can grant you a pardon. But if you've stirred up too much trouble, then his hands will be tied."

"And when, exactly, is your father going to grant me this pardon?"

I wrung my fingers helplessly. "As soon as he returns. Which should be any day now. The commander said he had only gone to St. Nevis."

"Godspeed his return," said Nicholas wryly.

I set my chin and spoke with all the conviction I had. "He'll come back in time, I know it. Providence did not bring us through so many trials to land on these shores for this. You will not hang." I wish I felt as confident as I sounded.

The guard took a step towards us. "Back to your cell." My eyes filled with tears. I wanted to latch onto Nicholas and never let go. How could I watch him walk away, knowing that the next time I might see him he could be swaying from a banyan tree? I watched dumbly as the guard led Nicholas away down into the dungeons. I hated that I couldn't say goodbye or offer a word of cheer, but I didn't trust my voice. I mouthed a silent prayer that my father would return before time ran out.

CHAPTER THREE

LORD DE LUCA LED me back to the carriage. "Is all well?"

I blinked back my tears and forced a smile. "My father will sort all this out. I pray he returns soon."

After helping me into my seat, he spoke briefly to the driver and joined me on the other side of the carriage. "We'll take a small tour of Basseterre before taking you to your home."

I nodded politely, secretly wishing to be left alone with my thoughts.

I only half paid attention as the carriage rattled along the cobblestone roadways flanked with swaying, emerald foliage. Lord De Luca identified points of interest—Brimstone Hill Fortress just up the hillside from Fort Charles, Wingfield Estate with its huge saman tree, St. George's church. As I looked at the impressive stone church, I found it oddly reassuring to see bastions of European culture in the wild, foreign lands of the West Indies. As we drove down Old Road, Lord De Luca pointed out the original settlements of the island. The Warner Estate—home of the first governor of St. Kitts—was treated as the capital of the island, though Basseterre had eclipsed it in size and influence. As we rattled past an elegant yellow mansion, Lord De Luca informed me it was the home of the current governor, Thaddeus Abner.

When the carriage turned in to a narrow driveway, my nose was tickled with a delightful floral scent. I craned my neck to see out the window and my mouth popped open at the site before me. The winding road before us was edged with small knobby trees, their branches heavy with clumps of flowers—each five-petaled flower sported a shock of yellow in the center that faded to pure white. Underneath the trees, stunning tropical blooms in shades of crimson, chartreuse, and fuchsia put on a spectacular show.

Lord De Luca reached out the window and snapped a small bunch of the white flowers with the yellow centers from a low-hanging tree branch. He handed it to me. "Frangipani."

I held the bouquet to my nose and inhaled deeply.

He scooted closer to me and pointed out my window. "Those are lantana. And there is cockscomb. See those hedges with the pink flowers?"

I nodded excitedly.

"Ixora."

"Ixora?"

"Sì. Also known as West Indian jasmine. They are my favorite. You suck nectar from the flowers. It's very sweet."

The carriage turned to the left. He craned his neck out his window.

"Ah, yes. Come, Miss Monroe. Look here."

I looked out his window to see more beautiful flowers. "The gardener must take great pride in his work."

"Yes, indeed, but that is not what I want you to see. Here—come closer." His arm hooked around my waist and pulled me close to him.

"There!" He pointed out the window.

I looked but was still unsure as to what I was meant to see.

With his arm still around me, the baron pulled me until I was leaning far over his lap. "There. Through the trees."

I looked, feeling improper and silly all at once. But those thoughts vanished as soon as I caught a glimpse of the two fountains flanking a snow-white mansion.

"It's called Amerscott House."

The white mansion bobbed in and out of my vision. I leaned precariously over my companion, my mouth agape, staring at the home before me. Set atop a foundation of black stonework were three glorious stories. Curving iron pillars and archways—all painted white—daintily wove around the house like intricate lace, creating countless balconies. Flowering trees in large pots decorated each balcony, vibrant blossoms cascading down the snow-white façade of the mansion. Large windows and vast French doors made it impossible to tell where gardens ended and the living quarters began. Despite all of London's glories, I had never seen such a beautiful home.

"Is this your estate?" I asked, still entranced by the sight of it.

"Actually, it is yours."

The carriage jostled to a stop and, as before, Lord De Luca lifted me from my seat. Leaning on his strong arm, we passed by the fountains and up a row of wide steps. He took the liberty of rapping the iron knocker three times. And then we waited.

Lord De Luca said, "It must feel strange to knock at the door of your own home."

"Nothing about this place feels like home."

A shuffling sounded on the other side of the door. I quickly smoothed my skirt and squared my shoulders.

A frail old man with white hair as wispy as spider webs answered the door. He saw me first, a look of confusion crossing his face, then recognized Lord De Luca.

"Good morning," the steward bowed deeply.

"Good morning, Mr. Dean," the baron replied. "Might we come in?"

"Admiral Monroe is at sea. No one is home." He looked bewildered but stepped aside.

Lord De Luca let himself in. Uncertain, I followed him into the foyer and tried to keep my jaw from dropping open as I admired the blue-veined marble floors, carved wooden walls, and crystal chandeliers.

"It is to you that I must speak," Lord De Luca addressed the steward. "You see this young woman?"

The steward adjusted a pair of small round spectacles on his nose while looking at me from head to toe. I fidgeted nervously. I looked like...well, I looked like a renegade stowaway who hadn't had a proper bath in weeks.

My escort continued, "Though presumed dead, this young woman is the admiral's daughter. She made port this morning."

Mr. Dean's eyes bulged. "Is it possible?" he exclaimed under his breath. He addressed a nearby footman. "Fetch Miss Maisley."

"Margaret Maisley?" I cried. "My nurse? She's alive?"

Mr. Dean's eyes shone with delight. "The fact you know her name tells me you are who the baron says. How I wish the admiral were here now."

"Miss Tessa?" I heard Miss Maisley's voice before I saw her ample figure trotting into the foyer. "Is it really you?" She clutched me to her breast. "My stars! It's like seein' a ghost!"

After a rather tearful embrace, Miss Maisley examined me better. "Nay, you're no ghost but you're practically a corpse! Your hair! What happened to your hair? Oh my! Your leg. When was the last time you had a hot supper? What have you done with yourself for the past three months? By my word, Miss Tessa, I've never seen a happier sight in my life!"

She smothered me with another hug.

"Lord Emilio, where did you find her?" Miss Maisley asked over my shoulder, refusing to let me go.

"On the docks like a crate of coffee. I was randomly asked to escort this woman to Amerscott since it was on my way. What a delight it was when I learned who she was."

Miss Maisley peppered my cheeks with kisses. "I thought you were dead!"

"I thought *you* were dead," I answered. "I thought my father was dead. I thought I was the only one. I have never been happier to be wrong. Did everyone survive then?"

Miss Maisley finally released me from her clutches. "The ocean took nearly as many as were spared."

"Lucia?" I asked, hoping that my personal maid might be tucked away somewhere in this imposing house.

Miss Maisley shook her head gravely.

The baron clicked his heels on the polished stone floor, subtly calling attention to himself. "If you'll excuse me, I have some urgent matters I must see to. Miss Monroe, it was more than a pleasure," he took my hand and lifted my fingers to his lips, "it was a true joy. You shall hear from me soon."

I bowed deeply. "Thank you, Lord De Luca, for the escort. And if it's not too much trouble, may I fetch my trunk from your carriage?"

"I had forgotten," he said. He snapped his fingers and his driver perked up. "Miss Monroe's trunk?"

The driver hopped down from his post and retrieved my small trunk. Mr. Dean took it from him.

"Do you not have more?" Lord De Luca asked, eyeing the single, small piece of luggage.

"No, my lord. My belongings are quite meager, as you can imagine."

For a brief moment, I saw his brows pinch together in concern. Just as quickly, he flashed a confident smile at me. "Very well. Good day."

I watched the black carriage drive away, surprised at the loneliness I suddenly felt.

Several more curious servants had gathered in the foyer. The attention was stifling. I looked at Miss Maisley with pleading eyes, hoping she'd sense my desperation and offer me some privacy.

All those years as my nurse did not fail. Miss Maisley smiled knowingly. "First things first. I will show you to your room."

* * * * *

Miss Maisley insisted on a hot meal before anything else. She let me eat in the bedroom away from the prying eyes of the rest of the staff.

The bedroom—*my* bedroom—was roomy. A canopy bed with an embroidered grey bedspread sat in the corner. There was a stately but empty oak wardrobe next to it. The other side of the room opened to a balcony with a view of the gardens. If I craned my neck, I could see the ocean in the distance.

After a quick exploration of my new room, I devoured the steamed potatoes and smoked fish that Miss Maisley had left with me. If only I knew how to cook like this I certainly I would not have lost so much weight aboard the *Freedom*. I vaguely wondered if Nicholas had lost weight because of my cooking. I hadn't noticed. Of course, he was used to hardtack and dried beef. It was a wonder he was as fit and strong as he was.

After eating, I asked for a bath. It was my first real bath since Curaçao. I kept my splinted leg propped on the edge of the tub while Miss Maisley lathered my hair and scrubbed my skin until it felt raw.

"Lord De Luca called while you were bathing," Mr. Dean informed me as Miss Maisley helped me limp back to my room.

My chest clenched in surprise. "He did? What did he want?"

"He asked that you be prepared for dinner this evening. He shall pick you up at seven o'clock. And he sent a few things for you."

We entered my room just then. A young woman was rummaging through a pile of clothes on the bed. She smiled warmly when she saw us enter.

"This is Margaret Quincy," Mr. Dean said, answering my unasked question. "She was on the baron's staff, but he thought your need for her was greater than his. And he sent the clothing too."

"Call me Meg, if you please. And I am pleased to meet you, Miss Monroe." The girl curtsied. She was about my age with honey-blonde hair knotted in a bun at her neck. She was quite pretty with wide hazel eyes, a petite nose, and an engaging smile. Her manners were spotty and her diction was rough. She had not been raised to serve a fine lady. But if the baron found no fault in her, how could I?

"The pleasure's mine," I replied tentatively.

She gestured to the clothing spread on the bed. "The baron said you had nothing. He sent for a few dresses. They're ready-made but we can alter them to fit you. If you pick, I can dress you."

Mr. Dean and Miss Maisley excused themselves. I was alone with my new maid. Why did this feel so foreign? Had the last three months erased my years of this standard of living? I wished fervently that I could refuse her assistance and simply take care of myself. But my injured leg—and the corsets of those fancy dresses—would not allow it.

I swallowed nervously and hobbled to the bed to assess my new wardrobe. At least a half dozen dresses were spread out —a variety of styles and colors.

Meg yanked my robe away before I knew what she was doing and coaxed me into a chemise. The silken fabric felt like butter next to my skin. A corset came next. I could only think one terrifying thought: Lord De Luca had purchased undergarments for me.

Meg directed my attention back to the dresses.

"I wish I knew more about the nature of this dinner," I muttered as my hand caressed the varied fabrics. I looked at Meg. "You must have some idea of how I should dress."

"You'll want something formal, I think." She gave me a sly smile.

I was beginning to like her. "Red or brown?" I asked her, holding up each dress in turn.

"The red is right romantic," Meg said whimsically.

"You think so?" I looked at the crimson gown with its cream accents. It was quite dramatic and I loved every intricate detail.

Meg nodded, her lips curling upwards.

"Do you think the baron intends for this dinner to be romantic?" I asked in shock.

"One can only hope!" she giggled.

I set the red dress aside. "Brown it is, then."

"Are you—" she stopped herself abruptly. "Pardon my manners, miss."

I raised my eyebrows, curious to know what she had been about to ask.

Meg shook her head slightly. "'Tis not my place. I apologize."

"To hell with social places," I said, sounding more like Nicholas than I thought possible. "Say what's on your mind. Please, Meg, your words have no less value than anyone else's."

Meg turned a shocking shade of pink. It was a delicious surprise.

She shrugged self-consciously. "I just wondered if you weren't attracted to the baron. Why wouldn't you want his intentions to be romantic? Every girl on the island would die for a formal dinner date with him."

I recalled Lord De Luca's bottomless eyes, his thick ebony hair, and sleek, strong profile. "He is an appealing man," I easily conceded, "but I am spoken for."

Meg kept her face impassive as she fastened my dress. She led me to a full-length mirror so I could see myself properly.

Perhaps this dress wasn't as romantic as the red one but it was more sumptuous. It was the color of coffee grounds, perfectly matching my eyes and making my alabaster skin look as pale as porcelain. The laced bodice hugged every curve of my torso, the bustle in the back erupting into a cascade of burnished silk that spilled to the floor. Smoked crystals were sewn into velvet trimming, each reflecting the candlelight like an ocean wave in the moonlight.

I pressed my lips into a thin line and fidgeted with my hair in disgust. It ruined the entire look.

"Here," Meg gestured to a chair. "Allow me, miss."

She rummaged through the drawers in the vanity and pulled out a brush and several hairpins. She set to work and within just a few moments, my boyishly chopped hair was pinned into small barrel curls on top of my head, though a few stray tendrils hung down by my eyes. She even managed to find a gilded comb to weave into my hair.

I admired her work. "Thank you, Meg. I have hated my hair since the moment it was cut. I finally feel myself again."

We chatted idly as Meg tidied up the vanity. Our conversation was easy, not too formal. Any reservation I had about this girl was gone. We were similar, with many common interests and desires. It was a change from my former maid Lucia, who was cold as a London rain and proper to a fault. As I laughed at one of Meg's stories, I knew we would be friends.

There was a rap on the door. Meg opened it to reveal Mr. Dean.

"Lord Emilio De Luca has arrived for Miss Monroe. He is waiting in the parlor."

I cast an uneasy look at Meg, who gave me a reassuring nod. "Please show me to the parlor, Mr. Dean."

CHAPTER FOUR

THE BARON WAS STANDING with his back to me when I entered the parlor off of the front foyer. It was an intimate room with a polished parquet floor covered in Oriental rugs. Two sofas faced each other, flanked by game tables and bookshelves. A fireplace hewn from black marble housed a crackling fire despite the heat of the day. Some things were too traditional to discard, no matter how impractical they may seem. The baron stood next to a harpsichord admiring a seascape painting on the wall. It was something I had painted back in England. A corner of it was discolored and the paint was cracking in some spots, yet it had survived the hurricane impressively well.

"Lord De Luca, Miss Monroe," Mr. Dean announced.

The baron turned at the sound of his name and his ebony eyes swooped over me. "*Signorina* Monroe," he smiled, quickly closing the distance between us. He kissed my gloved fingers. "*Sei bella.* A vision, truly."

I smiled self-consciously. "Thank you for the gifts. And for Meg. Your generosity is humbling."

"It was my pleasure. I trust you've had a pleasant evening?"

He still held my hand. I gently tugged it away from him. "Yes. Thank you."

"Good. I hope my invitation is not too forward. I loathed the idea of you dining alone."

"I have Miss Maisley," I waved my hand in the direction of the rest of the house. "And you sent your assistant. I would hardly be alone."

Lord De Luca reprimanded me with a click of his tongue. In his eyes, servants were not suitable company. Not long ago I would have shared that opinion.

"Ready for dinner, then?"

"Yes, sir."

"Very good."

I followed Lord De Luca out of the parlor. Miss Maisley was in the foyer and handed jackets to the two of us before donning one herself. A chaperone. I had completely forgotten. I felt my cheeks grow pink at the memory of midnight kisses with Nicholas under the stars.

"Are you all right, Miss Tessa? You look a little flushed."

I blinked rapidly. "I'm fine, Miss Maisley. Just an exciting day."

Lord De Luca's carriage was waiting in the drive. "It's a pleasant walk between Amerscott and Glencartha, my estate," he said as he settled in the carriage across from Miss Maisley and me, "but your leg prevents us from enjoying it. When you are fully recovered, I insist on personally showing you the grounds."

Miss Maisley nodded. "There's an enclosed garden on Lord Emilio's estate. But he has no qualms about any of our household visiting it. It's lovely."

"I'm looking forward to it."

"What happened to your leg?" Lord De Luca asked as the horses whisked us under a canopy of frangipani trees. It was a rude question and I expected my chaperone to say as much, but Miss Maisley stared at me with the same curious expression that the baron wore.

How should I explain? Would I start with how I had been kidnapped in Curaçao by the captain Nicholas had mutinied against? Should I include the part where Captain Black sawed off locks of my hair and left them around the city like breadcrumbs to lure Nicholas to his death? Or should I skip to their confrontation in a derelict church, then explain how their brawl had started a fire and caused the building to collapse on me?

I opted for oversimplification. "I happened to be in an old, rotted church when a beam gave way. It landed on top of me."

Lord De Luca's face clouded with concern. "You are lucky you were not injured worse."

"Indeed." I was lucky I hadn't burned to ash like Captain Black and his cohorts...although judging by the number of bodies, there was an unlikely chance that Captain Black had survived the fire. Nicholas insisted that too much evidence was lost in the fire and that there was no way Black made it out. But I had my doubts. He was the captain of a pirate vessel...he was more resourceful than your average man.

I looked out the window, detaching myself from idle conversation. My worry for Nicholas consumed me. My father must return over the weekend. He must. Or else Nicholas would hang.

The baron's dinner table was set with garlic-crusted lamb, roasted turnips in honey sauce, chestnut soup, spiced cabbage, and hot scones with fresh-churned butter. The food was delectable, but my appetite was less than generous. I absentmindedly pushed the food around my plate as Lord De Luca recounted stories of his youth in Italy and his first impressions of St. Kitts. The stories were meant to ease my transition to my new home, but I could hardly pay attention. Only once did Lord De Luca prompt me to speak of my seafaring adventures, but I waved away the topic, stating that my stories were better suited to be told over a deck of cards than at a mealtime. As distracted as I was, I simply did not have the mental capacity to sort my tales into what was appropriate dinner conversation and what was too dangerous to ever be shared.

As Lord De Luca bid me goodnight at the Amerscott House

doorstep, he bowed and kissed my hand and asked to replicate our dinner arrangements the next night.

"You are far too generous, my lord," I answered. "Please accept my apologies, but my voyage has been most exhausting. I think I will need a night or two to recover before any other social engagements."

I couldn't help but notice Miss Maisley's eyes widen with horror at my refusal.

The baron nodded courteously. "Your refusal forces me to attend a political engagement that will bore me immensely. But as you wish. I just hate the idea of you feeling abandoned in a new place."

"I assure you, I will let you know should I feel abandoned." My tone was more acerbic than I intended, but the baron laughed.

"I suppose I shouldn't worry about a girl who has endured so much already. Good evening, ladies." He tipped his hat and returned to his carriage.

"My, but he's persistent," I muttered as Miss Maisley unfastened my jacket.

"It's his best quality. Not much that man can't do. He was quite persistent with his company when your father first arrived."

"Perhaps he's cozying up to the family in order to influence Father," I said darkly.

Miss Maisley shot me a withering look. "Emilio De Luca would do no such thing. He came every night, invited or not, because your father was so devastated by losing you. He would not allow a widower who had lost his only child to find his way in a foreign land without a friend. Lord Emilio took many rough rebukes from your father in stride. I have never seen such integrity, and you should mind your manners concerning him."

Chastened, I uttered a hasty apology and excused myself to go to bed.

I leaned across the balustrade of my balcony, staring off into the shadows of the night. Miss Maisley was right. The baron had done things today that he didn't have to—from taking me all the way to Fort Charles to making sure I had an acceptable wardrobe—and I had bristled at his company the entire time. My guilt was so thick I could taste it in the back of my throat. I owed him my gratitude.

No more would I say whatever wafted into my mind. No more would I shirk off inconvenient acts of politeness. I was a lady and I vowed to act like it, especially where Lord De Luca was concerned. It was the least I could do for him. Or for my father.

CHAPTER FIVE

I HAD BEEN IN fits all morning. Meg, thinking she was doing me a favor, had closed the curtains in my bedroom to block the sun and allow me more sleep. I had slept past midmorning and felt that a good portion of my day was wasted. In less than twenty-four hours, Nicholas would hang unless my father stopped the execution. No one in the household seemed to have any updates from the harbor on ship sightings, so I quickly dressed and insisted on Meg accompanying me to the docks to inquire for myself.

Miss Maisley gave me a disapproving glance when I told her I was going to Christophe Harbor instead of church services. I tersely explained that it would be distasteful to announce my existence at church when my father still thought me dead. With a reluctant sigh, she called for the stable hand Clarence to ready a carriage.

When we arrived at the docks, I cowered at the foreign world of hardened sailors, greedy merchants, buskers, privateers, prostitutes, and thieves. Without even a moment of hesitation, Meg grabbed my hand and marched me to a cluster of naval officers.

"Hallo, good sirs," Meg bowed her head. "We were

wondering whether you had any news on the return of Admiral Monroe's ship?"

The seamen looked on in surprise. They weren't used to being addressed by servants. I nodded my approval at her question.

"No sightings yet, miss," a gangly ensign answered.

"You do expect him anytime, though, don't you?" I asked.

"Who wants to know?" another officer piped in.

"His staff," Meg said with squared shoulders.

The combative officer rolled his eyes and turned away to chat with one of his companions. The gangly ensign shrugged. "Our news isn't any newer than yours would be. Depending on winds, I would expect him back tomorrow or Tuesday. Wednesday at the latest."

"Is there any chance he could return today?"

The young man held his hand to his brow to shield the glare of the sun and squinted across the harbor. "We can see a ship at least five hours before it docks. And there's no sight of the *Majestic* as of yet. Maybe during the night," he quickly added after seeing my crestfallen look.

I stared at him expectantly, wishing he could offer me more, guarantee something solid.

He shifted uncomfortably under my fervent gaze. "Will that be all, miss?"

I nodded and turned away. I walked slowly back to the carriage, fighting against the constriction in my throat.

Meg tried to comfort me. "He'll be home before you know it, Miss Monroe. I know you must miss him something awful."

"It's not that," I began. "I mean, I do miss him terribly. But there's a legal matter I need his assistance with."

"A legal matter?" Meg quickly amended herself. "I'm sorry, miss, 'tis not my place to inquire."

I sighed. What did it matter? "The sailor who rescued me and escorted me home...he has some ties with piracy. He is to be hanged tomorrow."

Meg's eyes grew wide and she quickly looked away.

"But it's unfair," I quickly defended, "especially considering the danger he risked in seeing me safely home. I need to stop the execution. No matter the cost."

To her credit, Meg looked quite concerned, her brow deeply furrowed. "That's very brave of you. Shows that you have a just heart."

"I couldn't bear it if he died." It was as simple as that.

* * * * *

An hour later, I had eaten lunch and told Meg I was retiring for a nap. Instead of going to my room, I had gone to the stables to—as Nicholas would say—*procure* a carriage for an unauthorized journey. If only my leg weren't such a hindrance, I would be able to ride a horse, a much easier endeavor to do undercover. Instead, I told Clarence that Mr. Dean had requested an audience with him.

When I was alone in the stables, I tethered a chestnut mare to a small carriage, completely unsure if I was doing anything correctly, then climbed into the driver's seat and rode away. I kept looking over my shoulder, certain my departure down the long driveway had not gone unseen, but somehow I made my escape. I got lost a time or two as I neared the congestion of downtown Basseterre, but I eventually found myself standing before the guard at Fort Charles, asking for an audience with their prisoner.

I could not convince the guard to let Nicholas come to me like before. My only option was to go to his cell myself. With my sore and splinted leg, I hobbled down the stairs, doing my best to keep pace with the guard. I wrinkled my nose at the smell of the dank, rotting moss coating the stone-hewn walls of the dungeons, and I cringed whenever my skin accidentally brushed against it.

I smoothed my skirt and patted my hair. This morning I had chosen a dress with a cheerful floral pattern and Meg had pinned my hair up into large curls like the night before. Nicholas had never really seen me dressed as a lady. I hoped to impress him.

The hallway at the base of the stairs was lit by evenly-spaced torches. I peered into each cell as I walked by and the exaggerated shadows looked like distorted demons behind the bars.

"Right here, ma'am." The guard stopped before a cell.

"Nicholas?" I quietly called as I approached the cell. It was cloaked in darkness.

A small scuffle answered me. "Tessa?" His voice was full of astonishment as he emerged from the shadows. "What are you doing here?"

"I promised I would visit, didn't I?"

"Why didn't they bring me upstairs?" He glanced at my leg. His voice was laced with disapproval.

"Only Lord De Luca can make such things happen."

"You came alone?" He was shocked.

I looked at the guard, who had melted into the shadows to offer me privacy. "We're not exactly alone."

"But you're unescorted?" He draped his hands through the bars of his cell.

All my worries caught up with me and I burst into tears.

"What is it?" he asked me in a tentative voice. "What happened?"

"Nothing!" I blubbered. "Absolutely nothing! There is no sign of my father. There is little chance he'll be back before dawn tomorrow. I don't know what to do. This can't be happening!"

I pressed my face into the bars and Nicholas reached his fingers through to wipe my tears. "Shh, shh. Don't cry, luv. Not when I can't hold you."

I sank to the ground, my fingers tangling into my hair and destroying Meg's perfectly crafted coif. Sobs rippled through me.

"Come here," he commanded softly, crouching down and reaching out to me.

I ignored him. "This is it. These are our last moments. With thick, metal bars between us. We should have never come here. This is all my fault."

"No, luv, don't say that. We had to come. For your father. I wouldn't have wanted it any other way. It was my choice. I wrote the letter. You cannot blame yourself for this. Besides, the day is not over yet."

"What does that matter? Beyond the fact that I can still feel your breath at this moment, a few more hours or a few more minutes means nothing."

Nicholas reached for my hand and clasped it tightly. "I know your heart has been beyond brutalized, but I need you to stay strong for me." He lowered his voice to the quietest of whispers. "I need your help." His eyes were wide and hopeful, innocent like a child's in the glow of the torch light.

I leaned closer and lowered my voice. "What can I possibly do?"

Nicholas pressed my knuckles to his lips, his eyes closing briefly as he did so. "I need a weapon." His voice was so low I wasn't sure I heard him properly. He continued. "Go to your home and come back and visit me again. Hide a knife in your skirts. Even a letter opener will do."

His request instantly sobered me. "What do you plan to do?"

"What I have to."

I thought of the guard standing twenty feet from me now. Streaks of grey in his hair. Lines down his face. A slight limp from some past injury. "You can't mean... "

"I don't want to hurt anyone," Nicholas reassured me. "But I can't negotiate very well without something to negotiate *with*."

A weapon would certainly give him that. Even still, threatening a guard or harming one in any way would compound the charges against him. "If you do something rash, there will be no chance for a pardon."

"If I stay in here another night, there will be no chance of my survival."

I glanced at the guard standing halfway down the corridor. There was no indication that he heard anything Nicholas had said. I sighed and pulled my hand away from Nicholas and rubbed my brow. I felt lousy trying to talk him out of a confrontation. He only wanted to live. I wanted the same thing. I could either bring him the weapon or be an accomplice in his execution.

My eyes lingered on the guard. If it came down to it, Nicholas would kill him. I had no doubt of it. He would save himself at the expense of anything else. He was a pirate, it was the only way he'd ever known. If I brought Nicholas a weapon and the guard ended up dead, I would be an accomplice in his murder.

"There has to be another way," I mumbled into the darkness. "Something that doesn't involve violence."

"I've always found violence to be particularly effective."

"You're thinking like a pirate," I muttered.

"What was that?" Nicholas's voice was icy.

"Nothing."

We marinated in tense silence for a few minutes. I stood. "I don't have much time. If any of the staff find out that I have sneaked away, they'll never let me out of their sight again."

Nicholas stood and grabbed my hand through the bars. "Come back as soon as you can."

My brow furrowed but I nodded slowly. I interlocked my fingers with his. His hands—usually so warm—were like ice.

"I'll see you soon," I whispered.

CHAPTER SIX

THE GUARD HELPED ME to the carriage. As he tipped his head in a genteel nod and wished me a safe journey, I could only think that I may have signed his death warrant. I snapped the reins and rolled away from Fort Charles with a sick stomach.

I mulled over every scenario that might transpire. The most hopefully outlandish chain of events would include my father returning during the night and very quickly issuing a pardon for Nicholas. It was unlikely, but I couldn't let go of my hope of that happening. If I did nothing, if I did not return with a weapon, Nicholas would be killed. He would try to fight his way out, attack a guard with his fists, and probably be shot through the skull rather than having the formality of a hanging.

If I returned with a weapon, Nicholas would threaten—or kill—the guard with it and escape the dungeon. As a fugitive, he could not remain on St. Kitts. He would have to sail far away and never come back. I, of course, would never see him again. My heart hurt at the thought. I could go with him. He would have me. We would live like simple sailors for the rest of our windburned lives. And I would never see my father again. My only family. The only person on the planet who had known me and loved me my entire life. Could I turn my back on that?

I exhaled sharply. There had to be something else. Some alternative I was missing. Despite Nicholas's experience, violence wasn't everything. My father was a military man and certainly had inflicted and received plenty of violence, but he always told me that diplomacy reaches further than the longest sword. Diplomacy. If only my father were here, I could argue diplomacy with him.

World-weary, I didn't notice the beauty of the pinking sky in the west. I only knew that time was slipping away.

Could I live with myself if that guard were hurt or killed? Nicholas would have killed to save me. He incited a mutiny to disrupt my execution. He was willing to die for me, kill for me; how could I hesitate to do the same?

But how could I live with myself if Nicholas died? How could I return for a visit tonight empty handed and look into those eyes—eyes the color of the sky before dawn—and tell him I had decided to let him die?

My black-and-white ideals were quickly blurring into shades of grey. Nothing was right. So did it matter which wrong decision I made?

I couldn't return to Amerscott. Mr. Dean would certainly lock me in my room. I wasn't sure I was going to help Nicholas yet, but I couldn't go home. If I did want to help him, I would have to find a weapon somewhere else.

I rolled through the town, my mind racing. I became increasingly aware of the stares of strangers on the street. A girl with short hair, driving an empty carriage. I popped the reins to spur the mare on. I cruised past the town square, the shops of Main Street, the governor's mansion, and other fancy estates until the buildings began to thin, and I was in the countryside.

I steered the carriage into the drive of a small country house with few neighbors. I halted the horse halfway up the drive and made my way to the door. A bewildered housewife answered my knock.

"Pardon the intrusion, ma'am. I was riding home," I gestured to the carriage, "and my horse's bridle got tangled with the reins. Do you have a dagger or a knife I could use to free the knot? I would be most obliged."

The woman looked at me suspiciously then finally nodded. She did not invite me in. After a moment, she returned and handed me a worn and rusted butcher knife. "This'll have to do."

"It will. Thank you."

I clambered back to the carriage and with a spurt of courage akin to stupidity, hoisted myself onto the driver's seat, snapped the reins, and drove away. I closed my eyes in an attempt to ignore the shouts from the housewife who was none too happy about her butcher knife being stolen.

Once I was out of view from the little farmhouse, I slowed the mare and examined the knife. Square and blunt, it was probably not what Nicholas had intended me to supply. I slipped it into my splint where I could feel its cool steel against my leg. I was nauseous. My hands shook. I couldn't do this...but what else could I do?

I cursed my father again for not being here.

And suddenly, without thought or plan, I found myself in front of the governor's house, stepping down from the carriage. My father's words on diplomacy echoed through my mind again. I did not know what exactly I was doing.

A footman greeted me with a look of surprise but helped me up the mansion's sweeping steps without question, then led away the carriage.

I knocked on the door before I could think through what I was doing. It was Sunday evening. The governor was bound to be home. Probably dining with his family. Would he suffer my presence or be insulted by my insolence? I would find out.

More than once, my courage nearly failed me, and I all but dashed down the steps, but feeling the dull blade of the knife scraping against my leg gave me the nerve I needed to face the one man on this island who had the power to save Nicholas's neck.

The door opened. I took a deep breath. "I'm here to see the governor, please."

"I'm sorry, miss, but the governor is busy with matters of the state and is not receiving unannounced guests at this time. Good day."

A chorus of laughter sounded from inside the house. I raised my eyebrows at the butler and craned my neck to see inside. He scowled and shut the door.

I balled my fists and bit my lip. What I was doing went against everything I had ever been taught. I rapped on the door again.

The butler reopened the door and glared at me with ill-hidden contempt. "I do not make it a habit to throw young ladies off Governor Abner's property, but if you do not immediately remove yourself, I shall make an exception."

"Of course, sir," I curtsied and hoped to look contrite. "I do hate to impose. It's just that I need to use the facilities. My home is in the countryside and I'm not a fast rider with my leg."

He eyed me suspiciously and finally sighed. "I shall escort you every inch of the way."

"Understood." I bobbed in acquiescence.

I entered the foyer and the butler shut the door behind me. He turned to lead me to the latrine, but as soon as his back was turned, I followed the sound of voices and dashed towards the closed door on the far side of the foyer. I heard the butler call to me and hurry after me. My head start was all but lost with my splinted leg. I reached the door only a second before the butler did. He slammed into me. I slammed into the door and it unlatched. I fell face-first into the room and the butler landed with a groan on top of me.

I looked up into the faces of a dozen astonished men. The butler lifted himself off me and cleared his throat. He was going to make an excuse. Apologize. Force me out. I felt his gloved fingers curl around my shoulder. I lurched forward on my hands and knees, crawling into the smoking parlor, which was what the room was, I realized.

"Governor Abner!" I shouted as I desperately crawled out of the butler's grasp. I looked wildly around the faces in the room, not knowing whom to address myself. "Governor! Please, I must speak with you!"

The butler's hands firmly circled my waist and pulled me backwards. The slick brocade of my dress slipped easily against the polished wooden floor, allowing the butler to heave me like a sack of flour.

"Governor!" I shouted desperately as I skidded backwards over the threshold.

"Miss Monroe?" A face I recognized popped into view.

Lord De Luca, pipe in hand, rushed towards me, waving off the butler. "What are you doing here? Are you all right? Has something happened?"

He stored his pipe between his teeth and crouched down to help lift me from the floor.

I could feel my cheeks burning as I looked around the sea of curious faces. My hair was in disarray. My skirt was hitched up over my petticoat. I righted my appearance as best I could, then stood tall and clasped my hands in front of me. I may not have looked it, but I was a lady. I could do this.

"My name is Tessa Monroe. I came to see the governor. I apologize for the nature of my visit but it couldn't be helped." My eyes swept across the room and locked with every bewildered stare.

A man stepped forward. He was a compact gentleman with a heavily lined face. His sharp brown eyes gleamed under thick, black brows. He wore a burgundy smoking jacket and a teased white wig that made him seem taller than he was. He looked at Lord De Luca. "Do you know this woman?"

"Yes."

"Is she sane?"

I had to stifle a laugh at the question.

Lord De Luca looked at me as if he were truly considering my mental faculties. "I believe so."

I fought back a glare.

"Excuse me, sir, are you Governor Abner?"

Another man—a portly redhead—stepped forward. "Perhaps you should state your purpose first."

"I had hoped to be a little more discreet," I muttered, "but I suppose I have no choice. As I stated, my name is Tessa Monroe. I am the daughter of Admiral Archibald Monroe and request an urgent audience with the governor on his behalf."

A collective gasp rippled through the room.

The small man looked to Lord De Luca. "It can't be."

Lord De Luca was amused. "It is true. The staff at Amerscott—those who survived the crossing from England—recognized her immediately."

"Does your father know of your arrival here?" the governor asked.

"No, sir. He does not. I had hoped for a reunion today but he has not yet returned from sea."

The peculiarity of the situation dawned on the governor. He quickly dropped his pipe on a nearby end table, embarrassed, it seemed, to be smoking in front of a woman. "Mr. York, will you show Miss Monroe to the parlor. I shall be along in a moment."

I curtsied my thanks and turned to follow the butler, unable to hide the smirk on my face. He glared loathingly at me and led me to a lavish parlor with high-backed plush chairs the color of blood.

I wandered the perimeter of the room, staring wide-eyed at the intricate wall hangings and paintings.

As promised, the governor joined me. "Miss Monroe. Back from the dead. Please make yourself comfortable."

I sat in one of the blood-red chairs and spread my skirt to cover my splint.

"Lord De Luca said you practically fell into his carriage yesterday morning. Like manna from heaven. Though he didn't complain and I can see why."

The flattery made me itch. I tried my best not to show it, reminding myself that a lady's charms could only work to her advantage.

I cleared my throat. "I came here for a reason."

"Of course," the governor flipped his hand through the air as if swatting away a distracting bug. "First, I'd like to hear your story. I am sure it is quite the tale."

I blushed. "Oh, I don't know about that."

"Nonsense!" he barked. "You came from Curaçao with an infamous pirate quartermaster. I wouldn't be any less surprised if you rode here on a mermaid's back. And don't think I didn't notice that splint you are trying to hide. Tell me everything." He sat back and rubbed his hands along the tops of his legs. "I feel a bit devious, hearing all the details before Archibald!"

I swallowed hard. This was my cue to tell my story.

CHAPTER SEVEN

I TOOK A MOMENT to gather my wits. I hadn't really planned on how to plead my case for Nicholas. And blurting out a lovesick petition would certainly make things worse. This was better. I could tell my story and the events themselves would testify on his behalf.

I fidgeted with the buttons on my gloves. I cleared my throat. "As you know, my father and I were sailing on a naval vessel from England. Well, our ship went down in a storm near Grand Bahama. The mast broke and my father and I had to jump overboard to avoid it. And then...I awoke on a strange ship." I paused, taking a moment to filter through the memories of meeting Nicholas that first night. I wished I could keep those memories private, but in order to argue for Nicholas's freedom, the governor needed to understand why I would ask such a thing of him.

I continued my story. "A sailor found me wandering the main deck in the middle of the night. His name was Nicholas Holladay. He was the quartermaster and he had given up his cabin for me. He fed me, then sent me back to the cabin, making me promise not to come out. I did not understand why he would ask such a thing of me. I wanted badly to speak to the captain, but he made me promise not to speak to anyone but him."

The governor stared at me as if in a trance. His eyes widened with every revelation.

I nervously continued. "After a couple of days hidden in the cabin, there was a terrible noise. I thought it was thunder, a breaking mast, or another hurricane. I broke my promise and left my cabin. Two ships were battling. What I had heard was cannon fire. At first, I assumed my ship was under attack. And then I saw the Jolly Roger above. I saw Nicholas—Mr. Holladay—commanding the raid, other pirates following his orders. It was then that I realized I was on a pirate ship. Mr. Holladay ordered me to be locked in the brig."

My voice wavered under the intensity of the governor's stare.

He urged me to continue.

I wished to leave out the next part of the tale, but it was essential to showing Nicholas's character. I cleared my throat, looked down at my hands, and softly recounted the most horrifying night of my life. "One night, a drunken pirate named Wrack came down. He had stolen the keys to the brig. He...um...he..." I struggled to say it aloud. "He let himself in and...attacked me."

My eyes were fixed on my lap, but I could hear the governor's sharp intake of breath.

My voice dropped even lower. "I fought back as hard as I could. Mr. Holladay heard my screams and came to my rescue just in time. He nursed my injuries back in the cabin and explained that he locked me in the brig for my own protection, to keep me safe." I choked on the last word, lost in the memories of the horrific attack.

"Miss Monroe." The governor softly touched my arm. I jumped out of my dark reverie. He was standing before me with a handkerchief in his hand. "Here."

I looked at it quizzically as I accepted it. "What is this for?"

"You're crying."

I touched my face. My cheeks were wet. I looked down,

certain I was scarlet with humiliation, and dabbed my tears away.

"You needn't continue," he said.

I forced myself to meet the governor's eyes. "It's important for you to know what Mr. Holladay did for me."

The governor looked baffled. Did he even realize that the man I spoke of was the same man for whom he had signed a death warrant?

I began again. "The man who attacked me died the next day. Mr. Holladay thinks it was a result of unseen injuries from when I fought back. But the other pirates thought I had murdered him using witchcrafts. I was put on trial, found guilty, and condemned to death. Mr. Holladay rallied a mutiny and overthrew the captain, thus overthrowing the mandate to hang me. I wasn't safe, though. The crew was still suspicious of me and still wanted me dead. In the middle of the night, Mr. Holladay helped me escape in a jollyboat. He was planning to join me but was intercepted by his shipmates.

"I drifted at sea for a couple of days and finally landed near Port Winslow. I worked as a scullery maid in a tavern, earning my keep. I felt as though I had no future. I was an orphan half a world away from anything I had ever known. Meanwhile, Mr. Holladay managed to desert his crew and obtain a small fishing ketch. Knowing where the currents would have taken me, he searched for me and found me."

I carefully worded the next part. By hiding the true nature of my feelings for Nicholas, I felt I was offering him a bit of protection. I felt if the Governor knew of my affections for Nicholas, he would simply be branded as a villain taking advantage of a lonely girl. "Mr. Holladay planned to return me to England where I could seek aid from family friends. We stopped in Willemstad for supplies and heard news of a new British admiral named Monroe who was seeking out the lives of pirates as a sort of revenge for his slain daughter. Knowing that my father was alive, we headed directly to St. Kitts."

"What a tale!" The governor was thoroughly entertained. I liked the man. He was naturally jovial and warm. "Though I suppose it doesn't exactly explain why you burst into my study this evening."

I gave my most charming smile. "You will understand soon enough. While sailing here, Mr. Holladay and I were intercepted by the Royal Navy. He was arrested and I was deposited in Lord De Luca's carriage. I am here, safe and cared for, while my noble escort sits in a dungeon awaiting his execution."

Understanding dawned on Governor Abner's face. "The pirate officer known as Marks. He is your Mr. Holladay."

"And now you know why I so desperately intruded on your Sunday evening. He is scheduled to hang at dawn." I glanced at the indigo twilight darkening the windows.

He paused and cleared his throat. His bushy black brows drew together, the lighthearted sense of adventure gone from his eyes. "Your feelings do you credit. But this matter is bigger than you realize."

I knotted my hands together tightly so the governor could not see them tremble. This was it. I felt as if I were back on the *Banshee* defending my life against false accusations. I choked out a sorrowful appeal. "Please. Don't kill my friend."

There was a feeling of foreboding in the room. It made my heart heavy.

"Miss Monroe." He looked at me, then his eyes darted away. "Miss Monroe. I am not sure what you expect me to do."

I bristled. He certainly knew what I would ask of him. He was just too craven to confront it. "Are you not the governor? Is it not in your power to pardon him?"

He shifted uncomfortably. "Pardon? He's a criminal of the highest sort. Guilty of treason, murder, theft, and more."

"Isn't it obvious that he is no longer that man?" I could feel my temper stirring.

Abner smiled kindly. "It seems so, indeed. Yet a singular

noble deed performed on behalf of a pretty girl doesn't diminish the amount of blood he has spilt before."

My blood turned hot as hellfire and my nerves evaporated. Battle-ready, I scooted to the edge of my chair. "You govern the laws of the land on St. Kitts. Nicholas—Mr. Holladay has not committed any crimes here. You have no right to hold him."

"Do you presume to tell me how to do my job?" he snapped back at me.

Damn my temper. I stared into my lap, instantly contrite. Why would he ever want to grant the request of a demanding, spoilt girl? If I had ruined any hope of saving Nicholas…

"Miss Monroe, please look at me."

I lifted my eyes and prayed he saw the shame in them.

"You're right. My dominion at sea is limited. However, the admiral in charge of governing the sea—who happens to be your father—has established very clear laws with very clear consequences. There is a certain banyan tree along the coast—"

My strength wilted at the memory.

Governor Abner's eyebrows lifted. "From your response, I assume you've seen it."

My throat was parched. I swallowed hard, trying to find a trace of moisture in my mouth.

The governor continued. "Then you know I have all the precedent necessary to carry out Mr. Holladay's sentence. Truth be told, I do not have the power to grant a pardon. Only your father can do that."

Perspiration gathered along my hairline. I fanned myself with my hand as a wave of heat threatened to undo me.

"You do not look well. Are you ill?"

"I'm fine," I gasped, dropping my hand.

"You're flushed." He stood and held out his hand for me. "Would you like some fresh air?"

I nodded vigorously. Mr. Abner led me out of the parlor and to an open veranda at the back of the house. I drank in the evening air, willing my nerves to calm.

"Ah, Lord De Luca," the governor said.

I turned around. The baron had joined us on the veranda.

"How goes your visit?" Lord De Luca asked.

I wasn't sure how to answer. Fortunately, the governor answered for me. "It's been one revelation after another. We have more to discuss but Miss Monroe required some air. If you don't mind, sir, would you keep her company while I request tea service?"

"I'd be honored."

I could feel Lord De Luca's eyes on me once we were alone. He had no clue what I was doing here but he was too proper to ask. I couldn't stand the weight of the silence—or the pressure of my fear—and unleashed a dam of words.

"I have to convince the governor to pardon Mr. Holladay. He'll hang at sunrise if I can't. It's not going particularly well. If I don't do this, I'm worried about what Nicholas might do out of desperation." I groaned and massaged my temples. "I can't do this," I stammered. "I cannot listen to that man reduce my friend to a list of infractions. I cannot bear to hear him refuse my request. I've made my case and he is unmoved. I cannot bear to waltz around in pretense over tea. I should leave."

"You don't want to do that, not really."

"Yes, I do. He is not going to release Nicholas and I can't bear to hear it."

Lord De Luca placed his hands on my shoulders and looked squarely at me, his expression both passionate and fatherly. "I do not know much about you, but I do know that you'll hate yourself forever if you leave now."

I shivered as I felt the edge of the butcher knife secreted away in my splint. "I'll hate myself forever if he dies."

He released me and walked a few steps into the night. "I know the governor well. He does not want to turn you away or he would have done so already. Yet he is bound by law."

"What does is it matter then? He's a lame figure. I was foolish to have come here."

"He's not entirely impotent."

"Isn't he? He said he cannot grant a pardon. I am wasting time. I need to return to the fort."

Lord De Luca turned quickly, his head cocked in thought. "You're not here for a pardon."

"Yes, actually, I am." My tone was surly but I did not care. Manners meant nothing anymore.

"Listen, *signorina*, you're not here for a pardon...you're here to save Mr. Holladay's life. Perhaps as governor, he cannot grant a pardon. But there must be something else he *can* do."

The butler appeared on the veranda and asked me to return to the parlor. As I followed him, I thought about what the baron had said. He was right. All I needed to do was keep Nicholas alive past dawn.

I returned to the red chair. A steaming cup of tea was on the table beside it.

"Are you feeling better?" Governor Abner's concern was genuine.

"Much, thank you."

"Some worry that the night air brings illness," Abner waved towards the windows. "I find nothing more invigorating."

"Indeed," I smiled at the easy segue. "In fact, it has helped me think more clearly about the topic of our discussion."

"Oh?" Governor Abner was intrigued.

I sat as tall as I could. "I understand your limitations for granting a pardon. Really, it was selfish of me to ask for such a thing. It is your duty to execute criminals. I imagine you wouldn't fancy having a conversation with my father explaining why you failed to do so. Please consider the other conversation you might have with him—the one where you explain why you discarded the tears of his beloved daughter, back from the dead, and tied a noose around her rescuer's neck when it was in your power to look the other way."

"Miss Monroe—"

I held up my hand to silence him. "Please forgive my

impudence. I hope you understand my desperation. So here I sit, pleading with you, asking you to decide which of those conversations you would like to have when my father returns."

The governor's face was lined with true worry. "Miss Monroe, please understand, I *cannot* grant a pardon. I do not have the power, as much as I wish I did."

"Then do not pardon him, Governor. But do not kill him tomorrow. Keep him jailed. Let the charges stand. Delay the sentence until my father returns."

The governor pondered my request in silence. He took a sip of tea and ate a biscuit. He hadn't openly refused me, which I took as a promising sign. His brows were lowered, his lips moving in a thin line.

Finally, Governor Abner met my gaze. I held my breath.

"You are as shrewd as your father. Yes, yes. I'll grant a stay of execution until I have a personal consultation with your father."

CHAPTER EIGHT

I TEETERED PRECARIOUSLY AS I descended the steps into the fortress dungeons. Lord De Luca stood close by for support. When he realized I had come to Governor Abner's mansion without an escort, he insisted on taking me home. I, however, insisted on visiting the fort.

My hand slid against the dank stone walls, my fingers cringing over the slime. I focused on every step, making sure not to fall down the rough, narrow stairs.

"Here we are," I said when we neared the cell. I took the lantern from Lord De Luca. I had expected Nicholas to be waiting anxiously. He must have heard the shuffle-scrape of my step for the past five minutes. Alas, he was lying in the corner of the cell, snoring softly.

How he could sleep at such a time baffled me.

"Nicholas," I whispered. He didn't stir. I tried again. "Nicholas!" I struck my cane against the bars of the cell.

Nicholas awoke. He looked around, confused for a moment. "Tessa?" His voice was groggy. He rubbed his eyes and stretched before lifting himself off the stone floor. He squinted into the shadows behind me. "You're not alone."

"Good evening, Mr. Holladay," Lord De Luca answered with a tip of his head.

Nicholas nodded in return, but there was nothing genuine

about it. "The baron?" he asked me quietly, suspicious as to why I would bring someone into our escape plan.

I reached through the bars, clutching his hand. "We've just come from the governor's mansion."

Nicholas's face tensed slightly.

"I convinced him to delay the execution until my father returns. I couldn't get him to release you, but at least..." I shrugged. I couldn't say the words.

Nicholas stammered and made me repeat myself. Then he dared to smile, a genuine, heartwarming smile. He intertwined his fingers with mine and looked at me in awe. "You should not have had to do this. That it fell on your shoulders to beg—" he stopped himself and shook his head. "Thank you, Tessa. You amaze me."

"I was so afraid." My hands trembled at the memory.

"I know, I know." His tone was soothing. "But everything is fine. You did everything just right. It's more than I ever hoped for. How did it happen? Did he go with you?" His eyes flashed behind me towards the baron.

I smiled shyly. "I forced my way into the governor's house. Lord De Luca happened to be a dinner guest. He insisted on acting as an escort since it's dark and I was alone."

Two deep lines appeared between his eyebrows. "How very kind of Mr. De Luca." There was an edge in his voice. "Too kind, really."

Nicholas was jealous. How endearing.

"He has been very, uh, warm to me. It's taken me aback a few times." I wanted Nicholas to know that I wasn't oblivious of the situation—or his feelings.

Nicholas shrugged, feigning nonchalance, but the furrow between his eyebrows remained. "Italians are quite affectionate. It's their way."

"Yes," I nodded in agreement, trying to convince myself. "The Italian way."

I settled onto the floor, my back leaning against the stone doorframe of the cell.

Nicholas sat down too and reached for my hand again. "You're not going to stay here all night."

"Stop me," I smiled sweetly.

"You'll visit me tomorrow."

"I'll visit with you all night."

"Tessa." He cocked his head.

I cocked mine. "Nicholas." I couldn't help but laugh. It was contagious—Nicholas chuckled too. It was a reassuring sound.

"Fine," I conceded, laughter still in my voice, "I won't stay here all night. But only because I *know* I will see you tomorrow. And not dangling from the end of a noose."

Nicholas's face twisted into a look of mock horror. "Can you imagine?"

"Don't jest, Nicholas. I've been imagining it all day."

He lightly squeezed my hand. "Me too."

I saw the shadows shift out of the corner of my vision. I had completely forgotten that Lord De Luca was only a few steps away. I combed through our conversation, wondering if we said anything embarrassing. I was safe enough, but knew I would refrain from the goodnight kiss I so desperately wanted to steal.

"I suppose I shouldn't keep the baron waiting any longer." I hoped Nicholas heard the sadness in my voice.

Nicholas nodded.

Neither of us moved. We remained on the cold, wet floor of a fortress dungeon, holding hands through the bars and staring helplessly into each other's eyes.

And then Nicholas stood. "Go. Sleep in a bed."

He reached through the bars and helped me stand. Our touch lingered.

"Do you need anything?" I peered into the cell. Aside from its resident and a chamber pot, it was empty.

He looked around too. "If I'm to be here several more days, a blanket would be nice."

I nodded. "Have you eaten?" I asked. I didn't see a plate or any scraps.

He shook his head.

My heart lurched. Just because the guards thought he would be dead in less than a day gave them no right to deprive him of food. "I'll bring something," I promised.

Nicholas still hadn't let go of my hand. "Tomorrow, then?"

I nodded.

Lord De Luca shuffled again. No doubt he was bored by our prolonged farewell.

With tears in my eyes, I stepped away from the bars. If I didn't leave now, I never would. I took one more step towards the shadows, towards the baron. He caught my elbow, "Are you ready?"

I glanced over my shoulder at Nicholas. He looked as torn as I felt.

He nodded strongly. It was time.

I nodded at Lord De Luca, not trusting my voice for anything. He took the lantern from me, then offered his free arm as a support. It felt strange accepting it, knowing Nicholas was watching, but with my injured ankle, I had no choice. It felt so wrong to leave Nicholas here like this. I knew it wouldn't be forever. I knew my father would grant the pardon the governor would not. But there was no telling when that would happen. I felt like I was leaving my heart in the dungeon. In truth, I was.

* * * * *

I said very little on the carriage ride back to Amerscott House. Lord De Luca walked me to the door, bowed before me, and kissed the back of my hand like any gentleman would do. I fought the urge to pull my hand away. Why did I feel like he was disrespecting Nicholas?

"I wish you a *buonasera*, Miss Monroe. May I call on you tomorrow?"

I didn't know what to say. He was the most gracious person I had ever met, and my only friend in St. Kitts at the moment.

Yet the attention he lavished on me made me uncomfortable. Perhaps Nicholas was right. It was a cultural difference that I was not accustomed to.

He must have sensed my hesitation. "I will happily escort you to the fortress so you can visit your friend once more."

"Oh."

"Or I could send my driver, no extra company needed— although I do worry about you traversing the stairs all alone."

I pushed out a smile. I owed him my gratitude. "Yes, what a lovely offer. I would like to return to the fort tomorrow. My hope is that when my father returns, you won't have to visit Amerscott so frequently."

He raised a single eyebrow. "My hope is quite the opposite."

Uncertain how to respond, I gave him a polite smile and let myself inside my house.

CHAPTER NINE

THE HOUSEHOLD WAS STILL. Though I knew the staff were somewhere within the walls, I felt alone. It was a relief.

I shuffled through the foyer, my splint catching and scraping on the wooden floor. I sank down and removed the monstrosity, casting it aside in the middle of the floor. I didn't care that the physician recommended that I wear it for another fortnight. I couldn't stand it any longer.

Relishing the newfound agility, I walked to the parlor, still using my cane to support my weight. The house was dark and quiet. I breathed it in. How long had it been since I had been completely alone like this? It felt like tonic to my soul.

I gingerly eased myself down on the harpsichord bench and my hands naturally took their place on the white keys. My fingers drew out a melody without effort. The notes drifted around me, like intoxicating curls of smoke, but I paid no attention to the sound. My mind was wrapped up in thoughts of Lord De Luca. I had not imagined him to be anything more than a helpful neighbor until Meg put a different notion in my head. I hoped Nicholas was right—that the baron's eagerness to help and his profuse compliments stemmed from his Italian heritage. The *joie de vivre* of the Italians could easily be misinterpreted. But something in the pit of my stomach told me that Lord De Luca's behavior was more than that.

"My stars, Miss Tessa! Where have you been?"

Miss Maisley scowled as she crossed to me, a blazing lantern in her hand. Meg was on her heels.

"I, uh, needed some air."

"You've been missing all day!" Meg cried. "Mr. Dean nearly whipped me!"

Miss Maisley silenced her with a glare. She looked back at me. "First things first. Are you all right?"

"Yes."

"Now tell me exactly where you have been. No fibs!"

I sighed and tried to breeze over the story as quickly as possible. I was too tired for an inquisition. "I visited my friend in Fort Charles then visited Governor Abner about my friend's future."

If I weren't so tired, I would have enjoyed the identical looks of shock on their faces. After a beat, Miss Maisley looked as if she were going to give me a tongue-lashing.

I quickly added, "Lord De Luca just brought me home."

It worked. Miss Maisley's rage froze, then thawed. "Lord De Luca?"

"He was with me at the governor's house. He'll call again tomorrow."

Miss Maisley's expression went from fierce to impressed to resigned. It was amazing what the mere mention of the baron could do. "Very well," Miss Maisley sighed. "You best get some rest. Meg, help her to bed and do not let her out of your sight."

"Yes, ma'am," Meg curtsied.

My maid quickly ushered me to my room without her smiles and brusquely helped me into my night shift.

"I'm sorry you got in trouble on my behalf," I said as she unfastened what was left of my hairstyle.

She said nothing, but her lips pursed tightly together.

"It wasn't fair of Mr. Dean to threaten you," I continued. "You're my maid, not my keeper."

"It's my job to attend to you. That includes knowing where you are. I could've been beaten."

She brushed my hair furiously. I caught her hand and turned my face so I was looking into her eyes. "I am sorry, Meg. It was wrong of me. I was desperate and stupid and I should have at least brought you with me. Everyone would have worried so much less."

"You should not have gone at all."

I looked at her sharply. I had enough people telling me what to do. I did not need my *servant* to join them.

Meg looked down contritely. "It's not my place to say so, miss. I beg your pardon."

I turned back to my reflection as Meg finished. My unruly hair had grown a little, though it still didn't reach my shoulders. I cringed when I looked at it. Chestnut-colored waves had once cascaded to my waist. That was back when I was pretty. Before the hurricane and Captain Black and Nicholas.

Once, I'd had the type of beauty that made others take notice—gentlemen were kind to me and ladies were cold. Alabaster skin. Large innocent eyes—the deepest shade of brown—fringed with thick, black lashes. Shapely, sweet lips.

But now I looked like a pauper—brown-skinned and gaunt with wide, serious eyes and a spattering of freckles spreading across my nose. I was thinner than I had been before my Atlantic crossing. I hadn't thought I could get any thinner, but without more to eat than a few pieces of bread a day, my gamine figure looked even more skeletal. My collarbones protruded like blades.

In a few weeks, the bronze on my skin would fade and my porcelain complexion would return. Regular meals would pad my willowy figure. I'd be a lady again. Nicholas would like that. My hair would take longer to re-grow. And some things could not be undone. Like the scar on my throat where Captain Black had cut me.

My eyes wandered to the intricate embroidery on my nightdress. "Did the baron select these clothes himself?" I wasn't entirely sure I wanted to know the answer.

Meg was quiet for a while, and I wondered if she was too upset with me to answer. She must have thought better of her temper because she finally said, "No, miss. He sent his steward and me to shop for you."

"Oh," I said, feeling a rush of relief. "Is he always so generous?"

"When the situation calls for it."

Meg's answer perplexed me. I had hoped she would gush about his obscene generosity in every aspect. It would let me know that he did not view me as a special case. As it was, I was starting to believe he did.

"How long have you worked for him?"

Meg pulled down the covers on my bed dutifully. "Eight months."

"You must know him well."

"I couldn't say, miss."

She was such a treasure trove of information on Lord De Luca. I wanted to ask her a thousand questions but she made it clear she was not in the mood to chat. She had only been in my service a day and already she was in trouble. There was no reason she would divulge secrets about her previous employer for my benefit.

I studied Meg as she stoically straightened my room. She was different from any other servant I had met. There was a spark in her personality that made submission difficult for her. She had an ill-suited curiosity and an obvious temper. And from our interactions before, I knew she longed for friendship.

She was angry with me. But she would break.

"He seemed rather…well, I suppose I shouldn't say. You might think me a gossip."

Meg looked at me, her eyes hungry for details, and I knew I had her. "I would never think that," she said hesitantly, carefully choosing her words. "It's my job to listen. To answer your questions the best I can. If you request it, of course."

"Of course," I nodded, pleased that she had offered her services so willingly.

I held my tongue and twirled my hair, acting lost in my thoughts. Meg drifted closer, adjusting the clutter on top of the vanity.

"You must have had an interesting day." She tried to seem disinterested.

"I accomplished much. I had not expected to see Lord De Luca. It was rather embarrassing to be seen barging into the governor's home and demanding an audience with him as Lord De Luca and a dozen other gentlemen looked on. I fear he'll distance himself from me. And why shouldn't he? I am not proper."

Meg stifled a smile but kept quiet.

"You know him. What do you think? Have I utterly humiliated myself in front of him? Would it be a kindness to refuse his aid tomorrow when he turns up out of obligation?"

"From what I know of Lord De Luca, if he calls on you tomorrow, it is because he wants to see you."

I hobbled to the bed and sat on the turned-down sheets. "He's been very accommodating."

"Perhaps he fancies you," Meg shrugged.

I felt my heart quicken, but I tried to remain as measured as I had been. "Do you think he might?" I scooted over, an invitation to Meg. She accepted it and sat beside me. And suddenly we were a pair of girls again, no longer a lady and a servant.

"Every girl on the island vies for him," Meg leaned in. "He's never made time for a single one of them. But since he met you, he has been, as you say, accommodating. I've never seen him act like this. The clothing. Sending me. He is a kind man to be sure, but this seems beyond Christian goodness."

My entire face flushed and Meg giggled. I rolled my eyes and shrugged. "Maybe he means to find favor with my father." I leaned back against the pillows.

She sank back onto an elbow. "There is only one reason I can think of as to why he would want to win your father's favor—and that reason has to do with you. You said you were spoken for. Would you reconsider? Assuming Lord De Luca has eyes for you, of course."

I didn't hesitate to answer. "Maybe once I would have. But not now. My heart is not mine to give away."

Meg smiled shyly. "I know what you mean."

I cocked my head. "Do you?" A faint shade of pink colored Meg's cheeks and her hazel eyes danced. "You're in love!"

Her smile blossomed. "Is it that obvious?" She looked down and picked at the bedspread, her face darkening. There was sadness there, behind the love.

"What is it?"

Meg kept her face down and her voice was low. "I haven't seen him for so long. I miss him. I wonder if I'll ever see him again."

"What happened? Tell me about him."

"I used to be a sailor. Does that surprise you?" She looked up at me. "My father..." she cleared her throat and started over. "The life of a sailor was a fast way to escape a life with no future. The boy I love, he was a sailor too. Taught me how to sail as good as any man. He was so kind. And funny. Made sure the others respected me. When I had enough money to establish something more comfortable for myself, I moved on so we could be together. He had obligations, though, and couldn't leave the crew as easily as I did. I don't know where he is. He could be halfway to China for all I know. And he doesn't know where I am either. I still dream of him and wonder if I'll see him again."

Her tale had me captivated. "Does he love you in return?"

Meg smiled sadly. "He never said as much, but in my heart I think he does. Or, perhaps, did."

"If he loves you at all, certainly he'll find you." I thought of Nicholas scouring every isle and cay to find me in Port Winslow. He stopped at nothing to get me back.

"He has returned to the sea." Her statement was definitive.

I furrowed my brow in confusion. "So?"

"Loving a sailor is like loving the tide. It's teasing, it's powerful, it pulls you in, deeper and deeper...but it always returns to the sea. It's hard to vie for someone's love, especially when the competition is the ocean. The pull of the sea is too strong for any woman to compete with."

"That's terrible," I said. I was secretly reassured by how easy it had been for Nicholas to renounce his profession and commit to a future as a carpenter. If only Meg had been so lucky with her love.

"Meg, may I ask a favor?"

"I am your maid. Nothing is a favor, miss. It's part of my job to do as you ask."

She was right, of course, but I felt this request was slightly beyond her expected duties. "Would you come with me tomorrow to see my friend?" I didn't want Nicholas to see me alone with Lord De Luca again.

"Of course, miss. It will be my pleasure."

"Thank you, Meg. Goodnight."

Meg stood and pulled the covers over me, then shut the windows, blew out the lamp, and excused herself. I snuggled into my bed, hardly enjoying the feather mattress as thoughts of Nicholas curled up on a stone floor without so much as a blanket plagued me. I wouldn't feel at peace until I could lose myself in his arms again.

I fussed with the pillow and kicked off the blankets. It wasn't hot, but I felt claustrophobic. The air felt heavy.

I escaped to my private balcony and inhaled deeply. The air smelled of the flower garden below but if I tried hard enough, I could smell the distant scent of a salty ocean breeze. I left the veranda doors open and went back to bed, finally falling asleep to the distant rhythm of waves crashing on the beach.

* * * * *

Images of half-rotted corpses dangling from the banyan tree haunted my dreams. Nicholas was hanging there too, but still alive. I climbed the leathery trunks only to fall on the ground. I climbed again and again, falling each time. I stared into the faces of the corpses and recognized Lord De Luca, Meg, and my father. Finally, I climbed to the branch from which Nicholas was hanging. A dirk appeared in my hand and I started to saw the rope, his grey eyes staring up at me in terror the entire time. The dirk slipped and I leaned to grab it but lost my balance and slipped from my place on the branch. I fell and fell, only stopping when I reached the end of a rope around my own neck.

My eyes flew open. I looked around in a panic, uncertain where I was. Amerscott House. My new room. My new bed. I closed my eyes and exhaled, willing my heart to cease its pounding. I pushed myself out of bed and hobbled to the veranda. It was still dark, but a faint grey glow filled the sky.

I closed my eyes and remembered the dream.

What if the governor changed his mind? What if he didn't follow through with his promise or the guards never received word that the execution had been delayed? I felt nauseous. I had to get to Nicholas.

Back in my room, I lit a lantern and squinted into the shadows until I found a china pitcher and basin on top of a small table near the vanity. I splashed my face with cool water, hoping to wash away the images of my nightmare. I dressed myself in a pale yellow frock with Watteau pleats flowing from my shoulders to the floor. Leaving my hair in disarray, I left my room in search of Meg.

I needed to get to the fortress before sunrise.

I explored the first floor. My own home was still unfamiliar to me. I found the kitchen tucked in the back corner behind the staircase. Meg was stoking the fire.

"You're awake. Good."

She jumped with shock, a spray of cinders flying out of the oven door. "My goodness, Miss Monroe! You startled me!"

"I'm so sorry. Are you hurt?"

Meg brushed ash off her sleeves. "No, I'm fine. Did any get you?"

"No."

Meg looked me up and down. "Why are you awake? And dressed?"

"I need to see my friend. I just have to know that he is safe, that the governor issued the stay of execution in time." I looked anxiously at the sky. Sunrise wasn't far away.

Understanding spread across Meg's face. "I'll have Clarence ready the carriage."

"Thank you. Might I pack some food?"

Meg tossed me a muslin bag. "Help yourself to anything."

I was packing the bag with hard cheeses and fresh rolls when a knock at the front door drew me to the foyer. I could feel the weakness of my ankle, but I was determined to forgo the splint.

Mr. Dean answered the door to reveal Lord De Luca. The baron was dressed sharply, a hat tucked under his arm.

I curtsied around my cane. "My lord. Mr. Dean."

"Miss Monroe." The baron dipped his head politely as he stepped into the foyer.

"What brings you to Amerscott at such an early hour?" I asked.

His lips parted into a broad smile. He really was a handsome man. "You, of course."

My mouth slackened. *Me?*

"I thought you would want to be at the fortress before dawn...to make sure."

Meg found me then, a wool jacket over her dress. She held another jacket out for me and helped me shrug it on. "Clarence will have the carriage ready in ten minutes."

Lord De Luca stepped forward. "My carriage is ready now. Allow me to take you."

I was too desperate to get to Fort Charles to care who took me. I thanked the baron graciously and alighted into his carriage.

Twenty minutes later, we stood at the entrance of the fortress. I saw no signs of a pending execution. My anxiety settled a little. Lord De Luca convinced the guard to bring Nicholas to us again. If I had been wearing my splint, the persuasion would probably have gone faster, but my cane and limp proved reason enough.

My heart pounded as I heard footsteps coming up the stairs. Nicholas emerged, hands chained before him, blinking in the morning light. I struggled forward, eager to wrap my arms around him.

"It's you," Meg breathed, her voice barely audible.

"Hm?" I turned towards her, confused.

She was staring at Nicholas. Her eyes were shining, her mouth drawn up in a disbelieving smile.

I followed her gaze to Nicholas. He was staring back at her, his eyes full of recognition. "Quin?" Nicholas answered.

The baron gaped at Meg. "You have dealings with this pirate?"

Meg—who seemed on her way to throw her arms around Nicholas—stopped mid-gait. She ducked her head and trained her eyes to the ground. "No, sir. No dealings, sir. I knew him long ago."

I looked at her suspiciously. She was lying. My curiosity consumed me. I hitched my arm around her elbow and pulled her close to me.

"How do you know him?" I whispered in her ear.

"Please, miss, I need this job. If the baron were to put me out—"

"Answer me truthfully, Meg, or I will tell the baron everything. How do you know him?"

She was terrified. "He's the one I told you about."

I stared at her without understanding. She hadn't told me about any pirates. The only person she had told me about was...the realization hit me like a battering ram.

A sailor. The man she loved. The man she was certain loved her in return.

My Nicholas.

They had sailed together. Which meant that Meg had been a pirate, too. I reassessed her golden hair and slim figure, trying to imagine her with a sword in her hand. I imagined Nicholas teaching her how to tie off the lines and read the currents of the ocean as he had taught me. My stomach plummeted. I released her arm and staggered back a step.

Nicholas grinned like a child. "Quin! What are you doing here?"

Meg kept her posture contrite. "I'm Miss Monroe's personal maid."

"Impossible," he breathed. Finally, he turned away from Meg and looked at me. "Tessa, this is unbelievable. Quin and I know each other."

"Quin?" It was all I could think to say.

"Just a nickname. We were friends once."

Friends? She said you were in love.

"Amazing coincidence." My voice was flat.

"Can you believe it, Tessa?" Nicholas laughed. "I should be dangling from a rope right now but I'm free from that fate and I've been reunited with Meg Quincy. It's all because of you."

Nicholas moved towards me. He had that look in his eye that beckoned me to come to him. I took a step back. His look changed to one of bemusement. I glanced meaningfully at Meg. I couldn't show affection to Nicholas knowing how she felt about him—how she assumed he felt about her. Things would eventually sort out, but I couldn't do that to her right now. In a jealous fit she could accuse Nicholas of things for which he would hang.

Nicholas followed my gaze to Meg, but didn't seem to detect my platonic explanation. He looked puzzled and hurt. I hated it.

With a brittle smile, I looked around at my companions, my gaze resting on each in turn. Nicholas, the pirate, whom I longed to enfold in my arms. Meg, my maid who had fallen in love with Nicholas when she sailed with him—*as a pirate*—and was certain he loved her in return. And Lord De Luca—Meg's employer, Nicholas's advocate, and apparently my suitor. My knowledge to this mess was private and I had to keep it that way. I had to do everything in my power to keep the four of us from ever being together at the same time again.

CHAPTER TEN

MEG APPROACHED NICHOLAS, HER large eyes searching his face. He glanced from her to me. I struggled to read his emotion. Was he embarrassed? Apologetic? All that and more?

"I never thought I would see you again. I didn't even know if you were alive," Meg gushed, shyly brushing the backs of his knuckles with her fingertips.

I looked away.

Lord De Luca looked at me and cocked his head. I smiled tightly, completely unsure how I should respond. I wanted to rip Meg away from Nicholas. I wanted Nicholas to do it himself despite his shackles. I wanted Meg to vanish. I wanted Lord De Luca to vanish. If I could vanish, I would have.

Lord De Luca came to me. "Did you know they were acquainted?"

I shook my head. "I'm as surprised as you."

I tried to listen as Nicholas and Meg exchanged pleasantries and updated each other on how they both came to be in St. Kitts.

"Miss Monroe?"

I realized Lord De Luca had been speaking to me.

"I'm sorry. Did you ask me something?"

"You look peaked. Are you feeling like yourself?"

"I didn't sleep well."

"I imagined that you would have slept like an angel in a real bed."

Lord De Luca imagining me sleeping didn't lessen the lead in my stomach. "I had upsetting dreams."

"Tessa."

I turned at the sound of Nicholas saying my name.

"How is your ankle? Can you walk with me?" He twitched his head towards the expanse of fortress beyond us. He extended his elbow—the best he could do to offer me his arm with his hands confined. I took his arm and leaned heavily on him as he led me away from the others, acutely aware of Meg's gaze on us.

A thousand thoughts ran through my mind. I tried to sort them, tried to decide which—if any—I should bring up with Nicholas now. We had precious few moments. Should I waste them on jealously? Was that all it was? Or was there something to fear? Meg was sure Nicholas had loved her. Just as I was sure Nicholas loved me.

"What's going on in that head of yours?" Nicholas's eyes searched my face.

"The stay of execution worked," I replied safely.

"The governor came by last night."

"He did?"

Nicholas nodded. "Not long after you left. He wanted to tell me about the stay of execution personally. He even thanked me for bringin' you home. But he did warn me that I was still a prisoner and my sentence is still enforceable."

I closed my eyes. I didn't want to think about what would happen if my father would not grant the pardon. "Everything was supposed to be better when we got here," I whispered. I could feel a lump forming in my throat.

"It will be, luv. Just a few more days and everything will be as it was before."

"No it won't. Not ever again." I didn't bother holding back my tears.

Nicholas's hands clenched and pulled against the shackles. I knew he wanted me in his arms. I wanted that too.

I looked around the confining stone walls of Fort Charles. "There will always be something. Some ghost of the past to haunt us."

"My piracy," he said bitterly.

Meg.

"Please don't cry, Tessa. Not when I can't wipe your tears away."

With the back of my hand, I dashed the tears out of my eyes. "Look at me."

His handsome face shimmered behind the sheen of the tears in my eyes. A stray brown curl fell into his eyes. I reached up to sweep it off his forehead, but caught myself before I touched him. I lowered my hand and looked guiltily behind me, wondering what Meg was thinking. She was speaking with Lord De Luca, but she had positioned herself to watch our interactions. I stepped back.

"You're distracted," said Nicholas.

"You're in chains," I replied.

"You keep looking at Meg."

I shrugged unapologetically. "It seems as though you were close."

"All shipmates are. Part of the job. Can't leave each other's company, so you adapt."

"You weren't close to Wrack."

"He was…a pain."

I looked at my hands, the walls, the flagstones—anywhere but at Nicholas. "Why didn't you tell me about her?"

"She wasn't worth mentioning."

I'd only known Meg for a couple of days and she had already found it worth mentioning. I knotted my fingers. "The way she looks at you…it seems like you're worth something to her."

"She's just happy to see an old friend."

I knew Nicholas had a past. Everyone did. Why wouldn't he

tell me about her? And why did it matter so much to me? "An old friend?" I asked with derision.

"That's what I said." His tone held a warning.

"I've heard a million stories about Skidmore. Stories about Black and Beck and Porter and a dozen other of your shipmates. How is it that not one single story about the only female pirate on your crew ever surfaced?"

"Are you jealous of her? You shouldn't be."

"Maybe she's jealous of me," I mumbled, forcing myself not to look at Meg again.

"Who cares if she is? I'll tell her right now how things are."

"Shh!" I looked around hastily to see if anyone had heard him. "She can't know! No one can know. In her eyes we need to be nothing more than shipmates bonded by a long journey. Like you said before."

Like you said about Meg.

"What does it matter what Meg knows?"

"It's too dangerous for you. My father hates pirates. I am sure he will be *very* suspicious that I spent the past three months in your company. If he knew we're sweethearts, he'll think you preyed on my situation. Anyone would think that. We cannot claim to be anything more than friends. The truth is too dangerous."

Nicholas looked at me darkly. "The truth can be harsh, but it's never as dangerous as a lie. I don't want to lie to your father. I don't want to lie about you."

"Some lies are useful. This one will save your life."

He rolled his eyes. "You mean it will save your reputation. Yes, some lies are useful, indeed."

I dropped my voice dangerously low. "As if you're a paragon of honesty! You've had plenty of practice selling lies." I eyed Meg again as I folded my arms.

His eyes were sharp and narrow, his posture tense. Then suddenly, like a storm blowing over, his anger vanished. He sighed and his shoulders sagged. "I don't have much time and I don't want to spend it fighting. Especially when we can't reconcile properly." He smirked. Only Nicholas would be coy at a time like this, with shackles on his hands on the day of his intended execution in the midst of a heated argument.

I nodded, forcing out a small smile. God willing, there would be enough time for us to fight later. I laid my hand on top of his—a truce.

And just when our anger had been set aside, the guard came to collect Nicholas.

I called to Meg to bring the food and blanket. The guard examined everything but allowed Nicholas to keep them.

"I'll come back later," I said.

"I'd rather you didn't."

"What? Why?"

Tender concern laced Nicholas's eyes. "You don't have to worry about me anymore. Enjoy your day, your new home. Rest. You look bloody miserable."

I looked down at my dress, wondering if it was unflattering.

Nicholas cocked his lips in a half smile. "Not so much the way you're dressed as those black shadows under your eyes. Do this for me. Take today to recover a bit. Come see me tomorrow. I won't be going anywhere."

I swatted him on the arm. "This is no time for jesting. You're in jail."

"Aye, but a mighty fine one."

I scowled.

"Not a whiff of bilge water."

I tried to hold back my laughter, but couldn't.

Nicholas grinned. "I have missed your laugh. Now how 'bout a kiss from my girl?"

"Not now," I said, aghast that he would expect a kiss in public in front of Lord De Luca and Meg.

Nicholas pressed his lips together. "You'll deny a man his dyin' wish?"

I glanced quickly at my companions. They were in conversation, their backs to us, pointing at the horses. I snapped back, rose on my toes and planted a swift peck on Nicholas's cheek.

He shook his head in mock disappointment. "You've nigh lost your edge. I promise to tutor you."

If he was trying to goad me into something more, it didn't work. Meg couldn't see anything like that. It would devastate her.

"Goodbye, Nicholas. For today only."

"For today only." His voice was husky. He nodded to the guard, who led him deep into the belly of the fortress.

CHAPTER ELEVEN

THE RETURN RIDE TO Amerscott was as awful as I had
dreaded. Meg turned towards me, suspicion in her eyes. "What
a shocking connection. I would have never expected the pirate
you told me about would be an acquaintance." There was a
hint of a threat in her tone, a hint of hysteria. I had never
known a servant who would speak to her employer in such a
way. But this girl wasn't really a servant—she was a pirate.

I reminded her of her place. "It was shocking to know
you've had such close ties to a convicted pirate officer. Tell me
again how you two are connected?"

She shrank back and lowered her gaze.

After a moment of tense silence, Lord De Luca said, "I am
as confused as Miss Monroe. Will you explain your link to
this pirate?"

Meg swallowed and kept her eyes down. She had much to
lose. "I used to be a sailor. Nicky was a sailor, too. We were
crewmates. That's all." She risked a sideways glance at me to
see if I would reveal her lie.

Lord De Luca was not sympathetic. "You told me you
were a scullery maid before coming into my household. Was
that a lie?"

Meg stuttered out an answer. "I...I...I was a scullery maid

on a ship. I'm sorry, my lord. I was afraid you wouldn't hire me if you knew the truth."

"You should not have presumed to know my prejudices. Perhaps I would have hired you, perhaps not. We won't ever know. But as of this moment, you are terminated. I cannot allow dishonesty in my staff."

Meg's head was still down and I could not see her face, but I felt a slight tremble coming from her. I stared at her with cold, calculating eyes. She had been put out. I would never have to see her again. She would not have to act as my maid and companion while Nicholas courted me. He would not be reminded of his past with her or tempted into an alternative future. Lord De Luca had just removed all the dread that had been building up in me from the moment I realized Meg knew and loved Nicholas.

And I couldn't let it alone.

The situation was horrid, but it wasn't Meg's fault. No one dreamed of being a pirate. Just like Nicholas, she was a victim of circumstance; it wasn't wrong of her to want to change the course of her life. I praised that about Nicholas. I couldn't condemn her for the same act. Her connection with him was a bitter coincidence, nothing more. I could indulge my petty jealousy and see her put out where she would return to piracy or prostitution or die in the street as a gutter rat. Or I could defend her as my friend. "Begging your pardon, Lord De Luca, you sent her to me. She is a member of my staff. Not yours."

Meg lifted her eyes. They were red, but hope-filled.

"Not anymore," Lord De Luca said. "I am embarrassed that I ever sent her to you. I have endangered you and I cannot forgive myself for it."

"Please, sir," I said forcefully, "she is my maid and I wish her to remain in that capacity."

"She was on loan from my staff and I refuse to employ her a moment longer."

I thought quickly. I had to be insistent yet not humiliate him more than Meg already had. "I am not wise in such things and

I know I have the soft heart of a lady, but Meg's dishonesty has not threatened me. She hasn't stolen anything. Her work is honest and industrious. I struggle to find fault in how a past she chose to leave behind effects the quality of service she has rendered me."

Lord De Luca studied my face. He exhaled slowly and his eyes softened. Then he dropped his voice as if that would prevent Meg from hearing him. "Miss Monroe, she is affiliated with a pirate. Her past puts you at risk."

I looked at Meg for a long moment. She was a pirate. A killer. As my personal maid, she had intimate access to me. She could kill me on a whim if she so desired. Maybe it would be best to set her loose. "Let's hear her story," I said finally, my eyes still resting on her, weighing her. "Tell us who you are. I am inclined to trust you. Tell me why I should."

Meg looked warily from me to Lord De Luca. "I've told you true except the part about the ship, I promise. I've never been a bad employee, I swear."

"Tell me about your father, Meg," I said. A tremble went through her, just as I had expected. "Tell me what led you to become a sailor." I emphasized the last word.

She understood what I was asking and nodded ever so slightly. "My father...my parents...we were just a simple family. We had a small farm and my father was a tanner, too. My mother...she died. It was just two years ago."

"How did she die?" I pried.

Meg blinked and looked away. I thought she was going to refuse to answer, but she finally did. "She sold a deer pelt to the cobbler for too small a price. My father was upset. He...when he had whiskey...he said he had to teach her a lesson. She never recovered from it."

Lord De Luca and I exchanged a horrified look. I was sorry I had pressed her for the details. I grabbed her hand. "And then you were the oldest, weren't you? You took her place?"

Meg nodded. "I was in trouble all the time." Her voice

dropped and I strained to hear her whisper, "I didn't want to die. Not like that."

"You escaped to the sea," I finished.

Her tears were falling openly now. She looked at me with vulnerable eyes. "I never wanted to be dependent on anyone again. I joined the first crew that would take me." I knew she meant the crew of the *Banshee*. They probably took her on for reasons other than her housekeeping skills. "And with money of my own and some experience, I passed myself off as a maid and began working for Lord De Luca eight months ago."

I looked at Lord De Luca. The horror was evident on his face. He would not insist on putting out Meg now. I gave him a wan smile. He furrowed his brow and looked away.

"You'll stay on as my maid," I told Meg. "But I will not brook any ill behavior, insolence, or dishonesty from you. When my father returns, I'll speak with him about making you a permanent part of the Monroe staff."

"Thank you, miss."

It was still morning when we arrived at Amerscott, but between my restless night and the emotional ride with Nicholas and Meg, I was exhausted. I was ready to be alone for a few hours.

I started up the stairs on my own but my solitude was thwarted by my healing ankle. As I struggled up the first stair, Meg and Lord De Luca both rushed to me, eager to assist. I gasped in surprise as the baron scooped me into his arms.

"Please excuse this, but it is the easiest way," he said.

My arms automatically linked around his neck. Our faces were just inches away. I could smell the fine oils on his clothing and feel the warmth from his cheek so near to mine.

"If you insist," I said, nervously glancing into his bottomless black eyes.

"Meg, show me to Miss Monroe's room," he instructed.

Meg led the way.

I anticipated him releasing me once we reached my

bedroom, but he did not. Our gaze met again. His smile slowly faded, something new sparking in his eyes.

I wanted to look away, but I couldn't. "Are you going to put me down?"

He blinked, as stunned as I, it seemed. "Sorry." His voice cracked. "Where shall I deposit you? The bed?"

"Please." My voice was small.

He set me gently on the bed and nodded at me with pursed lips, barely able to look at me. "Meg, you'll see she is comfortable?"

"Certainly, sir."

My sense returned. "Actually, Meg, I am not in need of your services. I would like to rest."

"Of course, miss." Meg curtsied. "I could bring you up some tea if you like."

Tea sounded wonderful, but I just wanted Meg to leave. I felt sorry for her lot in life and I had just saved her job, but I still seethed to think about her and Nicholas together. I shook my head, declining her offer.

"Is there anything I can get for you, sir?" Meg asked as she and Lord De Luca left my room.

"No. I think I'll return home for a little while. I shall come back later to check on the lady of the house. Meg...I want to apologize for my brusque response before. I was judgmental and I am sorry."

"Your response was honorable, my lord, and the apology is unnecessary, though I gladly accept it. And thank you for allowing me to continue my employment."

"You should thank Miss Monroe."

"I have much to speak to Miss Monroe about."

I had hoped she would feel indebted enough to me for saving her job that she would not pry about Nicholas. Apparently not.

The voices were fading down the hallway. I heard Lord De Luca say, "If your services aren't needed, I can arrange for a carriage to take you back to the fortress, to visit Mr. Holladay."

I strained to hear Meg's response but they were too far away. What had I done? I had just driven Meg into Nicholas's arms.

My guts twisted and I crumpled into a mess of tears.

After a few moments of private sobbing, a soft rap sounded on my door. I stifled my sobs and smeared my tears with the back of my hand. The door swung wide revealing Meg holding a pair of gloves in her hand.

"Miss Monroe! What ails you?"

"I'm sorry," I wiped my face frantically. "I didn't think you'd return."

"I know you told me not to. I'm sorry for disobeying. It's just that you left your gloves in Lord Emilio's carriage." She held up the gloves apologetically, then set them on my nightstand. "Are you unwell?"

I smiled wanly. "Just a bout of hysterics."

"Of course, miss. You've survived so much." Meg fished a handkerchief out of her pocket and handed it to me. I wiped my nose and eyes. "Do you need anything?"

"Just a good cry and a good nap." I smiled self-indulgently.

Meg turned to go then halted and turned back to me. "I can't thank you enough, Miss Monroe, for convincing Lord De Luca not to put me out."

I nodded, my head still cloudy from my tears. "I'm sorry I had to pry. You weren't just a sailor, though, you were a pirate. On the *Banshee*."

Meg looked down and didn't answer.

"I was serious about wanting complete honesty from you."

"Yes," she answered. "I was a pirate on the *Banshee*. How do you know of the *Banshee*? Of Nicky? You don't have to answer," she added quickly. "It isn't my place to ask."

I waved aside her remark. She was as curious as I had been—maybe more so. She deserved to know that much. Plus it was the perfect opportunity to get her to see my connection with Nicholas the way I wanted her to see it.

"Yes. I was rescued by the pirates on the *Banshee* and barely survived my time on board. Nicholas was the only reason I came home alive and with my virtue intact."

"He's not quite like the rest, is he? How did he come to be here, arrested, and no one else was caught?"

"He was alone. He no longer sails with the *Banshee*." I doubt I could have said anything more shocking to Meg. I'd told my story so many times to so many people that I had forgotten that she didn't know anything of my ordeal. "After the mutiny, he had to leave."

"A *mutiny*? They mutinied against *Nicky*?"

I pinched the bridge of my nose, feeling a headache coming on. "Nicholas," I subtly stressed his full name, "led a mutiny against Black."

"That's impossible."

"Why is that impossible? That's what happened."

Meg blinked rapidly, her eyes wide with disbelief. "Nicky and Captain Black are like brothers."

"Like brothers?" It was my turn to gape in disbelief. "They couldn't see eye to eye on anything. Nicholas had said that anger towards the captain was brewing. And he was able to stir up a mutiny at the right time."

"What do you mean—at the right time?"

I swallowed, afraid of how much I was about to reveal. "The pirates were going to hang me. He did it to interrupt them and help me escape."

Meg stood in quiet confusion for a moment. "Maybe it was a ruse."

"It wasn't a ruse when Black kidnapped me and tried to kill Nicholas."

Meg's eyes grew even wider.

I nodded. I tugged at my short hair. "Black gave me the haircut." I gestured to my leg. "And a man named Mendoza who was working with Black gave me the ankle."

"Mendoza?" She obviously knew the name.

"Did you work with him too?" Just my luck, Meg would defend him as well.

"I knew *of* him," Meg answered. "This is all so strange. It sounds nothing like the *Banshee* I knew."

"Thinking of you as a pirate is strange to me." Again I tried to imagine the demure, pretty girl in front of me wielding a battle-axe or cutlass during a raid.

Meg looked at me with round, worried eyes. "Are you going to tell your father?"

It would definitely remove her from Nicholas's life. It would also earn her a rope on the banyan tree. I sighed. "No, of course not."

Meg sat on the stool at the vanity. "So they were going to kill you and Nicky led a mutiny. How did he come to be in a jail in St. Kitts?"

I couldn't tell her about how Nicholas had set me adrift in a jollyboat to save me, gave up his fortune for his own freedom, then spent weeks searching for me. Those were the actions of a man in love. "I don't know much about the political climate of the *Banshee*, but it obviously didn't sit well with Nicholas. He renounced his position as quartermaster, got a modified fishing ketch, and escorted me here. Only they arrested him, not realizing he was the only reason I was alive."

"Oh." She realized it then. He had done for me what he refused to do for her. He'd left his crew, left his fortune, left his position of power, and sailed alone with me for weeks to make sure I was somewhere that I would never be hurt again. "He must care for you a great deal to risk so much." Her voice was haunted.

"He has a noble heart. I believe he would have done the same for anyone." That part was not a lie. I believed every word of it to be true. "Our time and trials have bonded us. I love him dearly. I have never had a brother before, but I have one now." The lie came easily enough and sounded sincere on my tongue.

Her features relaxed with relief but my pulse sped up. "For a moment I thought...the other day you said you were spoken for and I thought maybe Nicky..." She trailed off and smiled sheepishly.

I smiled in response, but didn't answer. I didn't need to.

Meg smoothed her skirt and stood. "Lord Emilio said he would take me back to visit Nicky. Unless you need anything, I would like to take advantage of his offer."

My chest tightened. She was going to see him. Alone.

"Are you feeling all right, miss? You look flushed."

I could tell her to stay, I thought. I could be so demanding that she would never have the chance to see Nicholas again. Maybe I could insist on going with her. Nicholas made me promise not to come back today. Maybe he and Meg arranged this and he wanted her to come back alone. I sank back on my pillow. I supposed I would never truly know what—if anything—was between them if I constantly thwarted them. I would rather know sooner than later.

"I'm fine. I am going to sleep now. Enjoy your time off."

Pausing by the door, Meg asked, "Did he ever mention me?"

I shook my head slowly. "No. It was just as shocking to me this morning to realize you two knew one another."

She nodded, remembering the moment. Then with a genuine smile, she said, "Thank you, miss. Thank you for giving me this time off. Thank you for saving my job, for saving my life, for saving Nicky." She pulled the door closed behind her.

I pulled the blankets over my head and shut my eyes. Any hope of sleep was lost. If I had done something so wonderful, why did I feel so dirty? I hadn't done anything wrong. I had only spared her feelings. It was kindness.

She'd go to the fort and Nicholas would tell her the same thing. He'd agreed to keep our romance private—hadn't he?

What if he told her everything and she knew I had lied?

He wouldn't do that. He knew how things had to be. He would tell her what I had told her. We were close. We were friends. She would believe him as easily as she believed me because it was what she wanted to believe. She thought he loved her. Would she act on that? A million scenarios of what was taking place at the fortress paraded through my mind, each worse than the last.

I cowered under my covers until I heard a clock chime nine. I couldn't torment myself any longer. I made my way down the stairs and wandered around until I found Miss Maisley beating the carpets out back.

"Hello, darling." She greeted me with a kiss on the cheek. "Would you like something to eat?"

"Some tea would be lovely."

Miss Maisley disappeared into the house.

The surrounding beauty was a welcome distraction. A tiled patio stretched out before me, winding amid potted flowering trees. A quaint gazebo housed a wrought-iron table and set of chairs—a perfect spot for tea. Tropical birds chattered in the fronds above me and sunshine splashed in dapples at my feet.

Miss Maisley found me in the gazebo. "What do you think of Amerscott? It's quite different from the home in England."

My eyes scanned the blankets of emerald surrounding me. "It's strange to think of this as my home."

"I'm sure it will feel more like home once your father returns."

I nodded towards the meandering walkway. "How far back does that go?"

"It connects Amerscott to Glencartha, Lord Emilio's estate. His garden is back that way. It's enchanting."

"Everything here is enchanting." I gestured broadly. "The Caribbean sun. Living next door to a baron. The scent of frangipani on the breeze. No worry of snow or fog. It's practically unbelievable."

Miss Maisley nodded in agreement, a look of pure contentment on her face. "It was quite kind of you to allow Miss Meg to visit her friend. She seems to fancy him quite a bit."

No. Not this. Not now. Not Miss Maisley.

I smiled politely, but my lips were tight and my eyes cool.

My look was well interpreted. "I'll just be here, finishing the rugs." Miss Maisley resumed her task.

After tea, I wandered back into the house, trying to distract myself from the passing time. Meg had been gone for over an hour and a half now.

I found myself at the harpsichord in the parlor. I played every song I could remember then resorted to composing some melodies of my own. My eyes kept wandering to the grandfather clock in the corner of the parlor. What were they doing? She had spent more time with him than I had in the past two days combined.

Bored with the harpsichord, I found some spare paper and pencils and sat to sketch in a velveteen chair with a view of the driveway.

It was another thirty minutes before the De Luca carriage rolled to a stop in front of Amerscott. The driver helped Meg out. A moment later, she joined me in the parlor, flopping down on a chaise opposite from me. She was unhappy. My heart beat faster. Perhaps she knew. Perhaps he told her. I felt a pang of guilt.

"Good day, Meg." I did my best to sound indifferent as I casually glanced up from my sketch.

Meg's lip quivered.

I stiffened, preparing for a berating.

"We had a very long discussion. He told me everything."

"Everything?" I gulped.

Tears filled Meg's eyes. "The last time I saw him, I had decided to leave the *Banshee*. Nicky and I had become close. I told him how I felt. He told me that he cared for me but that nothing more than the stolen kisses we sometimes shared could ever happen because we were shipmates."

Stolen kisses?

"And honestly, that's why I left the *Banshee*. So we could be together. But he vanished to the sea. I knew he had responsibilities as quartermaster. But now he's told me that while he cared for me, the intensity of his feelings never matched my own." Tears flowed freely down Meg's cheeks. "He never loved me. He never intended to find me."

After an initial wave of relief, I felt genuine pity for Meg. Her supposed soul mate had rejected her.

"Oh, Meg. I am so sorry." I was still worried that she knew of Nicholas's affection for me and that she would react maliciously. I cleared my throat. "Do you think there is somebody else?"

"Oh, no." Meg shook her head violently. "He's too married to the sea for anything like that. I knew it then and I know it now—nothing can ever take him away from his first love."

I draped my arm around her shoulders and comforted her the best I could, my hypocrisy unfurling inside me like a red flag that could not be ignored.

CHAPTER TWELVE

THE DAYS PASSED LIKE molasses. There was no sign of my father. The most his commander could tell me was that he must have had an unexpected delay. These things happened with sea travel and no one seemed concerned, so I tried to keep from despairing.

Lord De Luca came to Amerscott at least once a day to join in a meal or offer his services in some respect. He took me to see Nicholas whenever I wanted, though Meg never returned to the fortress with me. I knew I had to tell her eventually, but she was so forlorn that I thought it best to give her heart time to grieve before cutting it anew.

After a few days without my splint, my ankle grew more stable. Lord De Luca noticed and asked if I felt strong enough to walk to the gardens with him. He led me down the winding, tiled pathway from the back door of Amerscott through lush jungle brush to a walled garden with an ornate iron gate. Miss Maisley had been wrong. The garden wasn't beautiful; it was a fairyland. A canopy of wisteria covered half the garden, their graceful lavender strands reflecting in pristine pools. More frangipani scented the air. Cherubic statues hid amongst the birds of paradise and miniature roses. Benches, gazebos, and secreted chairs beckoned me to sit with a book or sketchpad for hours on end.

"This is my favorite place in the world," Lord De Luca said proudly. "I never knew such beauty could exist." We watched a rabble of butterflies dance around a bed of snow-white orchids.

"I've never seen anything like it. Thank you for sharing it with me, my lord."

"Please, don't be so formal with me. I am not your lord. Call me Emilio."

I blushed and ducked my head. "If it pleases you."

"It does. It also pleases me that your ankle was strong enough to walk here. I meant to ask you...do you think it's strong enough for dancing?"

"I do not know. I have not attempted it."

Without warning, his left hand scooped up my right hand and his arm slid around my waist. He began to waltz me over the velvety grass.

"You are light on your feet. Like a ballerina." He twirled me under his arm. "You dance beautifully, broken ankle notwithstanding." He pulled me close to his chest and suddenly stopped. His deep eyes peered into mine, a longing in them. I cleared my throat and pulled back. He began the dance again, slower this time.

"This is what I needed to know," he said.

"What do you mean?"

"It would only be proper to welcome you to St. Kitts with a celebratory ball."

"I would not even know who to invite. I hardly know anyone on the island."

"All the more reason to give you a formal debut," explained Emilio as he twirled me around slowly. "Everyone on the island wants to meet you. It's only fair we allow them to—and we can do it in style."

I swayed with Emilio, thinking of his proposal. "I suppose it might be amusing. Though I must insist we wait until my father is home."

And Nicholas.

"Of course. We shall start preparations now but keep everything on reserve until your father returns."

A ball! For me! Despite how I felt about Emilio, I bit my lip to keep my smile from splitting my face.

* * * * *

Nine days had passed since I arrived at St. Kitts. It was Sunday morning and the sun was bright. I sat at the harpsichord and tinkered with a melody I had been inventing myself when I heard the clattering of a carriage rolling on the cobblestones in front of Amerscott. It would be Lord Emilio, of course. I hadn't yet visited Nicholas today. Perhaps he had come to do that. My fingers danced easily over the keys, weaving a song that had been playing inside my head. I would finish my song and then greet him in the foyer.

A small clatter startled me. I stopped playing and glanced over my shoulder just as I heard the sound I had been longing to hear: my father, saying my name.

"Tessa?"

He had me in his arms before I could stand.

"Is it really you? How can this be possible?" he asked. He knelt before me, tears tracing down the lines on his cheeks.

I laughed through my own tears. "Oh, Papa! My thoughts are the same."

"My Tessa. God has smiled on me this day. How long have you been here? Where have you been? Are you all right?"

"Slow down. Can you help me to the sofa?"

I rose unsteadily to my feet and took a limping step forward. My father wrapped his arm around my waist. "Are you injured?"

I pointed to my ankle. "It was broken several weeks ago in Curaçao. It's healing smartly."

"Curaçao?"

We settled on the sofa. "I'll tell you everything, but perhaps we should start with tea."

* * * * *

"My father has returned," I beamed at Nicholas as soon as the guard brought him up from the dungeons. The day was hot and bright, but a brisk wind blew from the harbor, snapping my skirt around my legs.

Nicholas looked towards the carriage and his posture changed instantly—his shoulders squared, his hands flexed. He licked his lips and asked, "Is he here?"

"No. He is settling in back at Amerscott. He barely let me out of his sight to come and see you, though."

"I can only imagine."

"He is eager to meet you. The infamous pirate quartermaster who saved his daughter."

Nicholas's eyebrows raised in apprehension.

"Don't tell me that the fearless Marks is nervous?"

Nicholas chuckled. "Let's see, which daunts me more…meeting the father of the girl I fancy…or meeting a pirate-hating, bloodthirsty admiral who could reinstate my execution with one word? Luck must be on my side because today I do not have to choose."

"Nicholas!" I chided playfully.

He laughed. Oh how I had missed his laugh. "Think about it!"

"If only you had some respect for your superiors." I raised my eyebrows at him.

"But I don't and that's the problem. How long before I say or do somethin' that will have him clap me in irons again?"

I shushed him. "My father and I will collect you later today in time for dinner."

"Would it be possible to arrange something else?"

"What do you mean?"

"I feel highly motivated to make a good impression. I cannot do it like this." He shrugged and looked down at himself.

I stepped back and assessed him. Black whiskers covered half his face. He was shoeless and his clothing was stained and rumpled. "I see what you mean. I imagine Lord Emilio can help."

"Lord *Emilio*?"

"That's what everyone else calls him," I quickly defended.

I beckoned Emilio over—he had politely remained by his carriage while I had my visit—and explained that Nicholas needed to freshen up before meeting my father.

"I shall talk to the admiral," Emilio said, "and convince him to have Mr. Holladay released by letter rather than a personal visit. You can refresh yourself at Glencartha, my home. Do you need clothing?"

"My belongings are still aboard my ship. If I could have access to them, I won't be needing anything else."

Emilio nodded, excusing himself. "As soon as you're done with your visit, Miss Monroe, we'll set this in motion."

"He's awfully helpful," Nicholas said, his eyes trained on the baron as he walked away.

"I know," I said happily. "It was a lucky star that led me to his carriage that day."

"Is that what it was?"

I didn't understand why he sounded so sullen. "You'll be free before the sun sets. Aren't you happy?"

Nicholas finally tore his eyes away from Emilio. "Can I just tell you how sorry I am that I kept you in the *Banshee's* brig for nearly three weeks?"

I touched the shackles around his wrists, then linked my fingers in his. "I can't wait to have you all to myself again."

"That thought's the only thing that's kept my spirits up, luv."

The wind tousled my hair. I futilely tried to tuck it behind my ears. Nicholas eyed me. "I can't wait until I can do that for you again."

I blushed furiously.

"You should go," Nicholas said, his face resigned.

"I don't want to."

"The sooner you go, the sooner I will be out of here and ready to see you as an unshackled, freshly shaven, bathed man."

I looked to see what Emilio was doing, hoping to sneak in a goodbye kiss. He was watching us from the carriage. I smiled apologetically at Nicholas and squeezed his hand instead.

"Tonight," I whispered, the word full of promise.

CHAPTER THIRTEEN

I HELD MY BREATH.

My father stood up from his chair, ready to greet our guests. I stood in turn, smoothing my gloved hands over the sea-green satin of my skirt.

Mr. Dean entered the parlor, two figures behind him. "Lord Emilio De Luca and Mr. Nicholas Holladay," he announced dryly, as though he were commenting on the temperature of his morning oatmeal.

I caught sight of Nicholas and my heart stuttered. The afternoon at Glencartha had agreed with him. He had donned the dress clothes he had purchased in Curaçao—a loose, ivory shirt, burgundy waistcoat, fitted brown trousers, brown velvet jacket, polished boots, and a tricorn hat.

I rolled my eyes at the sight of his ornate baldric, housing his flintlock and several daggers. His cutlass hung from his hip in an oiled leather sheath. I had hoped he had better sense than to display his weapons like an outlaw.

Nicholas swept off his hat and the glowing light of the chandelier illuminated his sharp cheekbones, his pillowy lips, and the strong line of his jaw. The soft waves of his brown hair were tied back at the nape of his neck, but a few sun-kissed strands had broken free to frame his dove-grey eyes. He stood tall: defiant, yet magnetic; graceful, yet commanding. Just one look around the room cemented his rebel status. He was a world apart from the rest of us in our white gloves, ruffled cuffs, and teased wigs.

Emilio nodded politely to my father, bowed before me and scooped my hand to his lips in a genteel kiss. My eyes flashed to Nicholas. He paid no mind to Emilio's kiss. He paid no mind to me at all. His stare was fixed strongly on my father.

Nicholas had a deep-bred distrust for authority in general and government specifically. I prayed he could keep his defiance in check for just one night. *Be polite, be polite, be polite,* I silently chanted.

My father's lips lifted in a smile that was courteous but cold. "Mr. Holladay, I am Admiral Archibald Monroe. Welcome to my home."

Nicholas tipped his head. "Admiral Monroe."

My father gestured to me. "I understand you are acquainted with my daughter."

Nicholas breezed over to me, forcing Emilio to sidestep awkwardly out of his way. He picked up my hands and kissed each in turn. "I know Tessa far better than either of you are likely comfortable with."

I shot Nicholas a poisonous looked that he only smirked at. Playing the part of the lady, I somehow managed to hide my mortification, knowing only I could save Nicholas from himself.

I smiled coyly. "And I know you far better than makes me comfortable, Mr. Holladay. As the only two people on a ship escaping pirates full of bloodlust, what was the alternative?"

My father looked at the scene before him in intrigue. I fought the urge to cower, knowing my mood would influence the entire situation. I held my posture, forced my smile, and fought against everything inside me that wanted to bow my head like a polite little lady. My father looked from me to

Nicholas, his eyes shrewd and judging. And then he laughed—a pure, rowdy guffaw that chased away the agitation in the room.

"As one seasoned seaman to the next, I know exactly what you mean." My father clapped a smiling Nicholas on the shoulder. "I hope you found better company in my daughter than the usual smelly sea dogs."

"Her smell was an improvement on the lot, but she makes an abhorrent drinking partner."

My father laughed again, then fixed his face in a stern look. "I pray you did not take advantage of her."

My stomach flipped as I guessed how Nicholas might respond.

"Believe me when I say there was no advantage to be had. Your daughter is quite threatening."

The three men broke out in boisterous laughter. I forced myself to join in with a girlish giggle, desperate to show that I was comfortable with everything about Nicholas and they should be too.

My father invited us all to sit and began speaking about his most recent venture to Nevus. When the attention was off me, I sagged into a stale sigh. I would have never expected such a response—my father, charmed by the brazen, direct, unapologetic pirate. The conversation ebbed and flowed around me while I basked in peace for the first time in months. My father, alive. My Nicholas, safe.

At dinner, Nicholas was on his worst behavior with irreverent jokes and a plethora of contentious opinions. Remarkably, my father and Lord Emilio loved every word he said. I shouldn't have been so surprised. He was charismatic, a natural leader. He had ushered more than a hundred men into battle, their lives forfeit to his decisions.

After apologizing for the cold temperatures of the meat pies, my father angrily asked Miss Maisley why the service was so slow. It wasn't until that moment that I realized that Meg hadn't helped at all.

"Father," I interrupted bravely, hoping the presence of dinner guests would prevent his ire from falling on me, "Meg is ill and can't assist Miss Maisley tonight. Miss Maisley, I think you're managing quite well on your own."

My father assessed me with the impatience bred from being a man of power. "What is the matter with her?"

I did my best to keep my eyes from wandering to Nicholas. "An upset stomach, I believe." It was the best excuse to keep her away from food. If I said she had a headache, my father might insist she help anyway.

My father grunted and stirred his dinner distastefully. Nicholas made some comment about cold meat pies being better than wormy hardtack and lightened the mood immediately.

My father prompted Nicholas to fill in details on his life as a pirate officer. The topic made me nervous. My father hated pirates so. Certainly discussing Nicholas's most recent profession would only disgust him. To my surprise, my father forgot his meal, leaned forward, and relished the information like he was hearing a forbidden secret.

Nicholas told his story. "I was orphaned as a lad. I knew a bit of carpentry but not enough to support myself. I would have died on the streets had I not taken to the sea; it was my salvation. I used my skills on board. But when pirates attacked the merchant ship I sailed with, I could either join with them or be killed. I didn't have a choice if I wanted to live. I turned pirate. I studied with a master carpenter and surgeon. I learned to fence and use firearms. I was a skilled marksman so they called me Marks. I was junior boatswain. Then senior. Then sailing master. By the time I was eighteen, I was quartermaster."

"Quartermaster at eighteen?" my father asked, visibly impressed.

"Aye," Nicholas confirmed through hardy bites of tepid meat pie.

"That's very young."

"I was very good at what I did," he said factually, no trace of arrogance or pride. It made him sound cold. I closed my eyes and wished him to tread carefully. Very carefully.

Lord Emilio jumped in on the questioning. "You were quartermaster for nearly three years, a position equivalent to that of captain, and you just walked away from it? Why?"

Nicholas looked at me, his eyes serious. "A lady's life depended on it."

"Why should I believe that you'll not return to the only life you've ever known?" my father asked.

Nicholas eyed him coolly. He didn't like being doubted. "Understand this—I love the sea, but I don't love piracy. When I was taken as a boy, I didn't have a choice. But now, I do. I'm done with it."

"Then what do you intend to do with yourself?"

I perked at my father's question. It was a question that had weighed on my mind since we decided to abandon our plans of a life at sea and sail to St. Kitts.

"Assuming I won't be killed for my crimes against the crown, I've thought on returning to carpentry."

My father shot a meaningful look at the baron. Then he said, "You have an impressive reputation, Mr. Holladay, and an unparalleled set of talents. What a shame to waste it. I could certainly use skills like yours. Have you considered privateering?"

Nicholas nearly choked on his wine. "You're offering me a Letter of Marque from the crown to hunt down other pirates?"

I almost choked, myself. A legal way to be a pirate. A sanctioned station at sea. How could Nicholas refuse the offer? Meg spoke true. I would lose him to the siren's song.

Nicholas raised his eyebrows, swirled his glass of wine, and mulled over the idea. "It's a flattering offer, but I am no longer interested in piracy—in any of its forms."

"Really?" I asked, the doubt obvious in my voice. "It seems like a perfect loophole."

Nicholas's eyes darkened. "I'm not looking for a loophole, Tessa. I'm looking for a new life. I told you I was done with it."

I flushed, shamed by his words, yet reassured by his passion. Despite everything—the surprises and the changes to our plans—he was still mine.

My father raised his eyebrows, no doubt curious about our exchange. "I wish you would reconsider, Mr. Holladay. I could certainly make use of your skill set. Christophe Harbor has been plagued by a rash of pirate attacks. I have reason to think we are being targeted."

Nicholas was suddenly very interested. "What evidence have you?"

"I've chased the pirates twice now, and though I have not caught them, I have gotten close enough to see them. Same men. But on different ships and flying different colors. The attacks are quite systematic. I suspect French privateers."

Nicholas steepled his fingers. "Why the French?"

"They've had their eyes on St. Kitts since it was colonized nigh a hundred years ago. Their attempts at conquering resulted in brief periods of French rule, but the British have always taken St. Kitts back and maintained dominance. The last attempt resulted in a series of shaky treaties, creating what we now call the Peace of Utrecht. If the French invade the island, they'll excite the wrath of the entire Royal Navy along with Spain, Portugal, and the Netherlands—all countries that signed the treaty. I have a pre-signed Declaration of War from King George himself to use in such an event. However, if we attack them, we have no such support. And we'd betray our allies. It makes me think—"

"They are trying to provoke you into an attack, leaving you helpless against a hostile invasion," Nicholas finished.

My father nodded.

I listened with curious horror. My father had never spoken freely about his work in front of me. I was always shielded from the dangers and politics of it all. My stomach soured. Our new home was a potential warzone.

"So you see," my father continued, "your experience would be invaluable in keeping my island safe. It would be a most profitable venture for you. I'd see to that. Sharing a prize with a hundred other men offered you, what? An even split of the bounty?"

"Double portion for officers."

"I offer you fifty percent of everything you take in."

Nicholas smiled and shook his head. "You have my answer, Admiral."

"Could I rely on you for consultation, at least?"

"It would be my pleasure, sir."

My father shrugged. "I'll take what I can. I'll have my commander call on us tomorrow with the most recent reports."

The conversation moved on and, little by little, my nerves settled. I learned that Nicholas had been let out of his cell as a temporary courtesy to my father. The formal pardon would have to be issued tomorrow—Monday—when my father could meet with Governor Abner. Luckily, Nicholas would not have to go back to the fortress. Emilio offered Nicholas a room at Glencartha and my father offered him a job at Amerscott. Apparently, my father had been renovating the manor and while most of the repairs were complete, he had yet to hire anyone to work on the servants' quarters out back.

After my father showed us the servants' quarters behind the house and settled the details of Nicholas's employment, Emilio invited us to stroll to his garden. Nicholas looked expectantly at me, his elbow extended. Emilio waited with a similar posture, possibly out of habit. I froze. I couldn't take Nicholas's arm. Doing so could reveal too much about us too soon. My father could change his mind about the job offer, or the pardon. I couldn't take Emilio's arm. Managing his expectations was a daily task already. Avoiding both of their stares, I sidled up to my father and slipped my hand into the crook of his arm. He patted my hand and kissed my forehead. Emilio smiled pleasantly, happy to see me reunited with my father. I cautiously gauged Nicholas's response. He looked confused. Hurt, even. I took a deep breath and pressed forward to the garden.

Once within the walls of the expansive garden, we spread out, each exploring distant groves and hidden alcoves. I quietly padded to a far corner of the garden where a ring of weeping trees secluded a shimmering pond. I glanced at Nicholas as I disappeared into the trees and waited on a wooden bridge overlooking a colony of lily pads.

Moments later he joined me. No words passed between us as he gathered me to his chest and lifted my chin, his lips sinking down onto mine.

This was the moment I had longed for ever since Nicholas had been taken away from the *Freedom*, yet I was too preoccupied to melt into Nicholas the way I wanted to. I pulled back and looked at him, my eyes full of my unspoken apology.

"Something amiss?" He wore that wounded expression again.

This wasn't the ideal reunion. But we knew it would be like this.

"It's too risky."

"I don't mind risks." Nicholas clamped his hands on my face and kissed me again.

I pulled back immediately. "Please. Not now." I jerked my head around, certain we were being watched.

"If it pleases you." He turned away from me.

I grabbed his hand. "My father has been so open already; I don't want to test his limits."

"Of course," Nicholas conceded. He squeezed my hand. I smiled tightly. "I'm not used to sharing you."

"Think of it as a game," I suggested. "Society's rules and all."

"There's a reason I've avoided society. I don't do well with its rules."

"It won't be forever." I took both of his hands in mine and stepped in close to him, a peace offering.

Nicholas leaned down and brushed his nose against mine.

"It won't be soon enough." He closed his eyes, as if in pain, a low breath escaping from his lips. He pulled back. "Best behavior, I promise."

CHAPTER FOURTEEN

THE EARLY SUNLIGHT STREAMED through my open windows, illuminating the dust motes as they danced in the air. I stretched lazily, a happy smile on my face. I couldn't remember the last time I had slept so well. My heart was at peace.

Standing in front of my new wardrobe, I carefully selected the day's attire—a pink overdress with a split skirt opening over an ornate brocade petticoat. I finished the look with an elaborate wig topped by a lace cap. I had often longed for Nicholas to see me this way—dressed to my full potential, a lady of high breeding. He would finally see the real me…and hopefully be impressed.

After a quick breakfast, I made my way outside to the corner of the yard where the servants' house was. Nicholas was there—as I had hoped—already sweating under the hot Caribbean sun. He was dressed like a sailor…like a pirate. Canvas breeches. Bare feet. White linen shirt open at the chest, transparent where it was wet with sweat.

I tiptoed up behind him. "Good morning."

Nicholas jumped in surprise, a strangled noise coming out of him. I laughed and clapped my hands together. He turned to me, his eyes still wide from the surprise, but he wore a boyish grin that made my heart race.

"Finally! I've been waitin' all morning just to catch a glimpse of you." He wiped the sweat from his brow with a bandanna.

He reached for me, hooking his hand around my waist, and pulling me towards him. He leaned in for a kiss and I did not deny him, though I kept it rather chaste.

He leaned in again, determined, so it seemed, to recreate the kind of lingering kisses we had shared when we were alone on the ketch.

I looked up at him with pleading eyes. "Best behavior, remember?"

His eyes swept the area around us. "No one's here."

I pointed at the building Nicholas was working on. "There is only a thin, cracked wall separating us from half a dozen of my father's employees."

He grinned wickedly. "I care not."

"Meg may be in there."

Nicholas's face darkened. "Why would that make a difference?" He let go of me and sauntered back to his tools.

"She's in love with you, Nicholas."

He set back to work removing rotted wooden panels on the house's exterior. "If memory serves, you seemed a pretty shade of green when you first learned of Miss Quincy's affections for me."

I placed my hands on my hips. "I was not!"

Nicholas raised his eyebrows.

I sighed. "Maybe. But that was before you clarified things with her. Now I pity her."

"You pity her?"

"You haven't seen her. Moping around, brokenhearted."

Nicholas pried off another rotted board. "Are you suggesting I do something to repair said broken heart?"

"No," I answered quickly. "I just want to be sympathetic. It would be in poor taste to flaunt such things in front of her."

He sighed. "I'll try to be sympathetic, too. Though I do not know how long I can manage it. I am not known for my patience."

I smiled gratefully. "You won't have to be patient for long. As soon as my father grows more accustomed to you, we can be more open."

Nicholas's eyes swept up and down me. "You're certainly coiffed." His tone was accusatory. Insulting even.

"You do not care for my dress?" I had spent so long picking it out just for him. Any other suitor I had known would have been pleased with my appearance. I struggled to understand Nicholas's preference for simple clothes and undone hair.

"I like your dress just fine," Nicholas corrected quickly. "A little more done up than I am used to, but the dress is fine. The wig makes you look absurd."

My hand flew to the wig as if I could protect it from his insult. "My cropped hair is absurd."

Nicholas turned back to his tools. "It's fetching. I quite like it," he muttered.

His secret comment flustered me. How was I supposed to answer that? "I can't run around corset-free with wind-tossed hair."

"Society's rules."

"Exactly," I said, glad he understood.

I turned at the sound of footsteps. My father, Emilio, and a third man I recognized as Commander Bidlack had come out of the house. My father was wearing a black jacket and matching pantaloons, drops of sweat beading on his pale forehead despite the early hour. Emilio was dressed similarly, his jacket trimmed with emerald-colored velvet. His heeled booties were adorned with golden buckles and his wool socks stretched over his calves to his knees. Commander Bidlack wore his uniform, heavy red wool with golden stitching and tassels. I was hot just looking at him.

"My darling girl, there you are." My father swept me into a tight hug.

"Hello, Papa." I kissed his cheek.

Emilio bowed graciously. "A pleasant morning to you, Miss Monroe. And to you, Mr. Holladay."

I curtsied. Nicholas grunted where he stood.

My father gestured to his commander. "Ephraim Bidlack, this is Nicholas Holladay. Ephraim is my second."

There was a frisson of tension as Nicholas's stare held Bidlack's.

"Have you met before?" Emilio asked.

Bidlack shook his head and Nicholas only smiled. Bidlack had been responsible for Nicholas's arrest.

Finally, Nicholas broke the tension. "I look forward to working with you to quell this pirate problem."

The flat-faced commander couldn't even give Nicholas the courtesy of a nod.

My father addressed me. "Lord De Luca has offered to host a reception for us in your honor, Tessa. A ball. Won't that be lovely?"

"A masquerade," Emilio added.

I pictured dancing freely with Nicholas with both of our identities hidden. "Very intriguing."

"Then it's settled," Emilio smiled. "This Saturday."

"I'll have to fashion a costume," I informed my father. "Mr. Holladay, too."

"Perhaps you can go to the dressmaker's this afternoon," my father said. His expression changed and he fumbled in the breast pocket of his jacket. "Mr. Holladay." He produced two pieces of parchment with official-looking calligraphy. "I've been to see Governor Abner. Your pardon is certified. Welcome to St. Kitts." He handed Nicholas the top piece of paper.

Nicholas accepted it reverently, unfolded it and read the words that set him free. "Thank you, sir."

"It was the least I could do, really, to thank you for returning my daughter to me in one piece—even if one of those pieces was broken." My father brandished the other piece of paper. "And here's this."

He passed the second paper to Nicholas, who took it with a perplexed look. He broke the seal and read it, his eyes growing wide.

"A Letter of Marque with your name on it, signed by the governor," my father explained. "It's yours if you'll have it."

Nicholas read it again. Then again. He folded it neatly, his expression growing impassive, then handed it back to my father with a curt nod. "Thank you, but my decision has not changed."

My father returned the Letter of Marque to his breast pocket. "I expected you to say as much. I hope you have no ill feelings towards me for trying."

"Of course not," Nicholas said. "It's quite flattering. I sincerely hope you have no ill feelings towards me for refusing."

"I understand completely. But I insist you discuss our most recent naval happenings with my commander, Lord Emilio, and myself. Your insight is much desired."

Nicholas scanned the tools and lumber scattered about his feet.

"Finish with that later," my father said, beckoning Nicholas to follow him inside. "This is far more important."

Nicholas wiped his hands on his bandanna, gave me a half-smile, and followed the men into the house. He looked so apart from them, his bare feet and linen blouse. I wondered if he wished he were wearing shoes. I certainly wished it on his behalf.

* * * * *

The night air was alive with the sound of crickets, their symphony a serenade on the light breeze. The ever-present perfume from orchids, jasmine, and honeysuckle seemed more intoxicating than usual. I lifted my nightdress and picked my way carefully down the winding tiled pathway, my heart throbbing in my throat.

My fingers trailed along the cold, bumpy stones of the garden wall. I peered through the gate before I entered, certain that in my eagerness I had arrived before Nicholas. I tiptoed under the canopy of wisteria, the moon shining through it to cast lacy patterns of silver on the emerald carpet of grass.

"You're early."

My stomach flipped at the sound of his voice—partly from the startle, but mostly from excitement.

"So are you," I replied, turning towards the sound of his voice.

A silhouette materialized, tall, muscular, and familiar. And then he was before me. Without so much as a greeting, I was lost in his kiss, his hands wildly tangling in my hair. I breathed deeply, drinking in his airy, marine scent. Like a sea breeze dancing across a meadow. Our kiss grew hungrier. I felt dizzy and pulled away before my knees buckled.

Nicholas pulled me back, refusing to let me go, his lips searching for mine as his arms pinned me against his chest. "You've been too far away for too long. I won't be letting you go so easily."

My fingers trailed along the planes of his face. I sometimes forgot how beautiful he was.

Our lips met again and I had as much power to withstand his passion as wax has against a flame.

"You're so beautiful," Nicholas murmured, his fingers grazing up and down my spine, leaving a trail of fire and ice in their wake.

"I was thinking the same of you."

He shook his head, "Not like you. Your skin in the moonlight—it practically glows. I feel like I have an angel in my arms right now. I am not worthy to kiss the ground you step on, let alone your lips. Still...you let me." He kissed me again.

"Will you come to the ball Saturday?"

Nicholas nuzzled into my hair. "Will you dance with me?"

"Of course."

"Then yes."

"What costume will you wear? I want to make sure I am dancing with the right man."

Nicholas shrugged. "I've not thought on it. I will make sure you can recognize me. I would hate to lose out on a dance with the most beautiful girl in the Caribbean over a case of mistaken identity."

"I'll be in red." I knew no other details of my dress, so it was all I could offer.

"The color of passion. So very fitting." His lips trailed along my jaw.

"I couldn't agree more," I murmured.

Nicholas stroked my cheek. "Come with me. You must see the pond in the moonlight." He led me deeper into the garden.

"How was your day? Did my father treat you well?"

"You never told me how funny he is."

Funny? I had never thought of him as so. Intelligent. Studious. Fair-minded. But not funny. I shook my head slightly, bemused.

"We're hunting fowl tomorrow."

"You and my father?"

"De Luca, too."

I blinked, my bewilderment growing. I struggled to find words.

Nicholas laughed at my reaction. "Apparently, they want to see my marksmanship skills firsthand." He tucked my hand into his arm and strolled with me under the wisteria canopy.

"I...I...I'm speechless. I had never expected my father taking to you so."

"I was well prepared for his hatred or begrudging tolerance at best."

A bullfrog sounded from the rushes on the far side of the garden, his bass voice echoing off the walls.

My eyes strayed to the looming mansion on the other side of the eastern garden wall. "How is Glencartha? What do you think of Lord De Luca?"

"A humble home, but I've seen worse," he replied diplomatically. We both laughed, knowing what an understatement that was. "De Luca is a decent chap. Benevolent in every way."

I nodded, thinking on how much he had done for the two of us.

Nicholas lowered his voice. "He speaks fondly of you, Tessa."

I looked at him apologetically. "I have suspected as much. In the beginning, I had no choice but to accept his help. I have worried that my reliance on him has given him the wrong impression."

"It has nothing to do with your reliance on him." Nicholas looked at me softly. "It has more to do with your spirit, your wit, and the way your lips curl just so when you hear a compliment you don't agree with." He brushed my lips with the tip of his thumb. "Any man would be a fool not to want you."

I felt myself blush. "I don't want him to want me. Besides, even if he thinks fondly of me, he is a gentleman. He'll be respectful. And in time, he'll realize his feelings are not returned."

In the darkness his eyes looked as black as flint, but his caress was as soft as moonlight on my skin.

We kissed again. "I should get back before I am missed."

Nicholas pursed his lips. "Can I walk you back to Amerscott?"

I shook my head. "Someone might see us together."

I could hear the longing in Nicholas's sigh.

"I'll see you tomorrow," I promised, "after your hunt. And we'll meet here again at moonrise."

Nicholas cupped my chin in his hand and kissed me sweetly. "I will be waiting for you. I'm getting very good at it."

"Patience is a virtue," I whispered.

"I despise virtue."

With a smile, I hurried away, leaving Nicholas and his underdeveloped patience in the shadows.

CHAPTER FIFTEEN

I HURRIED OUT OF the back of the house, my father's instructions still in my mind.

"I need Holladay now. Lord De Luca, too."

He was speaking to Mr. Dean, urgency in his voice. The steward began his slow shuffle across the room.

"Allow me," I volunteered.

My father looked at me with disapproval. This was work for a servant. I cocked my head, telling him without words that I could be much faster than the decrepit steward. My father looked at the newly arrived Commander Bidlack and then nodded at me.

"Go on, Tessa. Please hurry. This matter is of utmost importance."

As I neared Nicholas's worksite, the sound of laughter stopped me. I peered through the trees. Two men were working together, talking, and laughing. I had hoped to summon Nicholas first and have him accompany me to fetch the baron. I sagged with disappointment when I realized the other man with Nicholas was Lord Emilio.

Emilio was at the lathe, his unsteady hands holding a piece of wood the size of a sapling against the spindle, each turn smoothing and shaping the branch. Nicholas was guiding him, holding it steady where Emilio could not.

"Why do you want to learn this?" Nicholas asked as he showed Emilio how the pedal affected the spring pole.

Emilio copied what he had just been shown. "Call it a rich boy's whim. I've never done a useful thing in my life. I know tomes of useless knowledge. I've studied a dozen languages, fencing, sailing, and a host of other things without ever truly learning them. Away from the scrutiny of my family, away from the expectations of the Italian nobility, I am free to actually learn a few things. The De Luca family...it is a heavy legacy. It is liberating to be out from under it."

I knew I should interrupt them, tell them my father needed them immediately, but their exchange was so curious to me that I stayed hidden among the trees and watched. I hadn't expected such friendly dealings from Nicholas.

"Here, like this." Nicholas corrected Emilio's grip on the banister pole they were creating. "If I believed a word you said, I would think being an Italian nobleman was a terrible fate."

"There is much benefit. But much obligation too. Though less benefit and more obligation for a younger son. In my father's eyes, I exist only to strengthen the family holdings. You think my rank and my wealth would allow me more freedoms, but there is a price to pay for it all. Everything I do brings either honor or shame to the De Luca name." He chuckled darkly. "Understand that you truly have a unique life. Freedoms most have never experienced."

"I was never free. It's a common misjudgment."

Lord De Luca scoffed. "No laws. No limits. No reputation. No family. Money. Women. Power. Freedom."

I took a step closer, not wanting to miss any of Nicholas's reply.

"Power? Freedom? No. I was beholden to the fickle democracy of rebel drunkards. Backbreaking work. Hardtack. Nothing to eat but bloody hardtack. Women? The only women insane enough to tolerate our lot had the pox. The days were either a fight for my life or as dull as dust. But money," Nicholas's lip curled up. "Yes, there was money."

They finished turning the banister pole and Nicholas reached for another piece of wood to repeat the process. "How much money?" Emilio asked. He quickly retracted the question. "Forgive me, that is rude to ask."

Nicholas focused on Emilio's work intently, making small corrections as needed. "Loot consists mostly of life's necessities. Victuals, rum, tar, canvas, gunpowder, the like. Daily needs. Sometimes there were things you could sell: spices, lace, sugar. You got a few coins that way. But overtaking one Spanish treasure galleon a year can make a pirate a very rich man. My best prize ship left me with one-hundred and fifty-eight thousand pounds."

"One hundred and fifty-eight thousand pounds?" Lord De Luca sputtered.

I clamped my hand over my mouth to stop a gasp. I felt my eyes grow wide. My view of Nicholas as a poverty-stricken sailor barely subsisting on raided goods shattered. My father's new and sizeable salary was five hundred pounds a year. It was a trifle compared to Nicholas's wealth.

"With means like that, what business have you hiring yourself for manual labor? You could purchase the sugar plantation next to mine and be a king in the Caribbean."

Nicholas inspected the second banister and set it aside when he saw that it met his approval. "The money is gone," he said matter-of-factly.

I swallowed hard. Nicholas had told me that he bought his freedom from the pirates on the *Banshee* with his entire fortune so he could find me in Port Winslow. I had no idea his fortune was so vast.

Lord De Luca was in shock. "Certainly you didn't spend it all on frivolities such as drink and game."

Nicholas fixed Emilio with a poisonous look. I knew how he hated being fitted with the scoundrel archetype.

"I spent it saving the life of a certain young lass acquainted to us both."

The baron looked chastened. Rightfully so. "A smart expenditure," he conceded.

"A thousand times over," Nicholas answered in a low voice.

"She is quite the creature."

"That she is."

My skin prickled. I leaned in closer, praying I would remain unnoticed.

"You spent nearly three months with her in close quarters. You must know her well."

Nicholas grunted.

"Is she truly as enchanting as she seems?"

Nicholas smirked. He had such a haughty air about him at times. I wondered if it came from a life deprived of polite society or something more primal. "More so."

A satisfied smile graced Emilio's handsome face. "So many females excel at playing the part of a lady only to be unmasked with time. Yet I feel it isn't the case with Miss Monroe. Tell me what you know of her."

Nicholas shifted. "You know the lady."

"Not like you. Tell me the secrets you learned living so closely with her. I beg of you."

I held my breath, as desperate as Emilio to hear the response. Nicholas shook his head and sighed, but he answered. "I know that she is a terrible cook. I know that she has a lovely singing voice. That she looks best with a bit of sunburn on her nose." He paused and cleared his throat. "I know far more of her than a man of my station should. I do not claim to be a gentleman, but it would be beneath me to divulge more than I already have."

I couldn't tell if my heart had stopped or was fluttering so rapidly that it gave the feeling of stillness. I inched closer, hungry to hear what Nicholas would say next, what he would confess to Emilio that he would not confess to me.

Instead, I found myself hearing a different confession.

"I find myself thinking of her all the time. She consumes me," said Emilio quietly.

My palms were instantly damp and I felt a little dizzy. Emilio's words were alarming, thrilling, and terrifying all at once. I stared at Nicholas, anxiously awaiting his response. He was bent over the lathe. I noticed the thick cords of his muscled shoulders tense beneath his shirt. But he said nothing. He didn't even look up from his work.

After a beat of silence, Emilio continued. "I am going to ask the admiral permission to court her."

My heart quickened.

Nicholas stopped lathing abruptly and stared at Emilio with hot grey eyes. His mouth worked for a moment before words came out. "Perhaps you should wait. Her heart is not unfettered."

Emilio cocked a brow. "Is this one of the details you are too gallant to divulge? You must tell me. The way I yearn for her...I must know any obstacle I have to conquer."

Nicholas resumed his work. "I can only advise you not to rush into a courtship with her."

Emilio sighed but nodded. "You're right. There is time enough."

I stayed hidden as their conversation drifted to more mundane topics, then emerged on the path and walked quickly to the men. They took my breathlessness for urgency.

"Miss Monroe," Emilio bowed deeply, "an unexpected delight. Is everything all right?"

Nicholas straightened and smiled politely at me, but the tension in his shoulders remained.

I bobbed a curtsy. "Good afternoon, gentlemen. My father asked if you would be kind enough to join him in his study immediately. Commander Bidlack arrived a few moments ago and my father said the matter is of utmost importance."

The men exchanged curious glances. Neither of them knew what this summons was about.

"Lead on, Miss Monroe." Emilio offered his arm to me.

I glimpsed an amused glint in Nicholas's eyes. He knew how uncomfortable Emilio's affections made me. He enjoyed seeing me squirm. I covered my nose with both of my hands and feigned a sneeze, then I picked up my skirts so my hands would be too full to take the baron's arm.

Nicholas grinned broadly. He was taking far too much pleasure in the situation.

* * * * *

I sat in my bedroom, the flickering candlelight dancing across the pages of my book. The rooms in Amerscott had finally quieted down as the twilight deepened into night. A small fire crackled across the room, more for comfort and light than for a source of heat. The pop and sizzle of the sap was the only sound in the room. In the back of my throat, I could taste the dust burning in the chimney. Snuggling with an itchy wool blanket, I could smell the walls and rugs and the upholstery on the chair. For so long, I had only smelled the salt of the sea and the stench of a ship. These smells were so foreign, yet so familiar. They were the smells of civilization. The smells of society.

Outside, a glowing white disk crested over the palm trees. Moonrise. I tied my red dressing gown around me and stealthily made my way to Lord Emilio's garden.

"Good evening, Miss Monroe," Nicholas said as he glided through the shadows like a cat.

"Mr. Holladay," I curtsied formally.

He bowed deeply and kissed my hand.

"Such manners," I teased.

"Perhaps you find it attractive in a suitor," replied Nicholas with laughter in his voice.

"Perhaps I do not mind a little impropriety."

He took me in his arms. "If that's what the lady wants," he kissed the corners of my mouth, "then who am I to deny her?"

Before he could kiss me fully, I asked him why my father had requested an audience with him. It had been nagging me all day.

His brow furrowed. "An enemy ship nearly breached the harbor this morning. He wanted my opinion on some things."

"Which explains why his commander was there."

"Such a lovely man," Nicholas said sarcastically.

"You don't like Bidlack?"

"No."

"Neither do I," I said. "Were you rude to him?"

"Not as rude as he was to me."

"That's not what I hoped to hear. What happened?"

Nicholas shrugged. "Nothing *happened*. I overheard him tell your father that as a pirate I should not be privy to military discussions and I should have been hanged when they had the chance."

I gasped. "How could he dare question the judgment of his superior?"

"I don't blame him for being suspicious of me. His charge is to fight pirates. Not fraternize with them. I make him very uncomfortable."

"How good of you to be so forgiving."

He scoffed. "I said I didn't blame him, not that I forgave him. He was a right cuss and if I ever hear him say the like again, I'll truly make him wish he hanged me."

I quickly changed the subject. "So what were you discussing? Is there any danger?"

"Could be. A few sailors were able to identify the captain. A man named Mateus Salazar."

"Mateus Salazar? That doesn't sound French."

"Portuguese."

"Just another pirate then. What's there to fear of this man?"

"I've had dealings with him in the past. He calls himself King of the Pirates. He's a mercenary with no allegiance, no honor, nothing but hatred and bloodlust for anyone who is not pirate."

"The Royal Navy will take him out," I stated with confidence.

Nicholas clicked his tongue. "I have a feeling that is just what Salazar wants. We must protect the harbor without engaging him."

"*We*? Are you part of a 'we'?"

"No, no. Just sayin'. Though your father offered me the Letter of Marque again."

I blanched, angry that my father would be so pushy. Nicholas felt indebted to him. It wasn't fair for my father to exploit that. "You told him no. He shouldn't disrespect your wishes."

"I told him no again."

My heart settled a little, but I was still angry. It wouldn't take much to push Nicholas back to the sea. It was his home. "Isn't there a part of you that wants to accept it?"

He pulled me into his arms. "Not one bit of me."

"Good," I murmured, willing myself to believe it.

"You don't fancy me a privateer?"

I snuggled into his chest, inhaling the scent I found so irresistible. "I don't fancy you leaving me."

"And that, luv, will never happen." He pecked me on the nose.

"You won't leave me for the sea?"

"Never."

"Promise it."

"I promise it."

I heard a scurry in the darkness. I froze, listening hard.

"What was that?" I whispered.

Nicholas frowned, obviously uncertain. "An animal?"

I hitched up the skirt of my nightdress and started towards the gate. "It could be my father. I must go."

Nicholas kept pace with me. "It wasn't your father. Just the trees rustling."

"If I am caught—"

"Stop and listen." Nicholas grabbed my elbow and pulled me to a halt. We listened for a moment. "Nothing but the night."

"I cannot risk it." I began walking again. "If there is as much as a whisper of a pirate threat to St. Kitts, my father will be more paranoid about my safety than usual."

"Tessa, you only just arrived. We've had no time together at all. Please don't rush off."

I slowly eased open the wrought-iron gate, hoping the song of the crickets covered the wailing of the metal hinges.

"Tessa," Nicholas pleaded again.

"I'll see you at the ball. Save a dance for me?" I closed the gate and blew him a quick kiss through the bars, then dashed off to Amerscott, too preoccupied to fully register the crestfallen look on his face.

CHAPTER SIXTEEN

THE GOWN WAS BEYOND my wildest expectations.

Yards and yards of shimmering scarlet satin draped over my hoop skirt. The red fabric was slashed down the center revealing a silk underskirt of striking cerulean blue.

Tiny gold feathers were stitched into elaborate patterns along the hemline. The bodice of my gown was of scarlet brocade with cap sleeves made from a flouncing arrangement of red feathers dusted with crystals. My mask—encrusted with brightly colored jewels and framed by soaring feathered plumes—completed my transformation into a scarlet macaw.

The pavilion behind Glencartha was wreathed with bouquets of night-blooming jasmine that dwarfed me. A thousand flickering candles spilled their light over the guests, illuminating the fantastical masks that filled the dance floor. The flames reflected off of every cut crystal, filling the night with a spectrum of rainbows. Swaths of silk hung from gilded arches, the lightest of breezes rippling through them and bringing them to life. A small orchestra played from the north end of the pavilion, the strains of their strings filling the night air with romantic enchantment.

I felt like a princess in a castle ready to step into my happy ending.

I expected Lord De Luca to greet me and introduce me to his guests since I was the guest of honor and he was the host. I did not see him, though he could have been anywhere amidst the sea of masks. My father found that curious as well, but took the liberty of parading me through the upper society of St. Kitts.

Within a quarter of an hour, I found myself dancing with anyone who asked. Behind each mask was a mystery. I knew Nicholas was somewhere in the throng—he had given me his word—and with each new partner, I examined the height, build, and grace for any indication that it was my Nicholas.

I had just finished dancing a minuet when a touch at my elbow drew my attention to a man behind me. He was styled as a pirate but in high fashion with a black velvet jacket and dress breeches. A white mask completely covered his face. He wore a long, curling black wig topped with a showy tricorn hat.

My smile was so big it nearly dislodged my mask from my face. Nicholas said I would know who he was and he had delivered. He couldn't have picked a more ingenious costume.

He bowed with a flourish and I curtsied regally, my oversized skirt ballooning around me. He was trying to say something, but we were too close to the music for me to hear anything he said. We came together in a flirtatious rendition of the contredanse. Before the final strains of the song sounded, I cocked my head and gestured for my partner to follow me away from the festivities.

I slipped my arm through Nicholas's as we wandered to the edge of the pavilion, clinging to the shadows of the palm trees. I hadn't spoken to him since I had rushed out of the garden. I knew it had upset him. He deserved to be reassured. "I want to tell you something," I began. "I know you've felt a little lost and perhaps neglected over the past few days. I wanted to apologize for that. I'm still trying to navigate my new life here. But mostly, I want to assure that my feelings for you grow each day."

"Miss Monroe," Nicholas replied, though his voice sounded a bit strange behind the mask. "Your flattery moves me."

His response was so formal. Without a hint of his usual playfulness. The words were startlingly *genuine*.

Suddenly suspicious, I pulled my hand back and anxiously scanned the pavilion. I saw him then—Nicholas—walking the perimeter of the dance floor. He was dressed a little dandier than usual, but with a black half mask covering only his eyes and his untamed brown hair spilling over his forehead, I recognized him immediately.

Who was I with?

I stepped back from the man cautiously. It was probably some stranger who would be nothing but amused by my mistake.

The man unfastened his mask and revealed his face.

"Lord De Luca," I breathed, not willing to believe that I had just proclaimed feelings for the baron. My mind raced to concoct a strategy to undo the damage.

My head spun. Three months ago this would have been a dream come true. A handsome baron desperate to court me, pleased by the proclamation of my affections. He could offer me not only a life of comfort, but a life of nobility. He could change my destiny forever. And he was kind and pleasant and an easy companion. Truly what anyone could ever want in a mate. It had only been three months since I was that girl, but it felt like a lifetime ago. That girl had been replaced by someone who lost much of her sense when she lost her heart to a pirate. No matter how perfectly appealing the baron was, he would never be enough. He would never be Nicholas.

I looked at the dance floor again. Nicholas was still weaving through the crowd, no doubt searching for me. I wanted nothing more than to run to him. To run away with him. Flee to the ketch and leave behind a world of silly rules and expectations.

But that wasn't a possibility. I had to take care of the problem I had just created.

Lord De Luca caught up both of my hands in his and raised them to his lips. He showered my knuckles with a dozen soft kissed. "*Cara mia*. I told you once to never hold back and you never have. Your words mean everything to me."

I smiled falsely and removed my hands from his. "Perhaps I spoke too soon, my lord. I hardly know myself. The night has been far too exciting for me to manage. Please do not take what I said to heart."

My attention drifted back towards the pavilion. Nicholas was leaving the crowd, heading into the shadows of the night on the pathway towards the garden, towards Amerscott. Probably searching for me.

"If you'll excuse me, my lord." I curtsied sloppily and turned away.

"Give me a few moments longer. There is so much for us to talk about."

"I must go," I muttered as I rudely ducked away and traced Nicholas's steps towards the garden. "Nicholas?" I whispered as I approached the gate. "Hello? Nick?"

My mask cropped my vision, making it difficult to see anything in the tangle of plants and shadows. I unfastened it from my face and held it gingerly while I peered into the garden and called for him again.

There was no answer but I heard something in the distance. Footsteps? Nicholas must have gone to Amerscott to find me.

I walked the rest of the way to my home without seeing any sign of him. If he weren't so stubborn, we would have met up by now. I was aching to see him, especially after my encounter with the baron. Nicholas would help me laugh it off. Right now the thought of it just made me sick.

The backyard was empty but the back door of the house was ajar. Nicholas wouldn't let himself into Amerscott, would he? I saw the shadow of a man move through the window. The figure was tall and lean, definitely not that of the aged and withered Mr. Dean.

I quietly entered the house and scanned each room for

Nicholas. I heard footsteps and then a large crash. The noise came from my father's study. My stomach pinched tight against my spine. This was not right.

I ventured towards the study. "Hello? Is someone there?"

My questions were answered with a low curse and another crash—the sound of wood clattering on the stone floor. I peered into the room. A man was at my father's desk, ransacking his papers and belongings. Two drawers were on the floor, their contents spilled everywhere. The man was dressed in a fine, emerald-green overcoat, a snowy cravat, black gloves, and a powdered white wig. He was tall with black eyes and a strong jaw. His upper lip was split with a scar. If I weren't so terrified, I may have considered him handsome.

"Who are you?" I demanded. "You're trespassing!"

His livid black eyes locked with my startled brown eyes, and he said something I didn't quite hear, but I knew it wasn't pleasant. He scooped up an armful of papers from the top of the desk and barreled through the door, knocking me over.

I let out a small scream as I hit the floor, watching helplessly as the man rushed out of the front door into the night. I barely had time to register what I saw when Lord De Luca was kneeling beside me, his wig askew and his mask still on. He must have followed me.

"Miss Monroe, what happened?"

"I…I…I…there was a man," I couldn't form a coherent thought. I pointed at the front door.

Lord De Luca helped me to my feet. He peered into the study. "*Che macello.* You've been burgled."

As he led me to a sofa in the parlor, he peppered me with questions. "Are you hurt? Who was it? Did he say anything? Did he take anything?"

I nodded my head, words still failing me.

"You're hurt?" He knelt before me, his hands on my shoulders, and examined me.

I shook my head and tried my voice again. "No. I'm fine. He took papers."

The baron's face clouded. "We must send for your father. Where is everyone? Mr. Dean?"

"The servants' quarters?" I guessed.

Lord De Luca left, assuring me he would be back in a moment. I sat alone in the parlor—alone in a house that was just broken into—painfully sensitive to every pop of the fire, every creak of timber.

Lord De Luca returned in a matter of seconds, kneeling before me as before. He gathered my hands. "You're trembling."

"Am I?" I spread out my fingers. They were quaking.

"Perhaps you should lie down."

I did as I was told and reclined on the sofa. He paced the room tensely, peering through the house and fawning over me in turn.

The quiet house instantly filled with a flurry of excitement. My father, Miss Maisley, Nicholas, and Meg crashed into the parlor. I struggled to sit up. It wasn't the terror that kept me lying flat as much as it was my tight corset and oversized hoopskirt. My efforts certainly made me appear far frailer than I felt. I finally managed to prop myself on my elbows.

My father rushed to me and pulled me into his arms.

"I'm so sorry, Papa. If only I had arrived a few moments sooner, I could have spooked him away before he took anything."

"Are you all right?"

I nodded.

"What if he had hurt you?"

"He didn't. He pushed past me to get away. That's all. What did he take? Anything important?"

My father's face darkened. "I haven't looked. Sit down and try to relax. Meg?" He snapped his fingers and Meg hurried to his side. "Attend to Tessa. I need to see if anything is missing."

My father left for the parlor with Emilio and Miss Maisley on his heels. Meg and Nicholas stayed behind.

Nicholas was by me instantly. "You were attacked?" His black mask set off the ferocity in his pale eyes.

"I surprised a burglar. He knocked me over on his way out. That is all."

"A burglar?" Nicholas scowled. He reached up and removed the mask from his face and cast it onto a side table.

"He was in the study."

"What were you doing here all by yourself?"

I glanced at Meg then back at Nicholas. "I thought it was you. I saw a shadow moving along the path. I followed it."

Nicholas huffed. "That was stupid."

"I beg your pardon?"

"It was reckless. You put yourself in danger."

Now it was my turn to huff. "I was entering my own home."

His mouth pressed into a hard line. "Did you recognize the man?" He lowered his voice. "Was it Captain Black? Anyone from the *Banshee*?"

"No. It was not a pirate, unless he was in a very good disguise. He looked like gentry. Fine clothes. Powdered wig. He wasn't British, though."

"Oh?"

"He was dark."

"A negro?"

"No. Dark like Lord De Luca but not as dark as you." I touched the back of his hand. "Tan skin and black eyes."

Nicholas pinched the bridge of his nose. "Excuse me," was all he said as he left the parlor.

It worried me that he thought Captain Black might attack me here in my home. Captain Black was supposed to be dead. Nicholas was harboring secret fears.

I sank back onto the couch, my hoop skirts billowing around me and catching on the armrest. Meg helped me arrange the complications of my dress and kept me decent.

"Beautiful, but ridiculous," I said.

Heated voices moved towards the parlor.

"...told me he looked like gentry. White wig," said Nicholas. "But not British. Dark like a Spaniard or an Italian."

"He had to have known about the ball. That Amerscott would be all but empty." That was my father.

"Every move was calculated." And Emilio.

The men entered the room.

"What did he take?" I asked my father.

"Nothing we shall miss, I'm sure." My father reassured me with a smile, but it was forced. "There's still much to sort through. Now tell me, my dear, absolutely everything."

With my father sitting across from me and staring at me with his shrewd eyes, I recounted my brief encounter with the stranger. When the constable arrived, I recounted my story again. I was exhausted when the constable left an hour and a half later. I hadn't even thought about the ball. Apparently, it had continued in all its splendor without its host or guest of honor. I idly mourned my lost chance of dancing with Nicholas. The house emptied and I retired to my room where Meg helped me out of my monstrous costume and into my nightdress.

The idea of the burglar coming back kept me from falling asleep. Restless, I ventured downstairs in search of a soothing mug of hot milk.

I was pulled from my course by a flickering light and hushed voices coming from the study. I crept to the doorway and saw my father, Governor Abner, and Ephraim Bidlack gathered around the ransacked desk.

"...sailed about an hour ago," Commander Bidlack said.

"The same ship as before?" my father asked.

Bidlack shook his head brusquely. "A completely different vessel. Flying British colors. It went unnoticed for some time."

My father's face looked as if it had aged a decade. "Salazar?"

"My men were quite certain," Bidlack answered.

"A completely different ship," the governor noted. "He must have a massive fleet."

My father passed his fingers over his brow. "Or a powerful backer."

"Sir?" Governor Abner asked.

"The entire French force," my father clarified.

"Is that possible?" The governor had grown pale.

"I suspect it."

"But why?"

"The king issued me a very powerful document. A Declaration of War against the French. It is only to be used in retaliation of a French attack. But if that document somehow falls into French hands, if King Louis sees it, he will believe that King George has declared war on him."

"Why would the French want their king to think the British have started a war with them?"

My father continued, "It gives them all the excuse they need to recapture the colonies they lost to us while looking like the victim, winning allies away from us. The French would stand to gain unspeakable power and wealth."

"The entire hemisphere would be at war," Bidlack muttered. "I cannot imagine the scope of it."

"This document," the governor asked, "where is it?"

"It was stolen this night."

"What does that have to do with Salazar?" Governor Abner asked.

Bidlack chimed in. "Salazar is more than a pirate, sir, he's a mercenary."

Seeing the confusion still on the governor's face, my father explained further. "Salazar in Christophe Harbor the same night as my study is burgled of an edict signed by the king? It cannot be coincidence. Some French official must have hired him. It means only one thing—a war like the world has never seen before."

CHAPTER SEVENTEEN

MEG THREW BACK THE curtains and bounded to the wardrobe where she yanked out a plum dress. "This will do. Hurry, miss."

"Meg?" I asked groggily as I blinked back the sunlight in the room. "Is something amiss?"

"Lord De Luca is calling on you."

"So early?"

Meg gestured to the flaming sunlight. "It's not that early, miss."

"What time is it?"

"Ten thirty."

"Ten thirty?" I sprang up, then sank on the bed again. My head pounded. I pressed my fingers to my temples. "Can't you send him away?"

"No one sends the baron away."

"Well, maybe I do." I made no move to stand up again.

Pieces of the previous night floated into my tangled mind. The intruder. The questioning. Eavesdropping on my father in the middle of the night. Such serious things were at play. I wished I knew when I could discuss it all with Nicholas.

"Up, up, up!" Meg insisted, half pushing, half pulling me out of bed. I was barely on my feet when she began unbuttoning my nightdress.

I flapped my arms angrily, waving her off. I could undress myself. I stood behind a painted wooden screen and stripped. Meg handed me fresh pantaloons and a petticoat.

"Oh no," I mumbled, my words doused in shame. "No, no, no, no, no."

Meg's face popped around the screen. "What is it?"

Little by little, memories of last night sharpened. The things I had said to the baron, mistaking him for Nicholas. And now he was calling on me unannounced. He was here to court me. Officially.

"No, no, no," I stammered walking from behind the screen and throwing myself on the bed in a dramatic huff of white linen. "This can't be happening. I can't see the baron. He must be sent away."

"Miss Monroe, you mustn't give in to hysterics. There's really no time to lose." Meg picked up the dress and chased me with it.

Hysterics? No. This was dread. This was shame. This was humiliation.

"I'm ill." I insisted as she worked the taffeta gown on to me. I did not have the mind to fight her. "I can't be seen. He can come back later."

She clicked her tongue. "Nonsense. You're well enough to give him the message yourself. If you're truly ill," the tone in her voice told me she knew I was not, "then you'll only need to spend a moment or two with him. But he's here now, waiting in the parlor. One mustn't keep the baron waiting."

"And what if I do?" I retorted, concocting a plan of everlasting preening to delay our meeting beyond proper etiquette. "I suppose he'd have to leave after an hour or three."

Meg ran a brush through my hair. I batted her away but it was no use. "If you would hold still, I could do a fast trick with your hair. But if you'd rather, you can greet the baron looking like a ragamuffin."

I sighed in disgust. I needed to tell him of my mistake. Blame it on the champagne, something. I would undo the mess.

It was going to be dreadful but now was as good a time as ever. I could be back in my bed in fifteen minutes.

"Fetch my wig," I relented.

The foyer was empty when I emerged from my room. No one was in the parlor either. Perhaps the baron had left and I wouldn't have to see him after all.

"Ah, Miss Monroe." I spun to see Mr. Dean coming from outside the front door. "Lord De Luca is expecting you."

His absence was too good to be true. "Where is he?"

"Outside, miss."

Outside? How very odd. I took a deep breath and followed Mr. Dean through the grand foyer and out the front door. I only needed five minutes to tell him to keep his distance from me. What was it Nicholas had said? *Her heart is not unfettered.* A perfect line—effective, yet pleasantly vague.

"Lead on," I instructed Mr. Dean as I lifted my head and my skirts.

Mr. Dean swung the door wide, letting in a beam of blinding sunlight. I halted for a moment, squinting and blinking, annoyed that my composure had slipped even slightly. Finally, my eyes took to my brilliant surroundings. The first figure I saw was that of my father, standing on the veranda.

"Morning, my Tessa," he greeted me.

"Papa." I crossed to him and kissed him on the cheek.

Lord De Luca was at the base of the stairs, dressed in tan sporting breeches and a smart, navy riding jacket. He held the reins of two palomino horses, their creamy coats glistening in the sun like taffeta.

He beamed the moment he saw me. My heart filled with dread.

I looked awkwardly from my father to Lord De Luca, reins in hand with no one else around. A private conversation here was out of the question and there was no way he could join me in the parlor for a moment.

The baron's smiled widened—I didn't think it possible, it

was already splitting his face like a crack in an egg. "Forgive me for not greeting you properly." He nodded at the horses. "And I hope you're ready for an adventure."

I opened my mouth in protest, but didn't know what to say. I was overly aware of my father watching our interchange. Finally, I found the words. "I'm not sure this is entirely proper. I don't see a horse for a chaperone."

"It's just a little horse ride," my father said. I looked at him with surprise. "You could use some diversion after last night's events and the baron has my full trust."

The two men exchanged an amused glance and I knew, *I knew* Lord De Luca had spoken to my father about courting me. My father's response was obvious.

The horses pulled at the reins, pillows of dust growing around their restless hooves. Lord De Luca put his lips to their ears and spoke to them in lilting Italian whispers.

I looked from the baron to my father—it was awkward to have such a dominating audience. I nodded politely at my father, still in disbelief that he would let me leave with an older gentleman without a chaperone. Island culture had made him lax.

I descended the steps and approached Lord De Luca. "I'd rather hoped to talk with you privately," I said quietly. "There are things that need to be said before any kind of outing."

"Nonsense!" It was my father again. His enthusiasm was not to be hidden. "You'll have enough time for conversation along the way."

Lord De Luca nodded, his black eyes sparking with delight.

"Very well," I said, knowing I could never say what I wanted to while on an outing with Lord. De Luca. Breaking hearts was best left at the end of a social obligation. Too much pain came from poor timing with these types of things. "I'll have Meg fetch my hat."

I emerged a moment later with a shallow but broad straw hat that tied at the nape of my neck with a wide cream-colored ribbon. I wondered how long this outing would be. I quickly devised a way to find out. "Shall I tell Miss Maisley to plan on one more for lunch?"

Lord De Luca smiled as if he were hiding a secret. "Actually, Miss Maisley ought to expect one *less* for lunch. Would you let her know, Admiral?"

"Indeed."

"Here, Miss Monroe. Meet my horses, Ambra and Oro. Ambra is all set for you."

I noticed a specialty saddle intended for female sidesaddle riding. With a little guidance from Lord De Luca, I hoisted myself onto the horse and hooked my leg over the leg pommel. I always felt like I would fall whenever I rode sidesaddle. It would be so much easier with canvas breeches instead of petticoats and laced-up stays.

I reached forward and patted the pale gold neck of my mare. "What does Ambra mean?"

"Ambra and Oro. Amber and gold. Because of their coats." He gracefully soared onto his saddle.

"Ah, Mr. Holladay," I heard my father say. "Are you in need of something?"

I twisted in my saddle to see Nicholas coming around the east side of the house. He was looking at me, his pace slowing. The surprise on his face was quickly darkening to disapproval.

I wished to offer some kind of explanation but could think of nothing that could be said in front of our audience. I widened my eyes with an unspoken apology, hoping Nicholas would read my mind. *I do not want to be here. This is being forced on me.*

"Miss Monroe?"

I broke my pleading stare at Nicholas and noticed that the baron had trotted Oro a few paces ahead. With one last wistful look at Nicholas, I clicked my tongue and urged Ambra to follow her mate. As we trotted down the cobblestone pathway towards the dusty roads, I couldn't help but feel Nicholas's eyes boring holes in my back. I owed him an explanation. Several, it seemed. I had run out on him during our last meeting at the garden, I had not met up with him at the masquerade ball, and now this. There wasn't much I could do about the obligations I had to my father. Things would settle soon enough. Nicholas needed to learn patience.

After ambling down the main roadway for a quarter of an hour, the horses led us along a grassy pathway with views of the cerulean sea stretching out to our left. Occasionally, Lord De Luca would point out a landmark, but for the most part we rode in easy silence, the steady clopping of the horses standing out against the soft *wooshing* of the sea to form a soothing rhythm.

The closer we go to the ocean, the stronger the breeze blew. My skirts whipped around my ankles, exposing my kneecap a time or two. I was glad Lord De Luca was riding ahead of me and could not see it. I found myself enjoying the outing. The quiet skies, the botanical smells, and the feel of the horse beneath me gave me a sense of abandon that I hadn't experienced since leaving the *Freedom*.

I felt a little bit lost—lost and small—as the horses meandered through the St. Kittian countryside. As we emerged from a copse of trees onto a rocky hilltop, I could see for miles in every direction, my eyes taking in the impossible green of the rolling hills, the stretch of unending ocean, and small cottages that made random appearances. The air was fresh and sweet, though heavy with the feel of the sea. Time seemed irrelevant. And space too. So different from the back-to-back buildings of London—tall, thick, and grey against a grey sky full of grey clouds that would create a grey fog over the smudgy greyness of the Thames River.

After a downward descent through low green brambles, Emilio pulled his horse to a stop at the edge of a meadow that faded into a rocky beach. He hopped off Oro and patted his rump, giving the horse permission to graze among the grasses.

As the baron approached me, the sense of peace that had settled over me dissolved. I dismounted, acutely aware of the baron's hands on my waist as I did so.

I landed on the ground with a little hop and smoothed my skirt. The breeze was stronger by the water and threatened to whisk my hat away.

He hadn't said a word for a long time. His face reflected the peace I had felt riding through the trees and dales. Without granting me much attention, he grasped the lapels of his jacket with both his hands and walked to the meadow's edge. Intrigued by his quiet demeanor, I followed him, one hand placed firmly on my flapping hat. Lord De Luca stared into the horizon, his eyes bright with the reflection of the water. A placid smile lifted the corners of his lips.

He was quite handsome, I noted. Tall and thin, a graceful willow compared to Nicholas's muscles and angles. A high, straight, Italian nose ran like an arrow down his face. His lips were thin but curvaceous. Lashes so thick they looked like liner ringing his eyes—eyes that weren't entirely black, but so deeply brown it seemed the best way to describe them. His face was thin and long with a pointed chin. It was only midday but the growth of whiskers already darkened his jaw.

Emilio caught me staring at him and his lips quirked up in a grin. I flushed and looked past him, pretending I had been taking in the view and not his profile.

He closed his eyes and inhaled deeply. I felt a bit like an intruder, witnessing a personal ritual not meant for my eyes. After a moment, I followed his lead and closed my own eyes to inhale the wind.

"Come," he finally said. "Let's eat."

He pulled the saddle bags off Oro and spread a blanket at the meadow's edge.

"May I help?"

"No, no. Please sit." He gestured to the blanket.

I sat on the edge of the blanket and fussed with my skirts as Lord De Luca set out a variety of fruits, breads, and cheeses.

I glanced around at the meadow and beach. The beauty of the spot was understated but undeniable. "I am surprised you brought me here."

"Are you?" Emilio's eyes gleamed with curiosity. "Why?"

I shrugged, realizing my line of thinking may be a bit too forward to share. Still, I had started the conversation, and I had promised him I would never hold back. "I thought you might take me to your mansion or somewhere fancy in town. Impress me."

"Nothing I own is more impressive than this." There was a reverence in his eyes that told me he believed what he was saying. "Is it not lovely?"

"Mmm."

"Forgive me," he said, seemingly shaking off his placidness. "I shouldn't be so distracted." He offered me a small, plump, purple fruit. "This is hicaco." He pointed to an oddly ridged yellow fruit. "Starfruit," he said. "Here is a custard apple and a guava." He gesture to each in turn. "I thought you could use a better introduction to the island. It seems so many of the settlers do all they can to live purely European lives here in a place that is so obviously not Europe. It's a shame. They miss out on the Caribbean splendor."

I took a bite of the hicaco, sweet juice dribbling down my chin. I relished the taste. "You love it here, then?"

"Of course. How could you not?"

"Do you never miss your home?"

Lord De Luca's thick, black eyebrows pinched together. "Immensely."

"Oh," I muttered, a bit surprised. "You seemed so enraptured by St. Kitts."

"I am," he reassured me. "I would be a fool to not experience everything it had to offer because I am homesick for another continent."

I nodded, wondering if I would ever miss England the way he missed Italy. "Will you return, then? To Italy?"

"Sì. Someday."

"Why are you here, my lordship? Truthfully?" I regretted the question as soon as I asked it. It was too bold. It would be best for me to keep our interactions superficial. "I apologize. Your business is not mine."

"The only thing you must apologize for is calling me your lordship. Use my given name. My title means nothing here. My title means very little anywhere, really."

I cocked my head and looked at him quizzically, refraining from asking any more questions, but thinking about the conversation he had with Nicholas. I knew his reasons, but he was not aware I had overheard them.

He went on. "As the fourth son, the title is spent."

"At least you have the title without the responsibility," I pointed out, hoping it was helpful. He looked a bit wounded at my words.

"The De Luca family stands upon the brink of shame. It wouldn't hurt for all of its members to have a bit more responsibility."

"Why are you here, then? It seems you are shirking your duty to your family by eating fruit in the island breezes." My words were stronger than I intended. Yet again, I berated myself for being too outspoken. I marveled at how thoroughly a lifetime of manners had been unlearned in only three months.

Emilio's eyes grew stormy. I braced myself for his reprimand. I deserved it. "My purpose here is not to play in the sun, as many think. I am here to do what my brothers—what my father—refuse to do. I am working. Earning money instead of spending it. The De Luca line is ancient. That might make it prestigious, but it also makes it nearly bankrupt. Dozens of De Luca noblemen are intent on holding a reputation they cannot afford. But there is too much pride. And what will be left for such a proud family when the coffers are empty? Humiliation and suicide."

Emilio looked away from me, seeing sights in the distance that I could not track. "People think I am just sporting here. A delicate nobleman with money to spare playing in the new world."

"I have never thought that of you."

Emilio smiled at me. "Of that I am most glad. My plantation is a success. My involvement with local politics is educational. I now have the collateral and experience necessary to return to my family's baronies with something they don't expect—a future."

His passion surprised me. Though I had never pictured him as some kind of spoiled gypsy noble, I hadn't ever imagined he had such verve in his sense of duty.

"I think it's impressive," I said as I fought to keep my skirt pooled decently around me. "All those who think you are here for yourself are completely wrong. Your time here is a sacrifice."

"Indeed. And a rotten one. What with endless white beaches and perfect tropical weather. Though I must correct you. I am not altogether selfless. I enjoy living life away from the expectations and disappointments of my parents. I came to find success in a place where my name or title make no difference." Emilio looked down and focused on his fingers as they picked lint from the blanket. I thought I noticed a flush of color in his cheeks. "I want to find someone who'll love me for more than my title. Someone I can marry without political arrangement."

I felt a pang of regret. For the past weeks, I had seen Emilio as little more than his title—a nobleman within my reach. As I had admitted to Meg before, had I not fallen in love with Nicholas, the baron was *exactly* the type of person I would have pursued merely because of his social standing. I had learned to look past Nicholas's lot in life...why hadn't I looked past Emilio's? He wasn't just a handsome face with a noble pedigree. He was a boy with hopes and dreams and feelings and fears, looking for a chance to break free from the conventions of his station.

Wasn't that what I was trying to do? I thought of Nicholas. It was my heart's greatest desire to marry him. Such a thing would not have happened in England—not without being exiled by my family and friends into extreme poverty. I looked at the wild grasses bowing in the salted wind. Here in these virgin colonies, there seemed a hope for it. This land had a will of its own, a freedom that could not be harnessed.

Taking in the rugged beauty of the isle, I said, "This seems like the place to do that."

"You really think so?" Emilio looked at me with blazing eyes. His stare was so intense I lost all my thoughts, all my words. I stared back. A sudden pinching in my chest made it difficult to breathe.

My hand rested palm down on the blanket beside me. Emilio reached over and pressed his hand on top of mine. I watched the action in a daze, as if I weren't in my body experiencing it.

I flinched when he touched me and the spark in his eyes was instantly doused. He looked at our hands, blinked rapidly, and pulled his hand away with an apologetic smile.

"Who is he?" asked Emilio.

Nicholas! I wanted to scream, *Nicholas!* Wasn't it obvious? I was terrible at hiding it. I was tempted to tell Emilio everything, I felt that I could trust him implicitly, but I couldn't risk it. My father would not approve, especially with a suitor like Emilio asking for my hand. Nicholas could be fired, exiled, or even sent back to the gallows. My charade—as flimsy as it was—was saving his life.

Needing a moment more to think up a response, I feigned ignorance. "I am certain I don't understand you."

Emilio had the decency to look a bit ashamed. "Mr. Holladay told me that…I'm sorry, I must have been mistaken."

I let out a slow breath, unsure if I should have seized the moment to tell him everything. The wind gusted and nearly stripped my hat and hairpiece from my head. A spray of sea showered us with salty droplets.

Emilio pointed to a patch of dark, thick clouds off the coast. "Looks like an afternoon storm is blowing in. Shall we return?"

We scrambled to collect the remains of our lunch, fighting

with the wind. Emilio rounded up the horses and helped me onto Ambra.

"My lord." He shot me a disapproving look. I started over. "Emilio, I meant to ask you something about last night."

"Go on." There was a hopeful timbre in his voice.

"Something was stolen. Papers. I saw it. My father assures me it is nothing, but I know there is something to worry about."

"I imagine you should heed your father. If he says there is nothing to worry about, he is right."

"But why, then, would the governor call in the middle of the night?"

Emilio's shoulders stiffened. "I'm sure he was simply verifying his facts."

Whatever was going on, he knew about it too.

I tried to sound demure and not challenging. "I only ask because I am scared. Is it safe here?"

"Your father would never tolerate any harm to come to you. But you might be safer if you could convince that friend of yours to accept your father's offer."

I trotted Ambra in silence for a moment. "He's spoken his mind."

"You can influence him. He values your friendship."

"He values it because he knows I do not manipulate it." My tone was stony.

Emilio caught up with me. "Do not take offense at the suggestion. I'm trying to help you see the good it would do all of us. He'd be protected by the crown. Not to mention the wealth he would acquire. Your father offered him half of all prize money. It's more than he ever made as a quartermaster. His skill would certainly help keep the island safe and save hundreds, even thousands of lives. Frankly, I think it's selfish of him not to offer his services. Your father is beyond generous. He could have had him hanged and instead he offers Mr. Holladay a fortune and chance for fame."

"And you think I should repeat this logic to Mr. Holladay on my father's behalf?"

"On your father's behalf. On mine. Whichever builds your courage."

My stomach grew sour and I grew brave. "You've asked me to misuse my friendship with Nicholas. In doing so, you've misused your friendship with me. I'll have no part in it and I thank you not to ask me again."

I dug my heels into Ambra and shot forward. Emilio quickly caught up. "Do not be angry," he said. "Understand why I asked you. I am not misusing your friendship. I was confiding in you. As a friend. As more than a friend."

There was longing in his voice. It fell on deaf ears. I kept my silence and Ambra kept her quick pace. Emilio was not one for groveling and he offered no more apologies. I was grateful for the quarrel. Emilio knew I was displeased with him. There was no longer a need to redress what happened at the ball. Enough damage was done.

CHAPTER EIGHTEEN

I WAITED A WHILE before seeking Nicholas, just to make sure my proceedings were unnoticed. The shadows of late afternoon were growing long when I meandered to the servant's house. Disappointment hit me like tidal wave when all I found was a scattering of sawdust.

Dejected, I wandered to the garden in hopes of a chance encounter. I wound through hedges and blooms, hoping that one of the tree trunks might materialize into Nicholas. I was more worried than ever that my outing with Emilio had upset him. He had to understand—I was simply playing a role.

The fading sunlight—and my grumbling belly—told me it was time to return for dinner. With a wistful look over my shoulder, I did just that.

The minutes dragged on as I waited for night to fall and the house to quiet. I fidgeted on my balcony as I watched the twilight sky turn to inky blue and finally saw the cresting of the moon. I wrapped a dressing gown around me and ghosted down the stairs.

"Oh." I brought up short at the base of the stairs. My father, Mr. Dean, and Miss Maisley looked up at me with puzzled faces.

"Is everything all right?" There was nothing but concern on my father's face.

"I wanted something from the kitchen."

"Hungry? Thirsty?" Miss Maisley was at my elbow.

"Not entirely sure," I responded. "A bit peckish, I suppose. I'll rummage through the pantry. Don't worry about me."

I slunk past the trio, casting several backward glances to be sure I wasn't being followed. Perhaps I could manage a quick visit to the garden—enough to let Nicholas know how much I missed him and why I couldn't stay.

I opened the back door as quietly as possible, sucking in my breath as the hinges creaked. I pulled the door behind me but didn't latch it in hopes of avoiding more noise.

I set out slowly, waiting for my eyes to adjust to the night before quickening my pace.

"Tessa?"

It was my father.

I froze with one foot in the air, scrunching my eyes closed as if that would help me vanish.

"What on earth are you doing?"

I willed a placid expression on my face and slowly turned to face him, hoping my voice wasn't trembling like my heart. "I needed some fresh air."

"Your room has a balcony."

"Of course." I scrambled for an excuse. "It's just that...once I was in the kitchen, the moonlight on the path looked so lovely. I just thought I would enjoy it for a moment."

My father smiled kindly, his brown eyes crinkling into crescent moons. "The climate here is much more amenable to an evening stroll than our last home, is it not? Might I join you?"

"Certainly." I tried to sound pleased.

We strolled slowly down the pathway. "I am sorry your ball was cut short last night. Were you able to enjoy it at all?"

"I do regret not being able to enjoy it more, but it was absolutely charming."

"Lord De Luca has offered to host another one, considering you were present for less than a quarter of an hour."

I was surprised Emilio even had time to discuss such a

frivolous matter with my father. What a ridiculous offer. "No, of course not. That would be silly."

I had my sights set further down the path towards the entrance of the Glencartha gardens. If we could stroll close enough, Nicholas would see me with my father and understand my absence. But my father steered us off the path into the gazebo and took a seat at the bench. I looked longingly at the stone walls that surely encased Nicholas.

"What do you think?" my father asked.

I snapped my attention back to him. "I'm sorry. Did you ask me something?"

"I suggested we reprise the soiree on your birthday."

"Yes," I mumbled, barely paying attention to what was being offered.

"We have a couple of months. We can plan something lovely. There was a long time when I thought your eighteenth birthday would be nothing but misery for me. I can't tell you what it means to me to be celebrating it with you under my roof again."

I smiled tenderly at my father and rested my head on his shoulder. He smelled just as I had remembered—a mixture of leather, wool, and soap. "I'm happy to be here with you, too."

We talked for a few minutes more. My father asked me about the progress of my leg (nearly as good as new), Meg (I quite liked her), and my opinion of St. Kitts (unlike anything I had ever seen). It felt a bit like an interview or an interrogation, though it was very like my father to take stock of his assets— even his daughter.

"Lord Emilio seems to be forging a friendship with you."

I sighed, my pride still sore from my earlier quarrel with Emilio. "He felt it was his obligation to see to my welfare while you were away."

"May I make a bold observation?"

I nodded, bemused.

"The attention he has bestowed on you recently is beyond feelings of obligation, I think. I venture that he fancies you."

"Oh?" I was glad for the cover of darkness so my father couldn't see me blushing. My father had never spoken to me this way.

"I wondered if he has said anything to you."

I sifted through the conversation I'd had with Emilio at the meadow that afternoon. While his intentions were rather clear, he certainly hadn't said as much. "Not a word."

"He's a good man, Tessa. He's been like a son ever since I arrived. Helping me settle in, acquainting me with the town and its citizens, and dining with me almost every night so I would not be alone in my grief."

I pictured my father alone in giant Amerscott, the empty rooms echoing with sadness. Had he cried for me? Emilio had injected himself to assuage that pain as much as he could. My pride softened. Emilio was a good man and I owed him a debt of gratitude.

"I wanted to ask you a favor, Tessie."

"Yes?"

"Mr. Holladay…he seems to trust you. Would you speak to him of something for me?"

I knew exactly what he would ask of me. "Of course, Papa."

"I need him, Tessa. I need him in my fleet. His experience is invaluable."

"But he doesn't want that life anymore."

"It's for the greater good!" My father's unexpected passion made me wonder if the military situation was more serious than he let on. After last night's events, I wouldn't have been surprised.

"He's consulting you, isn't that enough?"

My father shook his head vigorously, his powdered curls bouncing on his shoulders in the moonlight. "His experience is vast. I've been sailing my whole life, commanding crews for over a decade, yet that young whip of a pirate has knowledge and skill beyond my own. His familiarity of these waters and the players in the Spanish Main are an asset. Plus, he knows the ways of the pirates. It would be like having a spy. Beyond that, he is a brilliant tactician. For one so young to be so insightful, so cunning, and yet so ruthless…"

Nicholas? My Nicholas? Slouching against the mast. Spouting off jokes and irreverent comments. Shirking duties to spend time with the captive. My father's praise took me by surprise. It pleased me to know that my father thought so highly of him. Perhaps it wouldn't be too much for my father to accept my relationship with him. At the same time, it seemed a bit dangerous for my father to laud Nicholas's seamanship so. Perhaps in his eyes Nicholas would always be a pirate—a weapon for my father to wield for his own purposes, but never to be trusted.

My father continued. "If Holladay would have it, I'd make him vice commander in the Royal Navy. I don't think such a thing would appeal to him. But perhaps his own ship, being a captain of his own crew, with a Letter of Marque allowing him to keep half the plunder…I think it must tempt him. And so mutually beneficial. Will you talk to him, Tessa? I think he'll listen to you."

I knew I would do no such thing. I did not want Nicholas off hunting other pirates. And Nicholas had said as much himself, though the temptation was surely there. *The pull of the sea is too strong…*

"But there's a price on his head, Papa. The pirates of the *Banshee* want him dead. It is too dangerous for him to return to sea."

"He's always had a price on his head, my dear. This time, he would have the English crown on his side. A better deal than a few dozen drunken sea dogs, I'd say." My father looked at me expectantly, his eyes piercing me through the darkness. I half expected him to sense my true intentions.

"I'll speak to him," I lied.

148 | L A R A   H A Y S

My father patted my knee. "Good girl. Do all you can. Our safety may very well depend on it." He stood. "Shall we go back inside? It's past both of our bedtimes."

I followed him down the gazebo steps and cast a wayward glance over my shoulder. "I think I'll linger a few moments alone, Father."

"Not tonight." My father grabbed my elbow and steered me through the doorway. "I'm not about to let you wander unaccompanied at night. The madman who broke into the house could still be lurking about." He bolted the door behind me. "Let's get some rest, shall we?"

With that, my father escorted me upstairs to my bedroom before retiring to his own.

Disappointment weighed me down like wet, woolen cloak. I leaned on the railing of my balcony, tears shimmering on my cheeks. I couldn't even see the gardens from here.

I whispered into the night. "Nick, if you can hear me..." I paused, not knowing what to say, how to explain. "Just know...I love you."

* * * * *

I sprang out of bed with purpose as soon as dawn flooded my room. I dressed hastily—and rather sloppily—without Meg to help me, my corset bunching loosely around my torso. After a quick trip to my basin to splash water on my face and run a brush through my hair, I hurried down the stairs and to the kitchen, hoping, perchance, that Nicholas had joined us for breakfast as he occasionally did.

Meg was laying out the table for two. My heart dropped in my chest.

"Breakfast must be nearly ready." I noted that I did not have time to sneak outside to see whether or not Nicholas was working.

"Aye, miss. Comin' out of the oven as we speak."

"Just two then?"

"Are you expecting the baron? Shall I put out another setting?"

I told her no as Miss Maisley brought out a tray of hot croissants, stewed plums, and fried sausage.

After breakfast, I checked for Nicholas at the guesthouse, but he wasn't there. I returned to my room and slumped into a velvet-upholstered armchair. I tried to remedy my sour mood with some light reading.

I was interrupted by a knock on my door. It wasn't Meg, for her knock was much softer. Before I could even stand up, my bedroom door swung wide and Nicholas strutted in.

His eyes quickly swept the room then came to rest on me. His lips lifted into a half-smile—that smug look he got when he was particularly pleased with himself.

My wide eyes darted around the room. "You can't be in here." I scuttled to my feet in a panic.

"I'm happy to see you, too."

"I am serious, Nick. You cannot be seen in my room."

"So I will not be *seen* in here." He shut the door with a devilish smile.

I shook my head.

He walked towards me. "It's been days since I have spoken to you. Where were you last night?"

"My father intercepted me and would not let me out of the house. He's nervous about the intruder. Afraid he might be lurking about or something, ready to snatch me away. Were you waiting long?"

"Two hours."

"I'm so sorry. I wish I could have somehow told you. It's likely that I won't be able to slip out tonight either. "

Nicholas wrapped his arms around my waist. "I don't want to talk about your father." His nose nuzzled the hollow under my ear. "I don't want to talk at all."

I sighed deliciously and then pushed him away. "Not here.

If my father were to discover us…he's become so overprotective with this whole Salazar situation."

"I thought you said it was the burglary that made him nervous."

"Same thing."

He was confused. "What does Salazar have to do with the burglary?"

"I overheard a conversation my father had with the governor and Commander Bidlack. Salazar was spotted in the harbor the night of the ball. They think he was behind the burglary. They think he's been hired by the French to start a war."

His brows furrowed and he looked away briefly.

"You said he was dangerous. Are you worried?"

"I need to speak to your father immediately."

CHAPTER NINETEEN

EVERY DAY I FELT more like a prisoner in my home. My father and the staff guarded the house so completely that I was never able to sneak out to see Nicholas. Nicholas's patience was growing thin, I could tell. He begged for time alone, but I couldn't manage it. He'd tried to visit me in my bedroom once more, only to be thrown out by Miss Maisley. I visited him while he was working as often as I could, but too many people were around and our conversations were never candid.

I convinced Nicholas to attend Sunday services with me in hopes that we might find a moment alone. He battled his conscience on the matter but decided to join us. Though we sat in silence during the sermon, our hands met under the folds of my skirt and we shared sly smiles sitting side by side on the pew.

After the service, Nicholas asked to walk me home. I was a little surprised that my father agreed to it, though he instructed Miss Maisley and Mr. Dean to follow behind us several paces. Perhaps my father expected me to use that time alone with Nicholas to convince him to accept the Letter of Marque.

Nicholas looked dapper in grey breeches and an oxblood waistcoat. He went jacketless and bareheaded, the former being common in the sweltering climate but the latter was markedly rebellious.

"I liked the service," I mentioned.

"Hot as Hades in that church, though." He tugged at his waistcoat. "I was sweltering. How do you manage in all your skirts and layers?"

I adjusted my pearl-studded gloves. "One gets used to it, I suppose."

"I feel like I am suffocating." My eyes followed his fingers as he removed his cravat and unbuttoned his waistcoat. His cotton shirt clung to the planes of his chest, damp with sweat.

"I was always cold in England. You could never shake the chill, even on a summer day. And here it's the opposite. Even the balmiest day boils you alive."

He looked towards the distant strip of blue on the horizon. "I took the ketch out yesterday."

"Oh?" I couldn't understand the sudden trepidation I felt. Nicholas belonged on the ocean. I knew that. Of course he would go out when he could. The sea was in his soul.

"Fishing," said Nicholas.

"How was it?"

Nicholas's eyes sparked at the memory and his lips curled into an easy smile. "Perfect."

He looked so happy. Despite that—or maybe because of that—a seed of worry bloomed deep in my stomach. "Maybe you should do more of that," I said. "Fishing. On your own." If he couldn't resist the siren's song of surf and wind, perhaps the occasional fishing trip would quell the hunger.

"Maybe so." Nicholas sounded wistful. His eyes held a distant look as if he were drinking in the sea spray at the helm of the *Freedom* rather than walking down the scorching streets of Basseterre with me.

As dangerous as it was, I felt I had to tell him of my father's request. I had to know if his conviction to stay landlocked had wavered. "My father wanted me to ask you something."

"Hm?" Nicholas seemed surprised that I was still next to him. He blinked away the distant look from his eyes and looked at me intently.

"He asked if I would convince you to reconsider his offer. Well, more than ask. He wanted me to persuade you."

I expected him to react with playful disregard. Instead, he pursed his lips and looked out into the distance. He felt a million miles away from me.

"You'd be wasting your breath," said Nicholas finally.

I felt my tension melt away. "I knew you'd say that." He looked at me but didn't return my smile.

"Tess, I really need to talk to you. I was hoping to speak with you last night…" he trailed off.

"I'm so sorry about that. Lord De Luca joined us for a game of piquet last night and then stayed for biscuits and tea. I couldn't get away. But we have time now." We were still several minutes from Amerscott.

"Maybe now isn't the best time."

I glanced over my shoulder. Mr. Dean and Miss Maisley were out of earshot. "I don't know how long it will be until we have another chance like this."

"I'd rather talk to you in the garden…alone."

I sighed. "I know. Me too. But garden visits haven't been working out. Maybe after a few more quiet days…"

"It must be today. Right when we get back."

"I can't."

"I need you to."

"My father—"

Nicholas snarled at me, his anger coming out of nowhere. "Blast it, Tessa. It's like you don't even care."

I flinched. "Of course I care. I've been trying. This is difficult for me too. It's tearing me up inside."

"Is it?" That darkness was back in his eyes. In the months I had known Nicholas, I had never seen it until the past few weeks. His eyes, normally the palest of greys, had become stormy and cool, like the shadows on the granite pathway we were walking on.

His unfounded temper fueled my own. "You have to know that," I lashed back.

"Well, I don't. Not anymore. You're...you used to be so fearless. You once took on a bloody pirate with nothing more than a candle, for hell's sake. And now breaking some societal norm and—heaven forbid—*offending* someone leaves you frozen with indecision."

I stamped ahead several steps and turned in to the winding pathway leading to Amerscott House. My blood thundered through my veins. I longed for a door to slam in Nicholas's face. With a huff, I spun and confronted him. "Is *this* what you wanted to speak with me about? How spineless you think I am?"

He shook his head sadly and took a deep breath. He was slightly more composed when he said, "Come straight to the garden after you go inside. I'll be there and tell you everything."

I resumed my dramatic stamping. "Is that entirely necessary?" My voice grew embarrassingly shrill. "Say your piece now."

Nicholas jogged to catch up with me. "Stop, Tessa."

I marched up the stairs to the front door. "It's a hot day. I'm eager to get out of the sun. If you want to say anything, now is the time." I poised my hand over the doorknob.

"I took the letter," said Nicholas, stopping on the flagstones.

"What letter?"

"The Letter of Marque." He paused and repeated himself, his voice quieter, apologetic. "I accepted your father's Letter of Marque."

The world stopped then. The sighing of the wind in the trees stilled. Nicholas made no sound. I couldn't even hear the thunder of my blood in my ears. I swam through feelings of shock and fear and betrayal, trying to find something to say. Nothing surfaced. Without looking back, without saying a thing, I set my spine straight and walked into my home, shutting the door behind me.

I slouched against the door and dashed the tears out of my eyes with the back of my gloved hands. I had only moments until Miss Maisley and Mr. Dean came through the door. I took two shaky breaths and escaped to my room.

I fought back the tears. I was too angry to let myself fall apart. He promised. *He promised!*

Rage infiltrated every corner of my heart. I had defended him to my father and Emilio, insisted they respect his decision because it would never change. He'd made a fool of me. And now, he would leave me. I was no different than Meg. Or Charlotte from Port Winslow. Another heart he had plundered, another name on his list.

I deserved an explanation. I deserved an apology. I deserved to watch him wither under my stare and tell me why he had deceived me.

With gritty determination, I stormed through Amerscott, ignoring the stares of the staff and made my way to the garden. I didn't expect Nicholas to be there. I thought I would check, though, before waltzing to Glencartha and demanding an audience with him.

But there he was, sitting a bit like a lost little boy, against the wall of the garden with his legs crossed and pulling up handfuls of grass, his waistcoat discarded by his side.

He rose to his feet and slowly came to me. "You've been crying." His voice was harrowed, as though he had been swallowing razorblades. He cupped my cheeks and planted a kiss as soft as butterfly wings on my lips. I was too livid to kiss him back and pulled away.

How could he act tender when he had betrayed me so?

"Why?" My voice was bitter as I choked out the question. "You promised."

"I know," he whispered. "Sometimes promises must be broken for the greater good. The threat behind Salazar is growing. War will come to St. Kitts unless we stop it."

"But why go to sea? Already you advise my father. If you must fight, you could do it from here." A dark shadow cast itself on my thoughts. I had been willing it away for the past hour, but it pushed on and could no longer be ignored. "Is it...me? Are you leaving to get away from me?"

"No. Of course not."

"Then undo it."

He ran his hand through his mussed brown curls and shook his head. "It's done, Tessa."

"Nothing's in stone." I pleaded.

"I leave tomorrow."

Tomorrow? He was leaving tomorrow and I had only just found out about it. He wouldn't return for weeks—months, maybe—if he ever returned at all. How little he must think of me to casually mention this on a stroll home from church. I knew we were standing on the precipice of something dark and awful. My heart screamed to understand him, screamed for him to understand me. But it seemed impossible. One moment he looked shameful, the next moment angry, and the next moment wounded. None of it made sense. I turned away. I couldn't bear the sight of him.

"I tried to tell you but I haven't had a moment alone with you." He reached for me. I recoiled.

"You should have tried harder."

"Really?" he scoffed. "I've waited for you in this garden every night. Every bloody night. I beat down your door. You haven't had a minute to spare for me, and I am forced to watch you faffing about with Signor De Luca."

"I do not *faff about* with Signor De Luca!"

Nicholas cocked his head. "You do, Tess. You do."

"Don't make this about him. You knew this would be difficult. You said it didn't matter so long as we were together."

Fire sparked in Nicholas's eyes. The precipice was looming closer. I could sense the edge. The edge of everything. There was no way to stop the momentum propelling me into the unknown depths.

"But we're not together. Everything you do, you do on your own. You're too concerned about what's *proper* and what's *right*. I'm left in the dark. Alone. With every bow, every curtsy, every chaperoned visit and spot of afternoon tea, you make a mockery of me."

Anger lashed inside of me. "You expect me to turn my back on my life because it's easier for you?

"*I did!*"

"And I owe it to you to do the same? Because you bought me with one-hundred and fifty-eight thousand pounds?"

Nicholas flinched as if I had thrown acid on him.

I raged on. "It's so convenient to blame everything on me, isn't it? This—" I gestured all around me, "was the agreement. But you're no longer in control, Quartermaster Holladay, and you despise it. You found an exit—an exit with fifty percent profit, no less—and you took it."

Nicholas's eyes narrowed into slits and his mouth twisted with disgust. "How dare you imply that I was bought."

I set my chin defiantly. "I should say the same to you. You act like you've *earned* me, like I am some possession. And now when I don't do exactly what you want, I've somehow betrayed you." My voice hitched. "It's regretful, isn't it? The girl you spent your fortunes saving, and now she isn't even worth it."

Nicholas's eyes were full of poison. In a sweeping motion, he grabbed his waistcoat from the ground and stormed through the gate, the clang of its metal startling the birds overhead to take flight. The sound echoed so loudly in the silence that I could feel it in my chest.

He was gone.

My rage disintegrated. I sank to the ground, my skirt mushrooming around me, and I tumbled blindly over the precipice into unknown anguish. Falling. Drowning. Suffocating. The most beloved thing about my world had been stripped and scattered like dry leaves before the violence of a gale. I felt empty. *Profoundly* empty. I clutched one hand to my chest, certain I would feel a hole there, a vacuum where my heart once was. I stuffed the other hand into my mouth to stifle the desperate keening that tore from my throat.

CHAPTER TWENTY

I took Clarence's hand and stepped into the carriage, ignoring Miss Maisley's protests. He shut the door behind me and in a moment, I was on my way. I had one chance in the world to stop Nicholas before he boarded his ketch and was lost to the embrace of the sea.

All night I had rehearsed what I would say to Nicholas. *You were right, Nicholas. I have been a coward. I wronged you and I don't blame you for wanting to return to your life when I haven't been the least bit hospitable with you in my life. I'll tell my father this very day that I love you, that I am going to be with you forever. Forgive me.*

There was no denying that I was hurt that Nicholas had accepted the letter without telling me beforehand. I was still stunned by all he said in the garden. But that did not matter anymore. As my father had often told me when my temper bested me, some things were more important than being right.

Nicholas was one of those things.

The carriage slowed as it approached the harbor. "Where do you wish to stop, Miss Monroe?" Clarence hollered from his driving station.

I pulled back the velvet curtain on the window and peered at the jumble of ships and boats in Christophe Harbor backed by a pastel pink morning sky. "Continue on. Slowly. I'll let you know when to stop."

Halfway down the pier, I spotted the *Freedom*. I rapped on the ceiling of the carriage. "Here, Clarence!"

The carriage halted, my door opened, and Clarence assisted my exit. Before he could ask to escort me, I marched with purpose into the bustle of the quay. Scents of fish, tar, tobacco, and wood engulfed me. I pressed a gloved hand against my nose to lessen the assault of it. I turned on to the dock where the *Freedom* was anchored and nearly ran to the ship. I clambered up the jack ladder. It was a clumsy task in my petticoat and dainty heels but I managed without disaster. Once on the main deck, I finally let out the breath I had seemed to be holding on to all morning. I was here. I had made it.

"Nicholas?" I called. "Nicholas?"

The ketch was a small vessel with a flush deck—it stretched unbroken without any other raised decks. It was easy for me to take it all in with a single sweeping look. It seemed empty, but I wasn't satisfied until I had walked from bow to stern, ducking under the lines, looking among the barrels and crates, and checking around the masts. I craned my neck and looked to the rigging. The sails were reefed, making the masts and spars look naked. The hatch in the middle of the deck was closed and secured. I tugged the square door open and eased myself down the ladder, my petticoat barely fitting through the small entrance.

The ladder deposited me into an open area that spread the width of the ship; portholes let in light on both starboard and port sides. There were four doors—the two in front of me led to a small cabin on the portside and the galley on the starboard side. The doors aft of me led to the cabins that Nicholas and I had stayed in—I had claimed the starboard cabin while he had chosen the cabin on the left side of the ship. They were both roomy, but the one I had stayed in was furnished lavishly with a four-poster bed, ornate wall sconces, and an upholstered chair.

"Nicholas?" My voice echoed off the wooden bulkheads. I peered into all the rooms—they were all empty. I even opened the hatch that led to the bilge below and peered into the festering darkness. "Nicholas?"

The *Freedom* was empty.

Nicholas hadn't said what time he was leaving, just that he was leaving today. He could still be enjoying a large breakfast at Glencartha.

When I emerged on the main deck, I saw Clarence approaching. "Did you find what you were looking for, Miss?"

"Mr. Holladay isn't here. The ship is empty. I wonder if he is planning for the evening tide."

"I could take you home if you like."

"I think I would like to stay and wait a bit longer, Clarence. Just in case." The ketch was small and more maneuverable than the large brigantines and galleons that relied on the tides to get out of port. Nicholas could sail it at nearly anytime he wanted.

Clarence's head bobbed automatically. "Yes, miss. If'n you like, I could ask around a bit. It's likely there's someone 'round here will know somethin' of it."

"That would be most helpful."

With a tip of his hat, Clarence strolled away. I turned my attention back to the *Freedom*, my fingers trailing along the caprail.

The weeks we had spent together on this ketch were the best of my life. I had never known what it was like to be so carefree, to drop all pretense and be truly myself. I had not been a slave to language, or fashion, or propriety. I had cooked like a scullery maid, worked like a man, laughed like a child, read and sang like a lady, and even cussed like a sailor. All those tenuous compartments forced on me by society broke down and I was more than *a lady*. I was Tessa. How easy it was for me to step back into the confines of my birth once I stepped back into proper society. Nicholas was right. I had changed.

I was desperately relieved that he hadn't set sail yet. I

couldn't bear not to see him again before he sailed away, not when our last meeting was so unpleasant. I was still cross at him for accepting the letter, but in time I could forgive him. I needed to tell him that. I needed to kiss him. Kiss him like I used to. And let him know that he needn't worry about me—I would be all right and I would wait faithfully for his return.

I descended below deck again and looked into Nicholas's cabin. When we first set sail, the only bed had been in my room. A swath of canvas hung from the ceiling served as a hammock until he built himself a wide, sturdy bed.

The blankets were still mussed from his last night on the *Freedom* over a month ago. I smoothed them back into place and lie on the bed, my arms behind my head. This is where he slept. How often had he stared at the boards above thinking of me the way I was thinking of him now?

I must have dozed off because I jolted awake at the sounds of voices on the main deck. My heart soared. I flew up the ladder to the main deck, wings on my feet, but slowed when I saw my father standing with Clarence.

My father's stern gaze fell to me. "You should not be here."

I wanted to wilt and apologize, but that's what I would have done yesterday. I wilted too often, as Nicholas had so kindly pointed out. I balled my hands to keep them from shaking. "I wanted to see Mr. Holladay before he left. I was unaware that you had persuaded him to sign on until yesterday afternoon and had no chance to issue a proper farewell. I insisted Clarence bring me down the first thing this morning."

"You're too late." My father sounded purposefully cold, possibly from my petulance.

"What do you mean?" I gestured to the ship we were on. "He hasn't sailed yet."

My father sighed, taking pity on me, it seemed. "He sails a different ship."

"He has no other ship," I stated smugly as if that fact would bring Nicholas back.

My father seemed slightly apologetic. "I'm sorry, dear. I

suppose I should have mentioned something. The navy gifted him a schooner called the *Seabird*. He put together a crew last week. This ketch would have been far too small for the manpower needed."

"He put together a crew last week?" I repeated weakly.

My father looked a bit confused by my repetition but nodded.

My shoulders sagged. "Last week?" My voice was soft, a whisper lost on the wind. This Letter of Marque business was not as impulsive as I had imagined.

My anger came back. I turned my attention back to my father. "He's gone then?"

"Caught the early tide. I'm so sorry. He should have told you."

"You should have told me. It's been nearly a fortnight since you asked me to recruit him for you. Don't you think an update would have been nice? *By the way, Tessa, Nicholas accepted my bloody letter—*"

"You watch your language, miss!"

I felt hot blood in my cheeks and knew I was as red as an apple.

My father was red-faced too. "I've made certain allowances for you since your arrival because of what you've been through, but I am telling you here and now that it is time for you to act like the lady you are."

"I've made a world of concessions since my arrival and I'm sick of it. Please excuse me." With my back as stiff as a rod, I walked past my father, certain he would grab my wrist and slap my mouth. He didn't. I climbed the rope ladder down to the dock. "Clarence. Please take me home."

My father nodded his consent. As soon as I saw Clarence start down the side of the hull, I marched across the quay and let myself into my carriage.

I fought back the burning in my eyes and focused on the jade scenery outside. The carriage turned and we were running parallel with the coast. I could see dozens of tiny white squares on the horizon. Ships. The thought that one of them was

Nicholas's brand-new ship made one single tear spill down my cheek. I brushed it away angrily and closed the velvet curtains.

The carriage rolled to a gentle stop. Clarence opened my door and offered me his hand. I took it and stepped on to the pavement. Another carriage was in the drive, a pair of champagne-colored palominos hitched to it. I closed my eyes and stifled a groan. Not now.

Emilio slid out of the carriage and smiled pleasantly as he approached me. The look on my face must have warned him of my mood. His smile slipped and his posture tightened. "Good morning, Miss Monroe." He was all business.

"Good day, my lord."

He looked like he was about to correct the title, but decided against it. He pulled a parchment envelope from his inside jacket pocket and handed it to me. "Mr. Holladay asked me to deliver this."

I lifted the letter out of Emilio's hands. Scrawled across the front of the envelope in rakish penmanship were the words *Miss Monroe.* I flinched at the sight of it. He had always disregarded propriety and addressed me only by my Christian name. I had never minded. It felt a insulting that he hadn't addressed the letter to *Tessa* but had opted for the distant and stuffy *Miss Monroe.* I tried to convince myself that it was because it was a letter delivered by someone else—a more formal situation altogether. Still, it made me wary of the letter's contents.

I barely remembered to thank Emilio as I walked into Amerscott. If he desired additional conversation or an invitation inside, I did not care. I needed to be alone.

I ignored Miss Maisley's condemning looks as I strode up the stairs and shut myself in my room. I sat in the armchair and stared at the letter. *Miss Monroe.* There was a lump in one of the bottom corners. Something hard, yet flexible. The envelope was sealed with a patch of crimson wax. I stared at it, confused by the pattern in the wax. It was neither a monogram nor a motif. It seemed a bit sloppy and ill-pressed. As I stared harder, I finally understood what the thin ridges were—it was the imprint of Nicholas's thumb. I placed my thumb on top of it as if it still held his warmth. Wanting to keep the thumbprint intact, I carefully ripped the envelope away, not really caring when a tear severed the words *Miss Monroe* on the front.

I tipped the envelope and a golden chain spilled into my hand. I lifted it up. A beautiful gold cross on a long chain. I recognized it immediately. I had never seen him without it. I never asked for its backstory—I was afraid of the sins it might hold. All I needed to know was that it was precious to him. And he had given it to me. As a token? A promise? A consolation gift?

With the chain laced around my trembling fingers, I unfolded the fine stationery—obviously that of the De Luca family. My eyes were already swimming with tears. I blinked rapidly to clear them so I could read the note.

Dear Tessa:

I've lain awake half the night with the words of your reproach echoing in my mind. Our conversation did not go the way I had planned. I meant to leave you with reassurance. Instead, I've left you with betrayal.

I need you to know two things. First: this was not an easy decision for me to come by. I broke my promise to you. Know that it was painful for me. Second: no matter what the future holds, it was worth every farthing.

Capt. N. Holladay

The letter offered me no comfort. No tender words. No promise for his return. It was crueler than if he hadn't sent anything at all.

I crumpled the paper in my fist and screamed as I threw it across my room, the golden cross and chain skittering across the hardwood floor after it. Two seconds later, I was on the ground smoothing out the crumpled paper and retrieving the necklace. I reread the letter, hoping to find a touch of solace. He was sorry for my pain, but he wasn't sorry for leaving. He wasn't sorry for lying. He was merely sorry for my pain.

"Miss Monroe?" Meg tapped at my door.

I stifled the tears in my voice. "Leave me be, Meg."

"Lord De Luca is downstairs."

"Dismiss him. I will not be taking any callers today."

"Certainly, miss. He said he had a message to deliver. From Mr. Holladay. Shall I take the message myself?"

Could I really handle another dagger in my heart from Nicholas? I stood and smoothed my skirt with trembling hands. I had not the willpower to turn away from anything regarding Nicholas, no matter how painful.

"Miss Monroe?"

"I'll see Lord De Luca in the parlor."

I walked to the mirror and examined myself. The face in the mirror seemed as if it belonged to someone else. Inside I felt black and ravaged and shredded. Shouldn't I look that way too? Aside from my disheveled hair and red-rimmed eyes, I looked completely normal. Pretty, even. Soft pink lips. Flushed cheeks. Glistening brown eyes. A dusting of freckles on my nose. It seemed wrong. I should look the part of a broken being. Everyone who laid eyes on me ought to know that my heart had been brutally clawed out of me.

I smoothed my auburn locks with a silver-backed brush. My hair had grown, ever so slightly, its ends tickling the tops of my shoulders. I didn't have the time or patience to style it. It hung straight. That was good enough for me.

With a steadying breath, I left my bedroom and descended to the parlor, making no effort to conceal my mood.

Emilio's concern was evident when he stood to greet me. I wondered how much I had changed in his eyes from ten minutes before when he handed me the letter. "Good afternoon, Miss Monroe. Are you feeling quite well?"

"Meg said you had a message?" I had no stomach for pleasantries.

Emilio cleared his throat. He wrung his hat in his hands before me, obviously uncomfortable with the force of my emotion. I knew he could feel the devastation pouring out of me like tidal waves. "Yes," Emilio stammered a bit, a strange fear in his eyes. "Upon his departure this morning, Nicholas— Mr. Holladay—handed me that letter. He asked me if I would deliver it to you and tell you...uh..." Emilio fumbled, afraid, it seemed, of hurting me more than I already had been. "...tell you that he'll see you when he returns, though he doesn't know when that will be."

I digested the words in heavy silence. I could not entertain hope. Not now.

"Was there anything else?" I asked flatly.

Emilio stepped towards me tentatively, his eyes wide and worried. They were beautiful eyes. Dark as night. So unguarded. How could he hide anything, a man with eyes as pure as that? His concern for me—his *affection* for me—was transparent. He reached out for me, but I stood stiffly rooted in the doorway of the parlor. Emilio tilted his head and pulled his hand back. "I can't help but think that something in that letter upset you."

"Everything Nicholas does upsets me." I should not have said that. I should not have let Emilio see into my pain this way, but his eyes were too disarming. What did it matter? Nothing mattered anymore.

"I know you're worried for him but he'll be back before you can even miss him. It's just a short voyage."

I closed my eyes and shook my head. "He didn't even tell me he was leaving." My voice was a whisper. "I deserved at least that."

"Oh, Tessa," Emilio crossed to me and gathered my hands in his. He corrected himself. "Miss Monroe, let us leave for the day. Allow me to take your mind away from it."

"I'd rather stay in today," I said, my hands still in his. I had removed my gloves upstairs and my bare skin was next to his. How intimate it was. And he had used my name. Is this the way it would be now? Nicholas gone and Emilio here instead, touching me and talking to me, trying to fill the holes within?

"Of course." Emilio did not let go of my hands.

"Tell me, Emilio, tell me everything he said."

In his eyes I could see that he would give me whatever I asked for.

He pulled me to the sofa and without letting go of my hand, he told me how Nicholas had taken dinner in his room last night. How he looked haggard this morning and was short-tempered, shoving his breakfast aside after only a bite. The way he stared out at the gloomy predawn sky, his hands on his hips and a distant look in his eyes. The obscenities he muttered when he thought no one could hear. Then he asked for a piece of stationary. And I knew the rest.

"When did you know?" I asked, my face pinched with pain. "About his journey?"

"I don't know if that's germane—"

I cut him short. "How long?"

"I suppose it's been about a week."

What was left of my composure splintered like a dam against the force of a river. I buried my face in my hands and wept tears of utter heartbreak. I felt Emilio's hand on my back. It hesitated momentarily, then with conviction, rubbed small circles of comfort. It wasn't long until I reached for him and cried onto his shoulder.

CHAPTER TWENTY-ONE

I HATED LOVESICK, HEARTBROKEN girls. I had seen plenty of them, mooning over their lost beaux. And yet I had become one. I gave myself one day—two days counting the Monday that Nicholas left—to lock myself away and do nothing but mope. On Wednesday, I forced myself into the world. I didn't enjoy anything, but I refused to yield to my despair. My deepest desire was for space and solitude. I wistfully thought about the promontory I would escape to at Port Winslow. I didn't quite have the same escape on St. Kitts, but I did have something—a horse.

I had never been fully practiced at horseback riding. I was a city girl. But St. Kitts offered the space and I asked Emilio to teach me how to handle a horse. Within an hour, he was at Amerscott with his two palominos saddled and ready. Blushing, I told him I would rather learn on the chestnut mare in my father's stables. Her name was Gypsy. She was old and not nearly as fine as either of Emilio's horses, but I had constant access to her. He taught me how to saddle Gypsy and how to mount and dismount by myself. Emilio conversed with me easily, but never pried.

My daily ride gave me something to look forward to. I loved the sound of the long grasses swishing in the breeze, the spray of surf on my face when I galloped the horse on the beach. The wind and sun cleaned out corners of my soul that I could not reach myself.

In a week's time, I felt comfortable enough to take Gypsy out by myself. Riding wasn't just about passing time or healing the hurt. When I rode up Brimstone Hill near the site of the new fort, I had the best view of the harbor. I squinted across the reflective water, longing for a glimpse of a schooner I had never before seen.

Once I worked up the nerve, I began to visit the quay daily. I befriended several of the stevedores. They knew that I waited for a ship called *Seabird*, and they helped me keep watch. Day after day, their news was the same. No *Seabird*. No Nicholas. I often boarded the *Freedom* and walked the cabins of the ship like a widow in mourning—I felt I was one, truly. I wrapped myself in the blankets that still smelled of him, dreading the time when their aroma would fade and they would begin to smell like me.

Memories rose from the planks of the deck like ghosts in a forsaken graveyard. I stood in the spot where he had very nearly proposed to me. Lying on his bed, I could almost hear him crying out from a nightmare. I could close my eyes and see him perfectly, the sun on his face and the wind in his hair. But when I opened my eyes, the ghost was gone.

What had happened to him?

This was the same man who had given up his colossal fortune, betrayed his captain and crew, and turned his back on everything he ever knew to search for my marooned corpse in the midst of the Caribbean. That was before we'd spent nights revealing our souls to each other; before I had confessed my love for him. What had changed? Had I really made it that easy for a man like that to leave?

Numbness set in. It was a welcome change from the stabbing ache and volatile fits of tears. I was eager for Nicholas's return, but I began to wonder if it would be the romantic reunion I hoped for. Our parting had been brutal.

Anger still festered in my heart. Surely, he held ill feelings for me, too.

I recalled the words of a Roman poet I had studied: *Always towards absent lovers love's tide stronger flows.* I hoped Sextus Propertius knew what he was saying. I pushed away thoughts of pirate revelry and ladies of the evening.

Lord De Luca called every day. Sometimes it was only for a horse ride. Other times, he stopped by conveniently at mealtimes or asked for help with his shopping—though I knew he had servants who could shop for him if he wished it. At first, his presence was an annoyance. But it wasn't long until I grew to expect his visits, then anticipate them, and then long for them when they were spaced too far apart. His companionship grew precious to me. I cared not how he interpreted the time we spent together. He offered me friendship when I desperately needed it, and I clung to it like a drunkard clings to his bottle.

"The pink or the blue?" I asked Meg as I stared into my wardrobe.

Meg eyed the dresses suspiciously, as if they had secret intentions, her head cocked and her hands on her hips. Her blond curls sprang out from the gathers of her linen mob cap. "You have so many day dresses in blue. I think pink would be a nice change for the theatre."

I nodded in agreement and Meg retrieved the pieces of the gown. After slipping on a fresh chemise and silk stockings, Meg laced up my whalebone corset and tied a pair of pockets around my waist. I selected a brocade ivory petticoat and an elaborate rosebud embroidered stomacher. Finally, Meg draped the gown on me, gathered the split skirt behind my waist into a swirling bustle, and fixed the stomacher onto the front of my torso.

The pale pink brocade was as soft as a sunrise in the English winter, complimenting the delicate cream of my skin and offsetting my dark eyes. The wide neckline left my shoulders exposed. Antique lace cascaded out from the elbow-length sleeves. Next Meg styled my brunette wig with tight curls and topped it with a plumed hat. A dusting of rouge and painted rose lips finished the look.

I had secretly worn the necklace Nicholas gave me, always taking care to remove it before Meg dressed or undressed me. I did not know whether she would recognize it, but I did not want to risk it. The neckline of this dress was too low to hide the necklace so when Miss Maisley came to retrieve me for Lord De Luca, I slipped the necklace into my pocket.

I sometimes forgot how handsome Emilio was with his black hair and bottomless eyes. I could not look beyond it now. He was dressed elegantly in shades of plum and gold, my eyes captivated by the way his waistcoat hugged the shape of torso. He had exchanged his usual cravat for a stylish steinkirk, flowing from his neck in deliberate disarray. The effect was dashing. Tucked under Emilio's arm was a decorated tricorn hat. I couldn't help the heat that stole into my cheeks as he bowed deeply in greeting. I curtsied graciously.

Emilio's eyes lingered on me like the heat of a summer afternoon. He cleared his throat twice before saying, "I have something for you." He extracted a small rectangular box from his jacket and handed it to me.

I untied the ribbon and lifted the lid. Inside was a cobalt-blue bottle in the shape of a seashell with a silver stopper. I couldn't believe my eyes. "Is this—"

Emilio beamed. "Parisian perfume."

"Where did you...how?" Even in England, real perfume from France was an exquisite luxury. I had relied on rose water for fragrance.

"I've been waiting for weeks for a shipment to arrive. It came just this morning. May I?" Emilio took the bottle from the box and removed the stopper. He held it under my nose and I breathed in the scent of amber laced with violet.

"It's intoxicating." I removed my gloves and Emilio dabbed a drop on the inside of each wrist. "I feel as if I should refuse such a gracious gift, but in truth, I adore it too much to part with it. Thank you." I gestured to Meg. "Would you please place this on my vanity? *Carefully.*"

I refastened my gloves and slipped my hand through Emilio's arm. Once we were in his carriage, Emilio took my hand and brought my wrist to his nose, closing his eyes and inhaling deeply. "Intoxicating, indeed."

His lips brushed the inside of my wrist. The gesture was so subtle that I questioned if it had been intentional or not. The result was so delicious—an unfurling of pleasure deep within my stomach—that I wished he would do it again.

Meg joined us a moment later—she was our chaperone for the evening. I kept my face down, knowing my cheeks were pinker than my dress.

The performance of *The Careless Husband* was the height of Kittian entertainment. Laughter and tears, a touching story of love lost and found. A steinkirk was a pivotal prop in the wife reclaiming her husband's affections, and I wondered if Emilio had worn his deliberately because of that scene. The thought was endearing.

"You enjoyed the show then?" asked Emilio.

The chirping of the evening crickets kept time with the staccato sound of my heels on the flagstones outside the theatre. "Absolutely. It's the most I have laughed since..." *Since I'd been with Nicholas.* "Well, in ages."

My hand rested in the crook of Emilio's right arm. He rested his left hand on top of mine. "I am glad. Your laughter is so beautiful. I want to hear it always."

I gave a disbelieving shake of my head.

"Would you accompany me back to Glencartha? My chef has prepared a lemon cake for us."

"That sounds delicious."

Emilio helped me into the carriage then sat on the bench across from me. A streak of moonlight sliced through the square window, casting a silver glow on his face. Even in the cover of night, I could see a burning in his eyes. I was drawn to it and I wondered what he saw in my eyes.

When we arrived at Glencartha, Meg vanished to the servants' quarters to visit with her former coworkers, leaving me alone with Emilio in his parlor. Sitting on a floral sofa, we discussed the play in depth over slices of cake and teacups full of creamed coffee. We were particularly fascinated by the use of female performers.

"It was quite shocking. A bit bawdy if you ask me," Emilio said.

"I thought it was brilliant and bold. If art is to imitate life, then why not make it as accurate as possible?" I countered.

"It's ludicrous to have women parading on stage like that."

"Men do it."

Emilio pursed his lips. "Men are just that—men. It's how it should be. Women should be sheltered from such things."

"It's acceptable for men to parade on stage, but not women?"

"You make it sound antagonistic."

I smiled demurely. "No, sir. *You* make it sound antagonistic."

Emilio gaped at me. I wondered if anyone had argued with him before—particularly a woman of a lower status. Finally, his mouth closed and he shook his head. But his eyes gleamed with humor. "It's rare that anyone challenges me, Miss Monroe. I quite like it."

"I'm glad you appreciate it. I'm afraid less tolerant men would have put me out by now. I've tried to control it, but I can't. Or maybe I don't want to. I believe things should be questioned. Life is worth exploring."

Emilio tilted his head to the side, the burning look returning to his eyes. He set his cup down and inched closer to me. So close I could smell the concoction of fine musk cologne and coffee on him.

"Life *is* worth exploring," Emilio repeated. He touched my face, his thumb tracing the curve of my cheekbone. My breath hitched. His eyes strayed to my lips, then back to my eyes. "May I?" he whispered. "Explore?"

My skin burned under his touch. Words failed me. Breath failed me. My lips parted and Emilio descended on me. My lips yielded to the soft pressure of his kiss. My hands lifted of their own accord and clasped behind Emilio's neck. His kiss engulfed me, gaining in strength and fervor as his hands caressed my face. I could taste him—lemons and cake and coffee—as our kiss deepened. He slowed his lips, ready to pull away, I could tell, but I could not stand the thought of it. With my arms still around his neck, I pulled Emilio to me again, eagerly meeting his lips with my own. I had been starving for the warmth of arms around me, soft kisses on my lips. I lifted my chin and exposed my throat, aching for Emilio to trail kisses along its curve the way Nicholas had always done. Instead, Emilio placed both hands on the sides of my face and kissed me harder, leaving the skin on my throat itching with unmet desire.

I gasped for breath and Emilio stared at me with hard passion. His chest was heaving too. I touched my lips. They were tingling from the chafe of his stubble. I shifted my weight and heard the faint tinkling sound of the golden chain in my pocket falling on itself.

I tore my eyes away from Emilio. "I should go."

Trying to control his breathlessness, Emilio stood and pulled me to my feet. "Of course."

In brittle silence, Emilio escorted me out of the back of Glencartha. My eyes strayed to the walls of the garden and the last time I was there. I put my hand in my pocket and felt the cool coil of the necklace. Why did I feel so guilty? Nicholas left me without so much as a goodbye. And Emilio kissed me. I didn't prompt it. My cheeks flamed at the memory. I had certainly kissed him back.

We were halfway to Amerscott before I remembered my chaperone. I stopped short. "Meg. I forgot to get her."

"I'll walk her back. Um," Emilio cleared this throat self-consciously. "I'm sorry. About the parlor. I...I shouldn't have been so forward."

I kept my eyes down, not certain how I should respond. Accept his apology? Tell him I enjoyed it? My cheeks grew hotter. I was grateful for the moonless night. "I was taken by surprise."

"Were you?" The question was sincere. I realized then that Lord De Luca was a man used to getting what he wanted. He was reserved where Nicholas was brash, modest where Nicholas was cocky, but in certain ways, they were more alike than I had ever noticed.

I didn't answer him. We rounded a bend and Amerscott came into view.

"I had rather hoped you had anticipated it," said Emilio quietly.

I looked at him with surprise. "The kiss?"

"Perhaps not the kiss but the emotion behind it. After what you said at the masquerade ball..." Uncertainty colored his voice.

I had never corrected that error. What else was he to think? In his mind, *I* must be the forward one. I couldn't undo what had happened. I didn't want to embarrass Emilio. Or myself. What kind of proper young lady would allow a man to kiss her in that way without feeling serious affection? Me, obviously.

I gave a reassuring squeeze to Emilio's arm. "There is no need for you to apologize. I am just overwhelmed."

"You were not...offended?"

"No," I answered without thinking.

Emilio let out a deep sigh, as though he had been holding his breath for the past ten minutes.

I felt a pang of pity for Emilio. I saw myself in him—caught up in condemned emotions. I thought of myself, of Nicholas, and said, "Passion is powerful. I can hardly fault anyone who falls victim to it."

"I'm glad to hear that." Emilio lifted my chin with his fingertips. "Because I feel myself falling victim to it once again."

As his lips softly touched mine, my hand in my pocket curled around the necklace and I pulled away.

CHAPTER TWENTY-TWO

FORTY-THREE DAYS.

It had been forty-three days since the *Seabird* left Christophe Harbor. At first, I only wondered if Nicholas would return to see me. Then I began to worry whether he would return at all. Terrible things happened at sea.

The shadows at the quay were long and soft in the early-evening sun. I dismounted Gypsy and walked among the barkers, sailors, merchants, and stevedores, the scent of fish and tar so sharp I could taste it. I was grateful that Emilio had taught me to ride, but lately it was getting harder to go out alone. He always wanted to accompany me.

I was tying Gypsy to a dock post so I could mope on board the *Freedom* when I saw a stevedore I recognized.

He was a toothless, white-haired man with a hunched back and arms as large as tree trunks.

"Hello, Mr. Roger," I said pleasantly as I finished Gypsy's knot.

"Evenin', Miss Monroe. Been waitin' for ya."

"Have you? I missed you too," I said with a wink. "I was too busy with an art lesson yesterday to visit." I patted the horse's shining neck.

"I'm glad to be the one to tell ya. Your *Seabird* came in."

"It did?" I was instantly lightheaded. He was back. Nicholas was back. He had survived his first mission as a privateer, attacking other pirates, and had returned safely from an unforgiving sea. I closed my eyes in a silent prayer of thanks. Despite the news of Nicholas's safety, a rabble of butterflies erupted in my stomach. How would he greet me? Had his anger towards me cooled in the past forty-three days—or grown?

"'Tis the ship you've been waitin' for, ain't it?"

My eyes were scanning the harbor greedily, scared and thrilled to spot the ship. I swallowed hard and nodded. I was ready. "Can you take me to it?"

His head bobbed. "It be at the far end of the quay." He started shuffling along then stopped as if he had remembered something important. He held out his arm. I smiled warmly and linked my arm with his.

We slowly walked down the quay, garnering a few curious stares. Mr. Roger reveled in the attention. Half a year ago, I would have found the gnarled worker abhorrent. His accent was crass and his hygiene left much to be desired. But time spent with pirates and prostitutes had softened my judgments. Beneath his stench and leathered skin was a kind, kind soul.

My heart hammered in my chest as my eyes flitted among every ship in the harbor. My hands grew wet inside my gloves. "When did it arrive?"

"Yesterday," said Mr. Roger with a confident nod of his grizzled chin.

"Late last night, you mean," I corrected him.

"'Twas in the morn. Round about seven o' th' clock."

I stopped short. Fear and euphoria had been warring in me since Mr. Roger had told me that Nicholas's ship was back, but the notion that I would look upon Nicholas's face again soon, inhale his scent, and touch his face had allowed euphoria to hedge of the fear. But now the tides had turned. My euphoria was crushed and the fear grew.

He looked at me, concerned by my sudden shift in mood.

I tried to hide my disappointment. "I suppose the vessel has been unloaded then. No more cargo? No more crew?" Maybe there was some extenuating reason that Nicholas had been in port for a day and a half without seeking me out.

"Empty as a church on Monday."

"Oh." I should have been prepared for that answer. It was logical. Standard. But I still felt crushed. "There's no reason for me to go there, then. What I wanted was on the ship, not the ship itself." I smiled apologetically and turned back to the direction from which I had come. "Thank you for the escort. And for watching the harbor for me." I kissed Mr. Roger on the cheek.

His papery skin flushed pink. "I'd escort you to the moon if'n I could."

"You're too kind. But how about an escort to the *Freedom*?" I slipped my arm back through his and he led me down the boardwalk past the monstrous oak and cedar ships anchored there.

My mind raced to understand why Nicholas would not call on Amerscott immediately after arriving—if not to see me, then at least to see my father. Dread buffeted me down as I walked down the dock to the *Freedom*, her sails reefed and stowed carefully, just as they had been the past few weeks.

"Thank you, Mr. Roger," I said as I turned towards the ketch. It looked like a toy next to the behemoths surrounding it.

"Any time, ducky!"

With trembling hands, I hauled myself onto the main deck. It was empty, but I could see that someone had been aboard since my last visit two days prior. I unlatched the hatch door, pulled it up, and descended into the ship's belly. I quieted my footsteps and listened intently. All I could hear was the swirl of the ocean against the hull and the muted thrum of chaos from the wharf.

The door to Nicholas's cabin was closed. I knew I had left it open two days ago. I held my breath and rapped my knuckles against it.

No answer. No shuffle of feet. I opened the door. The room was empty.

I had better go home. He was probably trying to visit me now. Perhaps he'd take dinner at Amerscott.

As I disembarked the *Freedom*, I noticed Mr. Roger standing next to Gypsy. He removed the cloth cap from his head when I approached him.

"Hallo, Miss Monroe."

"Good day, Mr. Roger. Were you waiting for me?"

He shrugged a bit self-consciously. "I knows you been waitin' for that ship for ages. Me thinks you might like to know that I seen the crew."

My eyebrows lifted. "The crew, you say?"

"Aye," he nodded. "Captain and crew."

I peered around the dock.

"They ain't here. Pardon the assumption, miss, but me thinks you might like to know that they be goin' to the tavern." He winked slightly at me. "You ain't the first lass I seen who got herself mixed up with a swabby. It's a rollick while it lasts."

I ignored his insinuation. "Do you know which tavern?"

"Aye. The Three Brothers Alehouse. Just this side of High Street." He pointed a gnarled finger towards the bawdier part of town.

My stomach tightened at the narrow alleys crowded with the city's riffraff. I was liable to be robbed of my horse and other valuables. My hand went clenched around the crucifix that dangled below my breasts. I tucked it into my bodice to hide it.

"Mr. Roger, could you…could you take a few moments and escort me. I am unsure of the way." I rummaged for a twopence.

Mr. Roger grinned, revealing a smile full of gaps and grey teeth and pocketed the coin. Taking Gypsy's lead rope, I followed Mr. Roger through the winding alleys. Mr. Roger barked greetings at nearly everyone he saw. It was more than a pleasantry—it was a way to offer me protection.

The Three Brothers Alehouse was a wide, wooden building

that dominated the street, its deeply pitched, green roof was sun-bleached and flaking. Strains of music poured out of the tavern—along with wafts of alcohol and tobacco smoke. I led Gypsy to an empty hitching post and gave a young street urchin two farthings to take care of her while I was inside. I thanked Mr. Roger for his time and stood on the pathway to the alehouse gathering my wits.

My reflection stared back at me from a large window. My striped gown of olive green taffeta was trimmed with satin ribbon and ivory lace. I wore grey kid gloves embroidered with flourishing navy stitches. My hair was swept back into a tight chignon—I had not made time for the wig today—and topped with an ivory fontange that stood on my head like a crown. My ruffles and lace drew unwanted attention from every passerby. I cleared my throat, gathered my skirts, and walked daintily into the Three Brothers Alehouse.

I choked on a billow of smoke that greeted me at the door and fanned the air in front of my face while my vision adjusted to the hazy, dim-lit interior. Customers bustled past me, and I was pushed and pulled from one direction to the next. My fish-out-of-water feeling subsided rather quickly, because of my time working at Mother Ivy's tavern in Port Winslow. I fastened a stern look to my face as I had learned to do before. Looking soft made you vulnerable.

I walked towards the center of the action, my eyes scouring the patrons for the glimpse of wind-tossed brown hair, the overconfident set of broad shoulders, or even a red bandanna.

A passing patron backed into me—rather hard—and his beer sloshed out of his mug and on to me. I bent over and shook the droplets off my skirt.

"Blast it. Pardon me clumsiness," the man said, humiliated. He handed me a handkerchief, which I took to soak up the beer. "I'm so sorry."

"You didn't mean to," I said, looking up at the offender.

We recognized each other instantly and simultaneously said each other's names.

"Miss Monroe?"

"Skidmore?"

With a squeal, I threw my arms around the pirate's neck. I hadn't seen him since I escaped from the *Banshee*, but he held a precious part of my heart—my friend, my confidant, and my guardian angel when I was locked in the brig for weeks.

"I wasn't sure I would ever see you again," I exclaimed as I stood back to look at him from arm's length.

His clothes were wool and canvas, dingy and shapeless. He wore a golden hoop in each ear and a knit cap on his head. His stocky build made him seem shorter than he actually was, though he would never be considered a tall man by anyone's standards. A shock of straw-blonde hair hung into his eyes and over his ears. His cheeks were pink with windburn and his beard was longer than I had remembered it. His blue eyes—the kindest eyes I had ever seen—crinkled with delight.

"Wasn't so sure myself."

"What are you *doing* here?"

"I feel that I should be askin' the same thing of ye."

I scanned the tavern again, the haze of pipe smoke blurring the corners of the large room. "I heard Nicholas might be here. Are you with him?"

Skidmore bowed his head and twirled his wrist in a grand gesture. "You are now looking at Simon Skidmore, privateer."

"Do you need a congratulations?"

Skidmore laughed. "At least I'm on the right side of the law for now. But you're right. Our good captain is here." Skidmore gestured with his mug of beer to a thick crowd standing around the bar.

As if responding to a cue, a man with his back to me turned around and visually swept the place, his eyes first finding Skidmore, then me.

His brown hair was loose and hung into his eyes. His clothes were in need of a good laundering and a black forest of stubble covered his chin. A cigar was stuffed between his teeth and he had a drink in his hand. I should have been ecstatic to see him. My heart should have been singing, but it felt as if it had been injected with lead. He had been in St. Kitts for a day and a half and I had to seek him out in a bar. My cheeks flamed with embarrassment. I was a fool to have come here.

"I really shouldn't be here," I said to Skidmore, though my eyes had never left Nicholas. He slowly stubbed out his cigar and finished his drink, laughing and clapping a nearby man on the back before sauntering towards me.

"It's not the first place I would've expected to see you, that's for sure."

"I heard that the ship...was in port..." my words were staggered and broken, my concentration occupied by Nicholas walking towards me. He did not hurry. His face was composed. "I...wanted to make sure...everyone...was...that the journey...went...well."

And then he was in front of me. Close enough to touch. I should have thrown myself in his arms. He should have crushed me to his chest. But neither of us moved. We simply stood before each other, our eyes locked, my breathing shallow.

"You're back," I finally said.

Nicholas nodded, his eyes sweeping up and down me. His expression was guarded, his lips pressed into a tight line. His eyes lingered on my neck. After a moment, he touched the golden chain hanging there. I could feel the heat from his fingers even though his skin never touched mine.

"Got in yesterday."

"I know," I said, a bit sharply.

Nicholas withdrew his hand.

I couldn't take my eyes off him. I felt like I was drowning, being pulled under by some unforeseen force. All I needed was for him to reach out to me to stop me from going under. But he didn't.

"I shouldn't be here," I said again.

Nicholas looked over my shoulder, a bit dazed. "Where is your father? Signor De Luca?"

Guilt sprang up in me and I had to look away. It took me a moment for me to remember that Nicholas did not know about my kiss with Emilio and there was nothing for me to feel guilty about anyway. Emilio had kissed me the evening of the play and I had not allowed it to happen again. I tried to answer his question honestly. "At their homes, I suppose."

Nicholas's gaze returned to me, astonishment mingled with disapproval. "You're here alone?"

"Yes."

"Unescorted?"

I raised my eyebrows and repeated the information slowly. "Yes, Nicholas, I came alone."

My words clicked into place for him. "You *shouldn't* be here," he said emphatically, taking my elbow and steering me past Skidmore and out of the door of the alehouse.

The growing shadows had engulfed the street and the sky was an indistinct color somewhere between blue and grey. The pedestrian traffic had grown thicker. In this district of town, activity didn't diminish as daylight faded, it flourished.

My heart thrummed with humiliation. I had endured forty-three days of tears and worry, exposed myself to the filth of the docks, and fostered the unseemly connections of stevedores and dockhands only to be kicked to the curb by Nicholas less than a minute after our reunion. I yanked my arm out of his grasp and marched to my horse.

Nicholas followed me to the sidewalk. "Where's your carriage?"

I gestured to Gypsy. "This is my horse."

Nicholas's eyes bugged. "Clarence didn't drive you? You mean to say you are completely and utterly unescorted?"

"I told you as much."

"Tessa, that was..." he seemed to bite back what he was going to say, "...risky."

"I thought it was worth the risk." I untied Gypsy. "Apparently, I was mistaken." I turned my back to Nicholas, ready to pull myself up into the saddle.

"Wait." Nicholas placed his hand on my arm. I froze, my breath catching at the feel of his skin on mine.

He ran a hand through his hair and looked at me through his lashes. "Blast it. I've not even issued you a proper hello."

His innocent expression only infuriated me. "You've never found use for propriety. Why start now?"

Nicholas blinked at my response, then straightened his shoulders. He took Gypsy's reins from me. "Let me hire a carriage for you. I'll return your horse tomorrow. I don't want you riding alone. It's getting dark."

I considered his offer. Not because I had any reservations about riding back to Amerscott alone, but because it would mean I would see him when he returned the horse. I pulled myself onto the saddle. If I were to see him, I wanted it to be because he *wanted* to see me—not to return my property.

"Tessa." My name in his mouth was equal parts pleading and warning.

Nicholas looked like a petulant child from my vantage, his hands on his hips and his head cocked angrily. Painting my face with my most angelic smile, I calmly said, "I once took out a bloody pirate with nothing but a candle. Riding a horse home in daylight is nothing more than a lark." With a cool wink, I tapped Gypsy's flanks with my heels and trotted away without a backward glance.

CHAPTER TWENTY-THREE

THE BOY'S PROFILE TOOK shape before me, the curve of his nose and set of his jaw. His hair was long, I remembered well, and always in his eyes. With a flick of my wrist, a thick strand appeared, slashing across his forehead and crossing down to his cheek. I fleshed out the line with the edge of my slim charcoal, smoothing the blackness with my fingers.

My drawing of Liam was somber. I had questioned myself when I had begun it. He was a happy child, one of the few good things about my time at the bordello on Port Winslow. I never understood how hateful Mother Ivy could have created such a joyous creature. As the drawing developed, I knew why I hadn't tried to capture the whimsy in his eyes or the mirth in his smile. He was more man than child, as fatherless children often are. He'd grounded me when I was drifting. He'd buffeted me and the other girls from the wrath of his mother. He looked at the sky with a longing that was painful to see, like a bird that couldn't fly.

He was just a little boy who helped me clear the dishes, but I thought of him every day.

Mr. Dean rapped on the drawing room door and poked his head inside. "Mr. Holladay is here and would like to call on you."

My stomach felt like it had hatched a nest of snakes. I was furious that he had returned without telling me, furious that he had left in the first place, yet I was excited to see him and petrified that he wouldn't feel the same way. "Send him in."

I had dressed in a burgundy gown trimmed in satin ribbons with a wide neckline. I had forgone the wig and twisted the front part of my hair back into pins, leaving most of it flowing loosely to my bared shoulders. I had dabbed a discretionary amount of my French perfume behind my ears and on my wrists. No matter how this meeting went, at least I looked my best.

As Nicholas stepped into the drawing room, I tore my eyes away from my art long enough to flash him a polite smile and ask him to sit, then went back to my sketching.

Nicholas sat in a chair across from me, his hands clasped in his lap.

I was too engrossed in my sketch to offer much in the way of conversation. Nicholas sat quietly for a while, then spoke. "I didn't know you were an artist."

"Just a pastime. I've been trying to keep myself busy. My tutor wishes I would hone my watercolor technique—so much more feminine. But I prefer the starkness of charcoal."

"May I see?"

"It's not finished, but yes."

"Who is it?" Nicholas asked, crossing to peer over my shoulder. My fingers flew skillfully, creating a hash of black lines then softening them with the side of my hand.

"It's Liam," I said, my voice a bit reverent. "The lad from Port Winslow." I caressed his cheek with my finger, blending away the harshness of the medium.

He leaned in for closer examination and his shirt lightly caressed the bare skin of my shoulder. I wondered if he had done that on purpose.

"You are very good. I had no idea."

"I'm almost finished. Do you mind waiting? I hate to quit now."

Nicholas sat back down.

"I hope I am not boring you," I said, peeking at Nicholas over the top of my easel. "Really, I only need five more minutes."

Nicholas settled into the chair and glanced around the room. He was clean-shaven this morning and I noticed a healing slash under his left eye that I had not seen the night before. Underneath an embroidered blue jacket he wore a collarless white shirt that opened in a deep V that showed his collarbones and the upper planes of his chest. His navy-blue breeches hugged his muscular legs and disappeared into knee-high polished black boots. Nicholas's style reflected the physical demands of his job—loose shirts allowed movement and fitted vests and breeches wouldn't get caught up in the rigging. Compared with men's current fashions of frilly doublets, high-heeled shoes, and ballooning petticoat breeches, Nicholas looked the part of a rebel. I could practically smell the scent of the sea on him from where I sat.

"I don't mind at all," said Nicholas. "Seeing you work in your element...it's a revelation."

Our eyes locked and the contact lasted well beyond what was comfortable. Feeling unsettled, I managed to tear my gaze away and returned to my sketch. I felt an undercurrent in his words, though I couldn't decipher it. Maybe I was assigning too much value to things that deserved far less. "I've seen you in your element. And now you're seeing me in mine. I imagine it's not entirely what you expected."

Nicholas *hmphed* but didn't say anything. I cocked my head and squinted, working in a curl of hair at the nape of Liam's neck. My fingers remembered the feel of that sand-colored hair, downy soft and wild, begging to be tousled anytime Liam strode by. "My birthday is Friday. Father is hosting a ball. Will you come?"

Nicholas's brows pinched together. "I'll be at sea."

I nearly dropped my charcoal. "Oh."

He propped his elbows on his knees and ran his hands

through his hair. "We're scheduled to leave that morning. I didn't know it was your birthday."

I pressed my lips into a thin line and nodded, keeping my eyes trained on my art. My hopes for a warm reunion were blighted. We would be courteous. We would be thoughtful. But we would not be what we once were. The forty-three days that had separated us seemed more like years. "How was your trip then? Is that what I should call it? A trip? A mission? A raid?"

"We made contact with Salazar. He's in possession of the Declaration of War."

My mind went to the night it was stolen. "Why did he steal it? How does it benefit him?"

"He was hired by the French to provoke the British to attack them, to start a war. He tried a few things, but your father's patience was too great. Somehow he found out about the Declaration. It seems he had spies infiltrate your father's fleet. He stole it to finish what he was hired to do."

"Did you get it back?"

"We didn't get that far." He subconsciously scratched the cut beneath his eye. "That's why my stay is so brief. We have work yet to be finished."

"It sounds dangerous."

"Mostly political. Should be a short mission." Nicholas trained his eyes on me. "De Luca will be accompanying me."

I kept my face stoic though I reeled inside. Both of them gone? Both in danger? I wouldn't survive it.

"Quin, too," he added.

I questioned him with a raise of my eyebrows.

"After the last mission, Salazar has marked my crew. I need people who aren't known to him—Skidmore and Meg."

"A few new recruits. It must be nice for you to be reunited with Skidmore again." I had a sudden longing for a reunion of my own with Skidmore. I yearned for his calmness—and his insight into Nicholas.

"It was the first stop I made. I needed my first mate."

"Why do you need Emilio? What can he offer you?"

"*Emilio*," Nicholas repeated the baron's first name with pointed interested, "is a diplomat not legally bound to the British Crown. Nor the French. Salazar is a mercenary. He has no loyalty to any country. He'll respond to prestige, to money. Signor De Luca—I'm sorry, *Emilio*—is in the unique position to offer political sway."

So that was it. Aside from my father, the three people closest to me would leave me, on my birthday no less, to track down a radical insurgent who wouldn't hesitate to kill them all.

"I didn't mean to announce it so bleakly. I thought you would've known." He picked at a loose thread in the armrest of the couch.

"Who would have told me?" There was a harsh edge in my voice that I couldn't conceal.

"De Luca."

I rolled my eyes. "You overestimate my friendship with him."

"Do I?" Nicholas leaned back in the chair, a display of assurance.

Memories of Emilio's heated lips on mine came to me unbidden. I blinked away the memory, praying that blood had not stained my cheeks. "Besides, when was this decided?"

"The day I arrived back."

So Emilio had known for two days that he was going to leave before the week was out. My father would have known. Meg too. She was probably giddy with excitement to be in the confines of a ship with Nicholas. What a perfect place to win back his affections. "No one said a word. But thank you for telling me about the raid, about Salazar. You're the only one who will tell me the truth. Everyone else thinks I'm too fragile or too stupid because I'm a woman."

Nicholas shook his head. "I'll never understand that kind of thing. You're savvy. You're strong. Besides, you're worth the truth."

Several more flicks of my wrist—laying charcoal, blurring it softly—and I was finished. I put the charcoal on the side table and wiped my hands on a rag. "*Finito.*"

Rising to his feet, Nicholas scrutinized the work with a cocked head. "Your Italian is improving," he said nonchalantly as he stared at the sketch. "I suppose it's the influence of the good baron. The drawing is lovely. I feel the boy's loneliness looking at it. I see what you mean when you called the charcoals stark."

I set the easel in the corner. "Let's walk. To the garden?"

"Unescorted?" Nicholas raised a brow. His sour mood was starting to grate on me.

"I wouldn't have it any other way." I shoved my hand onto his arm, even though he had not offered it. Nicholas's lips curled up at the ends and he escorted me out of Amerscott into the gardens behind Glencartha.

"Let's find some shade. It's too damn hot." Nicholas peeled off his coat.

I gestured to a secluded grove on the far side of the garden. Just as we stepped into the shade, my heel sunk into the soft grass and I stumbled.

Nicholas tried to catch me as I fell out of my shoe and on to my knees. "Whoa!" He eased me into a sitting position. "What happened?"

"My shoe." I pointed to the beaded silk mule stuck in the ground.

Nicholas bent down and worked it out of the soft earth. He held it up, clods of mud still clinging to the heel. "Who would have imagined that such a delicate thing could be so hazardous?" He brushed the dirt off the heel and knelt before me, holding the shoe out like an offering. I reached for it. He shook his head. "Allow me."

I sat back, my hands propping me from behind, my knees bent and my skirts concealing my legs and feet. With his free hand, Nicholas reached under the hem of my petticoat. I held my breath. He found my bare foot, his fingers curling around the arch. I inhaled sharply. Nicholas looked satisfied with himself. With a knowing smile, his fingers travelled upwards, caressing first my heel and then the angles of my ankle. His eyes were dancing with devilish mischief. I knew there was no smile on my face. I was too busy concentrating on breathing in and out to do much else with my body. I felt my eyes grow vulnerable and wide. When his hand reached my calf, he gently pulled my leg forward, exposing my foot from behind the folds of fabric. He slid the shoe into place, then guided my foot back under my skirt.

"Tessa, I—"

I sprang up onto my knees and cut off his words with a hungry kiss. After a second of frozen surprise, Nicholas pressed into me. His arms slid around my back and guided me to the ground so that he was propped over me. My fingers threaded in his hair as my lips traversed his face, his neck. I pressed a sweaty palm against the bareness of his chest. I felt the heated puffs of his breath across my face, my lips, my earlobes. I lifted my chin and Nicholas's lips found the tender skin of my throat. His hands caressed me, moving along the torso of my gown. I couldn't stop the moan that escaped from the back of my throat.

Body to body, our hearts hammered against one another. He kissed me and kissed me. I closed my eyes in a delirious pleasure that bordered on pain. My bones ached for us to be closer. My hands slid down Nicholas's back, feeling the tensing of his muscles under his thin, thin shirt. My breathing was shallow and rapid, my chest threatening to burst the ties of my corset. My hair fell rebelliously from its pins and stray locks tangled themselves into our kisses. His shirt had come untucked in the craze of our passion. Not caring that I was trespassing far beyond the bounds of decorum, my hands glided past the hem of shirt and spread against the feverish skin of his back.

"Bloody hell, Tess." His groan vibrated against my lips deliciously.

"Promise me," I said, my ragged breathing making my voice hoarse.

"Anything," Nicholas murmured, burying his face in my hair.

"Stay one day longer."

I could feel Nicholas hesitate. I arched my back and pressed my body closer to his.

"Oh, Tessa," Nicholas groaned, "I can't."

I tangled my hands into his hair and my mouth moved with his. "Don't leave me on my birthday. Any other day. But not on my birthday."

Nicholas's hands caressed my face, my jaw, my neck. His eyes—a soft dove grey—searched mine. I sensed a moment of faltering. I glanced my hands across his chest, feeling the dampness of sweat on his cotton shirt. "You're the captain," I whispered. "You can give me just one more day." I weaved my hands in his hair pressed my lips to his.

I could taste his sigh of submission. He nodded. "I'll stay."

Our limbs tangled together and I was suddenly hovering over Nicholas, my hair falling around our faces like a shining chestnut curtain. The scent of rumpled grass and heady loam blossomed around us. With my hand on his neck, I could feel the thrum of his pulse on my palm. Strong and swift.

Nicholas had spoken of my element. A drawing room in St. Kitts. Corsets and gloves and afternoon tea. Perhaps he was right. As my fingers traced the flexing of his arms, I pictured Nicholas at the helm of a ship, hauling sails in the rigging, brandishing a gleaming cutlass. That was his element. But this—our hearts thrumming in unison, our bodies so tangled it was hard to know where one of us left off and the other began—this was *our* element. My hands travelled down the flatness of Nicholas's stomach, feeling the structure of muscle, rippling and tense. My fingers fluttered at the hem of his shirt; his stomach contracted in a gratifying response. My thumb slowly grazed the skin there.

Nicholas's hand closed around my wrist. "Tessa," he whispered, his lips against my neck. "Oh, Tess, we have to stop."

I murmured unintelligibly through my kisses, refuting his words.

His grip tightened around my wrist and he pulled my hand away from his stomach. He then placed his hands on either side of my face, his thumbs drawing soft circles on my cheekbones. "Tessa," he said again, my name a plea, a litany, on his lips.

I sighed and collapsed on the ground next to him, my arms extended beyond my head, my hair pooling around me like a halo. My skin felt too thin against the power of my pulse, like a sail stretched beyond its limits by a sudden wind. I blinked at the brilliant blue sky, my chest heaving, my muscles coiled with tension. Bereft and wanting. Painfully wanting. Like a song cut short before the final chord of resolution could be played.

Nicholas propped up on an elbow. His cheeks were stained with pink. "You..." he said breathlessly, brushing the hair out of my face.

"I suppose I should apologize," I said. Nicholas raised his eyebrows. "But I don't want to."

Nicholas grinned and laughed softly. "I wouldn't accept an apology anyhow." He straightened the chain that had pooled behind my neck, pulling the crucifix onto my chest.

"Do you want it back?"

"What? Why?"

"It's yours. And you're back now."

He traced the lines of the chain with a finger. "I like knowing that you wear it."

I sat up and smoothed my dress. Nicholas pulled a blade of grass from my hair. I gave a shy smile.

Nicholas helped me to my feet. He retrieved his jacket and righted his shirt. "Let's walk."

I followed Nicholas around the edge of a pond dotted with water lilies. Colorful birds jumped between the branches overhead, their songs raining down on us.

"Are you happier now?" I asked.

Nicholas gave me a puzzled look.

"Having a place at sea again," I explained, wondering if he thought I was talking about the kiss.

"I feel I have purpose again."

"You didn't have a purpose before you left?" And all this time I thought both our purpose was to start a life together.

"I know what you're thinking, Tessa," he said, looking at me sharply. "It wasn't like that."

Five minutes ago everything between us was perfection. And now we were on the verge of arguing again. It seemed as though every recent conversation we had spiraled into a fight.

"Will you truly stay for my birthday?

"I said I would."

"I know. I just wondered if...if you meant it."

I saw him flinch. "Do you doubt me because I gave you my word while I was kissing you?"

It sounded so horribly wrong said that way. I changed the subject. "Why didn't you tell me that you returned?"

The distance between us grew slightly. A few inches only. But enough to notice.

"It's tradition to celebrate with the crew."

A voice inside was telling me to stay quiet. This conversation would only lead to heartache. But I had to know. "You were avoiding me."

Nicholas clenched his jaw tightly. "I was avoiding this very conversation."

I was bewildered. "If you hadn't avoided me, we wouldn't be having this conversation."

"It's the next question I don't want to talk about."

"As if you know what I am going to say next."

We stopped our leisurely stroll. A corner of Nicholas's shirt still hung out of his waistband. I had a maddening urge to grab its hem, yank it all out, and slide my hands across his stomach again. "Just say what you want to say. Ask me what you've been wanting to ask me ever since that Sunday."

I clenched my hands and felt my nails digging into my

palms. "Why? Why didn't you tell me? Why didn't you say goodbye? Why did you leave?"

He winked at me. "You do not fail to disappoint, Miss Monroe."

I reeled at him. "Fine. If you're dreading that question so much, you have my leave not to answer it."

"I have your leave, do I? How very gracious of—"

"But answer this instead. Why are you here now? If I am so painful for you to be around—"

"Stop, Tess." The sharpness in his voice silenced me. He reached out and removed another piece of grass from my hair. "Maybe I should go."

"It's been forty-three days and all we can do is argue," I muttered.

Nicholas looked as if he had been struck. "You counted the days?"

"I counted the tears. I counted the heartbeats. The days were the least of it. And now I must do it again. Not knowing if you..." I stopped myself before I said the words.

"Not knowing if I what?"

My eyes dropped to the ground. Blades of grass stood like an army, row upon row of soldiers at the ready. I stared, my hands fidgeting at my sides, terrified of what I was going to say. "When you were away, every moment was torment. My stomach sick with constant worry. Each day an eternity. Nights that were even longer. And if I am to survive that all again, I can. It will all be worth it if I were to know...if you were to say..." I looked up meekly through my lashes. "Do you love me? Do you mean to return to me?"

"Ah, Captain Holladay! There you are."

I snapped my head around. My father was striding towards us. "Hello, my girl," he said as he kissed my cheek. He nodded at Nicholas. "Captain Holladay. I believe we have much to accomplish before you set out again."

Nicholas nodded curtly. "I should let you know that I have delayed departure by one day." His eyes flicked to me.

"Is that wise?"

"Your daughter asked it of me. She thought it unfair that I take away Signor De Luca and her handmaid on the morning of her birthday. She can be *very* persuasive." The left side of his mouth lifted in a wicked half-smile. I looked down quickly, hoping to conceal the color that flooded my cheeks. "One day will not affect the outcome."

"I hadn't even considered my daughter's birthday. We're hosting a celebration. I am sure she will want the baron in attendance. Very good. You'll pull anchor early on Saturday then. Now, my Tessa, scurry off so we can discuss things far too ugly for your pretty little ears. I think Miss Maisley and Miss Quincy want to discuss the details of your birthday ball. Captain, Lord De Luca expects us presently at Glencartha."

I looked at Nicholas, my heart filled with longing. I searched his face for the answer to my question. He kept it guarded with a cool mask of indifference.

"Give me one moment to bid adieu to your lovely daughter and I will join you." Nicholas scooped my arm into his and led me several steps away. His voice was low when he said, "You know how I feel."

I looked across the gardens, the serene surroundings at odds with the turmoil within. "I know the last words we spoke to each other were hateful words. I know you left me without saying goodbye. I know you returned without saying hello. *That* is what I know."

I counted twenty-two beats of my heart before Nicholas said anything. "Why do you wish to wring such intimacies out of me during an interrogation?"

His refusal to answer seemed answer enough. I looked away, afraid to look too deeply in his eyes, lest he see how deeply his words had stung me.

My father cleared his throat impatiently.

I thought of the one time I had uttered those three words to him. We were in a blazing church facing a very real and fiery death and I told him I loved him. He didn't want to hear it. I now understood how he thought some kind of dire circumstance was all that had drawn it out. Those words deserved their own story. Their own space. He was right to refuse my question. I had cornered him, and I would always question the sincerity of his words, no matter what he said. "Very well," I said with more poise than I felt.

Nicholas faced me and took my right hand in his. "Know this. I have claimed you for my own. And I am a selfish man." He squeezed my hand gently, then with a sweeping bow, kissed it. He returned to my father while I stood frozen and reeling, the elation of the moment barely frosting over the deep-seated unease that still squirmed in my belly.

CHAPTER TWENTY-FOUR

THE BALLROOM AT AMERSCOTT was a gaping, echoing room with high ceilings and a parquet floor of polished hardwoods ranging from deep purplish brown to buttery blonde. Under Miss Maisley's direction, it had transformed from an empty tomb into a botanical delight; it looked like the inside of a greenhouse with hanging baskets of jasmine, small palm trees along the walls, and giant vases filled with mountains of orchids, the likes of which I had never seen in Europe.

I walked through the room the morning of my birthday, wonderstruck by the sight of all the decorations.

"Do you like it?" My father sounded a bit concerned.

"Oh, I love it!" I stroked the velvety petal of an orchid. "These trailing vines, the asymmetry of the orchids, the bright colors. Not at all like the pruned shrubbery and delicate blooms of any self-respecting English garden. It's just so untamed."

My father laughed. "You seem happy here."

I tucked my hair behind my ear as I bent to smell a nosegay of spider lilies on the refreshment table. "Mmm," I mumbled, avoiding the conversation. It had been too long since I had taken inventory of my happiness.

A painted portrait of my mother had been hung over the

serving table. I stared at it for a long time, even though I had memorized every brushstroke that had created it. Her eyes were round and brown like mine, though her hair was a bright auburn. As a child, I told myself that I couldn't truly miss her because I had never known her. It made sense—but the thought was no protection against the nights of crippling emptiness that my mother was meant to fill. I wished she were here today, the celebration of my eighteenth year. I wish I could confide in her about Nicholas and ask her about love and life and finding the right balance of it all. I wished the heavens were fair and I still had a mother.

"Did you and Mother ever argue?" I asked, my eyes still on the sweet, young face in the gilded frame.

My father looked at me quizzically, but his lips lifted into a smile as his eyes strayed to the painting of the lovely redhead. "Passion knows no bounds."

"Pardon?"

"It's what my grandmother used to say when she saw us bicker."

"So you did argue." I raised a brow.

He offered me a conspiring smile. "Ever since we were old enough to talk to each other. Oh, I hated that brown-eyed girl with the plaited hair. I pulled her pigtails every chance I got. And she stamped my toe something awful."

I smiled at the thought of it. I knew very little about my mother—littler still about my father's early years with her. I had not known they were children together.

"When our families arranged our marriage, we were both livid. I threatened to run away. She threatened to kill me in my sleep."

"Were you never happy together?" I had always imagined my parents as being perfectly in love.

My father brushed the tip of his nose with his forefinger. "That's just the thing. Passion knows no bounds. My grandmother saw it. We had passion for each other. As youth, we only knew how to express it with arguing. As we grew, our love was just as passionate. There was never a neutral ground between us. It was exhausting, mind you. But it was all I ever wanted."

My heart fluttered at the thought of a younger version of my father falling so fiercely in love with the brown-eyed girl with plaits. And I thought of Nicholas and how every other encounter with him was fire or ice. Maybe we were the same—passion without bounds.

Catching my elbow, my father steered me away from my mother's portrait. His face was serious. "I meant to ask you something. What is your opinion of Lord De Luca?"

"My opinion of him? You must know that I think highly of him. I value his friendship. Not just for myself but for you as well."

My father nodded, still a little unsettled. His lips moved without speech as he tried to find the right words. "He has recently asked me to trust him with something very important to me."

He must be referring to the mission. "Father, whatever it is, you know you can trust him with anything. Think on the way he took care of me. He would never, ever wrong you or anyone you care about."

My father looked relieved. "You're right," he said, his creased brow relaxing. "I'm satisfied then. Now let's sample the punch and start celebrating your birthday properly."

* * * * *

"There," Meg said, her smile proud as she finished brushing a rouge stick across my lips. "I did good, even if I do say so myself." She stood back with satisfaction.

I turned in my chair to face the vanity mirror but before I could fully glimpse my reflection, Meg pulled me out of my chair. "No, no. Look in the full-length mirror." She tugged me across the room and positioned me just so before stepping aside.

My eyes swept over my reflection and my lips parted to let out a small breath of wonder. I was beautiful. My newly tailored gown enveloped me in the finest ivory silk, a shimmering pattern of fleur-de-lis woven into it. The skirt was pulled back into a sweeping bustle to reveal a pale gold petticoat adorned with more lace than I had ever seen in my life. The stomacher probably cost more than the rest of the gown combined. Faceted crystals encrusted the golden panel on my bodice so that every breath I took scattered prisms of light like bits of falling ice in a winter storm. The neckline was wide enough to expose the gentle slope of my shoulders. The sleeves hugged my arms then spilled into a profusion of lace and ruffles at my elbow. Several strands of tiny pearls ringed my neck. When Meg wasn't looking, I had fastened Nicholas's necklace around my waist next to my corset. I wanted it with me always.

Meg had styled my wig with extra care, adding cloth pieces for extra height and style. Tucked into the brunette hairstyle were crystalline hair combs and more strands of small pearls. Sleek ringlets spiraled behind my right ear and over my shoulder.

I swished gently in front of the mirror, delighting in the ruffling sound of my skirt and the play of light on the crystals.

Meg watched my response with her hands pressed together in front of her mouth. Her eyes were giddy with anticipation.

I spun around, craning my neck to see myself. "Never in my entire life have I looked so beautiful."

"You look like royalty, miss. A right princess."

I couldn't help myself. I caught Meg up in hug, a surprised noise bubbling out of her. "You're an artist, Meg. Thank you. I must keep you around for my wedding."

"For your wedding?" She raised an eyebrow.

"I'm sure I'll have one someday," I said coyly. I pictured a quaint church wedding in Basseterre with Nicholas at the end of the aisle. "And I'll need to look as pretty as this."

"Right now, let's just get you to your party."

Meg had dressed for the ball in one of her Sunday dresses—a simple navy-blue shift with a split skirt and a black stomacher. Her blonde hair was a cluster of tiny curls close to her head like a gleaming halo.

At the threshold of the ballroom, I stood for a moment, overwhelmed by the sight before me. Dozens of couples glided across the floor and many more loitered about the edges of the ballroom, lost in conversation and grazing on hors d'oeuvres. There were so many guests, and I hardly knew any of them. I recognized a few of my father's associates, the constable, Governor and Mrs. Abner, and a handful of faces from church.

There was a whisper in my ear "A lady as lovely as you ought to be showcased—not hiding in the shadows."

I turned towards the voice. "You came!"

Nicholas admired me, his eyes on me like soft starlight. "I was a git for even thinking of missing this."

"Do you like my dress?"

Nicholas's eyes brushed over me again. He leaned in close to me, very close, his lips skimming my ear. His hot breath sent tingles down my back as he whispered, "I rather like the girl *in* the dress." He twirled a finger in my ringlet. "This, though. This is ridiculous. Your hair is softer than this. Redder, too. And not so...big."

I swatted his hand away.

"How long must we stay at this thing?" Nicholas asked.

"It's my party, I must stay for the entire event."

"Let me rephrase my question. How long must *I* stay at this thing?"

"Nicholas," I scolded, "it's my birthday. I want you to be part of it. What's your reservation anyway?"

He looked into the room with an expression of disgust. "All the people, for one thing."

"Oh, hush. Let's dance." I wheedled my hand into the crook of his arm and walked into the ballroom. He was dragging behind me.

"I don't exactly dance," Nicholas said.

"Of course you do. Sailors love to dance."

"Not like this. We didn't exactly practice the minuet aboard the *Banshee*."

The airy descant of a flute filled the air and joyous violins followed. Two lines—one of men and one of women—formed, ready for a contredanse. I took my place at the end of the women's line and lowered myself into a gracious curtsy. With a roll of his eyes, Nicholas stood across from me and bowed lazily.

Despite his unfamiliarity with the dance—and his general lack of enthusiasm—Nicholas was a superb dancer. He had a rare command over his body that was beyond grace. His tall, sinuous frame moved easily with the music. Even through his evening jacket I could see the pull of his muscles. Just a quick glance at the guests confirmed my suspicion that Nicholas was the most strapping man in the room. It was the result of his labors, but it was far more appealing to me than the willowy, pillowy men of high society. I longed to caress his shoulders and feel the way his muscles worked under my fingers as he wrapped me in his arms. But only our hands touched when it was our turn to walk down the aisle.

The music ended and we applauded the orchestra. I was about to compliment Nicholas on his dancing when a gloved hand holding a fluted glass appeared right before me. The hand belonged to Emilio. I took the spiced punch and sipped it as Emilio and Nicholas exchanged warm greetings.

The two were unlikely friends, I thought. Emilio was a bit taller than Nicholas and thinner. He stood stiffly, looking regal in a crimson coat and a crisp white cravat. Nicholas's posture was more settled. He wore black—ever the dashing pirate—but the fit of his jacket was not as stringent and he had left his top two buttons undone; he had skipped a cravat entirely so that his neck showed through the gap in his coat. Stray tendrils of wavy brown hair fell to the sharp planes of his cheeks, framing his vivid grey eyes. The prince and the pirate, I thought, a secretive smile teasing my lips.

Emilio took the drink out of my hand, gave it to Nicholas, and whisked me to the center of the ballroom. He took my right hand in his left, placed his other hand on the small of my back, and we waltzed. Emilio's every step was impeccable. This was his element.

Meg was talking to Nicholas, giggling and touching him on his arm. She was probably hoping for a dance. My eyes narrowed. Tomorrow they would be on the *Seabird* together. How excited she must be. I hated the idea of it.

The waltz ended and the dancers applauded the orchestra. I was on my way back towards Nicholas when the ring of a silver fork clinking against a crystal glass caught my attention. A hush settled over the room and all eyes fell on my father—commanding in his dress uniform—standing near the head of the refreshment table. Emilio joined him and my father gestured for me to do the same. I self-consciously walked to his side.

"Thank you all for coming tonight to celebrate the eighteenth anniversary of my daughter's birth. My little girl has always been the light of my life. Though as you can see, she's not so little anymore. She has blossomed into a smart, witty, and warmhearted beauty. She reminds me more of her mother every day." He gestured to my mother's painting on the wall. Several female guests sighed a collective, "*Aww.*"

My father grew a little misty and paused to steady his voice. "There was a time when I thought I had lost my Tessa. Her return was a gift from the heavens." He gave Nicholas a grateful smile. "And since her return at the hands of the brave adventurer, Mr. Holladay, her welfare has been my priority." He nodded at Nicholas, and Nicholas returned the gesture. My father's speech was a bit beyond that of publicly wishing me a happy birthday. A cool sweat glazed the back of my neck. I looked at Emilio expecting to see my feelings of confusion reflected in his countenance. Instead, I saw a confident smile. He was beaming. A glance at Nicholas told me he was as suspicious as I.

"Lord De Luca has been like a son to me. His friendship was precious to me during the dark times I thought my daughter was dead. And when she arrived home, his friendship was beneficial to her as well. Lord Emilio proposed unifying our families, and after speaking to my beloved girl about her regard for this man, I would like to announce the betrothal of my daughter Tessa to Lord Emilio De Luca. Please join me in congratulating them!"

The room exploded with clapping and cheering. I hardly knew what was happening as Emilio knelt before me and took my hand in his. He was poised and calm. The corners of my vision blurred and I latched on to Emilio's hand to keep from tipping over.

The party guests quieted again. I could sense the crowd pressing in, ready to hear what Emilio would say. He took a deep breath and for the first time, I saw a twinge of trepidation in his eyes.

"Miss Tessa Monroe, I offer you all that I am. And I offer you this as a symbol of my promise." He withdrew a small silver box from his pocket. Inside it was a golden ring. A large diamond was encircled with emeralds, like the petals of a flower. He slipped it on my finger with a victorious grin.

My eyes flittered from the ring on my hand to the man kneeling before me. My mouth hung open. I had no words. I had few thoughts. This couldn't be happening.

"A toast! A toast!" the crowd chanted.

Governor Abner raised a glass in our honor. "Hear, hear. I know the baron to be a true gentleman, a man of many virtues. I've known many ladies on the island who have chased after them." Soft laughter bubbled through the guests. "But not until spunky Miss Monroe arrived on my island have I seen Lord De Luca consider a life of domestication. I'd like to offer a toast to the newly affianced couple. May you both live as long as you want, and never want as long as you live. Congratulations to both of you. And to you, Admiral Monroe."

Emilio had risen from his knees at some point during the

Governor's toast and stood close by my side. I kept staring at my hand in his like it was a shimmering illusion that would vanish any moment and reality would return.

"Do you like it?" Emilio asked softly. "I had it commissioned just for you. The diamond is from Amsterdam and the emeralds are from Columbia. My family crest—*our* family crest—is carved into the gold band."

The ring twinkled daintily in the candlelight, glittering with ethereal beauty. Any other girl would certainly think it was spectacular but I only saw a viper wrapped around my finger.

"I'd like to say something." A voice pierced the din. A voice that was used to commanding crowds. The noise ebbed under its power.

Nicholas slithered through the crowd and people parted to make way for him. He walked like he danced, so sure of himself, so graceful. He did not hurry. He seemed distracted, bored even, as he walked to the refreshment table and selected a glass of punch. He took a sip and nodded in approval. His languid performance was offset by his eyes—sharp and vicious.

He raised his glass and appealed to the crowd. "There's much to congratulate tonight, is there not? First and foremost, I issue congratulations to Admiral Monroe. You've complimented me on my tactics before, but I must say this alliance is beyond anything I had ever imagined. You are a far superior strategist, and believe me, I am taking notes."

My blood chilled at his words. This was cruelty masked in flattery. Though Nicholas wore a broad smile, it was wicked and cold. His arrogance was clouding his sight. If he took but one moment's thought, he would know that this entire arrangement was a mistake. My heart ached for him, knowing that he thought I had publicly jilted him. I stared at him feverishly, willing him to read my mind.

Nicholas continued, animated and impassioned, and I steeled myself for his toast, silently praying to be spared humiliation. "Congratulations to my benefactor, Signor De

Luca. I know a thing or two about your fiancée, and I can confidently say she will make herself right at home in the noble house of De Luca." How dare he insinuate that I cared for nothing more than Emilio's money and title? My sympathies for Nicholas were quickly vanishing.

He turned to me and settled his impenetrable gaze squarely on my eyes. His jesting smile was gone. A cold cast was all that remained. I was frozen, horrified as he finished his toast. "Last of all, congratulations to you, Miss Monroe. Every girl has the right to pursue her heart's desires. I am impressed at how you have taken advantage of that privilege. Perhaps I should be praising you on your tactics rather than your father. You certainly know when to drop your anchor." He stepped very close to me and I flinched as he brought his hand up and gently stroked my cheek. "From the bottom of my heart, *Baroness*," he hissed out the title, "I truly wish to see you reap all that you have sown."

He lithely pivoted on his feet and raised his glass with a cheerful huzzah. The guests mimicked his enthusiasm and drank freely while I, still frozen, watched Nicholas walk away.

CHAPTER TWENTY-FIVE

A CLOUD OF PEOPLE closed around me, their smiles looming closer and closer as I rose to my toes to see over their heads. Through a gap of wigs and bared shoulders I saw Nicholas's silhouette leave the ballroom. I knew if I didn't speak to him right away, I would never see him again.

"Excuse me." I pushed against the growing crowd. I felt like I was being smothered. I grew more aggressive, no longer bothering to smile and make eye contact with those I wheedled past. Strangers grabbed my hands, patted my back, said cheerful words I didn't bother listening to. I barreled through, using my elbows like battering rams. I faintly heard someone call my name as I broke into a run.

"Nick!" I dashed down the front steps, my eyes looking for any movement. I didn't know if Nicholas had a horse or a carriage or had come on foot. With my skirts held high, I ran down the cobblestone driveway lined with carriages. "Nicholas!"

"Miss Monroe? Is everything all right?" Clarence stepped out from among the carriages.

I cast one last glance down the driveway, my vision obscured by the deepening twilight.

I turned back towards the house. "Ready my horse, Clarence. Five minutes."

I dashed back through Amerscott and flew out of the back door, thinking that Nicholas had gone to the garden or Glencartha. I called Nicholas's name through panting breaths. I cursed the darkness as my fingers fumbled with the latch on the garden gate. My voice echoed off the stone walls. No one answered me. I tried to fight the panic that ballooned in my throat.

When I returned to the stables, Clarence was finishing with Gypsy. He stepped back and nodded. Without a word, I pulled myself onto the mare and dug my heels into her flanks.

I almost slipped off the saddle as Gypsy banked around a corner, and I cursed the sidesaddle under my breath. The second time I nearly fell off, I reined Gypsy to a stop and remounted, riding astride like a man, giving no thought to my immodesty or the night air that chilled my legs.

Gypsy was covered in a sheen of sweat when I reached the edge of town. I hadn't seen another rider or carriage on the country roads. If Nicholas had come to town, he could have gone in a hundred different directions. I slowed Gypsy to a walk and steered her towards the harbor.

During the day, the wharf was overwhelming. Filthy stevedores, urchins, and sailors covered the pavement. Crates and shipping wears, coils of fragrant hemp rope, nets of hot, rotting fish. Carriages. Passengers. Barely room to turn around. At night though, the wharf was unsettling with too much space and too much quiet. The black harbor water drank up the light of the stars and splashed eerily against countless hulls. The skeletal masts of the ships rose in the moonlight like spears. Shadows prowled the water's edge, bits of dark conversations blown on the wind.

Squinting into the darkness, I passed by each ship. I knew the *Seabird* was a schooner, but nearly twenty of the ships anchored in the harbor were schooners. I had never seen the ship to recognize it and it was too dark to read the names painted on the hulls.

A holler of cursing sounded behind me. I startled in my

saddle and Gypsy jittered in a circle. Two men broke into a brawl only three feet away. The victim of a punch stumbled into Gypsy's rump, sending her rearing into the air. I grasped the saddle horn and yanked on the reins. The horse settled near a lonely female figure standing below a streetlamp. Her head was encased in a shawl so I could not see her features.

"Pardon me, ma'am. Do you know which of these ships is called *Seabird*?"

"Come again?" The woman dropped the shawl from her face. A thousand tiny bumps caught the light of the lamp, each a swollen mountain ready to burst with puss. Her eyes were gaping pits.

She had the pox.

I reared back on Gypsy. "I'm sorry."

I rode through the alleyway frantically, not caring that I almost trampled the drunkards and homeless that infested the streets. I found myself before Three Brothers Alehouse—the only other place I could think to look for Nicholas.

I tethered Gypsy to a lamppost and ventured inside. Bawdy laughter filled the hall. I felt for the crucifix under my dress as if it were a protective talisman. Ignoring the curious stares, I squared my shoulders and walked as strongly as I could, lapping the tavern twice until I was certain Nicholas wasn't inside.

I left the tavern quickly only to stop dead in my tracks when I was faced with an empty street. My stomach plummeted. Gypsy was gone. I ran to the lamppost and ran my hands over it, as if there were some invisible reins there that I couldn't see. I cursed something awful, kicked the post, and cursed again. I walked towards the wharf, longing to get out of the narrow alleys that closed around me like a labyrinth. I would have to hire a carriage—if I could find one at this hour. I didn't have any way to pay for one, but I could settle the debt at Amerscott. I idly fingered the diamond and emerald ring, wondering if a driver would take it in exchange for a ride.

I wandered the wharf aimlessly without seeing a carriage. I

must be missed at Amerscott by now. I had been gone for an hour at least. My father would come looking for me.

Across the quay where the storage yards ended and the bars began, a man dragged a woman out into the open, yelling vicious things at her. She spit in his face and he hit her hard with the back of his hand, the crack of his slap ricocheting around the emptiness of the harbor. She screamed. He hit her again. She fell to the ground. I gasped. The man saw me.

"What are you lookin' at?" His speech was slurred. He took a step towards me.

Backing up, I muttered, "I think that woman might be hurt."

The woman lifted her head and wiped a trickle of blood from her lips. "Mind your own business, princess," she snapped.

I ducked my head and walked away from the sparring couple.

Would my father think to look for me at the docks? No one knew that I frequented this area. I couldn't walk home. It was too dark and too far. Things happened to ladies on abandoned roads. I'd have to bide my time until a carriage happened by or until someone came looking for me.

I spun around at the sound of a gunshot, my heart thundering in my throat. Two drunkards were pacing out a duel twenty yards from me, their shots going wide from lack of coordination. Something brushed against my skirt and I almost lost myself in a scream, but swallowed it when I saw a mongrel dog running by me. My skin prickled like it wanted to peel off me. I could barely hear the sound of the ocean waves over the thudding of my pulse in my ears.

When another wide shot rang by me, I ran to the only place I knew I could lock out the night and hid in the depths of the *Freedom*. I paced the cabins below like a caged animal. Who would ever think to find me here? I'd have to wait out the night, but at least I was safe and had the comfort of a bed.

My head was pounding, my hands were shaking. I stared at the ring on my hand. I wasn't engaged. I wasn't. I didn't care that my consent mattered not in such affairs. I didn't care that my father had given his word and negotiated a contract. I didn't care how much money he had put in my dowry to entice a baron to marry so far beneath him. I wouldn't marry Emilio De Luca. I wouldn't.

Nicholas would never know. He'd be gone before I would have the chance to tell him.

I found myself in the galley staring into the liquor cabinet. The rum called to me like a siren promising me an escape.

I pulled the stopper from a jug and inhaled its acrid scent.

I remembered Nicholas's face. His angry words. He should have known I would never consent to marrying another. I was his. What hurt worse than his harsh humiliation was that he didn't see how sick I was at the idea of marrying anyone but him.

I lifted the jug to my lips and tipped a river of rum down my mouth. I swallowed, gagged, and sputtered, droplets of the foul stuff spraying across the galley countertops. My throat felt like it had been scored with a hot poker. I relished in the pain. A physical manifestation of what was happening within.

Nicholas would leave before the sun rose. There would be no letter this time. No hope of a future meeting.

I took another drink.

He would never know that I was just as upset about this betrothal as he. He'd be trapped with Emilio, whom he would consider to be my fiancé. Would Emilio even survive the trip? And Meg. I groaned. Hurt and reckless, Nicholas would turn to her.

I pulled deeper still on the jug, its contents searing my throat.

Heat spread through my belly. My head felt light and fuzzy. Tomorrow, there would be a price to pay but right now I needed the oblivion at the bottom of the bottle. My lips tingled and my fingers fumbled with the jug as I tipped the liquid fire down my throat, little rivulets spilling out of the sides of my mouth.

I have claimed you for my own, Nicholas had said. *And I am a selfish man.* His words echoed in my spinning mind. *I have claimed you for my own. And I am a selfish man. I am a selfish man.* I hinged all my hopes on his selfishness. It was the only chance I had that he would come back for me.

CHAPTER TWENTY-SIX

THERE WERE VOICES. I heard Nicholas and I tried to reach for him but I was frozen in some kind of dark prison. It was too painful to search for his voice and I let myself slip back into the blackness. The blackness cradled me for an eternity. Then my head erupted with pain. I opened my eyes and saw Emilio. His face was blurry and his voice muffled, as though his mouth was stuffed with cotton. Why had Miss Maisley let him into my room? A ray of sunlight pierced my eyes like a dagger. I groaned and shielded my face with my hand, opening first one eye and then the other. Emilio was still there, still speaking words I couldn't understand. I didn't want to speak with him. Why wouldn't he just let me sleep?

I reached for a blanket to pull over my head. Instead, I felt my tight corset, my showy gown, and a hard, wooden floor beneath me. My head felt as if it had been filled with sand as I struggled to sit up.

I was on the floor next to a bed. Why was I on the floor? Where was I? Was I ill? None of this made sense.

I looked around, still squinting in the brightness. Emilio crouched in front of me. He was still talking. Meg was standing behind him. She was wearing trousers. Was this a dream?

Emilio held his hand out to me. I took it and he helped me perch on the edge of the bed.

The cotton that had been muffling all the sounds dissipated and I was slammed with a wall of noise. I blinked back the din and shielded my ears.

Meg pulled my hands from my ears. She was shouting my name.

"By all that's holy, Meg, please stop shouting," I said. "And what are you wearing? What is happening?"

She retrieved something from the floor and held it up for me to see: a ceramic jug.

"You're drunk," Meg said, her voice still booming.

I covered my face with my hands. "How humiliating," I mumbled. My eyes flew open and my head snapped up. "Why are you here? Where's my father? Has Nicholas sailed yet?" I knew where I was now. I was aboard the *Freedom,* in my cabin. I must have lost consciousness and fallen on to the floor next to my bed.

Meg exchanged a loaded look with Emilio. "We didn't know you were on board," Emilio said. "We'll find some way to get you back to your father."

"What?"

"The mission is under way," said Meg. "We sailed with the early tide."

"What?" I said again, more desperate to understand.

"Can we get her up?" Emilio asked Meg.

Meg held out a hand. "Can you stand?"

I stood slowly, using Meg for support, my head feeling very heavy and very light at the same time. The stench of my own breath was enough to make my stomach sour.

Emilio and Meg steered me to a porthole. Instead of the bustle of the docks, I saw only the dark ocean and grey skies smeared with rain. "We're at sea?" I exclaimed.

"Yes," Emilio and Meg said in unison.

"The mission?"

"Yes," they said again.

"On the *Freedom*? Why aren't you on the *Seabird*?"

"Sailing the *Freedom* was always the plan," said Emilio. "It's swifter and less likely to garner unwanted attention. Just a small fishing rig."

I placed my forehead against the porthole. The chilled glass felt wonderfully calming. "How will I get back?"

"The captain will find a way."

The captain. Nicholas. Relief flooded through me. He was here. I could talk with him. He'd understand and help me find a way out of the engagement. "Does he know I'm here?"

"Yes," Meg answered.

That was strange. He should've been by my side, nursing me, helping me find a way to right everything that had gone wrong. "Where is he? Why isn't he here?"

"He wasn't exactly pleased to see you," Meg said sharply.

Emilio scowled at her.

"I need to see him." He'd fix everything.

Emilio slipped his arm around me. "Let's go to the galley and sit. You look like you're about to fall over."

The galley was empty. "Where's Nicholas?"

"On the main deck," said Emilio.

I sank on to a chair, my hands pressing against my throbbing temples. "I need him. Can you fetch him?"

Emilio nodded to Meg. She left. He sat beside me. "What in the world are you doing here?"

I closed my eyes and pinched the bridge of my nose, hoping to stop the pain that pounded with every beat of my heart.

When I didn't answer, Emilio asked a different question. "What happened last night?"

"I needed some air." I waved my hand dismissively. "All the excitement."

"You just vanished. We spent the night searching for you, worried sick. And I almost ruined the mission by staying behind. The thought of leaving without knowing where you were was too much. But your father commanded me to go."

"Was Nicholas looking, too?"

Emilio shook his head. "I don't know where he was last night. Only saw him this morning. He's barely said two words to any of us. He must not have known or he would have certainly been searching with us."

I sighed. Nicholas would be pickled in wrath when he saw me.

Emilio cradled my left hand and examined the ring. "I was petrified. I thought that maybe you were unhappy about—"

Nicholas breezed into the room. He was wet with rain, his shirt sticking to his shoulders, his hair clinging to his forehead. His eyes had that unpredictable glint in them that always made me nervous. He walked straight at me. I held my breath. He extended a hand and I thought he would pull me to my feet. Instead, he ripped the wig off my head.

"First things first." He tossed the wig into the burning stove.

"Nicholas!" I shrieked in dismay.

The burning wig stunk up the entire galley. I took shallow breaths through my mouth to try and keep from getting sick.

Skidmore had appeared in the galley. This was it then, the entire crew. Nicholas sat across from me. Meg and Skidmore settled in at the far end of the table. I looked up through my lashes at Nicholas, expecting him to avoid my stare. He caught my eye and held my gaze. I felt as though I was melting under his hot eyes, but I held the stare, willing my eyes to say everything I needed to say, to tell him how trapped I felt and how desperate I was for him to understand. I poured all my apologizes into that stare. I told him I did not want Emilio. I wanted him.

Meg shifted and her chair scraped loudly against the floor. I flinched in response, breaking the stare. Even that small jolt sent an aching ripple through my body. I had never hurt like this before. My head hurt. My jaw hurt. My arms hurt. My toenails hurt.

All of that pain was dwarfed by the hurt in my heart.

"Have you eaten?" Nicholas asked.

I gingerly shook my head.

Skidmore went to the pantry without being asked. A moment later a tin plate with a two strips of salted beef and an underripe banana appeared before me. I touched the beef but couldn't bring myself to eat it.

Emilio noticed my hesitation with the food. He put his arm around me and whispered in my ear. "You don't have to eat it. We can make you some tea in a moment."

Nicholas cleared his throat. "Our voyage will continue as planned with the exception of a brief stop in Antigua to send word to Admiral Monroe about his daughter's whereabouts. The women will sleep in the starboard cabin. The men will be portside."

Emilio stiffened. He pulled me closer to him. I was too dizzy to fight it and let my head slump against his shoulder.

Our posture did not go unnoticed and Nicholas clenched his jaw. He looked to Meg. "As for the watch bill, Quin, you and I will team up. Next watch is ours."

That meant he would be alone with her all day every day — whether they were working the deck or relaxing between watches. Meg's self-satisfied smile did not escape my notice. I clenched my hands into fists. I couldn't help but think he was being purposefully petulant. I wanted to tell him as much but I held my tongue.

Nicholas continued. "Skidmore and De Luca, you're together. Tessa will make herself useful as the ship's cook."

Emilio pulled his arm away from me and spread his hands on the table. "Pardon the question, Captain, but why aren't we returning my fiancée home?"

I cringed at the word *fiancée*.

Nicholas shrugged as if he didn't care about me at all. I couldn't blame him. He answered simply, "There is not time."

Emilio bristled. "Her safety is at stake. Not to mention the admiral's sanity. He'll be mad with worry."

"Our orders—orders from the admiral—are to intercept

Salazar. A stowaway doesn't change that." Nicholas sat lazily in his chair, a perfect picture of arrogance.

"That's rather cold," Emilio retorted. "As her future husband, I find myself responsible for her safety. I must insist we return her home immediately."

Nicholas examined something under his fingernails. "Your feelings do you credit, sailor. I wish I could oblige. More than you know. But remember why you are here. Our charge to intercept Salazar is our priority. We can see our orders through and keep our errant stowaway secure. But there is no way to guarantee the success of our mission if we turn back now. We are already one day behind schedule." He spoke evenly but the way he clipped his words told me there was an undercurrent of emotion there ready to explode.

"This is no place for a lady. In addition to the matter of her safety is the matter of propriety, the matter of her comfort—"

"Tessa's safety is paramount," Nicholas snapped. "Her comfort is not."

Neither of these men wanted to back down. I knew where it would lead—some kind of haughty duel on the deck where Nicholas would shoot Emilio. I softly touched Emilio's arm to get his attention. "Lord De Luca, I will manage."

He looked at me, almost as if he were surprised to see me there. He smiled gently. "I've asked you to call me by name before. And now that we are engaged, I must insist upon it."

I brought back the subject at hand. "Do not worry yourself about me. It is my fault that I am here."

"Asking me not to worry about you is like asking me not to breathe," he whispered, bringing my hand to his lips.

"Emilio," I gently resisted as I pulled my hand away.

Nicholas stood abruptly, nearly knocking his chair over.

"Nicky, wait!" Meg called after him as he stalked to the door.

I rolled my eyes. Even that motion hurt.

He turned and looked at her. "I'm going to monitor the

hourglass. Why don't you all take the rest of the watch to celebrate our departure? There's wine in storage. Open some bottles. Be merry." He left, closing the galley door behind him.

I slumped forward on the table, propping my face with my hands, exhausted from the encounter.

"I suppose I'll get the wine," Meg stood.

"Make tea for Miss Monroe first," said Emilio.

Meg moved towards the cupboards.

Skidmore cleared his throat. "If you want tea made," he said quietly but steadily, "you best make it yourself."

"But Meg is—"

"Not on this ship she's not," said Skidmore. "You two are equals here. And Miss Monroe is assigned galley duty. So if'n you want somethin' from the kitchen, you either ask Miss Monroe or you do it yerself."

Meg fidgeted. "I can make the tea. I don't mind."

"You best get the wine," Skidmore said. "I can make the tea. As a favor to Miss Monroe."

Emilio pushed back his chair. "I'll make the tea."

"I will do it," Meg said, looking nervously at Emilio. The shift in command was not easy for her to accept. Once the mission was over, Emilio would be her superior again.

Emilio hovered closely. "You get the wine, I'll make the tea."

"I don't want any bloody tea!" I slammed my hand down on the table. My teeth rattled in my skull. I groaned and stood up. "I am too sick for any of this. I am going to bed. Skidmore, I'll figure out meals later. Just give me a few hours to sleep."

"Aye." Skidmore nodded.

I pushed past Meg and left the galley before Emilio could insist on tucking me in. I bolted the door of my cabin and lay on my bed, the pitching of the ship threatening to turn my stomach inside out. I heard the banging of doors as Meg retrieved the wine. I heard voices in the galley. I heard my name. I didn't even care to listen to what was being said about me.

When I was certain no one was coming to check on me, I went in search of Nicholas. I didn't know what I would say, but I knew I needed to make him understand. I found him crouched on the deck picking at the seams of oakum, not even wearing a hat in the violent downpour. As soon as I approached him, he stood up and walked to the helm without so much as a glance in my direction.

"I was afraid I would never see you again."

I reached out for his elbow. He jerked it away, but at least he looked at me. I reached for him again. He dodged my touch.

"Why are you acting this way?"

His brows were pulled tightly over his eyes. "Must you ask?"

"I know you're upset, but you've never shrank from me before."

"I'll not betray my shipmate by tolerating a private touch from you."

So I was a leper now. I swallowed hard. "You don't understand, Nicholas. Last night was not supposed to happen like that. Emilio—" I shook my head. My thoughts were too clouded from the rum to say anything right.

"You don't have to explain anything to me." Nicholas threw up his hands as if that would silence me and walked towards the bow, gracefully dodging the barrels and pins on deck and ducking under the shrouds.

I followed him, tripping and stumbling and scraping my head on the lines with every step. "I am saying everything wrong. I owe you an explanation. It will all make sense."

"An explanation is not what you owe me." Nicholas stopped short midway down the ship and turned to face me with his hands on his hips.

I swallowed back a sharp retort asking what exactly it was he thought I owed him. "Please, Nicholas." I grabbed his hand. It was still fisted on his hip and I felt it tense. His eyes fluttered closed and I thought for a moment that my touch had penetrated his pride. He would finally hear me. But just as swiftly he snatched both of my wrists in each of his hands and pinned them at my sides.

His eyes were wild and dancing, only an inch away from mine. He was breathing heavily through his mouth, his carefully composed façade gone. My heart pounded, halfway expecting him to kiss me and halfway fearing he would shake the daylights out of me.

Maybe it was the fear in my eyes that woke him. He shoved me away and looked down.

I gasped. He had never been rough with me before. Never. Despite the chill from the rain, I was hot with anger. I glared at him as I wiped my wet hair out of my face with the back of my hand.

Nicholas gestured to my dress. "Go downstairs. You're getting wet."

I couldn't get wetter than I already was. "I need to talk with you," I demanded. I was done being polite.

"No, you do not. And I certainly do not need to hear whatever it is you have to say."

He was so infuriating. I wanted to throttle him. "Stop being such a—" I couldn't think of any insult that would fit, and nothing would surprise a master of cursing like Nicholas anyway. I shook my head. "You don't have to say a word. Give me five minutes."

He opened his mouth to speak. I waved my hand and cut him off. "Five minutes, Nicholas."

He reeled at me. "No," he said, his voice like a whip. "I have given you too much of my time already. I'm sorry if I won't let you purge your guilty conscience, but that's not my problem. Go downstairs."

He turned around and continued towards the bow.

"Stop running away," I yelled after him.

Hot anger flashed in his eyes. They looked like the storm clouds roiling overhead. "I'm *not* running away."

"Then what do you call it? Every time something gets difficult, you run away. Figuratively. Literally. You're doing it now."

"You don't know what you're talking about," he spat.

I finally found the insult. I hurled it at him with all the poison I had in me. "I know that you're a coward."

I expected him to react with fury at that word, to retaliate with claws bared. What I didn't expect was the pleading look in his eyes and the barely noticeable tremble in his hands as he pushed his sopping hair off his forehead. Even his voice trembled as he quietly said, "Can't you understand that I don't want to talk to you? I don't want to see you. I don't want you on my ship. I don't want anything to do with you. Ever. Can't you respect that? Leave me be."

I watched in bewilderment as he climbed up the ratlines and disappeared behind the mainsail. I never thought I would hear those words from him. And he wouldn't be saying them if he would give me five minutes to explain how I had become engaged against my will. But if he insisted on holding on to his foolish hubris, why should I even bother?

I gave him only a minute to change his mind. He re-mained hidden behind his precious sail. I stormed below, not bothering to shut the hatch behind me and slipped into bed to try to sleep off the effects of the rum.

CHAPTER TWENTY-SEVEN

"I'M SORRY, TESSA, I hope I didn't wake you."

Meg sat at the edge of the bed, pulling off her boots. She didn't sound sorry at all. I rolled over and rubbed my eyes. My dress was still damp where I had been laying on it and my hair was a fine display of knots.

"I hope you do not mind that I called you Tessa. Nicky—the captain said I couldn't call you Miss Monroe anymore."

I wondered if I was supposed to call her Quin. The thought was nauseating. "I really don't care. What time is it?"

"Afternoon watch just ended. First dog watch is starting now."

Four o'clock. I had been asleep for six hours and felt only slightly better. I was finally hungry. And thirsty. Heavens, was I thirsty. I felt as if I had swallowed an entire desert. I licked my lips and swallowed several times, trying to find moisture.

"I suppose I should think about dinner." I steadied myself against one of the bed's posters as I slowly sat up. The room spun lazily.

"No one would notice if you didn't bother with dinner."

I raised my eyebrows. "I'm pretty sure they would notice if there was nothing to eat."

"I just meant that we all know you're feeling out of sorts. Have you ever been plastered before?"

I touched my pounding forehead. "Is it that obvious?"

"Too much revelry? Congratulations, by the way. I didn't get a chance to tell you. You must be over the moon. The *baron*." She raised her eyebrows coyly.

I smiled weakly.

"Can I see the ring?"

I unhitched my hand from the post and looked at the ring on my hand. It felt foreign. Like a parasite. I held my hand out to Meg who cradled my fingers gingerly, rotating my hand back and forth so the ring made rainbows of the afternoon light.

"Can you believe it? You're going to be a baroness."

My eyes were still fixed on the shackle around my finger. "No, I can't."

"Remember when we spoke before, when I suggested he might have affections for you?"

I nodded.

"You spoke of your broken heart. I am glad it's mended."

I tried to recall the conversation. I don't think I had ever said anything about having a *broken* heart. Maybe that my heart was elsewhere...

"And my broken heart, it might be mending too."

"Really?" I looked directly at her, intrigued by a sick curiosity. "You've been able to move on from Nicholas?"

Meg's face drew up in a girlish grin. "Quite the contrary. He insisted I go on this mission. He picked me as his watch mate. We'll be spending twelve hours together every day. It won't be long until things are like they used to be."

My fingers knotted in my lap. "How were they? Before?" I cringed as the words came out of my mouth, but I had to know.

Meg was beaming. "Just...together. All the time."

"Did he kiss you?"

Meg turned bright scarlet. "Aye, and he is a fine kisser."

I felt the color drain from my face. The thought of his salt-laced kiss on Meg, on anyone else, made me seethe with feelings I had never felt before. The way I came alive under his kisses, the way my blood pulsed in agonizing and delirious ways. His kisses were made just for me. I pictured Nicholas kissing me in the garden, my hands fanned against the skin of his back, the way he said my name like it was all that tethered him to the earth. And then I pictured Meg in my place. Her name on his lips. Her hands, less shy than mine...

I stood abruptly. I tried to compose my face into a polite, excited expression. "Tell me if he kisses you again, would you?"

"A lady doesn't speak of such things." She smirked. "But then again, no one's ever accused me of bein' a lady."

* * * * *

Meg was right, I had a good excuse not to cook, but what else would I do? I didn't want to garner Emilio's sympathy or more of Nicholas's scorn.

I pulled myself out of bed as Meg nestled into it, ready to take advantage of her break before her next shift, and went into the galley. I lit a few lanterns and hung them from the ceiling. The habits Nicholas had taught me before came back. I examined the stove and the stones beneath it, looking for loose hinges or missing tiles. Either of those things could cause a disastrous fire. The brass bars in front of the stove were sturdy, as they should be. I had needed to catch myself on those bars more than once as the ship pitched to keep myself from tumbling in to the hot stove. Lastly, I examined the stovepipe that led to the open deck above. Aside from some excess ash, everything was sound. I shoved some scrapped planks into the stove and lit a fire.

As I worked, I could hear the voices and footfalls of my companions echoing through the ship. The noises set me on edge. Before, only Nicholas and I had sailed on the *Freedom*. It was a small ship, barely a ship, but it was something Nicholas could sail by himself and it was perfect for just the two of us. Quiet and intimate. Now it was crowded and noisy. I wasn't used to the acoustics of it and every sound made me feel like someone was walking in on me.

I took inventory of the cupboards and planned a meal with the perishable things that needed to be eaten first: melon, eggs, crusty bread, and greens.

Unlike the other watches which were four hours apiece, the two dog watches were both only two hours long. By splitting the watch this way, it created an odd number of watches, preventing the sailors from being stuck with the same rotation every day. It also allowed all members of the crew to eat dinner around a traditional time. Today, Nicholas and Meg were off duty during first dog watch.

I set the table and rang the dinner bell.

Nicholas entered the galley looking disheveled. He was tucking his shirt into his breeches and tightening his belt, a groggy look in his eyes. It was customary for sailors to sleep during their off watches. He seemed completely unfazed by my presence, as if no relationship besides that of captain and crewmember ever existed between us.

"Where's Quin?" he asked.

"Sleeping, I imagine." I shoveled spoonfuls of eggs on his plate.

"Are you eating now?" His tone was emotionless. Just the type of straightforward question the captain might ask of anyone.

"I thought we might talk."

"About the ball?" he asked, his eyes trained on his plate.

"Yes."

"I thought I made myself clear."

"Just talk to me!"

"Will you defy your captain?" He raised his eyes. They looked as if they had been chiseled from flint.

I dropped the bowl of melon on the table before him. "Of course not, *sir*." I walked out of the galley and let the door slam behind me.

I avoided my cabin and went to the main deck. The rain had ceased but the sky was still tumultuous and grey. Skidmore was at the helm, pointing across the deck and giving Emilio instructions.

"As we tack through the wind the leech is likely to twist. Put into the lines the slack of the mainsheet, increasing the tension on the boom vang, but not too taut. Careful not to let it get forward or hang down abaft."

Emilio looked desperately in the area Skidmore was pointing, unsure of what to do, though obviously eager to follow orders.

"The *leech*," Skidmore repeated. "The *leech!*"

"Like the worm that sucks blood?" Emilio asked nervously.

Skidmore gave a small headshake and led his charge to a fore-and-aft rigged sail. "This bit of canvas here is likely to twist up when I steer into the wind because it has too much slack. Pull on the lines—the ropes—to tighten the slack and adjust the vang tension like so," Skidmore gave a demonstration. "This is too taught and she'll snap." The loosened the tension. "This is too loose and she'll droop and get caught in other things. Aye?"

"Aye, aye," Emilio said, awkwardly taking over the boom vang as Skidmore returned to the helm.

"Ready about!" Skidmore called, leaning his mass against the wheel. The ship slowly arced into the wind and I grabbed a line to steady myself against the pitching deck. The sea was angry today.

Skidmore saw me approaching, battling the gusts.

"Squally weather, eh?"

"Shouldn't we avoid the storm?" I asked, glancing up at the sails.

"The captain means to ride through the storm."

I didn't know much about sailing, but I knew that a storm

like this could grow threatening very quickly. "He's putting all of us at risk."

"He's the captain," Skidmore said diplomatically, but I knew he agreed with me.

"He thinks that just because he's the captain, he can do whatever he wants. Treat people however he wants."

Skidmore shook his head. He knew why I was here.

"He thinks he can just neglect human decency. It sickens me. I know he's lashing out, but he's better than this. Isn't he? What do I know of him? I don't think I'll survive this, Skidmore."

He smiled sympathetically, keeping pressure on the wheel. "Your past and your future are colliding, are they?"

"Past and future?" I asked.

"Marks said you and De Luca became engaged." Skidmore nodded towards my ring.

I needed to throw the bloody thing in the ocean. Emilio was across the ship, yet I still dropped my voice before saying, "My father promised my hand to Lord De Luca, but that's hardly the same thing."

Skidmore raised a single brow but said nothing.

"I think I hate him," I whispered bitterly.

"De Luca?"

"Nicholas," I said with resignation.

"Sometimes I do, too."

"Really?"

Skidmore shrugged.

I sighed. "The way he looks at me, speaks to me. It's either full of venom or completely devoid of anything. I'm not sure which I prefer."

"There's a reason for his venom."

"Actually, there isn't," My voice was harsher than I meant it to be.

Skidmore gave me a patronizing look. "If you knew what it meant for him to go to that ball only to watch you become engaged..." He shook his head. "You could have given him some warning."

Would no one let me tell my side of the story? "You too?" I snapped.

I stamped into the galley, ignored the surprised look coming from Meg, who had joined Nicholas at the dinner table, loaded up a plate, and ate alone in my cabin to avoid the others.

CHAPTER TWENTY-EIGHT

IT WAS TWO BELLS into first watch—nine o'clock at night—and I sat over a cup of tea in the galley. Meg was asleep in our cabin. I'd successfully avoided her all day but I couldn't avoid her much longer—I was expected to share a bed with her. I couldn't stomach the thought of it. She'd be in there, dreaming of Nicholas all night, ready to tell me all her deepest thoughts in the morning. There had to be some other arrangements for sleep.

I finished my tea and wandered into the open area between the galley and the cabins and saw Nicholas sitting at a small table, looking at log books by lantern light. I'd expected him to be sleeping during his time off.

We glanced at each other uncomfortably, neither one of us saying a word. Nicholas turned back to his ledgers and I shrank back into the galley, trapped. I poured myself another cup of tea and drank it slowly in the dark, wondering if I would be able to keep myself awake for three more hours when Meg's next watch began so I could go to bed alone.

The ship rocked in the wind and I could hear Skidmore and Emilio on deck, booming commands to each other to do whatever it was they did to keep a small ship steady on a heaving sea.

A light blazed brightly behind me, my shadow growing

crisp and distorted on the table in front of me. I quickly glanced behind me. Nicholas stood at the threshold with the lantern in one hand.

"Oh. I thought you'd gone to bed."

I cleared my throat and stood up, taking my teacup with me. "Just finishing some tea. I'll leave."

I placed my cup in the basin and turned to go. Nicholas had followed me into the kitchen area and set his lantern on the wooden countertop. I was ready to brush past him when I remembered that it was my responsibility to serve him.

"Did you need something, Captain?" I asked curtly.

He gestured to the stove. "Tea sounds soothing."

I turned towards the kettle.

"I'll do it," he said, not unkindly. "Get some rest."

I left the galley and shut the door behind me. Now that I was alone in the foyer, I did what I had set out to do before. I unhooked a lantern from the bulkhead and, casting a glance over my shoulder to make sure I was alone, stepped into the men's cabin.

The bed had been pushed into a corner and two hammocks fashioned from extra sails were dangling from the ceiling, a duffel bag under each sleeping space. I held the lantern high to cast more light in the room and envisioned another hammock in the crowded cabin.

"What are you doing?"

I jolted at the sound of Nicholas's voice behind me, the lantern nearly jumping out of my hands. I backed out of the cabin guiltily.

"I was just looking for something," I said quietly.

"Did Skidmore need something? De Luca?" He didn't seem upset. On the contrary, he seemed eager to help.

How did I explain that I was looking for somewhere Meg could stay? I shook my head. "I was curious about something. Never mind."

"Do you need something?"

"No," I said shrinking farther away from him.

He looked at me as if he couldn't read my face. "As the captain, it's my duty to mind the crew. And passengers. Or whatever you are. If you need something, tell me."

I looked at him longingly. *I need you*, I longed to say. "I can't room with Meg."

"Why not?" He seemed genuinely concerned.

There was no way for me to explain it to him without sounding petty. "Personal differences."

"I see." Nicholas set his lantern on the small table in the foyer, then leaned against the bulkhead and folded his arms. "Do you propose a solution?"

I meekly gestured to the men's cabin. "She really ought to be staying with the crew."

"And you're not crew?"

"No. Technically, I'm a stowaway. I'm also a lady and the daughter of your superior."

Nicholas raised his eyebrows as if to say I was entering dangerous waters.

"I just mean that Meg signed on to be part of the crew and should be sleeping with them."

"So we move Quin here and you'd have the starboard cabin to yourself?" asked Nicholas.

A perfect solution. "Yes."

"No."

"Why not?"

He cocked his head. "You saw the men's cabin. It's at capacity."

"But the watches alternate. There are never three bodies in there at one time." My argument was logical, I thought, selfish as it was.

Nicholas shook his head. "Watch schedules won't be strictly enforced on this small of a vessel. There really isn't room for her in there. More than that, if I offer you special treatment, I'll have to offer it to my other guest as well."

"Who is your other guest?"

"Signor De Luca." Nicholas never used Emilio's title—a

subtle defiance. "He did not sign the articles like Skidmore and Quin did. He is immune from certain things. If I were to draw a hard line between crew and passengers, then Signor De Luca would be entitled to different sleeping arrangements, too. Although I suppose you'd be more than willing to share a cabin with him?"

There it was. The venom. His words sounded calm as ever, but there was a sting to them now.

"No," I said strongly. "I would not share a cabin with him."

"Are you certain? None here would think twice of it."

"No!" I insisted.

"What a relief. I don't think I'd like that arrangement much myself."

It was the first time he had hinted at his feelings for me.

"There has to be something else," I pleaded.

"Hmm." Nicholas put on a show of pensive thought. "I don't suppose you'd be willing to share with someone else. Skidmore, perhaps? Myself?"

"Nicholas!" I rolled my eyes.

"Oh, so me then. I can move my things over right away."

I shot him a withering glare, unsure if I should be pleased that he was teasing me or strictly offended. "I refuse to share quarters with anyone of the opposite gender, including you."

He shrugged. "Then I don't see a solution."

I sighed. Why did he insist on being difficult? "I know it would be an exception, but couldn't I please sleep alone?"

"Despite what you think, I'm not opposed to the idea. It's the execution that's the problem. We cannot fit another body into the portside cabin. You are unwilling to switch roommates in the starboard cabin. And if anyone were to have a cabin of their own, it would be *me*. The captain."

"What about the forward portside cabin?" I pointed to the cabin next to the galley, directly across from the men's. "No one is staying there. I could go there. Meg could go with the crew. And you could have your own cabin."

"Brilliant idea." Nicholas smirked a little as he unhitched

himself from the wall and sauntered to the cabin in question. "If you'd like to stay in that cabin, you may."

I followed him over to it, wondering why I hadn't thought of it earlier. When it was just Nicholas and me on the *Freedom*, we had no use for the spare cabin. We had stored a few things in it, but it was mostly empty. I had forgotten about it entirely.

Nicholas opened the door and backed away so I could look in. I raised my lantern and stepped inside. There was barely room for me to step across the threshold—the cabin was filled with crates, barrels, and jugs.

"Is that…?" I leaned forward and listened. "Is that a chicken clucking?"

Nicholas nudged the nearest crate with his toe. It responded with the undeniable cackle of poultry. "Three of them actually. We'll appreciate the fresh meat in a week or two."

I looked at him in horror. "They're for…eating?"

"They're not here for company. If you want to bunk with the chickens, this room is yours." He said it matter-of-factly. No sarcasm, no vitriol. If only he had been mean-spirited, my natural tendency to fight back would have been stoked. Instead, I stood staring at the crates and my throat tightened with hopelessness.

Nicholas returned to his ledgers.

I stood alone in the storage cabin for a moment, fighting back tears. I closed the door and crossed the foyer, keeping my head down so Nicholas wouldn't see my red and watery eyes. I tiptoed into my own cabin and closed the door behind me, shutting out Nicholas but trapping myself with Meg. She was sleeping, her breathing steady and slow. I listened for a moment, but couldn't bring myself to climb into bed beside her. I left the cabin, lantern still in hand, and ignored Nicholas's quizzical look as I went back to the galley. Time seemed to expand when I stood still, so I filled it with menial chores. I emptied all the cupboards and wiped each down, inside and out, then rearranged all the kitchen supplies the way I liked. I swept the floor and even washed the portholes.

I heard footsteps enter the galley. I expected to see Nicholas when I turned around, but it was Skidmore.

"Can I help? Not much happening above." He picked up a rag and helped me wash the portholes. "What's next? Polish the silver?"

I picked up a metal bucket and nodded at the stove. "Clean out the ashes."

Skidmore said nothing, only took the bucket from my hand, found a long metal spoon, and knelt before the pot-bellied stove.

"That's my job," I protested.

"The soot will ruin your dress."

"Skidmore. Let me. How else am I supposed to earn my room and board?"

Skidmore shoveled spoonfuls of ash into the bucket, little swirls of white dust billowing around his head. "No one would throw you off the ship."

I sat on the floor next to Skidmore and drew my knees to my chest. "Nicholas would."

"He's glad you're here. He just doesn't know it." Skidmore did not look at me; he stayed focused on the task at hand. He rarely made eye contact with anyone. For the longest time, I thought he didn't like me or trust me until I realized that was just his way. Taciturn and pensive, but always gentle. His presence reminded me of the ocean—an unfathomable depth and constancy that I found soothing. "Someday, you'll know him as I know him."

"I wish that were true. He makes very little sense to me."

"He has his reasons."

"He should share them." I picked a piece of lint off my skirt and stared at it, willing it to answer my questions. "I still don't understand why he accepted the Letter of Marque. He promised he wouldn't, but he did it anyway. I think it was to get away from me. I think our romance was splendid and beautiful when it was just the two of us, but it cannot survive the drudgery of daily life. I can't be a pirate and he discovered that he can't be a carpenter. And he left. He could tell me. I would understand."

"That's not why he left," Skidmore said as mushrooms of ash floated around his head.

"Oh yes, it was something gallant about Salazar and war," I said, rolling my eyes.

Skidmore was very quiet for a very long while, the sound of the metal spoon on the iron stove scraping a rhythm that was more soothing than it should have been. "I don't like to break confidences, but he never said not to say this and I think it would do you good to know. Mateus Salazar has been tracking Marks for some time because Marks owes him money. After the burglary, when Marks realized how close Salazar had come to you, he knew he had to do something. If Marks don't pay him, Salazar will punish him. You'd more'n likely be how Salazar would do that."

I sat forward, confused, but intrigued. Skidmore never told me privy things about Nicholas. That's how I knew he would never tell Nicholas privy things about me. "Why accept the Letter of Marque? My father was paying him as a carpenter."

"He could make a lot more money a lot faster as privateer. And it offered the chance to kill Salazar, besides."

I was afraid to ask questions, afraid my prying would shut Skidmore up, but I couldn't help myself. "How much money does he owe?"

He scraped out another spoonful of ash, his rhythm never halting. "A few thousand pounds, to my knowledge."

I blew out a long breath. "That's a lot of money owed to a very bad man. I don't understand why Nicholas would ever take money from him."

The *scrape-scrape-scrape* continued, but Skidmore grew quiet. He did not look at me.

"You know why, don't you? Tell me."

Scrape-scrape-scrape.

"Please. Tell me. If it offers me some sympathy for him, you'd want that for him. If it's something terrible, I need to know."

Skidmore put down the spoon and stared at the bucket of ash. "After he sent you off the *Banshee*, many in the crew wanted to kill him. In exchange for his life, he gave them all his gold."

"One hundred and fifty-eight thousand pounds," I murmured moodily, the number seared in my brain.

"Where'd you get that figure?"

I shrugged sheepishly. "I overheard him tell Emilio that he got one hundred and fifty-eight thousand pounds from his biggest raid."

Skidmore *hmphed*. "That's the figure from one raid. He had much more money'n that total. Much, much, more."

I gulped, feeling less worthy of his sacrifice than ever. "And he gave it all to his crew?"

"Aye. We left him on Cumaná and he made a deal with a man who brokers loans for Salazar. Marks was desperate, see, knowin' he needed to go find you. It were a bad choice and he knew it, but what else could he do?"

"And that's how he got the *Freedom*," I realized, my fingers spreading out on the wooden planks where I sat. The irony of the ketch's name was not lost on me.

Skidmore nodded. "Salazar loaned him the boat and a bit of money. I don't think Marks even cared about the terms of the loan. Just needed to get to you. He figured he'd wind up in England with you and it wouldn't matter much if he didn't settle his debt."

"This is my fault," I mumbled. "I made him go to St. Kitts."

"The way I see it, he made a choice. You didn't."

"And after all that, now he wants nothing to do with me. How can I blame him? He thinks I am treacherous." A tear rolled down my cheek. More were pressing against the backs of my eyes, threatening to drown me out, but I dammed them and wiped my cheeks dry. "The things he said...he's never spoken to me like that before. I hated him for it. His childish pride wouldn't grant me thirty seconds to explain. He doesn't care. He'd drop me at the next port if he didn't have to answer to my father."

Skidmore shook his head slightly as if to say I was wrong.

"It's true!" I insisted. "Do you know what I was doing last night? I was looking for him. He left Amerscott so suddenly. I left Emilio, my father, all those guests without a second thought. I rode my horse alone to the quay, which is a terrifying place at night, I might add. Emilio and my father and probably half their friends searched all night for me but did Nicholas even care? I was as good as dead to him the minute my father announced my betrothal.

"What gives a father the right to do that? Shouldn't there be some kind of discussion?" I knew I was ranting, but it felt cleansing, to pour the poison out of my veins. "I am not just a piece of property to be shuffled from one household to another."

I took a shaky breath and tried to compose myself, grateful I'd had my breakdown here instead of in my cabin where Meg could hear me. "I suppose I can't avoid bed forever."

"Why were you avoiding bed?"

"Meg." I sighed. And then I realized something. "Wait. You knew her before. On the *Banshee*. Meg and Nicholas...were they...? What was she to him?"

Skidmore had been so forthcoming already. Maybe he would divulge a little more to me.

"'Twas a convenient romance," he answered.

I traced patterns on my skirt with my finger tip. Such a lovely dress. And now it was accessorized with water stains and black smears of ash. "Maybe that was me, too. A convenient romance."

Skidmore scowled at me. "You ought to know better. It's rather obvious."

"What's obvious?"

"That he is in love with you."

I leaned my head against the cupboard behind me. "I asked him and he wouldn't say it."

"It's not an emotion he understands well. The only other woman he ever loved destroyed him."

I lifted my head. I had never heard of another woman. "Who was that?"

"His mum."

Sophronia Holladay. The daughter of an African slave and a white landowner who turned to prostitution. She died when Nicholas was twelve, leaving him an orphan. He'd spoken of her only once to me, but his memories were full of bile. Not the usual reverence someone reserves for speaking of a dead mother. "He told me a bit about her. He did not have kind things to say."

Skidmore shifted so he could face me, both of us sitting on the floor between cabinets. "She was the only person he ever loved. The pure love of a child. And she never loved him back."

"She was his mother. She *had* to love him."

"Not all mothers love their children. Marks was little more than an inconvenience to her. Leftovers from whoring."

"And then she died and he had to turn to the sea for survival where no one would love a penniless beggar boy." It was a revelation.

"Love is a risky thing. For anyone—"

"But especially for him." I held back a yawn. "Skidmore, how do you know so much about love?"

He smiled kindly. "I've been blessed to cross its path time and again."

"Has there ever been anyone special?"

"My wife."

"You're married?" I felt my eyes bulge.

"Aye. My wife Mary and my three children—all daughters."

I was flabbergasted. "Children, too? I had no idea. I'm sorry I have never asked before. Do you see them often?"

"More often than I did when I sailed for a merchant."

My jaw dropped. "You sailed for a merchant? Why did you turn pirate?"

"Captains are ruthless. They are vicious to their crew,

focused only on speed and profit. Hard hours. Corporal punishment. I had a mate who was sick and was late for watch. The captain ordered him to be nailed to the deck for the remainder of his watch."

I gasped.

"The navy fares a might better with the threat of court-martialing," he continued. "I'm sure you've never heard such things from your father. After a run-in with pirates, I learned that pirate ships are democratic. Captains and officers are voted in. Voted out. Even split o' th' spoils. Security against injury. The job ain't easier. But the conditions are fairer."

I sat quietly, soaking in this new information. Skidmore the sailor. Skidmore the husband. Skidmore the father.

I yawned.

"Best get some sleep, Miss Monroe."

Nicholas was still at his table when I bid Skidmore goodnight. I flushed with embarrassment thinking he may have overheard our conversation. But then I secretly wished he had. If he wouldn't talk to me, eavesdropping may be my best chance to explain myself to him. He conversed quietly with his first mate before Skidmore returned to deck. I steeled myself for a night with Meg and went to open my cabin door. My hand was on the latch when he said my name.

"Tessa?"

I turned.

"One moment." Nicholas held up a finger, took his lantern and disappeared into his cabin. He reemerged carrying something folded and white. He handed it to me.

"You can sleep in this."

It wasn't until I was in my cabin that I examined what he had given me under the faint light coming through the portholes. It was one of his downy-soft, cotton shirts.

CHAPTER TWENTY-NINE

PRIDE HAS ITS USES. It's what made me discard Nicholas's shirt and sleep in my ball gown, barely caring how the corset bruised my ribs. It's what made it bearable to be in the same room as Nicholas. It's what kept me composed when Meg flirted with him. Pride built up a wall that held in the tears.

Emilio spent much of our second day at sea painting the hull with the insides of his stomach. I had my moments too, but recovered quickly. I had spent more time at sea. It was painful to watch him try to carry out his duties. If he wasn't heaving over the rail, he was trying to puzzle out what was being asked of him. I couldn't help him with his duties because I didn't know much myself, but I could help him decipher the jargon: fore was towards the front of the ship and aft was to the back; portside was to the left and starboard to the right; a rope was a rope when it was coiled, but a line when in use on the ship; the larger mast was the main mast and the mizzen mast was the smaller one at the aft; stairs were always called ladders; the walls were called bulkheads. I cringed when Skidmore sent him aloft to provide lookout from the masthead. He was shaking, unsure with his footing in his polished boots. One slip and he'd fall a hundred feet to certain death.

Towards the end of the second day, Nicholas told me he needed me to holystone the deck after dinner and I wasn't dressed for it. Meg was appointed to help me find something more suitable. I refused to wear any of her trousers. She stripped me down to my chemise and lent me a studded, leather corset and large, plaid scarf to tie around my waist like a skirt. I borrowed a pair of her boots, too. Skidmore praised my new look; Emilio looked appalled and promised to buy me everything I needed at our very next stop; Nicholas eyed me approvingly as he handed me a holystone.

On our third day at sea, Emilio spilled on his shirt during lunch. I helped him dab at the stain, then offered to wash his shirt for him. He obliged and I figured I might as well extend the offer to the entire crew. Nicholas shrugged off his canvas jacket. "Mind the pockets," he said as he handed it to me.

As it turned out, the entire crew had things in their pockets. Papers, whistles, screws, and other odds and ends. I put everything on a pile on the foyer table. Skidmore helped me fill a wooden vat with ocean water. Then with a washboard and a lump of lye soap, I scrubbed the clothes and hung them to dry in the sunshine while I prepared a dinner of fresh-caught fish, hard cheese, hardtack, and lemons.

On our fourth day at sea, we arrived at Antigua. The docks were full, so Nicholas dropped anchor out in the harbor and we all took the jollyboat to shore. British officials were waiting for us as soon as our boat hit the shoals, a young, arrogant constable at their head.

"What's this about?" Skidmore muttered to Nicholas.

"Damn pirates have made everyone paranoid," replied Nicholas with a conspiratorial wink.

I stifled a smile.

"State your business."

Nicholas ambled out of the jollyboat, splashing in the shallow water to the beach. "We're British citizens and that's all you need to know."

Why did he always sound belligerent?

The constable eyed the rest of us. "You're no merchant. And you're not navy."

"And who said God wasn't merciful?"

I rolled my eyes.

"Papers." The official held out a white-gloved hand.

"Pardon?"

"You either have papers or you're a pirate."

"Pirates steal papers, you know." Nicholas said as he reached inside his canvas jacket. His hand came back empty. He searched another pocket. Then another.

The constable gestured behind him and several uniformed men stepped forward.

Nicholas took his jacket off and pulled out every pocket, even shaking the coat. He shot Skidmore a loaded look. "Get your letter."

Still sitting in the jollyboat, Skidmore began searching his pockets in vain for the letter. He gravely shook his head.

"Quin?" Nicholas asked, his voice edgy.

She had begun searching before he had asked her to. She, too, turned up empty handed.

Nicholas's eyes fell on me. "What did you do with the letters?"

"What letters?" I looked around anxiously, wondering what I had done to attract this accusation.

"The Letter of Marque from your father," Nicholas said between clenched teeth. "It was in my pocket before you washed my jacket."

The constable gestured to our small party. "Arrest them."

In an instant, Nicholas's wrists were pulled in front of him, iron cuffs locking around them. "Tessa, I told you to *mind the pockets.*"

"I did," I snapped back. "I emptied all your pockets. I didn't wash anything."

"You certainly didn't put anything back!" Nicholas said as he was guided to the nearest dock.

"You never told me to. Your letter—your responsibility."

The official gestured for the rest of us to exit the boat. Skidmore went first, his wrists chained together as soon as he stepped on land. Meg was next. Then it was my turn. Before I could stand up, Emilio grabbed my arm and stepped out of the boat into knee-high water.

"*Scusi.*" Emilio raised his gloved hands above his head. I hadn't realized until that moment how different he looked from the rest of us. He looked like a nobleman from his embroidered brocade jacket to his polished heels to his perfectly coifed hair. The rest of us looked like the renegades we were—Nicholas in sailor's garb with his fancy baldric covering his half-open shirt; Meg in men's trousers; Skidmore in patched canvas and a knit cap; and me in my rumpled and sorely inappropriate ball gown (I had refused to go ashore dressed in pirate cast-offs).

The constable looked at Emilio differently. "You're not British. Are you being held against your will? Are these people pirates?" The constable eyed us all with unmasked suspicion. He turned his attention back to Emilio, who still stood in the water. I overheard one of his men whisper in his ear, "He wears gold buttons. And purple trim. Given the sumptuary laws, he must be nobility."

"Or he's a pirate who stole that costume from its rightful owner," the constable whispered back.

Emilio's hands were still raised above his head. "My name is Emilio De Luca, Baron of Basilicata, Italy. We are not pirates. We hail from St. Kitts on business of His Majesty King George." Emilio reached into his jacket pocket and miraculously produced a trifolded piece of paper. He held it out to the officials. "*Per favore.*"

The constable gestured for Emilio to approach. Emilio sloshed onto the gravelly beach and handed the paper over. The constable examined it and handed it back to Emilio. "Thank you, Baron."

Emilio relaxed and offered me a hand. He lifted me out of

the boat and onto the beach so I wouldn't have to step in the water. Once we were on the deck, the constable turned his attention towards me. "Your papers, miss."

I looked wide-eyed from Emilio to Nicholas.

Emilio stepped forward. "She is my fiancée."

The constable's hard expression did not change. I tightened my hold on Emilio's hand. "I need to see her papers," he said. "Yours do not identify her."

With those condemning words, one of the officials handcuffed me before I could protest. Nicholas rolled his eyes dramatically. Emilio held up a protective hand. "The other papers are on our ship. They were misplaced before we disembarked."

"Then I suggest you retrieve them," the constable said coolly. "Until proven otherwise, we must assume your companions are pirates or traitors."

With a nod from their leader, the uniformed men marched Nicholas, Skidmore, Meg, and me towards the town.

Emilio scampered to keep up with us. "Where are the papers, Captain?"

"Ask Tessa. She's the one who forgot them."

"I did not even know about the papers! How can you blame me for forgetting them?"

Nicholas chided me over his shoulder. "I don't recall removing my Letter of Marque from my jacket pocket."

I huffed. "You told me to mind the pockets!"

"It would have been nice if you would have minded putting everything back in them!"

"Stop your bickering!" Emilio interjected. "Tessa, where did you empty the pockets?"

"Below deck. On the table."

"I will hurry." Emilio spun around and went back to the jollyboat. It would take him at least an hour to row all the way out to the *Freedom* and then return with the papers without help. Maybe longer.

Nicholas watched Emilio go with a look of disdain. I got the impression he didn't like being at his mercy. Then he looked at me. His gaze was accusing.

"Don't you dare make this my fault," I lashed out before he could say anything.

"I'm not *making* it your fault. It *is* your fault."

"It seems to me that a former pirate with a price on his head would be a little more judicious about double-checking his pockets before he left his ship."

The officials exchanged looks.

"Shh!" hissed Nicholas.

I couldn't let it alone. "Blame the rest of the crew. They forgot their papers, too."

"Because you washed everybody's clothes!" Bits of spittle sprayed from Nicholas's mouth. Tendons were bulging on his neck. I'd never seen him so unhinged. I found it funny.

"Emilio remembered his papers," I taunted.

"Thank you for reminding me how perfect he is. I had nearly forgotten."

The officials led us into a low, stone building and through a network of hallways until we reached a row of cells. Nicholas, Skidmore, and Meg were stripped of their weapons and belongings before being ushered into a cell. I had nothing on me save my dress, but I had to endure a formal search anyway.

"Lift your skirts." I lifted them. "Higher." I glared at Nicholas and hiked my skirts up to my thighs. The official cleared me and sent me into the cell with everyone else.

As the iron door clanged shut, I shot Nicholas a poisonous look. "Why is it that every time I sail with you, I end up behind bars?"

"Why is it that every time *I* sail with *you*, I end up having to come to your rescue?"

"*You* are going to rescue me?" I laughed haughtily. "For some strange reason I thought we were in the same jail cell together. I don't see you doing any rescuing whatsoever."

Skidmore and Meg watched our quarrel with timid fascination.

"Correct me if I'm wrong," I continued hotly, "but Emilio is the one doing the rescuing right now."

Nicholas cocked his head. "What happens when your beloved returns with papers for only three of us? Someone's going to have to get your bones out of here. I don't see you doing it yourself."

I turned away from his challenging stare and started wailing loudly, clinging to the door, the chains on my wrists clanking loudly against the bars of the cell.

Nicholas was annoyed. "Hysterics now?"

I cried harder, pressing myself as far from the others as possible.

"Don't mind the captain." Meg said, awkwardly patting my shoulder. "We'll all get out of here."

I flinched away from her. "Don't touch me!" Meg sank away from me and I continued my racket.

"Oh, for the love of all that's holy, Tessa, if you don't stop that caterwauling, I swear I'm gonna—" Nicholas cut himself off as the warden approached the cell.

The warden was a wire-thin man with an angry silver scar on his cheek and small, beady eyes.

He pointed a flintlock at the cell. "Are you threatening this woman?" he asked.

Nicholas started to respond but I cried over him in mock desperation. "Let me out of here, please Warden, please. He'll kill me if I stay in here, I know it."

"What's your business with them anyhow?" The warden's eyes swept over Nicholas, Skidmore, and Meg.

I dropped my voice. "They say they're privateers. But they don't have papers."

The warden stepped closer to me. "How did you get mixed up with them?"

"I'm on their ship against my will. Kidnapped from my own birthday ball. My father's an admiral in the Royal Navy. They think they'll get a ransom."

"She's lying!" Nicholas interjected.

The warden shot a look at Nicholas that could freeze the ocean. He visually inspected all of us—the three sailors in their rough wardrobe and me standing separate from them in my fancy gown.

"Please, warden," I summoned a hitch in my voice, "I don't care what you do with me—put me in another cell if you must—just don't leave me in here. I need to get word to my father where I am. He'll send for me." Real tears were raining down my cheeks. Deep inside, I was applauding myself on my performance.

He shook his head slowly, disgust contorting his already twisted face, and pulled a ring of keys from his belt. He unlocked the cell and let me out. "This is no place for a lady."

"Thank you, sir. I wasn't sure I was ever going to get out of there since I have no papers of my own." I glanced over my shoulder and winked at Nicholas.

The warden nodded sympathetically. "It's obvious you don't belong with them. You shouldn't have been arrested at all."

I gestured to the pile of the crew's weapons and belongings on a table near the cell. "Warden? They took my coin purse."

"Take it back."

I coyly plucked Nicholas's coin purse off the table with my thumb and forefinger and dangled it for him to see. I mouthed *thank you*.

I followed the warden out of the jail, unable to suppress my huge grin as the echo of Nicholas's spectacular swearing faded behind me.

CHAPTER THIRTY

ONCE I WAS ON my own, I set out for Antigua's market district. I was in need of a wardrobe. And lunch. I jingled Nicholas's coin purse without an ounce of guilt.

An hour later, I had sent a letter to my father and purchased everything I needed—and a few things I wanted—for a month-long journey. I intercepted Emilio and convinced him to have lunch with me at a public house before taking the papers to the jail. Nicholas deserved to sweat behind bars for a while longer.

"How did you get out and the others did not?" Emilio asked as we ate our lunch of fried plantains and shredded chicken.

"I think the warden felt sorry for me."

"I am so, so sorry that happened to you." Emilio cast his eyes down in shame. "And I just walked away."

"You did what no one else could do."

"How can you trust me to take care of you?"

I cocked my head and furrowed my brows. "Does it seem as if I need someone to take care of me?"

Emilio gave a reluctant chuckle.

"I don't need anyone to take care of me. I don't *want* anyone to take care of me."

Emilio watched as I brought a forkful of food to my mouth. "Your ring! It's missing."

I looked at the back of my hand. "Oh. No. I should have told you. I took it off on the ship. I work so much with my hands in the galley and with the laundry, I didn't want to damage it or lose it. It's safe."

"That's smart." His response was less than enthusiastic. I suddenly remembered the way Nicholas touched the chain around my neck, how he told me he liked seeing me wear it. Men liked to brand their women. I wondered if Nicholas had noticed my bare neck the past few days. As upset as he was with me, would it bother him to know that I still wore it around my waist under my dress?

After lunch, I conceded that it was time to liberate the others. Emilio went to the jail with the Letters of Marque while I strolled the open market. He was reluctant to leave me alone, but I assured him I could take care of myself—and besides, I couldn't risk the warden seeing me vouch for the people I accused of kidnapping me.

Plenty of money still jingled in Nicholas's purse. It was as good a time as any to restock on perishable food. I picked up a basket and filled it with apples, lemons, mushrooms, and sweet potatoes. At the bakery, I asked for a half-dozen baguettes. While I waited for my order to be packaged, a tall, thin figure brushed by me, covered from head to foot in a hooded black cloak. I instinctively shrunk away, remembering the woman with the pox on the wharf in Basseterre.

A hand reached out from under the robes to examine a loaf of bread. It was masculine and white as paper, an edge of pink around the fingernails. I stared at the long, scarred fingers, a tickle at the back of my brain.

The figure spoke to the baker. "I'll take this."

I knew that voice.

I shrank back farther, hoping to go unseen.

The baker's assistant emerged from the back. "Miss Monroe? Your order."

I considered running away, but thought it would be less conspicuous to take my order and disappear into the crowds. I thanked the young man and loaded my arms full of the bread. But when I turned to go, Captain Black was standing in my path, his eyes like watery rubies. My heart pounded in my chest. This man was supposed to be dead.

"I know you," he said.

I glanced behind him to see if any other of the *Banshee* pirates were with him. As far as I could tell, he was alone. I didn't trust appearances, though. This man was far too cunning to be found alone where pirates were unwelcome. "I think you must be mistaken. Excuse me." I ducked my head and tried to walk past him. He blocked my way.

"You're that little bird that flew away. Where's Marks?"

I didn't answer.

"Don't play coy, witch. I'll never forget the face I was betrayed for. If you're here, Marks can't be very far. You can tell me where he is or we can wait together."

My palms were moist where I gripped the bread. "The last time I saw Nicholas, he was behind bars on suspicion of piracy."

Captain Black clicked his tongue as if I were a child. "Lies."

"Actually, it's quite the truth. What do you want with him anyway?"

"Why, he's an old friend. My right-hand officer," he said rather jovially. He picked his teeth and assessed my shocked response. "I've been worried about him. Did he survive the fire?" Black slipped the hood off his head. Shimmering white scars stretched across his scalp where flowing white hair had once been. Half his face was deformed, making him uglier than he had been before.

"He should have killed you."

Black smiled, his teeth yellow against his pale pink lips. "And I should have killed you. But let's not dwell on should haves. Such a regretful set of words. Absolutely hate 'em. Now, shall we find a spot in the shade and wait for your lover?"

I should have been more afraid than I was, staring at a man who should have been a ghost, a man who had tried to kill me twice. But I was too exhausted from Nicholas and his antics to care much about Black. "He is not my lover. And he is not with me. Wait as long as you like, but all that will come to you will be a sunburn."

"Tessa, are you all right?" Emilio weaseled his way past Black and put his arm protectively around my shoulders. I felt him inhale sharply when he looked at the scarred albino man in front of us.

Black cocked his head and eyed Emilio. "And this strapping young lad is...?"

"My fiancé." I answered, leaning into Emilio. It was the first time I had used those words, and even though I wielded them only as a shield, they left me with the aftertaste of betrayal.

He shook his head slowly, a disbelieving smile on his lips. "The last time I saw Marks, he was fighting to the death—for *you*. He was a prince of the ocean, poised to inherit the kind of fame, fortune, and glory of which legends are made. And he traded it for the fickleness of a woman." A low chuckle rumbled out of Black and grew into a full-bodied laugh. His genuine delight sent shivers down my spine.

Emilio looked on in suspicious confusion. "Come on, darling. The others are waiting."

Still laughing hysterically, Black stepped aside with a flourish to let us pass, and Emilio scurried me towards the docks. "Who was that?"

"He was someone from the pirate ship that captured me."

"What did he want with you?"

I shrugged. "Nothing, I guess. He recognized me, is all."

* * * * *

The rhythmic sound of chanteys sounded on the deck above me as the crew heaved the anchor out of Antigua's harbor. The bread was heating in the oven, its yeasty smell making my stomach growl as I set the table for five. All hands were on deck to set the ketch sailing on the open sea. After that, we would all eat supper together, then resume the regular rotating watches.

The chantey changed and I felt the ship pick up speed and I knew full sails had been unfurled against the wind. A moment later, my four shipmates filed into the galley.

I placed the steaming bread on the table and ladled beef stew into everyone's dish. I sat in an empty seat beside Emilio and across from Nicholas, smoothing my hands over my new skirt. I rather liked my new ensemble—a dark green skirt and a black sleeveless bodice that laced overtop a white blouse.

I avoided Nicholas's gaze as I passed him the plate of bread. He hadn't spoken to me since I had left him in the custody of the warden. He hadn't even inquired after his coin purse. Even in his worst moods he found it appropriate to mock and ridicule. His silence scared me.

Meg carried the conversation, rehashing the arrest and imprisonment. She asked Emilio a few questions about his part in our rescue. When she asked why it seemed take him so long, he exchanged a quiet smile with me and expertly avoided the question.

When Meg had finally stopped talking, Emilio turned to me. "That man at the bakery, he was intense. Was he deranged?" Nicholas stiffened, listening to every word.

"I've questioned his sanity many times," I said, stirring my stew.

"What did he say to you?" Emilio asked.

"Not much. Just that he remembered me."

Nicholas's curiosity got the best of him. "Who? What happened?"

Emilio didn't hesitate to answer for me. "When I found Tessa at the bakery, a man was harassing her. Trying to frighten her, I think."

"Hmm." Nicholas reached for a slice of hot bread, turning it over and scowling at the blackened bottom.

"Tessa handled herself well. Never a frayed nerve with her. Perhaps you know the man. Tessa said he was from your ship."

Nicholas's hand holding the bread stopped halfway to his mouth. "My ship? The *Seabird*?"

Emilio looked at me. "The pirate ship, wasn't it?"

I was suddenly afraid of how Nicholas was going to react. "It was Captain Black."

"What?" Nicholas's bread fell out of his hand. "Captain Black? Are you sure?" His nostrils flared and I felt his fury thicken. I looked back into my stew.

"Peculiar fellow," Emilio said, oblivious of the tension in the room—Skidmore and Meg were hanging on our conversation too. "I have never seen eyes that color before. Sickly and pink." He shuddered.

Nicholas turned his anger on me, his hands slamming on the table. "Why didn't you say something?"

Before I could answer, Nicholas sprang from the table, Skidmore close behind, each man assessing the weapons that hung from their baldrics and belts. Meg was on their heels, an axe appearing in her hand as she climbed the ladder. Exchanging confused glances, Emilio and I took up the rear and followed everyone onto the main deck. By the time I had blinked back the low evening sunshine, Nicholas was poised on the topgallant yard with a spyglass at his eye. It made my stomach churn to see him so high in the air, barefoot, and casually holding on to a single line for balance as the ship pitched and tumbled.

Skidmore climbed after Nicholas. They passed the spyglass back and forth, pointed across the distance, and conversed with each other. My eyes followed their gestures to see what they were talking about. Antigua was still a green smudge in the distance, its harbor punctured with a hundred masts. A few ships sailed nearby, but none were close enough to be a threat.

The men shimmied down to the main deck and Nicholas

came at me. His hands locked on my upper arms, his eyes ablaze. "Why didn't you tell me?" He was nearly shaking me. "What did he say to you?"

Emilio was next to us in an instant. He laid a hand on Nicholas's shoulder. "Captain Holladay." His voice was stern.

Nicholas loosened his grip, but his hands remained on me. "Did he hurt you? Did he threaten you?" I felt as if I were a child being scolded. "What did he want?"

"I-I think he wanted you."

Emilio grew more concerned watching Nicholas's reaction. "Should we be worried about that man? Is he dangerous?"

"Seeing as he kidnapped Tessa and tried to kill her a time or two, it's safe to assume he wasn't asking her about the weather." Nicholas exhaled in exasperation, then let go of me. "Tell me, Tessa, verbatim, what Black Jack said."

I pressed my lips together and cast a quick, sideways look at Emilio. Nicholas understood. He turned to the crew. "I need to speak with Tessa alone. Go eat dinner before it gets any colder."

Skidmore and Meg disappeared below deck immediately. Emilio hesitated, his brow creased with worry. I walked over to him. "I have reservations about leaving you alone with him." Emilio had lowered his voice to a whisper but I could tell from the expression on Nicholas's face that his words had carried on the wind. Emilio brushed my arm where Nicholas had grabbed me.

I hugged myself to keep Emilio from touching me. "I will be fine. He was just scared."

"I can stay here, if you like. On the bow, out of earshot."

"That's not necessary."

Emilio's face fell. "Why does he need to be alone with you anyway? I was there. I can provide a second witness."

I looked at Nicholas then back at Emilio. I could not recount what Captain Black said with Emilio nearby. "I think his pride is sore over Captain Black. He thought he killed him. I'm really the only one who knows what happened."

Emilio held steady for a minute, then nodded. Men, it seemed, all understood the sacredness of pride. He offered me a tight smile then disappeared down the hatch.

To my surprise, Nicholas closed the hatch door after Emilio left. "Come on, then." He walked to the bow of the ship and draped his arms over the railing, looking out across the neverending expanse of sea and sky. A swath of orange arced across the horizon. The edges of the thin, wispy clouds glowed as if they were ablaze with heavenly flame. The warm light sharpened the planes of Nicholas's face, casting an angelic glow on him too. His hair blew in his eyes. My fingers itched to brush it back.

Nicholas turned with a look of expectation in his eyes. In that instant, the past few weeks vanished and it was just the two of us alone on the ketch, watching the sun cast its colors over the water together as we so often had done. Only we weren't touching. And the look of wanting in Nicholas's eyes was not for me—it was for information on Captain Black.

Before he could ask it of me again, I recounted my meeting with Black, though I left out what Black had said at the end— about Nicholas giving up everything for my fickleness. When I had finished, Nicholas nodded calmly. "You were clever to have said what you did. About me being arrested."

"I hoped it would dissuade him from following me."

Nicholas's grey eyes swept the open sea around us. "It very well may have. Did you recognize anyone else from the *Banshee*?"

I shook my head. "It seemed as though he were alone. That's odd, isn't it? Wouldn't he have had someone from his crew with him?"

He lifted a shoulder in a half shrug. "The men he had with him in Curaçao were all killed. The *Banshee* pirates mutinied against him. It's unlikely he'd trust any of them ever again. He could have found a new crew by now. But if his sole purpose is revenge, he could be working alone." Nicholas steepled his fingers and pressed his lips against their tips, his thoughts as deep as the waters around us.

The temperature was sinking with the sun. I shivered.

He turned to me, putting a hand on my arm. "Did I hurt you before?"

"No."

"I am sorry if I frightened you."

"You didn't."

"I frightened De Luca." His eyebrows pulled down.

I gave a hollow laugh. "He is taking his role as my protector rather seriously."

"Someone should." His eyes swept over my face, the reflected sunlight turning them into liquid gold. He looked down at his hand on my arm and quickly pulled it away. "I'm sorry."

My arm was instantly cold where the heat of his hand had been. I could tell he was ready to flee, the way he always did when he felt out of control, but I wanted the moment to last longer. I didn't care that we were speaking about Captain Black. I was ecstatic that we were speaking at all.

"Do you think Black will follow us?"

A shadow passed over his eyes. "I didn't see Black on Antigua so I do not think he saw me. You told him I was imprisoned, but not where. Neither Skidmore nor I spotted the *Banshee* in the harbor, though he probably wouldn't be sailing with them anyway. I do not think he will find me today."

I shivered again. "But you think he might find you?"

"If he wants to, aye."

"How anyone could find *anyone* in this place is beyond me. Every island days away from the next one. No roads. No routes. The open sea must be the safest place to hide."

Nicholas scoffed. "The currents might as well be roads. And gossip among the islands is strong. We leave our footprint everywhere we go. Black can find me. He knows people. He's smart. He's a skilled tracker. From Florida to Venezuela, the entire Spanish Main is his."

"Are you worried about what he'll do? If he finds you?"

His face was expressionless, his eyes steely. Like those of a soldier. "I cannot afford to be worried."

We stood in silence, watching the twilight leech the color from around us.

"Why didn't you tell me, Tessa?"

"I don't know," I answered honestly.

"We could have all been in danger."

My fingers were clenched on the caprail, my knuckles white. "I'm sorry."

After a quiet moment, he asked, "How is the boarding situation with Quin?"

If nothing, he was a dutiful captain. I shrugged and shook my head, not finding any words worth saying. "May I be excused?" I didn't wait for his reply.

I was halfway to the hatch when he said my name.

I turned to him, "What?"

His brows pulled together. "It's...nothing."

That night when I went into my cabin, a canvas hammock was hanging in the corner, Meg's duffel underneath it.

CHAPTER THIRTY-ONE

WITH RANDOM BITS OF information, I pieced together the intent of the mission. On Nicholas's previous mission, he confirmed what my father suspected—a French governor named Laval hired the Portuguese mercenary Mateus Salazar to goad the British into attacking the French. If the British colonies drew first blood, the Royal Navy would not support them, leaving them defenseless and easy to overthrow. It was all for naught—the English never engaged and the French did not have a fight they could win. Salazar, failing at his task, turned to subterfuge and planted spies in St. Kitts. He learned about the Declaration of War and had it stolen, knowing how valuable it would be to the French. If King Louis saw it, he would consider it an act of war and would retaliate with full force in Europe as well as in the Caribbean. Thinking that England had violated the Treaty of Utrecht, England's allies would abandon her, giving France an uncontested war against Britain. The colonies would be wiped out. The declar-ation would change France's position in the world forever.

Salazar was travelling to Laval on the island of St. Lucia to ransom the document—surely Laval would pay a good deal of gold for something so powerful.

We would reach St. Lucia within the week and intercept

Salazar there. Salazar's loyalties went to no crown, but rather to whomever had the largest purse. Lord De Luca—an Italian nobleman impartial to the strivings of either nation—had a purse much larger than Laval's. As one of the most successful plantation owners in the Caribbean, his money was all his own with no ties to any government. He would convince Salazar to sell the declaration to him.

I could tell Nicholas was concerned that Emilio would not be persuasive enough in his efforts to lure Salazar away from Laval. Nicholas would have preferred to impersonate Emilio himself, his natural charisma and time as a leader of rebels had honed his persuasion skills to a fine weapon indeed, but Salazar knew Nicholas. Meg and Skidmore were strangers to the man as of yet and would accompany Emilio on the mission. Nicholas would remain behind on the ship. With me.

In the days before we arrived at St. Lucia, my pride softened enough that I approached Nicholas again about the night of my birthday, but he cruelly dismissed me as he had before. Meg often took meals to him on deck so I rarely saw him in the galley. I ached every time he refused the dinner bell. I tried to remind myself that my current situation was better than the other time I was on a ship against my will. But something in the back of my mind would have preferred the mortal fear I lived in on the *Banshee* over the crushing finality of Nicholas's disregard for me.

As much as I tried to prevent it, I was becoming Meg's confidant. She narrated every encounter with Nicholas in detail. Every glance he gave her. Every time their hands brushed or he offered to go aloft so she didn't have to. Part of me was annoyed with Meg for misinterpreting normal human interaction as courtship. But part of me wondered if she was right, if maybe he was wooing her.

"...and he even said that I wielded a hammer smartly!" After breezing into the galley glassy-eyed, Meg prattled on about every interaction she had with Nicholas during her watch.

I hadn't listened to much of what she said. I'd kept myself

busy grinding oats for gruel. My annoyance finally got the best of me. "What do you expect to happen in the coming weeks, Meg? When the mission is over and you and I return to St. Kitts and the captain will… what?"

Meg looked as if I had slopped cold water on her. "He'll…maybe…"

"He'll return to the sea. It's what he does."

"But the way he's been treating me —"

"Enjoy it while you can, but your heart has been broken before. Be prepared." I said.

She jutted her chin. "I'll return with him."

"If he asks you to." Meg's face blanched at my words. I was sickened by the satisfaction I felt. "Don't forget that you aren't a sailor. You're an employee of the Monroe household. You'll return to St. Kitts as sure as I will. Nicholas will leave us both."

"Leave us *both*?" Meg asked. "Oh, yes." Her tone grew callous. "I forgot how much he means to you, the brother you never had. You don't like him sailing away forever any more than I do."

"No, Meg. I don't." I twisted the pestle with renewed vigor.

Meg stepped closer. "You're jealous."

"I'm not jealous." I turned my back and checked the boiling water on the stove so she would not see the traitorous blush of my cheeks. "I told you. I have a deep…camaraderie with him after what we went through together. A *familial* affection."

Meg leaned over the countertop. I quickly glanced at her costume and wondered how she could stand to wear men's breeches. It was so incredibly wrong. "Yes, *familial*," she repeated sardonically. "It explains everything."

"It explains what?"

"The tension between you two is palpable."

I didn't know what she was hinting at, but I didn't like the tone in her voice. "What are you implying?"

She barked out a laugh. "You're giving me advice on how to cope with Nicky's inevitable rejection when you really ought to be speaking to yourself. Your affection for him is well beyond brotherly. It's obvious. But he's always kept you at arm's length. You may have hoped that this inconvenience of being trapped on the *Freedom* might have developed into more, but Nicky doesn't want that. Not with you. You are jealous, whether or not you want to admit it. You're trying to make me doubt my standing with him. It won't happen. I won't allow you to sabotage me. Nicky and I are in love. He values you as a friend, or leastways he used to. I will respect that."

Of all the things she said, only one thing really stung. "He *used* to value me as a friend? What the hell do you mean by that? We are still friends."

Weren't we?

Meg sneered. "He avoids you. He doesn't talk about you. He doesn't want to have anything to do with you. He's sending you a very loud message. You'd save yourself a lot of pain if you listen."

I wanted to lash back and tell her that in all our time alone Nicholas had never once mentioned her name, but it was a futile, petty fight anyway. I just wanted her gone. "Thanks for the advice," I muttered, keeping the venom in my voice to a minimum.

She raised her eyebrows as if she were challenging me. After I failed to rise to the bait, she smiled insincerely and left the galley.

I placed my palms on the counter and sagged out a sigh. She was dead wrong about many things, but she was right about others. I needed to tread carefully or she would become even more vicious. It was the last thing I needed.

Nicholas entered and I snapped up, wondering how much he had heard of my conversation with Meg. It was easy to forget how sound carried through the ship. He crossed behind me towards the back of the galley without so much as a glance at me. He poured himself a mug of watered-down rum. "What's for lunch?"

"Gruel," I said flatly.

Nicholas made a noncommittal noise in his throat, then

tipped the contents of the mug into his mouth. "Make chicken for dinner, luv, won't you?" He tossed the pewter mug into the washbasin and strode out.

I waited until I was certain he was gone, then threw his pewter mug after him. "*You* make the chicken!"

* * * * *

The chicken writhed and wriggled and tufts of white feathers floated through the air.

"Now!" Emilio shouted.

I brought the cleaver down in a swift chop, but stopped before it could connect with the chicken's neck. "I can't."

"Would you rather hold the chicken?"

I shook my head violently, gagging at the thought of the chicken's severed head in my hand. "I say we don't bother. If the captain wants chicken for dinner, he bloody well can kill it himself."

"It's been ages since I've seen snow."

I turned to see Skidmore entering the galley, grasping at the airborne feathers with fascination. "Chicken for dinner?" His voice was giddy.

"No." I laid down the cleaver and crossed my arms. "I can't kill the chicken. Maybe I'll stop feeding it and let it starve. We can have chicken in a week."

The chicken flapped free. Emilio jumped back in surprise. Feathers floated all around while distressed clucking filled the air. I rushed to the door and slammed it closed so the chicken couldn't escape. Emilio and Skidmore scuffled around, hunched like apes, chasing it around the legs of the table. Skidmore cornered the bird and snatched it by its legs, hanging it upside down. Emilio went for the cleaver just as Skidmore placed his boot on the chicken's head and snapped its body up, effectively beheading it.

My hands flew to my mouth to stifle the gasp that slipped out.

Skidmore smiled apologetically. "I always found that to be the easiest way." The headless, upside-down chicken flapped its wings, a dribble of red ooze splattering the floor.

"There is no way I can eat that," I said, my hands still covering my mouth.

Skidmore took the bird to the basin, a dotted red line marking his path across the floor. "Nonsense! It will be delicious."

I stood like a statue, staring at the severed head on my galley floor.

Skidmore laughed loudly. "I take it you've never dressed a chicken before?"

My look gave him all the answer he needed.

He looked at the bare stove. "Boil some water. Enough to cover the chicken."

"Shouldn't we roast it over the fire?" I was still frozen by the door.

"Just a brief scalding," Skidmore said as he drained the chicken carcass into the basin. "Feathers'll come off easier."

My stomach turned and I made a gagging noise. Emilio looked at me with horror; Skidmore looked at me with mirth.

"Take her outta here," Skidmore said to Emilio. "Dinner'll be my doing tonight."

The breeze off the Caribbean took the scent of hot blood from my nose, but nausea still lingered in my stomach.

"How barbaric," Emilio said as he guided me to a bench along the starboard railing.

"I have an entire new perspective on Miss Maisley's duties. When I return, I'll insist father raise her wages."

"May I fetch you a glass of wine?"

I shook my head. "I can't even think about drinking or eating anything."

Emilio smiled. "When I first met you, I knew you were different from any other woman I had met. But I had never imagined seeing you brandishing a cleaver, trying to kill a chicken." We both laughed. "Though I would never have imagined that I would be holding the chicken." His eyes softened as they sought mine. "You do amaze me, Tessa Monroe. Every minute with you is an adventure."

My eyes lingered on him, drinking in the planes of his face. I could wake up to this every morning. I wouldn't tire of his appearance. Lean and handsome with giant black eyes. This face could be my future. My lips drew up into half a smile. I touched his cheek with my fingertips.

He watched as I dropped my hand into my lap. "I wish you would wear the engagement ring."

I followed his gaze to my bare fingers. "The ring is—" I wanted to say *important* or *special* but I couldn't bring myself to lie, "—irreplaceable," I finally said. "I couldn't stand the thought of losing it or ruining it. Imagine if I were plucking a bloody chicken with it now!"

Emilio smiled then pulled my left hand to his lips and kissed the base of my fourth finger. "Of course. There will be decades and decades ahead of us for you to wear it."

For the very first time, I imagined what those decades may be like.

* * * * *

The moonlight spilled through the hatch, a square of silvery light illuminating my way up the ladder. I walked to the aft railing, breathing deeply to clear my head of the nightmare that had woken me. I was still taken aback by how heavy the Caribbean air was. The breezes here varied in temperature, hot and cool, but they were never crisp or sharp or even caressing as they could be in England. The air was too thick for anything but a clumsy bypass. Even so, the thick wind glanced across me, drying the sweat that matted my hair to my forehead. I had been dreaming of death and fire. Memories of the church fire in Curaçao.

I splayed my toes on the deck. The wood was smoother than I anticipated. Nicholas went barefoot all the time. It gave him better traction up on the ropes he spent half the day climbing. I wriggled my toes thinking of Nicholas's bare feet and my bare feet. Our bare feet together. Why did he always invade my thoughts? I was tired of pushing thoughts of him away, but what else was I supposed to do?

We would arrive in St. Lucia tomorrow evening. Our journey was half over. I had been confined to a small ship with Nicholas for more than ten days and still had not been able to explain myself to him. I would never have a better opportunity—there was only so far he could run on a small fishing ketch. It wasn't as easy as all that, though. No matter how confined we were, if he wouldn't talk to me, there wasn't much I could do. Trying to have a meaningful conversation with him was as useful as shouting into the wind.

The sound of a giggle surprised me. I turned around, my eyes still adjusting to the dark. Meg hadn't been in her hammock when I awoke. She and Nicholas would be on watch. I hadn't thought of that when I came up. I bit my lip, hoping they weren't mocking me from a distance. But when the moonlight spilled from behind a cloud and lit the deck, I saw something much worse.

A strange, contorted figure leaned up against the foremast. I heard a lower voice on the breeze, speaking so softly I couldn't make out the words. The giggle sounded again. I stepped closer, ducking under the lines and rigging, then halted. What I thought was a single person was actually two figures so closely entwined I could barely distinguish them.

Nicholas had Meg pressed against the mast, her blonde waves cascading over her shoulders. His hands circled her waist. Their faces were close. Too close. They whispered and giggled. Her hands linked around the back of his neck. She tilted her chin up and pressed her lips against his.

I'd seen enough.

More concerned about speed than stealth, I dropped down the hatch, missing the ladder completely, and landed hard with an audible gasp.

I choked on sobs as I cowered in the galley. I couldn't go back to my cabin. It was Meg's cabin, too. I fell to my knees in front of the pot-bellied stove, glowing red in the night like a portal to hell, and rocked back and forth, my arms cinching around my waist to keep the sobs from escaping.

The cinders popped and crackled, a final burst of beautiful brightness before settling down in to a pile of ash. I sat in the dark and stared at their hypnotic display. I took up a long wooden spoon and slowly stirred the coals.

I heard footfalls come to the threshold of the galley, graceful and steadfast. Familiar. I didn't need to look to know they belonged to Nicholas. He paused briefly, but did not enter my domain. The footsteps retreated, more quietly than they had come. He'd seen me here, there was no doubt about that, a pathetic creature in the corner of the dank, dark kitchen, playing with ashes. Just my presence had driven him away.

I suspected he had been avoiding me, but now I knew. The realization hit me like a splash of acid—sharp, painful, and scarring. I had held to the hope that his pride would heal and he would come around, or at least he would be too curious to ignore my pleadings.

I was done pleading. I was done with him. What other choice did I have? He was repulsed by me.

The image of Nicholas and Meg kissing appeared every time I closed my eyes as though it were etched on the backs of my eyelids. I shook my head, trying to erase the memory.

Another set of footsteps approached the galley, their soft shuffle as equally familiar as Nicholas's. I had heard them every day for a fortnight when I was imprisoned in the brig of the *Banshee*. I had grown to associate the sound of Skidmore's step with reassurance and hope.

I straightened my posture and quickly wiped my face. Skidmore dragged a chair next to me and sat down.

I stirred the cinders. "Have you ever wondered what the future holds?" Without waiting for Skidmore to answer, I went on. "Ash. Everything becomes ash." I poked the crimson embers. "See there?" I used my spoon to point to a particularly bright patch of coals. "It's trying to last. Burn a bit brighter. Fight its fate. We might even help it a bit." I blew on the coals and they roared with glowing ferocity. "They try…" I poked at them again. They crumbled under the pressure of the spoon and faded to grey. "…and then they die. It's what becomes of everything. Ash."

I tore my eyes from the oven and looked at Skidmore, his face looking more scarred and worn than usual in the shadows of the embers. His eyes were glued to the coals, hypnotized as I had been.

My voice hitched. "Is that all we are now? Ash?"

Skidmore slowly shook his head. He wasn't disagreeing with me…just pensive.

Speaking with Skidmore had always been a bit like writing in a diary. I could pour out the contents of my soul without pretense or fear of repercussion. I attributed it to his trademark silence. "I thought we would be forever. I thought we were worth fighting for. But I've lost it now. Like these coals—our love once burned hot and brilliant, equally dangerous and beautiful. But it's doused now. Just a pile of ashes. Gone forever."

"Do you really think it is a love worth fighting for?" asked Skidmore.

"I *did*," I said quietly.

"Then, I think now is the time to fight."

"What's the use?" I moaned. "He can't stand the sight of me. He'll never listen to what I have to say."

Skidmore shifted his weight and pulled a scrap of paper from his pocket. He smoothed it out on his thigh. With a flick of his wrist, he flung the paper into the oven. It glided in the air, propelled like a pendulum by waves of heat until it finally settled on top of the mound of cinders. Curls of smoke bloomed above the paper, white and dense. Then the paper combusted and tongues of orange and red flames devoured the fuel.

Skidmore nodded knowingly. "There's fire in there yet."

Just as easily as he'd come, Skidmore left, replacing his chair and leaving me alone, blackened bits of paper swirling through the air like hellish flakes of snow.

CHAPTER THIRTY-TWO

THE STORMY WEATHER REFLECTED my mood. No rain fell, but thunder sounded across the roiling sky. An angry wind bit at the sails. The green, jagged mountains of St. Lucia rose ominously before me. We had anchored in Castries harbor sometime the night before. I stood at the bow with a cup of tea and let the storm wrap its arms around me.

"Tessa." Emilio appeared at my elbow. "We are leaving now."

I offered him a smile. "Are you worried?"

"No." He looked down at the choppy water. "Yes."

I slid my hand into the crook of his elbow. "You have my faith."

"I wish you could come, too. We could spend the day away from the ship, just the two of us."

"Maybe after you've neutralized Salazar."

Emilio leaned into me. "We'll certainly want to take time to celebrate our victory."

Skidmore called for Emilio. We both glanced behind us. Nicholas had opened a bulwark door and positioned a plank from the ship to the dock. Emilio kissed my forehead. "Until later."

I wished him luck and watched as he, Skidmore, and Meg descended the plank and walked towards the heart of St. Lucia.

Nicholas cast a wary glance at me. We were alone. I turned

back around and continued my vigil over the stormy harbor. Once my tea was gone, I retreated to my cabin and curled up with a book for the better part of the morning.

When lunch was ready—a helping of fried plantains, hard cheese, hardtack, and salted pork—I thought about ringing the bell, but that seemed silly since only Nicholas was on board. I dished a plate for him and took it to the main deck. His carpentry tools were strewn about—he'd been prying loose a rotted board on the deck—but he was looking over the railing at the flint-colored harbor. The water was frothing and boiling like a witch's brew. It was rare to see Nicholas still. He hated waiting here, not knowing how the mission was going.

"Captain?" He turned, startled. I held out the plate. "Lunch."

He took the plate. "Where's yours?"

"In the galley."

He gestured to a bench. "Fetch your food. Join me."

"Is that an order, Captain?"

He blinked at me and stepped back. "No."

"Then I'd rather not."

There was a spark of something in his eyes that I didn't bother trying to decipher as I returned to the galley and ate alone.

It was twilight when Emilio, Meg, and Skidmore returned. I saw them walking down the docks and immediately knew something was amiss. I went below deck and knocked on Nicholas's closed cabin door.

"Captain?" I knocked louder.

"Tessa?" His voice was groggy.

"The others are returning."

He opened the door. His eyes were puffy with sleep, his hair mussed. And he was shirtless. I blinked and stepped back quickly.

"You say they are back?"

"Um, yes. I saw them on the dock." I failed in my attempts to keep my eyes off his bare chest.

Nicholas ran a hand through his hair then retrieved a clean

shirt from his trunk. He pulled it on and stuffed the ends of it into his breeches.

"What time is it?" Nicholas asked.

"The sun has barely set."

He frowned. "They took longer than I expected."

We went onto the main deck and waited. Emilio boarded first and immediately pulled Nicholas into a far corner. He was shaking his head. He looked a mess. I only heard snippets of the conversation. *Paris...King Louis...retaliate with full force...war...war...England...Europe...Caribbean...war for all...*

I wanted to know the details. Skidmore joined Emilio and Nicholas, so I couldn't ask him. I went to Meg but as soon as I saw her, hate boiled inside me. I turned away from her, but she caught up with me.

"Did you hear? It's a disaster. Salazar wouldn't hear a thing Lord De Luca said. He said he *wants* a war. He didn't even care that Lord De Luca would pay him more."

"Why would he want a war? He has no allegiance to the English or the French."

"He calls himself King of the Pirates and says all European governments are a threat to *his kingdom*. Lord Emilio says that the more stabilized the colonies are, the less stable piracy is. So Salazar wants war so pirates can rise to power amidst the chaos. He's taking the Declaration of War to King Louis himself."

"Tessa." Emilio was at my side. "Will you join me?"

It was so unlike Emilio to interrupt a conversation. His eyes were gleaming with boyish excitement.

Nicholas approached us. "De Luca, let's go to the galley to plan what we do next. I need more details."

Emilio nodded politely at him. "Yes, Captain. But first, I need to spend some time with my fiancée. We can discuss everything in depth after Miss Monroe goes to bed."

Nicholas glared at me as if the failed mission was my fault. "Your romance is not my concern."

Emilio turned on him, his eyes steady. "Thirty minutes, Captain." Before waiting for permission, Emilio grabbed my hand and led me to the plank.

Ten minutes later, we were entering Castries, the capital of St. Lucia. Emilio held my hand as he led me through the streets. We had touched before. Danced. Kissed even. But this felt more intimate than any of that. He squeezed my hand. With a smile, I squeezed back.

"I hope we didn't upset the captain by leaving like that," I said.

He shrugged indifferently. "Our romance may not be his concern, but it concerns me. I need time with my girl and I am going to take it." He guided me into an open-air restaurant. "Here we are." He pulled out a chair for me then spoke to the proprietor. A moment later, two large porcelain mugs filled with thick brown liquid were placed before us. The aroma was beyond decadent.

"Have you ever had chocolate?"

My eyes grew wide. "This is chocolate? I've always dreamed of it. I told my father that the next time we went to Paris, he had to take me for chocolate."

"Instead, you're drinking it in St. Lucia with your foreign fiancé."

I lifted my mug and clinked the rim against Emilio's. "A surprising turn of events, indeed."

Emilio watched me with interest as I sipped the fabled liquid. "What do you think?"

I took another sip and swished the chocolate in my mouth to appreciate its flavor and texture before swallowing. "I think I could drink this every day." I grinned. Emilio grinned back.

As we chatted and sipped, Emilio removed his gloves and grimaced as he fanned out his fingers. He examined his hands, front and back, as he flexed them and stretched them. His palms were red and raw and his knuckles covered in healing scabs.

"You're turning into a sailor," I said with a smile.

"I think my hands are slowly turning to stone."

I held up my palms and flashed my calluses. "They are like badges of honor."

I couldn't complain about sea life to Nicholas or Skidmore or Meg. I was trying too hard to prove my worthiness as a mate. Emilio felt the same way. But together we could commiserate about the constant nausea, the raw hands, the lack of sleep, the stench in the privy, the poor food, and the pervading dampness without being mocked for our softness.

We finished our chocolate and slowly walked back to the *Freedom*, our hands interlocked again. The stormy skies from earlier had broken up, revealing a patchwork of stars overhead. Emilio halted me as we came to the end of the dock and pulled me close.

"Tessa. *Mi tesoro*. I never expected to spend our engagement this way. It's not ideal. I had hoped it would be full of wedding plans and celebratory balls, not spent working under the rule of a surly captain. He is not a man who manages pressure well. He never acted so churlish in St. Kitts. But I am glad you are with me now. I want to make you as happy as you make me. I promise I'll never stop trying."

I almost corrected him about Nicholas. The captain could manage pressure better than anyone I knew. He was poor at managing his temper—especially concerning me, it seemed.

Emilio's hands slid around my waist. Under their light pressure, I felt the gold chain I still wore underneath my clothes. I leaned my head against his chest. His heart was beating wildly. He lifted a hand and stroked my cheek.

"*Significhi tutto per me*. You are my world. *Te amo*."

I gazed at him in awe. He spoke the words with such reverence that I felt their meaning even though I didn't understand the words. Emilio tilted my chin with his finger. My eyes fluttered closed and his lips met mine in a sweet, tender kiss.

When I started up the plank, I noticed Nicholas looking down from the railing, his face taught. I quickly looked away.

What did I care if our kiss upset him? I had seen him kissing Meg. Still, I couldn't meet his eyes when I walked past him.

Everyone gathered in the galley. I offered to brew tea but everyone seemed happier with the idea of rum. The smell of the drink still made me nauseous.

"We return to St. Kitts and consult Admiral Monroe," stated Emilio.

Nicholas shook his head. "We don't have time. We have to stop Salazar."

"How?" Meg asked.

"Killing him would be a start."

I nervously sat down next to Skidmore, fully expecting that I would be asked to leave, but my presence didn't faze anyone. I wasn't used to that. My father never allowed me to sit in on discussions meant for men.

"Is killing him necessary?" I asked.

Nicholas smirked at me, though not unkindly. "I reckon it would put a damper on his plans."

I suppressed my urge to roll my eyes. "Yes. But what if he has a…a first mate…or a lieutenant or something. Passes the Declaration of War on to him. He can stir up as much trouble as he pleases, but the real problem is that paper signed by the king."

Nicholas chewed his lip and stared at me. "We have to get that bloody declaration. That paper is all the difference between an act of piracy and an act of war."

"We'll have to get it by force," Skidmore said.

"Aye." Nicholas nodded.

"How?"

Nicholas looked at Emilio. "Do you have any idea what his intentions are? When will he set sail for France?"

Emilio shook his head. "Immediately. There's no time to intercept him. He said he's stopping at a place called Port Winslow to switch ships, then sailing for France."

I gasped.

"Are you familiar with the place?" Emilio asked me.

I ignored his question and looked at Nicholas. "Port Winslow."

A ghost of a smile flickered across his lips. "If we can intercept him anywhere, that place be Port Winslow."

CHAPTER THIRTY-THREE

WE SPENT THE NIGHT in the turquoise waters of Castries Harbor. The following morning, Meg and I were sent to shop for fresh provisions as Nicholas and the others learned all they could about Salazar. They learned that Salazar had a fleet of four ships and personally sailed a brigantine crewed by more than one hundred men. It would take us ten days to sail to Port Winslow, but in the small ketch we would easily beat him there. Nicholas sent a word to my father explaining the change of plans.

Meg gave me a detailed retelling of her kiss with Nicholas as if she were waving a flag of victory in my face. I kept my mind busy with other things to block out the tale. I still registered some of it. They had gotten a bit tipsy. She said they had been speaking of me, but Nicholas insisted they stop. And then they were kissing.

She asked me what had happened the night before with Emilio. I somehow felt we were in some kind of contest comparing beaux. Her goading worked and I told her about the chocolate and she swooned at the thought. I exaggerated the story a little, even going in to details on the kiss, either to make myself feel better about her kissing Nicholas or in hopes that she would pass the story back to him. It was a childish thing to do, but I did it anyway.

We were two days into our journey to Port Winslow when I walked in on Nicholas at the counter in the galley with his back to me. Despite our collaboration over intercepting Salazar, the icy distance between us remained.

I was about to slink out of the kitchen unseen until I heard a clatter and saw Nicholas tense. "Dammit!" he cursed. He cradled his hand by his stomach, his posture hunching inward like a protective cocoon. He was hurt. Badly.

I found myself rushing to his side. A crude bandage was wound haphazardly around his right hand. It was red with fresh blood.

"What happened?" I breathed, grabbing his injured hand.

Surprised to see someone behind him, Nicholas jumped a little and pulled his hand back. "It's nothing," he said, winding the useless bandage a little tighter.

I looked around and noticed a large butcher knife on the counter and a papaya that he must have been trying to cut. I scowled at him and grabbed his hand again. "That's not nothing." I gingerly unwound the bandage. A very deep gash across the back of his hand oozed blood. "Did you do this while...dicing papaya?" I asked, looking at the knife.

"I was repairing that rotten board. Had my saw out. The ketch pitched at exactly the right moment," he explained sarcastically.

Still holding his hand, I looked into his face, my eyes pleading. "Nicholas, this is bad. If this gets infected..."

I trailed off, suddenly lost in Nicholas's grey eyes. My stomach flipped. I looked away.

Nicholas pulled his hand back. "I have suffered worse."

I took a step away from him and wiped my hands on my skirt—a futile attempt to erase the heat of his hand in mine. "You'll end up with a hook for a hand."

Nicholas gave half a smile. "I'll be like other pirates."

His typical flippancy was aggravating. "You always told me you weren't like other pirates. You're ready to be like them now? With a hook for a hand, a wooden peg for a leg, and a cruel, black heart?"

Nicholas looked up at me, anger flaring on his face. "Excuse me?"

I shook my head and mumbled, "Nothing."

I pushed my way behind Nicholas and retrieved a small crate of medical supplies and a bottle of brandy from the cupboard. I carried them to the table then looked over my shoulder. "Are you coming?"

Surprised, Nicholas took a step forward. "What are you doing?"

"I am going to clean your cut."

"It's fine."

"Why are you always so stubborn?"

"Why are you always so damn pushy?"

I pointed to a chair. "Just sit down."

Huffing, Nicholas sat and reluctantly held out his hand.

I spread a towel on the table, placed his hand on top of it, then slowly poured brandy over the wound. Nicholas sucked a breath in through his teeth. He balled his good hand and pounded the table, grunting in pain.

"I'm sorry," I murmured.

Fresh blood poured out of the cut. With a clean rag, I gently blotted the wound. I reached for a clean strip of canvas and began to wrap the wound. Nicholas shook his head and nudged the medical crate towards me with his other hand.

"Suture it."

"Pardon?"

"Sew me up."

"Excuse me?" I stammered again hoping he wasn't asking me to do what I thought he was.

Nicholas glared at me with annoyance. "Take a needle. Take some thread. And sew me up."

My pleading eyes met his angry eyes. "I can't."

Nicholas formed his injured hand into a fist. The wound pulled open across his sinews. I felt dizzy looking at it. "You're right. It's bad. It won't stay closed unless you suture it."

Fighting the dark spots that swam around the edges of my vision, I retrieved a large needle and some coarse thread from the spare room where we kept the sewing supplies. I tried not to think about what would happen next as I threaded the needle and swallowed hard.

Nicholas pressed his hand down on the table, bracing for the pain.

Pinching the needle between my thumb and forefinger, my hand hovered over his, shaking. I looked at Nicholas, terrified. He nodded strongly.

I slowly lowered the needle into his raw flesh. The tip went into his skin and my hand trembled. The needle danced. I yanked it out quickly.

Nicholas roared in pain. "Dammit to hell, Tessa, just do it fast."

I pulled my hand away and shot back, "If you think you can do it better, be my guest."

"I'm sorry," he grumbled, not sounding sorry at all. "Hurts like hell."

I closed my eyes and took a deep breath. "I can do this," I whispered to myself. "It's like mending a sail." I clenched my teeth, opened my eyes, and plunged the needle into his hand.

He flinched and moaned.

"Hold still," I muttered. I pulled the needle through, cinched the stitch, then did it again.

Nicholas looked straight up, a steady stream of curse words pouring out under his breath.

After eight stitches, I knotted off the thread. "Done," I announced coolly.

Nicholas exhaled and looked down at my handiwork. He nodded in satisfaction, then grabbed the bottle of brandy and poured a few more drops into his wound. The muscles in his jaw rippled and he cursed again. He lifted the brandy to his lips and drank deeply, then slammed the bottle down.

After wiping my fingers clean, I mopped the blood and brandy off his hand. I wrapped his trembling hand with a swath of clean cotton.

"All better," I announced when I was done. Standing up, I placed the medical supplies back in the crate.

"Don't I get a kiss?"

I froze, bloodied rags in my hand, and stared him down. "I beg your pardon?"

He scoffed, a devilish smile on his lips. "My hand," he lifted it up. "Won't you kiss it better?"

I picked up the crate and spun on my heels, marching to the far side of the galley. *Have Meg kiss it better,* I thought. "That's a child's superstition." I put the crate away and turned to Nicholas's original purpose. "What were you doing down here? Did you need to cut this papaya?"

Nicholas shrugged. "Just trying to be useful. I'll be in the galley a while."

"And why's that?" I asked, defending my territory.

"Wounded men are useless sailors. Off they go to the galley." I'd heard of the practice before. It was common enough. But I didn't need his help and the ketch was small enough to forgo one worker.

"You're not exactly needed here."

He smiled broadly. It was a cold smile. "It's my boat and this is where I will be fulfilling my duty."

"Fine." I tried to keep my face impassive as I chopped the papaya.

He stood. "You don't seem very happy with this arrangement."

"You don't either."

"Why do you say that?"

"You're in a foul mood." I kept my eyes down. "I pray it improves with your hand."

Nicholas scoffed and crossed over to me. He was close. Too close. Cornered, his face was inches from mine. I could smell him—the scent of fresh marine air, the burnt-sugar smell of brandy, the sharp tang of blood.

He looked down at me, his eyes dark with anger. "My foul mood has nothing to do with my hand."

"Salazar. Of course."

"Not Salazar." He pressed closer.

My chin jutted out and I stood a little taller, matching his pomp. "The brandy has made you bold. Tell me then, what reason do you have to be so disagreeable?"

Nicholas breathed a hollow chuckle. "Stuck on this small ship, watching a man I despise and the woman I...watching your...*mating ritual*. Is that not reason enough?"

He came closer. Closer still. His eyes were the color of flint. Cold and hard and glinting. A shiver prickled at my scalp and danced down my spine to my toes, a combination of fear and longing. I sucked in a breath. He grabbed my chin and before I knew it, his mouth had claimed mine. Before I could return the kiss, he brusquely shoved me away. "Go to your fiancé."

I stumbled away from him, horrified and stupefied, and found myself in my cabin, trying to catch my breath.

CHAPTER THIRTY-FOUR

I SLAMMED THE DOOR to my cabin and sank against it, my chest heaving. My fingers flew to my lips and lingered there, still feeling the pressure of Nicholas's kiss. Tears flooded my eyes. *How could he be so harsh?*

My head was awhirl with everything that happened. The heat I felt at our touch. His cruel dismissal. Being trapped onboard a small boat with Nicholas, Emilio, and Meg certainly wasn't paradise for any of us. But Nicholas acted as if he were the only one put out by the situation. And I was paying the price.

Fuming, I threw my cabin door open and marched back to the galley. Nicholas sat at the table, his head in his hands.

He looked up in surprise, then turned his face away. "Go away," he murmured.

"I have something to say."

Nicholas looked at me, his eyes settling on mine. They flashed with emotion I could not read. "I can't be alone with you. Leave. It's an order."

"No." I crossed my arms in defiance. "You have no right to be so unkind to me."

Without acknowledging me—or the tears that flowed freely down my cheeks—Nicholas stood and pushed past me, heading for the door.

"Oh, no you don't." I hustled in front of him and closed the door of the galley, bolting it shut.

"Fine," Nicholas gave in. He took a step back and looked at me expectantly, his hands on his hips. "Say your piece."

I angrily dashed the tears from my face. "You think you're the only one who finds this difficult? Stop being so selfish. This is hell for me, too, in case you haven't noticed." Nicholas began to interrupt me but I raised my hand to silence him and continued. "Do not forget that *you* left *me*. Do not forget that I am not on this ship by choice. You think it's any easier for me to try to put all I felt for you behind me when I see you every day? To see you kissing Meg?" I wiped my cheeks again.

Nicholas looked away, refusing to meet my gaze. He looked chastised, but it was difficult to be certain. He may have been hiding his anger.

Giving him the benefit of the doubt, I crossed the distance between us and peered at his face, making him look at me.

"If we're both going to be in the galley for the next little while, we must both be more compliant."

Nicholas met my gaze, a pained expression on his face. His shoulders fell, as if in defeat.

"We'll work out a system," I suggested. "Take turns." I gestured to the papaya on the chopping block. "For now, I had better help you with lunch."

Nicholas shook his head and shuffled backwards a step. "I can't be alone with you."

"Why do you keep saying that? If you're afraid of what the baron will think..."

Sneering, Nicholas shook his head. "I despise De Luca and care not what he thinks. He can go to hell for all I care."

"Nicholas!" He certainly was in a foul mood.

Nicholas shook his head. "Fine. I'll be civil." He walked to the back of the galley. "I was going to make lentil broth along with the papaya."

Nicholas gathered the supplies while I lit a fire in the stove.

An occasional whispered curse escaped his lips when he moved his hand wrong.

We worked in silence side by side. Like a team of horses, we anticipated each other's movements. I held the pot while Nicholas filled it with water. I measured the dried lentils while he sprinkled them with seasoning. Still, the silence was awkward.

"So..." I ventured, unsure of what to say but compelled to say something.

"So," Nicholas responded. "I said I would be civil. Tell me, how are you?"

I raised an eyebrow. Is this how we would play this? Pretend as if nothing happened? "Well enough. Thank you."

I stirred the soup mindlessly.

"Are you...happy?"

I looked over my shoulder, trying to read Nicholas. He wasn't even looking at me. He was scraping the chopped papaya on to a square wooden plate.

"Right now?"

Nicholas's shoulders lifted in a shrug.

"Not particularly," I admitted.

He wiped the chopping block with a rag. "I am sorry I made you cry."

Now it was my turn to shrug off the emotion. "It's a common occurrence. Don't give yourself too much credit."

"Will you be happy, though? When the mission is over and you're back to St. Kitts?"

I wasn't sure what Nicholas was getting at. Tired of his games, I answered honestly. "I am beginning to think happiness doesn't exist. It's a lie told to gullible children."

"You're not happy at all?" There was a change in Nicholas's voice.

I took a minute to gather my thoughts. "I wouldn't say that. St. Kitts is beautiful. That makes me happy. Being with my father again—that makes me happy."

"And De Luca?"

"I don't want to talk about Lord De Luca."

"I do."

I closed my eyes and sighed. This conversation was like playing with fire. "The baron is a fine man. I consider myself very fortunate that he fancies me so," I averted my gaze, afraid of what I might see in Nicholas's eyes.

"So you're happy with him?" his voice was husky.

"He treats me well. He behaves himself." I shot a quick glance at Nicholas. He leaned backwards against the counter, drying his hands on a towel.

He snorted. "I figured you would be ecstatic."

I whirled around and faced Nicholas. "Stop being so cryptic and say what you mean."

His face twisted with contempt. "You have everything you ever wanted. A man of good, nay, *excellent* breeding. Riches. Leisure. A formal courtship. A celebrated engagement. And a title to go with it all, *Baroness*." He tipped his head slightly as if bowing to a queen.

Anger flowed through my veins. "Once upon a time, I thought you—more than any other person on this earth—understood me. Though you've dropped your charade, I still find myself surprised at how little you know me at all."

"What the hell is that supposed to mean?"

"Would you mind your language?"

"Stop being cryptic," he mimicked. "Tell me what you mean."

"You should know exactly what I mean, we've had this conversation before. A life of riches, a life of leisure, can never replace a life of passion."

"So you're not happy with De Luca?"

"Given the circumstances, he is absolutely the best I can do."

"Given the circumstances, you're no better than a prostitute."

Nicholas tossed the towel aside and stared at me. His eyes burned.

"Tell me how you really feel." I was livid.

His voice dripped with derision. "You're whoring your ideals for comfort and convenience."

I wheeled at him. "You have no right to judge me. You broke my heart, Nicholas, you broke it and you left me. You disappeared for *weeks*. You moved on…and so did I. Emilio will never hurt me like you did."

"You give him so much credit," he said bitterly.

"I give him no credit. It's not that he *won't* break my heart," I muttered quietly, "it's that he *can't*. My feelings for him…he simply doesn't have the power to."

Nicholas smiled sadly. "You ought to pity me for what I am going through."

My anger flared. "How dare you say that? You created all of this. I have no pity for you."

The ship dipped down from a large swell, pitching me forward into Nicholas. I found myself against his chest, my eyes wide with surprise. He had instinctively caught me, his hands on my arms. Our eyes met. I froze in place and a fire ignited instantly. It was not the fire of fury that had been coursing through my veins one second before, but a burning I only felt with him.

I searched his face, looking deeply into his eyes. They were dangerous and wild. Nicholas leaned towards me. I closed my eyes. Our noses touched, our lips a breath away from a kiss. I thought of Emilio and pulled back. Stern hands slid around my waist, spreading across the valley of my lower back, and pulled me closer. Nicholas's lips descended upon mine, yearning and hungry. My breath rushed out of me. He spun me around, trapping me in the crook of the counter. One arm remained around my waist while the other one tangled in my hair.

I met his kiss with equal fervor, raising higher on my toes and melting into his body. His cording of muscles tensed in response. My hands slid up his chest, my fingers lingering on his bare collarbones. Nicholas froze, my touch on his skin stunning him. I laced my fingers into his hair and pulled his head down, moving my lips against his, willing him to never stop. The feel of his kiss, the taste of his lips, the scent of his skin…everything felt so familiar. I was home again. I was afraid if this kiss ever ended, I would never be in his arms again.

Nicholas stiffened and pulled away. I reached for him again, but he pushed me back.

"I'm the most hateful fool you've ever laid eyes on. If I don't earn your pity, I don't know what will."

Wanting him back in my arms, I reached out for him. He recoiled as if I were dangerous. "I told you, I can't be alone with you."

CHAPTER THIRTY-FIVE

MY HANDS TREMBLED AS I prepared dinner. I stopped frequently, trying to find my equilibrium. Every time I closed my eyes, I was back in Nicholas's arms, under his passionate assault. That's what it was. An assault. I wanted it then but now...I hung my head, unsure of what I wanted. Of all men, why did this one have my heart? I knew he was hurt, deeply, but by some misunderstanding. I gave him a wealth of leniency for it, but this was too much. My heart was too bruised and he was passing beyond the lengths of my forgiveness.

I managed to keep my wits about me during dinner. Nicholas acted as if nothing had transpired—addressing me only as needed and ignoring me otherwise.

Skidmore helped me clear the dishes. By the basin, I leaned and whispered in his ear, "I think I might murder that man in his sleep."

He gave an understanding smile. "What did he do now?"

I remembered the kiss. For any other man, a kiss would've meant affection. But that kiss from Nicholas was a display of defiant fury. "I'm convinced that he hates me."

"At least your feelings towards each other are mutual once more."

I laughed out loud. Nicholas eyed us speculatively.

"Skidmore," he barked. "Main deck. Bring your flute and a jug of rum."

By the time I had cleaned up after dinner and made my way to the deck, the sun hung low in the sky, fingers of orange threading through violet clouds. Everyone was gathered round a portside bench passing the rum and talking animatedly. I slid up through the hatch, wary of an evening of drunken abandon.

"The lady appears!" Emilio bellowed, crossing to the hatch in three long strides and helping me onto the deck. He clamped me in an uncharacteristic embrace. The smell of rum roiled off him. I balked at the stench.

"Why is no one working?" I asked, sidestepping Emilio's lumbering affections.

Meg piped up. "The captain has called for a night of revelry." She held out a cask of some kind of whiskey. I dismissed it with a wave of my hand. She shrugged and took a drink.

I joined the scene with apprehension. I had never seen Emilio so loose and carefree, his black hair disheveled and hanging in his eyes. Nicholas sat loosely on the bench, another jug of rum next to his feet. He had a wicked grin on his face as he examined me.

"What's this about?" I gestured to the scene around me. Apparently, I was the only one unhappy about being surrounded by a crew of drunken mariners.

"Seems like a mighty fine night to get sloshed," he grinned.

I feared this had something to do with our earlier encounter.

Nicholas looked at Skidmore. "Time to dance."

"Aye, Captain." Skidmore fished a flute from his jacket. After a few tentative notes, Skidmore let loose and a vigorous melody weaved its way through the night. Nicholas clapped and stamped a foot to the beat.

"Dance!" Nicholas shouted. "Your captain commands it!"

Meg lifted her skirt and jigged around Skidmore. Emilio swept me into his arms and before I knew it, he was spinning me wildly across the deck. He pulled me close, lifted his knees and galloped to the music. He was folk dancing—not the proper waltzes of the Italian court. I doubted that Emilio had ever danced like this in his life. I let myself get swept away in the merriment.

Skidmore stamped and danced, the sound of his flute growing faster and faster. I spun away from Emilio and linked arms with Meg. We lifted our skirts and twirled with each other. At the next shift in music, I twirled away from Meg and found myself in Nicholas's arms. He pulled me to his chest, grasped my right hand in his left, and placed his bandaged hand against the small of my back. I placed my left hand on the swell of his bicep. He danced me across the deck with the grace of a man who had mastered his body. Our steps were quick and light, but the air between us crackled with tension. His smile was gone and his eyes had lost their playful gleam. My smile faded as I met his scorching gaze.

Suddenly my feet felt sluggish. The sound of my pounding heart overpowered the sound of the flute. Nicholas was slowing too, a new rhythm overtaking both of us. He looked like he wanted to kiss me. I wished he would, but knew it would never happen here with the rest of the crew nearby. If only we were alone. Nicholas said he couldn't be alone with me. Was that why? Every time we were touching alone, Nicholas seemed to lose control over his seemingly impenetrable composure. Something was burning in his eyes — a shadow of desire. It stirred a long-lost hope deep in my belly. Skidmore's words returned to me. *There's fire in there yet.*

"Switch. Hey! Switch!"

The moment shattered. Nicholas and I both looked around, stupefied. The other dancers had been waiting on us. Nicholas found the rhythm of the music in an instant, lifted me by my waist and deposited me in front of Emilio before scooping Meg into his arms. I watched them twirl by with longing. I fell in step with Emilio, suddenly aware of how rigidly he moved compared to my last dance partner. I tried to find the gaiety I'd felt before, but it had been burned out of me by Nicholas's eyes. Emilio spun me away and I was back to linking arms with Meg. We raised our skirts and danced around. My eyes rested on Nicholas, anticipating the next change in music when I would be in his arms again.

The music changed, I let go of Meg, and danced towards Nicholas. He sidestepped me, pulling Emilio over to take his place. Nicholas nodded to Meg and clapped Skidmore on the back, leaving our makeshift dance floor. He sauntered back to the bench by the portside railing and took a deep swig from a jug of rum. He was watching me as I flitted between Emilio and Meg. I stared back at him, trying to mask my disappointment.

The song ended and Skidmore offered to play another. Emilio, Meg, and I all shook our heads as we panted for breath. Emilio went to Nicholas, who offered him the rum without a word. I cocked my head, intrigued to see the baron behaving so. The dancing. The drinking. He said he wanted to experience the fullness of life outside of the confines of his title—I guess he was doing just that.

Meg produced a small guitar and sat down with Skidmore to plink out a composition. I sat with them, near the bow of the ship, listening halfheartedly at the refrains of their new song. My mind was busy replaying the events from earlier. Nicholas had kissed me today. Twice. Violently. Aggressively. And the way he looked at me while dancing. My cheeks grew hot at the memory of it. Nicholas hadn't shut me out, not completely, not yet.

The sky was dark now, lit by dozens of lanterns hanging around the perimeter of the ship. The laughter from the portside bench grew louder and louder. Nicholas and Emilio were on their second jug of rum. I had never seen either of them drunk. I disapproved, of course, but I couldn't take my eyes away from them—laughing merrily, talking constantly, for a brief moment they were the close friends they had been before. Acting, again, like long-lost brothers.

I perked up at the sound of my name on the breeze. They were talking about me—and not quietly. I left Meg and

Skidmore to their music and walked to Emilio and Nicholas.

Nicholas gestured to me, though still talking to Emilio. "And she comes unbidden. Are you sure you want that in a wife?"

They both laughed riotously. I felt as if I had just been insulted, though I wasn't sure I had been.

"She is a beauty, I admit," Nicholas went on, his voice louder than necessary—a result of the rum. "I suppose you won't complain to have that on your arm. A decorative accessory fit for court."

"Indeed!" Emilio guffawed. "I'll go nowhere without her. She'll be in higher fashion than a golden pocket watch."

The moronic laughter continued.

I crossed my arms. "Excuse me?"

The men looked at me and erupted with more laughter.

"Promise me this, dear Emilio," Nicholas said, taking another drink from the jug. "Cover her in jewels. She needs to be absolutely dripping in jewels."

"*Certo*! Only the finest for such a beauty."

"And it might help you keep hold of her."

"Well, I must do that. Can't afford to lose one like this," Emilio attempted to give me an inebriated wink, but it looked more like a stifled sneeze.

I was quite certain I was being insulted now. "Excuse me? Keep *hold* of me?"

Nicholas leaned close to Emilio and in an exaggerated whisper, said, "She speaks out of turn, too."

They laughed loudly again.

Nicholas continued in his ineffective whisper. "I know a lot about Tessa. We spent a lot of time together on this boat. Boat? Did I just say boat? How foolish of me. I meant ship!"

More laughter.

I looked on in disgust.

"Tell me," Emilio prompted. "Tell me everything you know."

"Oh, she wouldn't want me to tell you." Nicholas smiled at me wolfishly, then turned back to Emilio. "But you're my friend and you're about to yoke yourself to her for the rest of your life so I'll tell you anyway."

Emilio leaned in unsteadily, greedy to hear the gossip. I couldn't help it—I shuffled a little closer, too.

"Tessa is..." Nicholas paused for dramatic effect, "...a terrible cook. She botches *hardtack*. She ain't gotta do anything but dig it out of the pantry and put it on a plate and she botches it." He shook his head gravely. Emilio mimicked him. I sighed with relief.

"Amusing, Nicholas," I said, my arms still crossed. "Though, I don't remember you much complaining when you refused to cook for yourself."

Nicholas looked at me unapologetically. "*In vino veritas*, luv. Or in rum, rather." He lifted the jug high, displaying it to me. "Tessa doesn't like rum," he told Emilio.

"I think you've had quite enough," I grabbed the jug. Despite his sloppy reflexes, Nicholas was stronger than I was and managed to wrestle it out of my grasp.

"Don't be rude, Tessa," Nicholas chided. "I am giving Emilio a wedding present. I have very special knowledge and I am going to share it all with him."

"Nicholas, this isn't fair," I begged.

I noticed that the music had stopped. We had an audience.

Nicholas pressed a finger to his lips and shushed me, then turned back to Emilio. "Do you want to know what we did all those weeks alone on this very ship? We kissed. A lot!"

I prickled with embarrassment. "Hold your tongue, Captain, I am warning you!"

I looked guiltily at Emilio, afraid of his response. He smiled devilishly at Nicholas. "You scoundrel!"

Nicholas laughed and puffed his chest. "So believe me when I say I know a thing or two about romancin' Miss Monroe. She's fascinated by the stars somethin' powerful. Say something sweet to her under the stars, and she'll throw herself at you, lips first."

I couldn't stop the words coming from Nicholas so I just listened in helpless horror. Hot tears burned my eyes.

"She's quite particular about her hair and cares about it far more than she should. But as long as you keep her stocked with a wardrobe of wigs, her vanity should be right satisfied."

Emilio nodded intently as if the secrets of the universe were being revealed to him.

"Keep her in jewels. Not because they befit her beauty, which they do, but because it might just help you keep her interest. She's fickle. Fickle as they come, lad."

I was weeping openly. "Stop it, Nick, please."

"Here's the most important part," Nicholas leveled his eyes at me, arctic, pitiless, and unmoved by my tears. "Don't let her out of your sight. As soon as you do, she'll be lost to you, chasing the nearest jewel chest she can find."

"That's enough, Marks." Skidmore stepped in. He looked at me with crushing sympathy. "You best go to bed, Miss Monroe."

I shook with rage and humiliation, not even trying to hide my hurt. Skidmore handed me a bandanna for my tears. "Go on, now."

I made my way to my cabin where I sank on to the bed and sobbed.

Meg was not far behind me.

"Is it true?" Her voice was sharp.

I shook my head in confusion. Was any of it true? No. I wasn't anything like that! But then again, yes, it was all true. Everything he said was true.

"I need to know." Her words were growing hotter. "Did he romance you?"

My heart screwed tightly in my chest. She had heard that. I kept my face buried in the bandanna, hoping Meg would just go away.

"Did you kiss him? Did you fall in love with him?" Her tone was dangerous and brittle, with a hint of hysteria.

"Yes!" I erupted, glad to finally have it out. "Yes to everything you ask!"

"You lied to me," she seethed. Then she mimicked me in a mocking tone. *"Poor me, poor me. My heart belongs to someone else. Good men fall in love with me at every turn and I must have them all."* She shook her head in disgust. "And it was you all along. I thought it was the sea or maybe the time was wrong...I never thought it would be someone else...*you*. You're a selfish, spiteful pig." She spat out the words like poison in her mouth.

I sighed, defeated. "I've tried to spare your feelings. I've tried to be decent. I give up. If you want to hear how he staged a mutiny to save my life, I'll tell you. If you want to hear how he abandoned his crew and sailed across the Caribbean to be with me, you'll have it. I'll tell you about every whisper, every kiss, every second of every day, but what does it matter now? He doesn't love me and he doesn't love you. You're wasting your hate on me and your tears on him."

She rocked back, slammed by my words.

Meg's eyes narrowed. "I trusted you. I'm sorry, but I can't stand to be near you now." She slowly backed away.

"Praise heavens!" I threw up my hands dramatically. "You think it's been easy for me to hear you pining over the man I love—loved—while I sat silently by, trying to spare your feelings? Your leaving is a relief!"

Meg's hands clenched into fists and I was scared she was going to attack me. Her face twisted: rage and disgust and then pain. Her lip quivered and a tear spilled from her eye. She dashed out of the cabin, leaving the door open behind her.

I flopped back on the bed, wallowing in my own humiliation.

I lie there until my cries turned to sobs and then to heaves, purging the poison of the last few weeks. The night grew deeper and deeper and eventually my tears ran dry. Meg didn't return. The cabin door was still ajar from her departure. I saw the glow of a lantern and voices outside my cabin. I strained to hear them.

It was Nicholas. "I don't know what the hell happened, but she's been crying for hours."

I groaned. He'd found Meg and was here to chastise me for upsetting her.

He continued. "Go to her. See what she needs. Make her happy. I hate it when she cries."

"No." It was Skidmore.

I had never heard him refuse Nicholas before. I listened harder.

"Come again?"

"No, *sir*."

"This is an order. Go talk to Tessa." There was undisguised fury in his voice.

My throat went dry. He wasn't talking about Meg—he was talking about me. I was surprised he had even noticed I was upset. How unlike him.

"I won't do it." Skidmore's voice was soft as always, but firm. I could picture him standing his ground, his eyes downcast, his hands wringing in front of him. "Every other day, you have me see to her, just like on the *Banshee*. I'm done following this order. It's your responsibility. You do it."

"How is this my responsibility?" Nicholas was seething with rage.

"The morale of your crew is your responsibility. Not to mention this is all your fault besides."

"I am your superior, Mr. Skidmore, and you are dangerously close to a lashing."

"You won't lash me," Skidmore said. "I have something to say and I'm going to say it. I'm tired of cleaning up yer messes when it comes to her. She's a right decent girl and she don't deserve this." There was a slight pause. "Don't walk away from this," Skidmore continued. I held my breath. I had never heard Skidmore so forceful. I had never heard him say so much at one time. "I'm telling you this as yer friend, Marks. And as my captain, ye ought to be right interested to hear what your first mate has to say."

"Go on," Nicholas huffed.

"You're a naïf."

"You're right, I am interested in this." His voice was dark. I was suddenly very worried for Skidmore.

"That girl in there is in misery. You say you hate it when she cries? Then stop making her cry! Simple as that. What you did tonight was bloody heartless—"

"Me? Heartless? If you knew the half of what she's put me through—"

"Shut your mouth and listen for a festerin' minute!" he bellowed then took a deep breath. "You told me everything, remember? It's been a type of purgatory for ya here with Tessa and De Luca. *I know.* But there are things that *you* don't know. Oh, you should, but you've been paper-skulled enough to let it slip past ya. You constantly send me to see if she is all right. Well, she's not. If ye would use yer sottish brain, you could figure it out for yerself. She ain't here to make your life hell. She doesn't want to be here at all. She doesn't want to be engaged to De Luca. She doesn't want to be trapped with Quin. And least of all, she doesn't want to be abused by you!"

"What do you mean she doesn't want to be engaged to De Luca? I told you what she did—how she begged me to her birthday ball just to flaunt it—"

"Oh, would you put away your pride!" Skidmore exploded. I sat up and gripped the edge of the bed, tense, hopeful, terrified. "Her father arranged the engagement without her consent. She doesn't want it."

"She told you this?"

"*She didn't bloody have to!* Piece it together, Marks. Why else on the night of her engagement would she leave her own celebration and come aboard yer *Freedom*—a place that be special to the both of you—and get so crapulently drunk on rum—a drink she abhors—that she loses consciousness? She didn't know you'd be on this ship. She figured you'd be on the *Seabird*. Those ain't the actions of a woman *flaunting* her engagement. She came here to mourn, Marks. She's sufferin'. And you've been nothin' but a baleful ass. She loves you, or leastways she did. I wouldn't blame her if she hates you for the rest of her days. Is this any way to treat someone who has pledged you her love? Who saved your neck from the gallows? Least of all—is it any way to treat a shipmate?"

There was a long pause. I could imagine a heated stare-down between the two men. Skidmore's voice sounded again, darker than I had ever heard him, but not without sympathy. "You've been a right coward. Dust off your heart, mate. Be decent. It's your responsibility to make the tears stop this time. I'm done with it."

CHAPTER THIRTY-SIX

THE *HEAVE-HO* OF sea chanteys drifted through the overheard boards, waking me. I stretched languidly, my mind blissfully blank. But it only took a few seconds to remember the night before.

I blew out my breath with a groan.

Meg.

Emilio.

Nicholas.

I pulled the covers over my head and hid from the world.

A quarter of an hour later, someone knocked gently on my door. I ignored it. The hinges creaked as it opened.

"Miss Monroe?" It was Skidmore. "Are you awake?"

I flopped the covers back and gave Skidmore my most pitiful look. "Must I get out of bed?"

With a kind smile, he shuffled to me and handed me a tin cup. "Orange juice. Squeezed it myself."

"Thank you." I gulped it down.

"How are you?"

I returned the empty cup "You don't have to look in on me just because Nicholas asked you to."

Skidmore's ruddy face grew redder. "You heard that, eh?"

I nodded. "Thank you, though. For saying what you did."

Skidmore shuffled back, uncomfortable with my praise. "I'd

hoped he would come 'round on his own. I told him to talk with you several times before. He got right livid every time I suggested it. But I couldn't stand it no more. Not after last night. And just so ye know, I'm here for myself right now. I've been worried. When you were late to your post...I don't blame you or nothin', just thought I would pop in."

"I'll survive."

"I can start the fire."

I pulled myself out of bed and wriggled my feet on the floorboards. "Nah. I've got to botch the hardtack at some point. The thought of facing everybody fills me with dread. Everybody but you. I had a bit of a confrontation with Meg last night. I don't know where she slept." I glanced at her empty hammock.

Skidmore cocked his head and sighed. "Ah. That's why she worked through the night."

"What of Emilio? What temper is he in?"

"He's not said much. Sick from too much drink, I think."

I bit my lip, dreading all the explaining I would have to do. "I don't suppose he or the captain were too drunk to remember last night."

Skidmore shrugged noncommittally.

"I guess it's time to face the day. Though I have a mind to fix breakfast and let everyone serve themselves while I return to bed."

He validated the option with a raise of his eyebrows. I walked him to the door of my cabin and thanked him again for the juice. Across the threshold I saw Emilio waiting, his face anxious. He smiled at me tightly and nodded. I offered an embarrassed smile in return and shut the door.

Of all the men on board, Emilio was the only one who managed to keep his manners. Nicholas and Skidmore had no issue entering my cabin without invitation or seeing me in my nightdress. Frankly, I'd given up on many of the rules of propriety as well. Emilio's good breeding ran deep. He was obviously waiting for me, but was too proper to let himself in as Skidmore had done.

I took an uneasy breath. No more dawdling. I padded to the basin and washed myself, rinsed my teeth, and dabbed on my favorite lavender and mint oil. I brushed my hair and framed my face with a braid, letting the rest of it hang in loose chestnut waves. Finally, I shuffled into a sapphire-colored skirt, linen blouse, and a black lace-up vest.

I took a deep breath and opened the door. Emilio was still waiting, his dark eyes expectant.

"Good morning," he said, his voice quiet.

"Good morning."

Meg dropped down the hatch just then, curtly looking at Emilio and completely ignoring me. She pushed past me, her shoulder clipping mine, and went into our cabin. I let out a dreadful sigh.

Emilio cleared his throat. "I know you're on watch, but may I have a moment?"

I closed the cabin door behind me and walked to him, my eyes down. What did he think of me now? I was not the makings of a baroness. I had known it all along, and now he knew it too. I didn't mind him putting me out. It would be a relief to have the charade ended. I simply dreaded the humiliation. At least he was kind enough to do it privately.

"Last night..." Emilio began, fumbling for words, "I should not have drunken like that. I am sorry."

He was apologizing to me? I dared to look at him. He was utterly shamefaced.

"And what Captain Holladay said about you was uncalled for," Emilio said, his eyes contrite. "I should not have allowed it. But I did. I disrespected you last night, Tessa. Can you forgive me?" His face was agonized. I stared back in astonishment. This was not at all what I expected.

"Of course," I whispered.

With a sigh of relief, Emilio grabbed my hands and pressed

my knuckles to his lips. "I am so sorry, *dolcezza*. I will restore your honor. I will challenge the captain to a duel if you wish it."

I balked. "Don't be foolish."

"I was foolish. I wish to make amends."

"It's unnecessary, Emilio." I squeezed his hands. "A duel would serve no one. I overheard Skidmore giving him a thorough reprimand last night. "

Emilio cleared his throat. "I may have reprimanded him myself this morning."

"You didn't!"

He nodded.

"What did you say? What did *he* say?"

"He didn't say much at all. I told him that he is not to talk about my fiancée that way, romantic past or no." Emilio's lips curled into a sheepish smile. So he remembered...and apparently he didn't care.

"Thank you. My honor is completely restored."

"Time for breakfast, then?"

"I suppose." I glanced towards the galley. "Have you seen our good captain?"

"I saw him splicing rope on deck, but that was some time ago."

I relaxed a little. The longer I could avoid Nicholas, the better.

I ventured into the galley—it was thankfully void of Nicholas—and started a pot of mush. Meg sauntered in and snatched a piece of hardtack and an overripe banana but left before I could offer her a hot breakfast. Emilio and Skidmore stayed nearby and I served the three of us as soon as the mush was ready.

I took the bowls from Emilio and Skidmore to the basin and was beginning to clean up when the atmosphere in the galley grew tense. I glanced back to see what the catalyst was. Nicholas was standing in the doorway. He looked terrible. His hair was a windblown mess, his eyes were bloodshot and underscored with shadows, and the scruff on his chin made him look haggard.

"Is breakfast ready? I didn't hear the bell."

Skidmore and Emilio uneasily looked from the captain to me. "Everyone else was right here. I guess I forgot," I answered.

"Might I have some?" He walked towards the table.

I picked up the large pot of mush and when I was certain he was looking, spooned it all into the rubbish bin.

Nicholas scowled. "What the..."

I feigned a look of surprise. "It was tasteless...worthless...rubbish, really." I dropped the pot into the basin with a loud clang.

Nicholas's expression darkened. I was picking a fight I wasn't sure I could win.

He walked towards the pile of hardtack on the counter. Before he could grab a piece, I dumped all of them in the bin on top of the wasted mush.

He raised his eyebrows.

I gave a nonchalant shrug. "They were botched."

"Really?" There was an undercurrent of amusement in his voice. It made me a bit braver.

"The way I see it, if you want the food prepared to your standards, you best do it yourself."

Nicholas shook his head, but there was a ghost of a smile on his lips. "It's only fitting I go hungry after last night. Tessa, I would like to speak with you. Alone." He directed the last word at Emilio and Skidmore.

They both looked at me expectantly. I swallowed hard and nodded. Nicholas escorted them out, managing not to react to their loaded stares. He closed the door behind them.

"Now that we're alone, I'd like to talk candidly with you."

I turned my back on him as I scoured the kettle. "It seems you have no issue speaking candidly, alone or not." I knew I shouldn't antagonize him—he was actually behaving himself for once—but I couldn't help it.

"I've made you miserable, haven't I?" His voice was nearly a whisper.

With my back still turned to him, I muttered, "You flatter yourself."

I steeled myself for a sharp retort, but was only met with silence. I turned around, unsure of what to expect. Nicholas stood on the other side of the counter from me, his hands braced on the countertop. His head was down and he looked up at me through his long eyelashes.

"I've been a baleful ass."

I pressed my lips together to avoid smiling.

"I owe you an apology of epic proportions. I've been selfish and cruel. I'm sorry I have made this harder for you. I'm sorry I haven't listened. I'm sorry I have been spiteful—on more than one occasion. I'm sorry I got drunk last night. I'm sorry I said what I did. I'm sorry I didn't stop when you asked me to. I'm sorry I yelled at you. I'm sorry I forced myself into your work."

This was not some shallow, blanketed apology. I nodded slightly with each acknowledgement of fault.

And then he said, "I'm sorry that I kissed you."

"I'm not," I said quietly, feeling bold.

Nicholas stopped short and cocked his head. I blushed and looked away—my boldness had its limits.

"I want to ask you something, Tessa. And I want you to answer me truthfully. Be as brutal as you must, just be true." He closed his eyes briefly. "Do you love De Luca?"

My answer was quiet but without hesitation. "No."

Nicholas took in a sharp breath. He continued. "Skidmore thinks your engagement to De Luca happened without your consent. Is that so?"

I debated rattling off a smart remark, but the sincerity in Nicholas's eyes dissolved my pride. "Yes," I answered simply.

Pain washed over Nicholas. It was as if that one word had stabbed him in the heart. "Why didn't you tell me?"

I shook my head in disbelief. "When did I have the chance? From the moment you rushed out of the ball, you've not given me the courtesy of a conversation."

Nicholas dropped his head into his hands, his elbows on the counter, his fingers tangling in his hair. "He's a good match for you, though."

"Perhaps he is a *smart* match," I corrected, "but he is not a good match. It matters not. The marriage will not happen."

Nicholas lifted his head. "What do you mean?"

"I do not intend to marry him. I've known it from the moment my father promised my hand against my will."

"De Luca does not know this."

I looked down at my hands, my fingers knotting together. "I didn't fancy breaking the engagement on the ship and being forced to see the man in such confinement for the remainder of the voyage."

"But you didn't mind putting me in that position."

I looked at him achingly then turned my attention back to the stack of dishes. As I poured water over the dirtied bowls, I tried to settle my mind. I still bristled at Nicholas's callousness. If I didn't check myself, this conversation could easily spiral into an ugly war of insults. As gratifying as that sounded, it was not what I wanted, ultimately. Nicholas was here, open and contrite and speaking to me like a human being—the conversation could just as easily build into something I had barely dared dream of.

"You left me." My response was a broken plea, too little, too late.

"I told you, I had a debt to pay."

"You had a job at my father's household. He paid you well. You did not have to leave to earn your money."

His voice was a whisper. "You pushed me away."

I stared at my hands as they trailed through the soapy water. "I know." It was easier to talk to him this way, unable to see the look on his face. "It wasn't fair. I'm so sorry. But when you left…did you ever imagine what that did to me? You took my heart with you. I was gutted. I wept every night. I walked the beach. I lingered in the ketch—"

"The ketch?"

"It reminded me of you."

"So that night of your engagement was not the first time you came here?"

I shook my head. "It was the only way I could feel close to you again."

After a beat, Nicholas's voice took on a new authority. "Stop with the dishes, Tess."

I wiped my hands on a rag and turned to face him, anxiety prickling in my belly. Nicholas stalked around the counter block, a commanding swing to his hips. He closed in on me. I held my breath, my eyes growing wide, as Nicholas lifted his hand to my face and tucked a stray lock of hair behind my ear, his fingers grazing my cheek.

"You told me you loved me once." His voice was tender. He took a deep breath, his eyes soft pools of silver. "Do you still?"

Did I? My mind was momentarily blank. His soft touch on my cheek had seen to that. But then the memories rushed back. His leaving. The abrupt note. Crying alone on the ketch. Discovering he had returned without telling me. His humiliating toast. The days of icy silence on this voyage. I was certain that I hated him.

He had been cruel and I still nursed the wounds. Could I love someone who had broken my trust and hurt me so deeply?

Nicholas's expression recomposed, the vulnerability in his eyes vanishing behind a stony mask. He dropped his hand. I had been quiet too long. "Thank you for the truth. And I'm sorry for my behavior. It's come at a price. I know that. I'll do what I can to earn back your friendship."

He pressed his lips into a thin line and nodded politely, his hair scattering across his forehead. Suddenly I was alone, still fighting my bewilderment, sorting through my feelings for the man who had just disappeared.

CHAPTER THIRTY-SEVEN

A TENUOUS BALANCE FORMED among the crew. Emilio hovered over me possessively since Nicholas was spending more time in the galley with his healing hand. Meg was curt with Nicholas and vicious with me. Skidmore was Skidmore. Solid and steady, never taking sides. I ran to him for solace when everyone else was too much. And Nicholas...as promised, he did what he could to be a friend. It wasn't natural. The ghost of our past romance haunted every conversation, every accidental touch. In a way it was easier to hate him than to pretend to feel nothing for him. My father's words echoed in my mind: *passion knows no bounds*. I had to bind it now, deep in my heart, no more love, no more hate— only a pretense at camaraderie.

With Nicholas helping in the galley, I had more free time. One night when Nicholas was preparing dinner, I found Emilio on the deck at ship's waist patching a sail.

"Would you like some help?"

He looked up in surprise from where he sat on the deck. The slanted evening sun was behind him, igniting his hair in a halo of fire. He smiled with surprise, pleased to see me.

"I would like nothing more."

I sat down across from him and began examining the mountain of canvas between us. "I'm always surprised how heavy sails are." I glanced up at the sails on the mast, weightlessly curving against the power of the wind. "They look as light as clouds up there."

"Here." Emilio helped me find another hole that needed to be mended.

I reached for scissors to cut a patch out of the extra canvas, then threaded my needle. As I started my first stitch, I tried not to compare the differences between sewing sails and sewing human flesh. I distracted myself with conversation.

"Have you decided exactly how to intercept Salazar?" I ventured a look at Emilio. As I expected, he looked wary, as if this were something he should not be speaking about with me.

He concentrated on a line of stitching, then finally answered with a shake of his head. "Whatever we do must be done by force. Salazar knows all of our faces. The captain discussed bringing on more crew for an offensive attack but there isn't room to house anyone. It would be best to return to St. Kitts and rally there. You and I will be back to safety. Your father can advise on the situation. The captain can take the *Seabird* with a full crew and thirty cannons. The entire naval fleet could be on task as well."

"The captain doesn't like this idea?" It seemed sound to me.

There was bitterness in Emilio's voice. "He's certain Salazar will get away. It will take weeks to go to St. Kitts, prepare another ship, then sail back here. Salazar will not have remained in Port Winslow, we won't know where he is, and it could take months to track him down. The captain thinks it is too risky."

That made sense too. I frowned. "So what do we do? Keep pursuing Salazar without a plan?"

Emilio scoffed. There was venom in his voice when he spoke of Nicholas now, an edge that had never been there before he knew of his romantic interest in me. "That is the captain's brilliant notion. He's certain he'll receive some kind of divine epiphany telling him what to do before time is out. He's intent that the way to defeat Salazar is through trickery, not military force. I can't see how it could be done. Salazar keeps that declaration on his person at all times. Someone would have to peel his clothes off to retrieve it. I doubt even his washerwoman has access like that. We'll need an army to get that close."

I gasped and clapped my hand over my mouth. Emilio looked at me in alarm. "I have an idea," I said, letting my hand drop slowly down. "Oh, it's a very, very bad, very stupid idea."

Emilio looked at me quizzically. I slowly shook my head, disbelieving my own irrational thought. It would work, though. It really would. "Get the captain. Get everyone. I know how to get the declaration."

Within ten minutes, the entire crew was in the galley. I helped Nicholas with the final preparations for dinner so we could eat while I explained my idea. After serving up hardtack, salted beef, and pickled vegetables and saying a brief grace over the meal, Nicholas looked at me expectantly.

"Tessa, go ahead," he said.

I tapped the weevils out of a piece of hardtack, took a bite, and slowly chewed it, stalling. I knew that my idea would work, but I also knew it would not be popular. I dreaded Nicholas's and Emilio's reactions.

No one else was eating. Everyone was staring at me. I finally swallowed my food and took a languid sip of watered-down rum. I cleared my throat warily. "We need to get the declaration back from Salazar," I began. Meg's cynical eyes stared at me as if to challenge my mental capacity—I was stating the obvious. "He will not willingly give it up. That leaves us with the option of taking it by force, but his crew outnumbers ours twenty to one. And he has the backing of the French, besides. We lack the resources to recruit a force big enough to challenge him without losing precious time."

I paused to gauge the expressions around the room. Nicholas was nodding with encouragement, ready to hear what I had to say. Skidmore was listening politely. Meg simply looked angry to have to be in the same room with me. Emilio's expression tripped me for a moment. His eyes held a strange mix of horror and esteem, as if he couldn't believe I understood such things

I tried to ignore Emilio's unnerving expression. I took another drink and continued. "We cannot gather an army to take Salazar on by force. But obtaining a single piece of paper does not need to take an army." I paused and steadied my nerves. I avoided Emilio's stricken gaze and focused on Nicholas, who was assessing my words more like a general rather than a would-be suitor. "All we need is a single person who can get close enough to Salazar, physically close enough, to simply take the paper away."

Emilio spoke. "Pray tell, how would this one person simply take the declaration from him?"

I sheepishly met Emilio's antagonizing stare. "You actually inspired the idea when you said someone would have to peel his clothes off him."

Emilio's brow furrowed. "None of us could do such a thing. He knows us." Emilio gestured to the crew. "His guards would shoot us before we could get within twenty paces of him."

I held up a finger to silence Emilio. "Salazar doesn't know me," I said quietly. Nicholas's eyes narrowed. Meg looked exasperated. Emilio still looked angry and dismayed. I went on. "Emilio mentioned that Salazar is always guarded. Not always. I know Port Winslow. It's a pirate haven that caters to pirate appetites."

Nicholas exhaled deeply and rocked back in his chair. He understood. Our eyes met and his jaw tensed. I quickly looked away. "There is a bordello there. Salazar will certainly pay a visit, will he not?" I looked around expectantly. No one disagreed with me, though Nicholas was looking down. "I know the proprietor. I am certain that she would allow me to pose as...as..." I looked at my hands twisting in my lap, "as a prostitute."

Disapproval rippled through the crew. I could not show any doubt or weakness. I forced my chin up and made steady eye contact. "Salazar and I would be alone. He would not have his guards with him. I would be close enough to touch him. In fact, I would be expected to touch him. I could remove his jacket, reach into his pocket, and retrieve the declaration without his knowledge. He'd be more than willing to let me, uh, peel his clothes off him. No force necessary."

I folded my hands in my lap and kept my posture dignified, waiting for the censure that was bound to erupt.

Emilio barked out a derisive laugh. "You cannot be serious!"

Skidmore slowly shook his head.

When Nicholas finally looked at me, his expression was pained.

"You know it would work," I quietly said to him. He pinched the bridge of his nose.

Emilio gesticulated wildly. "Captain! Did you hear her? It's preposterous. You should not let her entertain such notions. She is a *lady*! She has no mind for such things."

Nicholas swung his scorching gaze on to Emilio. "How very antediluvian of you. I am not sure *you* have a mind for such things." He turned his attention back to me. "Tessa, this plan is—"

"I know."

"—pure genius," he finished, surprising me. "But it's damn risky."

I nodded knowingly.

He shook his head. "I can't allow it."

"Thank you!" Emilio slammed his hands on the table, rattling the dishes.

I entreated Nicholas with my eyes. "It will work."

"Aye. Maybe. But I will not put you in that position."

"I'm offering! It will work. It's so *simple*!"

"Make someone else do it." Meg piped in.

"You couldn't," I said. "Salazar knows you."

Meg rolled her eyes. "Not me. Someone *else*. One of the regular prostitutes who know how to handle themselves around greedy men. Charlotte."

I cringed at the name of the prostitute who had fancied Nicholas.

Nicholas cocked his head and raised his brows.

"I cannot believe you are considering this catastrophe!" Emilio cried.

Nicholas held up his hands in a calming gesture. "We still have days to decide how we want to proceed. Tessa's idea is just that—an idea. If nothing else, it has shown us a new way to approach this problem. We don't need numbers and force. We simply need stealth. Thank you, Tessa, for sharing your idea. It's clever, really, but we'll find a way that's less risky."

I nodded politely and returned to my dinner, feeling like a small child who had been indulged by adults, then put away to bed.

After everyone had finished eating, Emilio asked if I would like to help him finish mending the sails. I politely declined, saying I needed to help with galley duties. In truth, I was too offended by his disbelief in me to be close to him. Besides, I wanted to speak with Nicholas.

Emilio and Skidmore left. Meg sidled up against Nicholas by the counter. "Here, let me do it. You'll hurt your hand." She grabbed a jar of marmalade from him and began to twist on the lid. Before my brain had time to process what I was doing, I closed the distance between us and snatched the jar from her. Her hazel eyes narrowed.

I closed the jar with a solid crank of my wrist. "Meg, the galley is already double-staffed. It's crowded. Aren't you on watch?"

She gave me a withering glare and stalked away without saying a word.

"That was rude," Nicholas mumbled.

"She doesn't need to drape herself on you like that."

Nicholas looked at me with poorly hidden amusement. "What concern do you have with Quin's draping habits anyhow?"

I looked at him sternly. "I don't want to talk about her. I want to talk about my idea."

"Tessa, we already discussed it."

"No, we didn't. You brushed it aside to appease Emilio." Nicholas shook his head but I cut him off before he could say anything. "You know it will work. You know that we don't have anything better."

"I'm the captain and I say no."

"You haven't even considered it!" I cried. "It's a good plan!"

"Perhaps if there were someone else…"

"Why? Why does that matter? I am volunteering. I am making a choice to do something valiant to save the world as we know it."

"I don't care."

"Why should you?" I rubbed my hands across my face. "Why should anyone care what I want?"

My words took him by surprise. His mouth popped open and it was a beat before he could find words. "I care what you want."

"No you don't. No one does."

He looked hurt. I continued on in explanation. "My sham of an engagement. You accepting the bloody Letter of Marque. My imprisonment here. The willful way you ignored me. Your presence here in the galley. These things are just forced on me, no consideration of what I want." Feelings that I didn't realize were related suddenly collided. The way I bowed to society's expectations and forsook Nicholas. The way he left me. The way my father changed the subject whenever he was around me. The way Emilio treated me as though I were some exotic pet he had captured for no other reason than to show off to his rich friends.

My words burst out like a waterfall. "I am so tired of being treated like some inept and fragile little thing. I might not be smart or strong or very useful, but I ought to be able to make my own decisions. I have thoughts and passions and hates and likes. Isn't it my right to act on them? I might be irrational. I might make mistakes. But bloody hell, can't someone please allow me my agency for once?"

"I do not mean to make you feel as if I am takin' away your agency," Nicholas said calmly. "I have to think of the entire crew. And the mission as a whole."

"I know you do," I said, embarrassed by my outburst. "I should not have made this about me. I know you have a responsibility to all of us. But this plan could save hundreds of lives."

"It's an abhorrent idea!" he pleaded.

"I know! But it's the best chance we have."

"It's dangerous," Nicholas said, as if it settled everything. He turned his back on me and piled dishes into the basin.

I touched his elbow. He glanced over his shoulder at me. "It's so simple, Nick. It's simple enough to work. And we can control the risk. You and Skidmore and everyone will be within earshot. Salazar will never suspect me."

"Until he sees you steal the piece of paper he has been guarding like treasure for the past month. If things go wrong, he could kill you. If nothing else, he'll think you're a prostitute and he'll—"

"You'll prepare me."

"There is no preparation for that!" Nicholas threw a large stack of dishes in the basin with a clatter.

I pulled his shoulder, forcing him to turn and face me. "Tell me what you think we should do instead? We are sailing in his path right now, outnumbered. A target. The way I see it, if we don't try this, we're facing death anyway."

His lips twitched, his eyes narrowed. "Charlotte might help."

"You'd rather risk her life over mine?" I asked with disgust, but the second I said it, I knew he would. "The danger to her is no less than it would be for me."

"She's used to men like that. She can stand her ground against him."

I rolled my eyes. "It won't even come to that. I will find the paper. I will leave *immediately*. You will be right on the other side of the door with your flintlock at the ready. You can prepare me. Teach me to fight and use a weapon. We have nearly a week to get me ready. With Charlotte, you'd only have a day."

Something shifted in Nicholas's eyes. He stepped back suddenly. "Are you doing this to retaliate?"

"Retaliate? For what?" I couldn't even fathom the question—or the motives for it.

Within a split second, his impassive expression returned. "Salazar knows me well. Knows me and Skidmore and De Luca and Meg. If he saw any of us, his suspicions would be raised. I have crossed him—he might kill me on the spot."

"That's the beauty of this plan. There is no reason for any of you to have contact with him. Only me. He'll literally put the declaration in my hands and I'll simply walk away. You and everyone else can be hiding around corners with weapons if it makes you feel better, but Salazar won't even see any of you."

"I do not like the idea," he said coolly.

I leveled my gaze at him, even though I was wilting inside. "I don't either."

"Then why are we having this discussion?"

"Because it might be the only way."

Nicholas frowned.

"Put aside your emotions. Think like a captain. How else will any of us get in a position where we can touch him? Rifle through his clothing? With his consent?"

My words had hit a chink in his armored façade; he began thinking about the plan, logically. I saw the light in his eyes that was always there when he was plotting against a Goliath. He fancied impossible situations. I briefly wondered if that's why he had ever fancied me. I pushed aside the thought and seized this moment of true consideration.

"I can do this," I said, my voice ringing strong. I could see that he was warring with himself. "All I ask is that you think hard about it, Captain."

He rolled his eyes at the title but nodded. "Aye. 'Tis an ingenious strategy. We'll think of something else, certainly, but I promise to consider it."

"Good." I smiled and began to dry the dishes.

Picking up a fresh towel, Nicholas joined me. "Now, luv, you never answered my question. What care do you have where Quin drapes herself?"

CHAPTER THIRTY-EIGHT

A WHISPER OF A breeze tousled my hair, my locks taking on a hue of auburn in the sun's last rays. I sat on the main deck with a book on my lap, the words of the pages holding little interest for me. The sky held my attention instead. Cloudless and aquamarine overhead, it faded into shades of cobalt framed by a burning stripe of gold at the horizon. The crests of the waves reflected the impending sunset, the water stretching before me like an army of flaming torches. I inspected each hue of the sky and the sea, how everything was blue but so much more than that at the same time. I imagined how I would capture such a sight if I had my watercolors before me. How easy it would be to blend one shade into the next.

A sword clattered across the desk, skidding towards me.

"Whoa, Tess! Watch out!"

I stuck my leg out and stopped the weapon with my foot. Nicholas jogged across the deck to retrieve it. Still admiring the artistic light of the evening, I studied him. His hair was damp with sweat and hung in his eyes; his open shirt revealed a smattering of soft chest hair; his shoulders were broad and powerful; yet his body lean and graceful; the magic glow of twilight seemed to make the angles of his face even more dramatic. What I wouldn't have given for a charcoal and easel at that moment to capture his haphazard beauty.

"Nice reflex." Nicholas grinned boyishly and picked up his sword then ran back towards the ship's waist. My eyes followed him as he returned to his fencing match with Skidmore. I smiled at his carefree fun. I hadn't seen him like this since we'd arrived at St. Kitts. My smile grew sad, thinking of my part in his recent stormy tempers.

"I disarmed you fair!" Skidmore said.

"My hand slipped."

Skidmore shook his head. He was smiling. I'd seen enough of their fencing to know that Skidmore was better with the blade. Nicholas's skill was not to be underestimated, but when he was flustered, he opted for an ingenious way out, whether it was climbing into the ratlines, ducking under a swinging boom, throwing a punch, or pulling his pistol. Skidmore called him a cheat because he didn't fence his way out of a pinch. Nicholas said it was smart tactics.

"Let's go again!" Nicholas said breathlessly.

Emilio and Meg joined Nicholas and Skidmore with raised swords. "*En garde!*" Emilio shouted. They all assumed their defensive positions. "*Prêt!*" They raised their blades above them, the soft evening light glinting on the sharp metal. "*Allez!*"

With the sharp sound of metal ringing against metal, the swords came down and the fighters parried. Shouts and laughs floated above them, swallowed up by the evening sky. Meg was disarmed first, her sword flying high and bouncing off the ratlines. They laughed as it plummeted back down. I cringed, uncomfortable with how unsafe this was. That sword could have impaled somebody. Meg reclaimed her weapon and stepped out of the fray.

Emilio would be next, I thought. He knew fencing well enough. He insisted on calling out the French fencing terms. The pirates made no bother with such formalities. Their formations weren't stringent and Emilio often whined of their ad hoc use of thrusts and lunges. For Emilio, fencing was a rich boy's sport; for Nicholas and Skidmore, fencing was life and death.

"Let's get Skidmore," Emilio said, standing next to Nicholas. Shoulder to shoulder, the two of them advanced on Skidmore. I hadn't seen Nicholas unite against Skidmore before. Sometimes it seemed he and Skidmore took on Emilio together, making swift work of dispatching his weapon, then enjoying a more equally matched duel with the just the two of them. I leaned forward and watched the new scenario intently.

Skidmore beckoned them with glee, holding off the dual onslaught for an impressive length of time. But when he was cornered at the bow, Nicholas disarmed him with a quick flick of his wrist. Instantly, the captain whirled on the baron and disarmed him in two quick moves.

Nicholas raised his arms over his head, his sword piercing the sky, and cried, "Hail the captain!"

I rolled my eyes. He had the sense of an immature boy! I cocked my head and watched his juvenile bravado as he strutted in front of the losers and my heart suddenly clenched. He'd never had a boyhood. It had been stolen from him. He was grasping for bits of it now.

"Again!"

The cry startled me from my sad thoughts. It was Emilio, his sword already hoisted in front of him.

Nicholas turned in surprise to find the point of Emilio's weapon leveled at his chest. "You want another go?" Nicholas gestured to Skidmore and Meg.

Emilio was panting. "Just us. *En garde.*"

Nicholas took his position.

"*Prêt. Allez.*"

Their swords crashed. Nicholas danced around Emilio sinuously, parrying every thrust and lunge. He grabbed a line and swung himself over Emilio's head, then came down, taking Emilio's sword with him.

Emilio was heaving for breath, his hair hanging in his eyes like streaks of ink. "Again," he said, claiming his weapon once more.

Nicholas furrowed his brows, a look of bewildered mirth in his eyes. He took his position.

"*En garde,*" Emilio choked out between breaths. Before he could issue the other commands, Nicholas advanced. Emilio parried and lunged, an aggressive assault. Nicholas danced backwards to avoid the sharp tip of Emilio's blade.

I stood, letting the book slide from my lap, and slowly stepped closer for a better view. The sky had erupted into a blaze of orange fire, igniting the fencing opponents with a sinister red light. The look of boyish bravado was still evident in Nicholas's eyes. Emilio's eyes were different. They blazed with a ferocity that scared me.

Emilio advanced with a cross over, then taunted Nicholas with a well-crafted feint. Nicholas parried and Emilio deceived, a direct lunge sending Emilio's blade straight at Nicholas's gut.

I gasped, my hands flying to my mouth.

Nicholas drew back, arms in the air, and pivoted, but he wasn't quick enough to avoid Emilio's sword. A red line appeared on his shirt where the tip had glanced him. Emilio halted at the sight of the blood and Nicholas took the advantage, disarming his opponent. With his opponent neutralized, Nicholas dropped his sword and pulled up his shirt.

I crowded closer, my hands still at my face. The wound was long and shallow, nothing more than a scratch. It had already stopped bleeding. I looked at Emilio, aghast at what he had done.

"So sorry," he panted.

"These things happen." Nicholas shrugged, quick to forgive, but I still saw the darkness in Emilio's eyes.

"Are you quite finished?" I picked up Emilio's sword. "I think that's enough peacockery for one night."

Nicholas smirked at me and smoothed his shirt down. "Are you ready for a bout, luv?" He clanked the tip of his cutlass against the sword I casually held. I felt it vibrate up my arm.

My first instinct was to shrink back, but I couldn't resist the playful challenge in Nicholas's eyes. *"En garde."* I smiled, sinking into the defensive beginning position I had seen the others use.

His lips pulled up in a surprised half smile. *"En garde,"* he repeated, his eyes as golden as a cat's from the light of the setting sun.

He held steady and waited for me to initiate. I lunged awkwardly, thrusting my blade at him. He blocked me easily but offered me an encouraging smile. I tried again. Again, he blocked me.

I sighed in frustration.

"You're doing well, luv. Come at me again."

I smirked. "I see you've decided to train me." I advanced with two successive lunges. Nicholas blocked them both but was a bit surprised by the second thrust.

His eyes sparked at my words. He advanced on me, slowly and deliberately, giving me time to deflect his blade with my own.

Before I knew what was happening, another sword was in the mix, clattering against Nicholas's blade and disarming him.

Emilio had grabbed Meg's sword from her. Nicholas looked at him incredulously.

"That was bloody dangerous," he said to Emilio, gesturing at me.

"I wasn't finished." Emilio aimed to sound playful, but there was challenge in his voice. He tossed the sword back to Meg, then grabbed his weapon from my hands.

Nicholas slowly crouched to retrieve his cutlass, never letting his eyes stray from Emilio. I stepped back, wary of the tension that thickened around the men. As soon as Nicholas had his fingers wrapped around the hilt of his cutlass, he sprang into action without any formalities, his eyes mirroring the ferocity in Emilio's.

"Nicholas!" I hissed. Emilio had goaded him, to be sure, but Nicholas was far more dangerous behind a blade. If his emotions were misaligned, real blood would be spilt.

The blades clashed with force. I stepped back again.

Emilio slashed at Nicholas in a frenzy, eyes wide, teeth clenched. Both hands on the hilt, he chopped down. Nicholas cursed as he threw his blade above his head and blocked the blow. With equal fervor, he advanced on Emilio, his movements deft and deliberate.

"Nick, no!" I cried again. I looked at Skidmore, my eyes begging him to do something.

"Marks, easy." Skidmore called.

Nicholas pressed Emilio against the rail and clutched the front of his shirt. "Yield."

"No," Emilio panted. "I will disarm you." He launched himself forward and Nicholas staggered back. The blades ground together, their screeching raising chills on my scalp.

No longer playful, Nicholas unleashed all his skill on Emilio, a flurry of sliver glinting in the dusk. Emilio's fighting style grew more desperate. Gone was the elegance of his formal training. He was out for blood.

"Emilio, stop!" I cried.

He countered violently, his blade chopping heavily against Nicholas's parries. "I will disarm you." He emphasized each word. He jockeyed for a change of engagement, then with a compound attack, he spun wildly and thrust his blade at Nicholas's sword hand.

Nicholas swore loudly as Emilio's blade drew blood, but he did not drop his cutlass. Emilio cursed in turn—the first time I had ever heard him say anything profane—and threw himself at Nicholas. Nicholas was distracted, looking at his cut, and did not have time to dodge. Instead, he threw his shoulder forward and caught Emilio in the chest. In an instant both weapons were cast aside and they were brawling.

Skidmore rushed forward but he was too late. Nicholas landed a punch on Emilio's face and sent him sprawling on his backside.

Nicholas shook his fist out. He stared at Emilio in shock. Emilio stared back, blood spurting from his nose. The frenzied look in his eyes had vanished. He looked as shocked as Nicholas.

"I'm sorry, Captain. I do not know what overcame me."

Nicholas flexed his fingers, still working the pain out of his knuckles. "Work it off, sailor. Get cleaned up, then pump the bilge. Dry."

Emilio lowered his eyes and nodded without retort.

I looked back and forth between them, mystified by what I had just witnessed. I was furious with both of them.

I watched as Nicholas examined his latest wound. The cut stretched across the back of his wrist. It was sticky with blood, but he still had use of his hand and the bleeding wasn't life threatening. Satisfied that it was not a mortal injury, I offered my hand to Emilio. "Come. I'll help you clean up."

He was utterly disgraced. He didn't take my hand but stood up and followed me down the ladder into the galley. He sat at the table while I fetched the medical crate.

I handed Emilio a rag for his nosebleed. "Tilt your head back. Pinch your nose."

I found a clean shirt in his trunk. When I returned, his nose had stopped bleeding. Still shamefaced, Emilio avoided my gaze as I dampened a fresh rag and mopped away the drying blood on his lips and chin. I was gentle but not compassionate.

"What happened up there?" I finally asked. "Were you possessed?"

Emilio shook his head and cast his eyes down. "I don't know."

"You shouldn't have done that. It was ridiculous. Nicholas has a temper. You are fortunate he did not break your nose."

Emilio scoffed, finally looking at me. There was a new arrogance to his countenance I had not seen before.

"He's a coward. Like Skidmore says, he won't fight out of a tough situation. He turns to other methods. Like punching."

I remembered Emilio's delusional assault. What else was

Nicholas supposed to do? I wanted to chastise Emilio, but I held my tongue.

I held the clean shirt out. "Bring me your soiled shirt. I'll see if I can soak the blood out."

Emilio took the clean shirt and left the galley. I cleaned up the dirty rags. A moment later he returned with his bloodied shirt. I poured water in the basin and began to scrub the shirt with lye soap.

"Tessa."

I hadn't realized he was still in the galley. "Yes?"

"I want you to wear your ring."

I stilled. "It is so precious. I do not want to risk damage to it."

"I want you to wear it."

I gave him a pleading look and gestured to the sink. "All day I scrub things, my hands in filthy water…"

"Take it off when you are washing clothing or dishes if you want. But other than that…I gave it to you for a reason. I want you to wear it."

I sighed. How could I tell him how uncomfortable it made me?

He prickled at my sigh. "Is there a problem? Do you not want to wear it?"

"It's the most valuable thing anyone has ever given me," I answered honestly. "I worry about it in this environment, that's all."

"If it gets damaged, I will buy you a new one. Now you have nothing to worry about. Is it in your cabin?"

"Yes."

He crossed to the door and waited expectantly. I resisted the urge to sigh again, dried my hands, then went to my cabin with Emilio following like a shadow.

I retrieved the ring from the bottom drawer of my chest.

"May I?"

I passed him the ring. As he picked up my hand and slipped it on my fourth finger, he relaxed. He brought my hand to his mouth and kissed the ring. "Mine," he softly said.

"I need to tend to your shirt."

Nicholas dropped down the ladder. His expression was cold.

"I should retreat to the bilge," Emilio said, gauging the captain's face coolly.

I smiled tightly and watched Emilio disappear into the foulest part of the ship. In the foyer, Nicholas went to the table, browsing his ledgers. A half-dozen lanterns blazed from hooks in the bulkheads, bathing the room in a golden glow.

"How are you?" I asked, quietly approaching.

"Hmm?" Nicholas turned towards me.

"Your wrist?"

Nicholas examined it at arm's length. "'Tis fine."

I knew better than to trust his assessments of personal injury. I grabbed his hand and pulled it into the light. Nicholas winced. "Sorry," I muttered halfheartedly. I realized I was still angry with him.

It had stopped bleeding. It could use a good washing, but he would be fine. My eyes drifted to the wound on his stomach, just below his baldric. I reached forward with my left hand, my fingers skimming the dried blood on his shirt and his hard flesh underneath. He flexed under my touch.

As I was about to pull my hand away, Nicholas grabbed it and grinned widely. "He asked you to wear the ring." It was a statement, not a question.

"What of it?" I couldn't understand why he would be smiling over such a thing.

Still holding my hand, Nicholas looked into my eyes. "What happened on deck—that was about you, you know."

I blinked in shock. "Emilio was just tired of you winning all the time."

"Exactly."

I blushed and pulled my hand away. "You should not have hit him."

"I had to defend myself." He held up his wrist to remind me of the cut.

I sighed. "You didn't have to punch him in the face. You're much stronger."

Nicholas beamed.

I glared at him. "That was not a compliment."

"If that's what you think, then you, luv, do not know the nature of a compliment."

I rolled my eyes and Nicholas laughed loudly. It was a sound I had missed. Playful banter had been in short supply.

"You did well with the blade," he said. "I was impressed."

"You should teach me."

His eyebrows shot up.

"It would be part of my preparations to intercept Salazar."

He shuffled back a step and raked his hands through his hair. He looked at me through his lashes, a strange pleading in his eyes. He knew this plan would work, but he could never ask it of me.

"I can do this. You can train me."

He shook his head. "You could get hurt."

"We will *all* get hurt if we try some brazen attack. Or if we do nothing and the world falls to war. Who's to say I won't die some horrible death then?"

His face twisted.

"This is worth trying. Trust me to do this. Let me choose my fate."

Nicholas still stood frozen, staring at me with an unguarded expression. I was surprised at the pleasure I felt seeing the worry etched in his face—he cared about me.

"Be honest," I prodded. "Do you think me incapable of this? Will I not learn the training? Will I cower and fold?"

"No."

"You're worried about Salazar."

"Of course!" he snapped, his jaw tense.

"He is what we worry about then. Not me. *Trust me to do this*. First thing tomorrow, we will begin. How much time do we have?"

"Four days to Port Winslow, if the wind holds."

"It's settled," I said, knowing that Nicholas hadn't truly

agreed to anything. "Tomorrow after breakfast, we'll begin."

Nicholas scrunched his eyes shut and pinched the bridge of his nose. He opened his mouth but I cut him off.

"You will train me to the best of your abilities. If you have doubts, you will ignore them. You will not tolerate doubts from the crew. I cannot do this without you, Captain. You cannot fail me."

"Never." His voice was husky. "I swear it."

I nodded, my façade slowly melting. I knew this had to happen but I was terrified. I let my vulnerability show only because I knew I could now, but only with Nicholas. "I need you," I whispered hoarsely.

Nicholas barreled towards me, as if my confession had dissolved the walls holding him frozen. He engulfed me in his arms, his nose buried in my hair. "I will not fail you. Not again."

Everything about him overwhelmed me. His warmth, his arms around me, his breath in my hair, his smell, his words. Tears threatened at the back of my eyes. He radiated compassion and it warmed the parts of my heart I thought were frostbitten and dead. My arms rose of their own will, holding Nicholas to me. I balled my hands into fists against his back to prevent them from twining into his hair and pulling him into a more intimate embrace.

But, really, could anything be more intimate? His oath, his body against mine, his heart thudding next to my cheek.

I dreaded moving and breaking the precious contact I finally had with him. My breathing was ragged and I felt as though my legs would give way any second. Nicholas pulled back and looked at me with a longing I relished. His thumb skimmed my bottom lip. I held my breath. "How is it that you can rattle me so? No one has ever made me so crazy before. I cannot trust my judgment around you."

I took a depth breath, feeling just as rattled as he claimed to be.

He tilted his head, burnished tendrils of hair hanging in his eyes. "Your insane plan is against my better judgment, but seeing as I have so little when it comes to you, I default to your judgment. Is this what you want?"

My breathing hitched, my eyes wide. I searched his face, dreaming that his words meant something more than an attempt to keep me from dying. He released me with a sad smile and pushed the hair out of his eyes. I nodded.

"Then we'll begin tomorrow. I vow to give you all that I can. All that I am. My pistol. My sword. My life."

CHAPTER THIRTY-NINE

IN MY DREAM, I was in the bordello. Instead of doors, each room had bars. Dark sinister eyes loomed before me. I knew they belonged to Salazar. I knew what I had to do. He clanked a key against the bars and let himself in. His breath reeked of rum. It made me sick and I vomited. I vomited blood. Enough to fill the entire room and I was drowning in it.

I awoke gasping. My blood pounded in my ears and a thin sheen of sweat plastered my hair to the back of my neck. I sat up and rubbed my face with my hands. Meg's soft snoring drifted from the hammock. An opalescent glow came in through the portholes. It was early. Almost dawn.

Still shaken from my dream, I staggered to the galley to brew a cup of tea. I didn't bother to change my nightgown—it was too early for that. I would dress before serving breakfast to the others. With my cup of tea, I ventured upstairs. My eyes swept the deck. No one was immediately visible, though I didn't trust my eyesight in the predawn glow.

My muslin nightgown was useless against the night breeze. I pulled the long sleeves down over my hands to keep them warm and wished I had stockings or even shoes as a barrier against the chilling sea spray that misted on deck.

My dream was an obvious response to my plan to thwart

Salazar. Could I truly follow through with it? I had sworn to Nicholas I could. In that moment, I believed myself. But now I wondered. It would be like going back into the brig with Wrack, the pirate who attacked me on the *Banshee*. I shuddered.

"Cold?"

I whirled around, tea spilling on the sleeve of my nightgown. Emilio was behind me. I felt a stitch of disappointment and realized I had secretly hoped he was Nicholas.

"A little."

Emilio draped a jacket over my shoulders. It was still warm from his body. "You shouldn't be out here undressed."

I was taken aback by the tone of his voice. His statement wasn't concern—it was censure.

I frowned to myself. This was where I was at odds with myself. I had been raised a proper lady, one who would shun ever being seen underdressed by anyone, especially a suitor. At sea, though, those rules didn't seem to apply. It wasn't just because I was so comfortable with Nicholas. If it were only him, I would still be shy and reserved around Skidmore and Meg and Emilio, too. But I wasn't. As Nicholas had explained to me so long ago, life at sea was free from the social conventions I was used to. And I obviously did not hesitate to shirk them. I couldn't blame Emilio for being appalled at my transition. Any more than I could blame Nicholas for being upset by the way I had fallen back into the social constructs of St. Kitts. Why was it so easy for me to simply slip in and out of these roles? Did this make me a hypocrite? The thought was uncomfortable. I didn't know the answer.

"My dear Tessa." Emilio played with a lock of my hair blowing in the wind. "I cannot wait to make you mine. We'll be married within the month and I'll finally be able to keep you safe."

I raised an eyebrow. "What makes you think things will be any different then?"

"You'll be my wife," he said proudly.

I snorted. "Again, I ask, what makes you think things will be any different then?"

His expression was bemused; he was utterly lost at my question. My heart sank. I had once thought that Emilio was freer than other men of his status. I was wrong. I turned away from him and focused my gaze on the slate-grey morning. The color of the sea made me think of Nicholas's eyes. "When we met, you told me never to hold back. I thought you appreciated that about me."

"*Certo.* Sometimes, though..." he trailed off.

"Tell me."

"I think that you are like an ocean wave. Fierce and unpredictable. I fear that you might pull me under, drown me." He turned me towards him and cupped my chin with his hand. "I want to keep you safe."

"Making me your wife won't change who I am. It won't keep me any safer."

"I know," he murmured softly, then kissed me very gently on my lips. "I fear that, like an ocean wave, you'll career into some unforeseen reef and break yourself upon it."

A sad smile spread on my lips. I saw myself as Emilio saw me. It was the same way I saw Nicholas. As something wild and free and majestic, yet dangerous in spite of its glory. But the difference between Emilio and me was that I never wanted to tame Nicholas. And Emilio wanted nothing more than to lock me away.

I touched his face. A painful realization hit me. "You do love me, don't you?" The words fell from my mouth quietly before I could stop them. I was a risk for him—for his status, for his heart—but he thought me worthy of it. I could see it in his eyes.

Emilio caught my hand and brought it to his lips where he kissed my palm. "Yes. I thought you knew. I'm sorry you had to ask. It means I've failed you."

His words hurtled through me. *I'm sorry you had to ask. It means I've failed you.* They were the words I should have said to Nicholas when he asked if I still loved him. Of course I did. There had been moments I was certain I hated him. But hate and love were two sides of the same coin. My hate, my pain, my resentment did not lessen my love. Like bold shadows cast by the noonday sun, they somehow defined the light with their presence.

I had always known that I would break the engagement. In that moment, I realized I would also break Emilio's heart. My own heart wrenched within me. My fingers traced the bow of his lips. I considered telling him then. Instead, I said, "No ocean wave survives the shore."

* * * * *

The silence was crushing. I knew it would not last. I kept my eyes locked on Nicholas. He stood at the head of the table, his posture powerful and casual simultaneously, a glint in his eyes. I wanted to stare at my hands knotting in my lap, but looking down would make me appear uncertain, and I could not afford to look weak.

"This is madness," Emilio whispered, a shred of control barely holding his words together. I could feel his fury. I dared not look at him.

I was waiting for Nicholas's temper to ignite. I watched closely for the flare of his nostrils, the bunching of a fist, or the flexing of his jaw—clues I had become very familiar with—but saw none of that. He had prepared for Emilio's reaction and kept a cold front against the baron's hostility. I had to do the same.

"It's decided," Nicholas said evenly, his hands slung on his hips.

Emilio's voice rose. "You are abusing your position as captain. You're power hungry and it has made you stupid."

Nicholas cocked his head, a little smile breaking through his stoic expression. "I thank you for your opinion, sailor. But your usefulness to this mission has been exhausted."

"This is asinine!" Emilio stood violently, his chair screeching against the floor. I jumped, my heart rate spiking. "You ought to be protecting this girl," he threw his hand in my direction, "not sending her to her death!"

"Sit down, De Luca," Nicholas said. He sounded bored. How did he do that?

"Dammit, Holladay!" Emilio pounded his fists on the table. I jumped again. "You are insane with jealousy!"

Nicholas's eyebrows shot up. "Explain yourself." His tone was still calm but held an edge.

"You had feelings for the girl. She said you developed a *familial* compassion towards one another," his words were heavy with sarcasm, "though I know your feelings were beyond that. Whatever you had with Miss Monroe is threatened now because *I* have been granted her hand in marriage. And now you are seeking your retribution through her. It's selfish and stupid."

The muscles in Nicholas's jaw rippled.

Emilio's tone softened to a plea. "I implore you now to resurrect those feelings. If you cared for her at all, you would not allow her to do this."

Nicholas leaned upon the table and met Emilio eye to eye, his gaze burning with barely controlled rage. "You dare challenge my feelings for the girl? My feelings—familial or other—and my respect for *her* feelings are the reasons why I will allow Miss Monroe to make her own decision—as suicidal as it may be."

Emilio and Nicholas glowered without wavering for several excruciating heartbeats. I clenched the edge of the table, the band of my engagement ring pinching my finger. Finally, Emilio broke and huffed. "I cannot condone this," he retorted before turning away.

With little patience in his voice, Nicholas turned to me. "Tessa. Understand that I do not like this plan. Not in the least. I do not recommend it. *I do not like it.*" I tried to interrupt. Nicholas silenced me with a glare. "However, I know you are capable of this. You are strong. And this is the best chance we have. I trust you." Despite the vitriol in his voice, his words were reassuring. "Before you commit to this, think of what could happen if things do not go as planned."

"I have," I insisted in a small voice.

"No, Tessa," Nicholas snapped. "Imagine it. Imagine what will happen to you. Close your eyes and picture what he will do to you."

Emilio blanched at Nicholas's command.

Unbidden images of Wrack's assault resurfaced. I closed my eyes against the memory, knowing I was putting myself in a cage with another shark. Willingly, this time. I swallowed, my mouth suddenly dry.

Emilio shook his head violently. "You cannot let her do this, Captain. Have you no sense?"

Nicholas peered at me, his steely eyes fixed to mine. An entire conversation seemed to transpire through our eye contact. With just his look, Nicholas was telling me how much he hated this idea and how, as captain, he could forbid it, but that he would not take away my agency and he would support me in every way he could.

"I can do this," I insisted, my voice stronger than before.

"Tessa, please!" Emilio hissed.

Neither of us paid Emilio heed, our eyes still connected. I reassured Nicholas silently and his eyes transformed from a beseeching gaze to a resolved stare. "Miss Monroe has made her decision."

Emilio stormed towards the galley door. "I cannot be part of this."

"Then don't be," Nicholas said haughtily, his eyes sliding to the baron. "The least I can do—any of us can do—is to prepare her for what lies ahead, ensuring her safety and the success of the mission. If your disdain for the plan hampers your ability to contribute, by all means, leave."

Emilio hesitated at the door. Uncertainty flickered in his eyes. He wheeled back at Nicholas. "I understand what you are trying to do as captain. But Nicholas, as your friend, as a dear friend of my fiancée, I implore you: find another way."

"My orders stand, sailor," Nicholas answered, his voice dangerously calm and quiet.

Desperate, Emilio turned his efforts to me. "This is madness, Tessa. You can't do this."

"Actually, I can."

"I won't allow it. As your fiancé, I forbid—"

"You are not my husband!" I erupted. "You are not my father! And you're not my captain! You cannot forbid me to do this—or anything for that matter."

"It would serve you well to remember your place," Emilio growled darkly.

He did not like being challenged.

Neither did I.

I knotted my shaking hands so they would not belie my icy façade. "The decision has been made, my lord, and it would serve you well to mind your threats." I turned my attention towards Nicholas. "Captain," I said with exaggerated respect, "let's begin the training."

Emilio stormed away, slamming the galley door with a flourish. A landslide of dishes crashed from the shelves, punctuating his departure. I let my head fall back against the chair and released a trembling breath. I had never known Emilio to be so frightening. He wasn't hot-tempered like Nicholas—or myself—but his resolve was undisputable. I feared the consequences.

I understood the expectations he had for his future baroness. *Remember your place.* No matter. I would not be his wife. I rebuilt my composure with a few deep breaths.

Nicholas was watching me apprehensively. "I shouldn't be lettin' you do this."

I shrugged but my eyes were hard.

Skidmore shook his head. "It's dangerous, Miss Monroe. Your father wouldn't approve."

"Not you, too."

I scanned the faces in the room. Everyone looked uneasy. "It's done!" I barked. Skidmore and Meg both jumped, looking a bit sheepish. I turned an expectant gaze to Nicholas.

His eyes were pleading with me again, but seeing my resolve, he shook his head once, then stood a little taller, turning from Nicholas into Captain Holladay. "You'll need to learn to defend yourself—use a weapon, fight back. And we'll talk with Mother Ivy about some training, too."

I blushed crimson. "I'm not actually going to—"

"Of course not," Nicholas snapped. Oh, he hated this plan. "But Salazar can't know that."

A greater understanding of what I had just sworn to do slowly dawned on me. I could not let the others see my trepidation. I polished my composure. "I am sure Hannah will help me."

Nicholas turned to our audience. "Skidmore, under my bed in my box you'll find my weaponry. There's a dagger about this long," Nicholas held his hands about six inches apart, "with a steel hilt and a black leather scabbard. Bring it. See what kind of belts I have. We'll need something that can fit around her waist and hide under her clothing. Meg, go through your and Tessa's wardrobes. Fashion something appropriate for her to wear."

"Appropriate for fighting?" Meg asked, perplexed.

Nicholas wiggled his eyebrows suggestively. "Appropriate for the bordello."

"Aye, aye," Meg said and left the room, never bothering to look at me.

"Tessa, to the deck. Your training begins now."

CHAPTER FORTY

"LIKE THIS." NICHOLAS ARTFULLY wrapped his fingers around the hilt of the knife, his thumb resting on top. "It is the most natural." He passed the knife to me. I mimicked his grasp and locked my fingers around the hilt.

Nicholas smiled and my heart threatened to falter. He was so close to me, acting more natural than he had in months. He had a playful gleam in his eye—the pirate with his weapons was like a child with a toy. He leaned over me, his hair tickling my nose.

Nicholas wrapped his hand around my forearm. My blood was singing in my veins and it was all I could to keep my mind focused on the lesson. My hands were obviously shaking and my breathing was erratic. Nicholas was as poised as ever, doing what he knew best. I felt even more flustered knowing that our proximity wasn't affecting him the way his was affecting me.

"Loosen your wrist." He wagged my arm until the rigidity in my wrist vanished. "Better. Your power comes from here." He touched my upper arm. I gazed into his eyes, doing my best to concentrate. I knew this lesson was critical. "But your precision and your technique come from here." His hand lazily drifted down my arm and his fingers tapped my wrist. "Always keep your wrist loose."

I shook out my wrist and reevaluated my grip on the knife. It felt more natural.

Meg sat on a barrel, watching us with ill-concealed disdain. She slid off her perch. "I can do it." She reached for the knife.

"We're fine, Quin." Nicholas didn't so much as look at her.

"C'mon, Nicky. This is pointless. She's a *lady*," Meg said the word like an insult. "She can't even draw her own bath. We've got a better chance, the two of us, with a brace of pistols. She's going to get us all killed."

Nicholas wheeled around. "You've a smart mouth. It'd serve you better if some of those smarts were in your brains. Since you're so adept at drawing baths, get one ready for me. Hot water."

Our baths were never heated. It was a tedious job.

She looked incredulous, then hurt. "Nicky—" she began.

"Do I have to repeat myself, sailor?" His tone brooked no argument.

"No, sir. I'll heat the bath, sir." With a surly glance at me, she pivoted on the heel of her boot and dropped down the ladder, slamming the hatch door after her.

"I can do this," I said meekly, worried that Meg's outburst had made him question me.

"Of course you can," he said dismissively, not wasting a moment on Meg and her moods. "Try again."

I did as I was told.

"I know you can do it. I've seen you draw. Heard you play the harpsichord. Same thing. Loose wrists. Here." He reached for the knife and I passed it back to him. He demonstrated the hold again. "See how loose my wrist is?"

While I examined his technique, I noticed a web of thin white scars across the back of his hand. I brushed them with the pads of my fingertips.

He answered my unspoken question. "Knives are sharp. Don't forget that. Unlike a firearm, they cannot be disabled. A knife can harm the wielder just as easily as the attacker. Your turn." He handed me the weapon.

I gripped the hilt securely with my fingers but made sure to keep my wrist fluid. I twisted and flicked my wrist, watching the blade flash in the sun with each tiny movement.

"Good," Nicholas observed. "Look at me."

I did as I was told, drinking in the sight of his angular face. His eyes grew serious.

"I pray to God you will not have to use this weapon. But if you do, it is because you need to fatally injure Salazar. There are only four strike areas for you to know. The neck, the armpit, the gut, and the groin." Nicholas gestured to each area on his own body.

"The largest and easiest target is the gut, so that's what we'll focus on. A wound here won't be immediately incapacitating. But the bile from the belly spills into the body, and it's a deathblow for sure."

He took the dagger from my grip and tucked it into his baldric. He stood directly in front of me and took my right hand and balled my fingers, as if I were still gripping the dagger's handle. I took a deep breath, trying to focus on the lesson. If I let his touch distract me, I would never learn what I needed to, and he would never let me set foot in Port Winslow. "First, you thrust the knife straight in." He jammed my fist against his stomach. "A sharp blade will sink into flesh like it's butter. It won't take much strength, but do not hesitate. The stomach is an easy area to protect. A swift dodge and you've missed your chance." Nicholas pulled my fist towards him again, but twisted his torso out of the way, showing me how easy it would be to sidestep the strike. "He won't expect any fight from you, so I doubt you'll have issue. But if you must strike, do it deliberately and with power." He pulled my fist against his stomach again.

He looked at me pensively. "One thrust won't be enough. Twist the blade like so," he twisted my fist against his stomach, "and slice across." He directed my fist horizontally across his abdomen. He pulled my hand away from him and dropped it by my side. "Good. Now show me."

I grasped my imaginary dagger and stabbed Nicholas's stomach. He stopped me before I could go further.

"More power, more depth. Don't hesitate. You're going in for a kill—don't be shy about hurting the bastard. Lunge into the thrust with your leg and you'll have more power than you know what to do with."

I tried again, stepping into the thrust, my fist barreling against his stomach.

"Ugh," he exaggerated and screwed his face with mock pain. "Go ahead, finish me."

I twisted my wrist and dragged my imaginary dagger across Nicholas, smiling at his dramatic reaction.

"Just like that," he said proudly.

I squinted back the sun. "Would this disembowel him?" I asked.

Nicholas cocked his head in thought. "It could, but that's not the intention. There's another technique for that. This will simply sunder the stomach and intestines, inflicting a mortal wound."

I nodded and practiced the motions again. Lunge and thrust. Twist. Slice. I did it again. Nicholas told me to keep practicing my form. He eased himself down the hatch and a minute later reappeared with a gunnysack of flour. He propped it on a bench and gave me back the dagger.

"Here's your man." He stepped back.

I felt slightly silly, but I did as I was told. Lunge and thrust. The dagger sunk silently into the bag with a poof of white dust. Twist. I could feel the gunnysack popping under the will of the knife. Slice.

And I suddenly thought about what I was learning to do. And I thought about why Nicholas knew so much about it. Why he was such a good instructor. The flour spilled on to the deck in a ghostly waterfall but I saw the flour as red and wet— guts and blood.

My expression must have given my thoughts away. "Is this too much?" he asked quietly.

I shook my head, quelling my nausea.

"I can call Skidmore and have him demonstrate the rest," offered Nicholas. The fact that he knew what I was thinking made it worse.

I shook my head again. "You're a good instructor," I stated flatly.

Nicholas blanched at my words, knowing they were an observation, not a compliment, then nodded, fighting back the self-loathing that had cracked his usual poise.

"All right. You've mastered that. You'll certainly strike fear into any bag of flour on the high seas."

Our laughter at his joke was a little too forced and a heavy silence followed.

"What else?" I asked as I tried to reengage my focus.

Nicholas unstrapped a leather belt from around his waist and transferred it to me. "There is another way to hold your knife, and a few more strikes you should learn." He gave the belt a hearty cinch and it pinched into the golden chain I wore hidden around my waist under my dress.

"Ow!" I gasped, rubbing my waist.

He looked at me with worry. "Did I hurt you?" He quickly unfastened the belt.

"No—" Before I could drum up an explanation, Nicholas's hand was probing my waist, searching for the origin of my pain. Surely he thought it had to do with some strange button or accessory of fashion. His fingers pushed against the hard rope of chain under my clothes. He looked at me quizzically. "What's this?"

"'Tis nothing," I said, afraid to look him in the eye.

He pressed against it again. "No wonder the belt hurt. Is it part of your dress? Can you remove it? You must be comfortable in your belt."

"One moment." Still avoiding his gaze, I turned my back on him and untucked my blouse. Once I found the clasp, I removed the necklace and sheepishly wondered what to do with it. I hid it in my left fist and restored my dress. I turned back to Nicholas knowing my face was as red as a beet.

Nicholas stared at my fisted hand. "What is it?"

There was no way to hide the necklace. I uncurled my fingers and revealed the golden cross on a coil of chain.

Still confused, Nicholas picked it up. The necklace fell and spun to its full length. Recognition spread slowly across his face.

When he spoke his voice sounded tinny. "You've been wearing this?"

I waved my hand through the air as if his question were nothing more than a nuisance. "Show me what you were going to show me."

I chanced a glance at him, being careful to keep my expression stoic. He was staring at the chain hanging off his fingers as though it was a legendary relic that he didn't know what to do with. With furrowed brows, he unhinged the clasp then fastened the necklace around his neck. The crucifix nestled against his sternum, glinting handsomely against his tawny skin. I instantly missed its presence. I had hoped to keep it always.

He picked up the belt where he had dropped it on the deck. I lifted my arms and he fastened it snugly around my waist without a word. Then he cleared his throat. "Now, your knife is here at your hip." He sheathed the knife in the belt at my right hip. "You're under attack. Grab it."

Doing my best to put the necklace incident behind me, I grabbed the knife with my right hand, my thumb wrapping the same direction as my fingers, but then fumbled because that was not the way Nicholas had taught me to hold the weapon. I quickly switched my grasp so that my fingers went under the hilt and my thumb rested on top of it.

"Two things, Tessa," Nicholas said, moving sinuously to face me. He seemed to have regained his emotional equilibrium. I was still fighting for mine. "First and most importantly—you took too long. You're dead. Second, your grip was right the first time."

"But you told me—"

"I know, I know." He smiled as if he knew I would make the mistake. "If you are grabbing across your body, you would use the forward grip—the grip with your thumb on top." Nicholas moved the knife to my left hip and had me unsheathe it with a forward grip. "But if you are extracting the weapon from the same side, the reverse grip is easier." He moved the knife back to my right hip and showed me how to unsheathe it.

"The forward grip is more versatile, more comfortable. Used for thrusting, jabbing, slicing, and deflecting. The reverse grip—" Nicholas took my dagger and grasped it in the reverse grip, his pinky nearest to the blade and his thumb on the butt of the handle, "offers you a powerful stabbing motion." He demonstrated a stab.

"Like I told you before, your preference should be to use a forward grip and lunge into the belly like we just practiced. But if that is not an option for some reason, hold the dagger like this and drive it into the neck or the armpit. The victim will be as good as dead in half a minute."

"Not the heart?"

Nicholas shook his head. "Going through the ribcage takes practice. It's easy for the blade to get redirected by bone and miss the heart if you do not know what you are doing. Understand?"

I nodded, fighting thoughts of the experiences behind the advice.

"Practice drawing the dagger from your right hip with a reverse grip and stabbing into my neck."

I practiced my form several times, first on Nicholas's neck, then on his armpit.

"You're a quick study," said Nicholas. "We'll practice more later." He wrapped his arms loosely around me and unfastened the belt from my waist. It was the perfect moment to stare because he was too preoccupied to notice. His face was covered in stubble and he bit his bottom lip as he concentrated. His eyes were serious, shaded by his long, thick eyelashes. I resisted the urge to brush his tousled hair out of his eyes.

He caught me looking at him and raised his lips in a smile. Concern flashed through his eyes though. "We can change tactics, Tessa. We will find another way."

"No. This is a solid plan," I kept my voice from trembling. "Besides," I added, hoping to reassure both of us, "it's unlikely I will even need to use the dagger. We're just being overly cautious."

"Right," Nicholas agreed, not looking very reassured at all.

CHAPTER FORTY-ONE

STEPPING ON THE BEACH at Port Winslow was like stepping back in time. Not wanting the ketch to be seen by Salazar and his men, Nicholas anchored the *Freedom* at the beach where I had landed with my jollyboat nearly six months before.

In the predawn darkness, I led the crew through the untamed island and into the backend of town, my memory of this route strengthening with every step. I approached the bordello and knocked on the door.

It was too early for business but I knew someone would be grinding flour for bread. My knock was answered by a young boy who stood a head taller than the last time I had seen him.

His face split with a smile of instant recognition. "Tessa!" he screeched, his whippet-thin arms pumping up and down.

I put my fingers to my lips and crouched to be eye level with the boy. "Shh. It's a secret that I am here. My how you've grown!" I pulled him into a hug. "Is your mother awake?"

"Not yet."

"Can my friends and I come in? I can help you grind the flour."

Liam's eyes lit up at the offer. I signaled for my companions to join me as I followed Liam inside the bordello that was my home for a short time.

Mother Ivy's House was the first tavern I had been in. I had no reference to compare it to at the time, but I now knew that this establishment was uncommonly clean and tidy. Elegant, even. None of the girls here bore the scars of pox. None were toothless and sickly. They dressed with deliberate precision in well-made costumes; even the mussed and tumbled hairstyles were artistic and lovely. Instead of society's castaways, each girl was presented as a piece of art, a delicacy meant to be sought after and enjoyed.

I received an icier greeting than I expected from Mother Ivy when she discovered me in the kitchen with her young son.

Despite her name, there was nothing matronly about her. She was a shrewd woman rubbed raw by the brutalities of life. There was no room for emotion in her stony heart. Her dull brown hair was knotted severely at the back of her head in her usual style. Deep lines pulled the corners of her mouth down in a perpetual frown, making her thin lips look like drooping twigs. Her eyes were two sharp needles. I often wondered how the spirited Liam could be her son.

When I told her of our plan, she was predictably hesitant to play a part—Mother Ivy valued nothing more than clean business practices. Nicholas spent nearly an hour convincing her how her bordello would be affected in the event of a transoceanic war and she finally consented to let me pose as one of her workers. I had to beg her to let me spend some time training with Hannah, a dark beauty whom I had grown close to during my stay.

Meg, Nicholas, and Skidmore were familiar with the bordello from their *Banshee* days and made themselves comfortable at the bar with the staff. Emilio grew tenser with every passing moment. The pirate underworld was new to him and things were still edgy between him and Nicholas. His manners shone through, but I could sense his deep distaste for the ever severe Mother Ivy, the bordello, and everyone working there. Even Liam. How would he ever make peace with the fact that I had earned my keep at Mother Ivy's bordello—even though I had only worked in the kitchen?

When Hannah saw us, she wrapped her ebony arms around me and kissed me on both cheeks. "My sister has returned," she whispered warmly in my ear.

Charlotte was another of Mother Ivy's employees. She was the most beautiful girl I had ever seen: white-blonde hair, pale green eyes so light they were almost colorless, and skin the color of cream. Her personality was as icy as her beauty. She shot me a hateful stare by way of greeting but gave Nicholas a much warmer welcome. During the time I lived at the bordello, she spoke of Nicholas as if he were her long lost beau. She hated me for my ties to him and did all she could to play up hers. He swore he had never had any interactions beyond conversation with her. Still, my stomach grew sour to see the way she paraded by him with greedy eyes. I wasn't the only one unsettled—Meg's eyes were narrowed at Charlotte too.

"Oh, I hate her," Meg seethed through closed teeth as we watched Charlotte drape herself on Nicholas's arm.

"Glad I'm not the only one," I muttered in assent.

Meg looked at me, surprised that I had heard her. I braced myself for an insulting remark. Instead, Meg stepped closer to me. Our distaste for Charlotte bridged the bitter waters that had been flowing between us.

"Do they have a, uh, history?" I asked.

Meg gave a derisive snort. "She wishes."

Nicholas was laughing at something Charlotte said. She brushed his forearm with her long, feminine fingers, leaning in closer to him than was proper.

I was terrified of Meg's answer, but I had to know. I pressed on. "He told me they were friends and nothing more. So, they never...?"

Meg looked at me warily, as if it pained her to have a real conversation with me. We hadn't had a polite interaction since she discovered that Nicholas and I had been sweethearts. "Nicky'd always seek her out and pay for her company—"

"He *what*?"

Nicholas and Charlotte looked at me.

"Shh," Meg said, leaning in to whisper. "He'd hire her, then talk with her in the tavern all night."

"Why?" I asked. "That doesn't make any sense."

"The most I've been able to figure," Meg said as she crossed her arms and popped out a hip, "is that she reminds him of his mother."

"Why in the world would he hire someone who reminded him of his mother?" I stared incredulously as Charlotte began rubbing his shoulders.

Meg shook her head. "Captain Black explained it to me. It's the one way he can save his mother. She's dead, but something in Nicky's heart replays the past as if he could undo it. Gives Charlotte the chance that his mother never had. He buys Charlotte a real meal. Gets her some money. Keeps her away from the back rooms if only for a night."

"That's sad," I said, my jealousy fading a twinge as I looked at Charlotte pawing at Nicholas. I thought I could see it in his eyes—the way he looked at Charlotte—there was kindness there, but not desire. Something more akin to pity. "Why would a single night's reprieve make a difference?" I asked.

Meg shook her head and shrugged. "A victim needs to be rescued."

"Charlotte chose her fate, same as Nicholas's mother. They aren't victims. They're dissenters."

Charlotte had always spoken kindly of Nicholas, though. She held him in a place of reverence, I thought. Maybe that's the difference it made. It seemed more intimate than a night of casual usage.

I couldn't take my eyes off them—Charlotte employing all her feminine wiles and Nicholas seemingly impervious to her touches and giggles. He bought her breakfast and beckoned the rest of us to join them.

* * * * *

"Swing. Swing! SWING! Tessa, you aren't swinging! Start over."

I walked back to my starting point at the far side of the room and began walking towards Hannah once more, trying to make my hips swivel seductively like she had shown me.

"Shoulders back," Hannah said, walking next to me. *Walking* was not the right word. *Slinking* was more accurate. "Chest out. And swing."

I popped out a hip with each step I took. I hoped I looked less awkward than I felt. A snigger from Nicholas told me that was not the case.

I glared at him.

His laugh turned in to a cough. "It's dusty in here. Isn't it dusty in here?"

He insisted on supervising my instruction. He said it was a matter of safety—if I didn't learn the proper techniques, he would cancel the mission. When Emilio heard that Nicholas would be present, he insisted on watching as well.

With the two men as my audience, Hannah was teaching me the art of seduction. She instructed me to smile coyly, flutter my eyes, toss my hair, and heave with every breath I took. Now we were working on my walk. Apparently my posture was too modest, too regal for such a situation.

"Your hips need to swing, Tessa," chided Hannah.

"They are swinging!"

She looked at me as if I had told a boldfaced lie.

I patted my narrow, gamine hips. "I don't have a lot to work with."

"Try again."

I did as Hannah bid me, but the results were the same.

Nicholas hopped from his chair and crossed to me. "You loosen up more when you dance. Let me remind you." Hannah backed up as Nicholas took up my right hand and placed his other hand on my waist. He began waltzing me around the room. My body responded to the silent rhythm, growing more fluid with every step. Emilio sat stoically, his arms clenched across his rigid frame. Then Nicholas pulled me tighter to him, erasing any respectable distance between us.

"Oh!" I said as his hips pressed against me.

The predictable pattern of the waltz broke down and Nicholas led me in an unknown dance. I fought him at first, trying to find proper form.

"Let me lead," he said. His hips swiveled against me and my face grew hot. From the way his hand pressed against the small of my back, I knew he wanted me to do the same. My hips circled against him.

He spun me out and pulled me back, swaying seductively against my body. "Banish your bones, luv. You are water. Liquid. Fluid." He placed both of his hands on my hips, guiding them in circular motions. "You are flame. Undulating. Weaving around your surroundings. Free."

My hands found their way to his shoulders where I could feel his strength, his muscle and sinew. I was no longer fighting my body. It swayed with his, as if we were one being instead of two. I didn't feel foolish anymore. Like he said, I felt free.

"Good!" Hannah clapped her hands. "Try walking again."

Nicholas's fingers slowly skated around my waist as he let me go.

This time when I crossed the room, my body moved seductively—my hips, my shoulders, my feet, my arms all flowing together, like the flame of a fire, the wave of an ocean.

"I doubt you'll have any trouble luring the man," Hannah mused.

Nicholas nodded. Emilio glowered.

"So I've lured him. Now what?"

Nicholas addressed me from where he stood against the wall. "Once Salazar has chartered you, Mother Ivy will assign you a room. Obviously, it won't be a random assignment. We've designated a room on the first floor near the tavern and kitchen so that Skidmore can stay nearby—he'll have to be in disguise. De Luca, Quin, and I will have to remain out of sight, just up the stairs. Once you're alone in the room with Salazar, you will have to be perfect. The mission depends on it—and so does your safety."

I was very aware of what it would mean to be behind a closed door with a man like Salazar.

Hannah nodded. "The most important thing is for you to be in control of the encounter—do not let him take charge. He may be inclined to, thinking you are untrained."

"Agreed," Nicholas said. "The quicker you can lift those papers off him, the quicker this is over."

I nodded impatiently. I knew all this. "What next?"

Nicholas answered me. "We know he keeps the declaration on his person. When you're with him, it's likely he'll have his guard down. With any luck, he'll be inebriated."

"I do not trust inebriated men," I muttered.

"A slow-witted demeanor will serve us well," Nicholas reminded me.

I still didn't like the idea of a drunken Salazar, but I didn't argue the point. Nicholas nodded to Hannah, who took back the training.

"First thing—do not be afraid to get close." She pushed me towards Nicholas. I stumbled into him. He reactively caught me, holding me close to his chest. Hannah beamed. "Never underestimate the lure of the touch. Put your hands on his chest."

I hesitated for a moment, then slowly placed my palms on Nicholas's chest, feeling the beat of his heart as my fingers splayed over the thin linen fabric of his shirt. I looked nervously at him, my breathing suddenly shallow.

"Too timid, Tessa," said Hannah. "You must make him think you are overflowing with desire."

Overflowing with desire. I was familiar with the concept.

"Try again," Nicholas commanded in a husky voice. He was as affected as I.

I cleared my throat and stepped back, but before I could get any closer to Nicholas, Emilio stood in a huff and crossed to us. "Captain, I think your services are better rendered in observation." He glowered down at Nicholas without bothering to mask his disapproval.

Nicholas winked impishly at Emilio. "A little to close for comfort, eh mate?" He stepped back several paces, his hands raised in mock surrender. "She's all yours."

Emilio looked at Hannah. "Proceed."

I stepped up to him and placed my hands on his chest with exactness.

"Better," Hannah said. "Keep your overall strategy in mind. You need to find the paper in his overcoat. The least conspicuous way to do that, I imagine, would be to get his overcoat off him. Like this."

I stepped aside. Hannah pranced to Emilio, practically slammed her palms against his chest, then swept her hands up to his shoulders and pulled his jacket down around his elbows in a fluid, graceful motion.

I had to stifle a laugh at the look on Emilio's face.

"See? Smooth. Aggressive. In control. Like a tigress. Feel for the paper the entire time. Listen for it to rattle." She helped Emilio shrug his jacket back on. "Try it."

Like a tigress, I thought repeatedly as I mimicked Hannah's demonstration. I placed my hands on Emilio's chest, then slid his jacket off.

"Well done," Nicholas added. "Now you have access to his jacket. Drop it to the floor, trip over it, topple the candle…buy yourself a few moments however you can to empty his pockets."

"It might not even be in the jacket," Emilio said, rather defensively.

"Indeed," agreed Nicholas. "It could be in his waistcoat."

Hannah pointed to Emilio's waistcoat. "Unbutton it," she instructed. "Remove it."

Emilio was beyond displeased, but kept his composure in

check. I fumbled with the buttons of his waistcoat, knowing full well a tigress would never tremble this way. Finally, the last button was free and I slid the vest off his chest.

Hannah and Nicholas exchanged concerned looks.

"Your nerves will get you into trouble, luv."

Emilio looked down at me. "It's time to call this off. You did what you could, but we can all see that it is just too risky."

"No, no, she's doing really well. She needs more practice, that's all," Hannah gushed. "Besides, there's one more trick that will draw any man's attention away from fumbling fingers."

"What's that?" Emilio, Nicholas, and I all asked simultaneously.

"Kiss him."

We all looked at her in shock.

She shrugged apologetically. "Don't look so surprised. You didn't think you could get through this without kissing, did you?"

We all exchanged anxious looks. Apparently we all had.

Hannah rolled her eyes. "You'll need to kiss him. Not only will his view be limited, he will be far too distracted to concern himself with what is happening to his clothing. In fact, he may help you unbutton it."

Nicholas frowned, but said, "Try it."

Emilio's eyes were unreadable. I couldn't be sure if they held anger, disgust, or fear. Whatever it was unnerved me. He re-dressed and stood still, waiting for me.

Besides our first kiss after our night at the theatre, our encounters had been quite chaste. And now I had to throw myself at him aggressively, while Nicholas watched. Seducing Salazar couldn't be any more uncomfortable than this.

I closed my eyes and gathered my wits. With my façade erected, I flattened my body against Emilio's and kissed him. His mouth was resistant at first, but with a little coaxing, our lips melded. I heard his breathing hitch as the kiss deepened. I ran my hands up his rigid body, slinking his jacket off. I unfastened the buttons on his waistcoat, fumbling more than before, and slid that off him as well, our kiss lasting the entire time.

I stepped back and looked up apologetically at Emilio. I almost erupted with laughter at the sight of his wild, wide eyes. Nicholas was nearby, a stoic expression fixed on his face, though I noticed a tightness around his mouth. Hannah was immune to the tension and applauded my performance.

"No man will care how much your hands tremble when you kiss him like that!" Hannah teased. I looked down, my face hot and flushed. "Let's try it again. Lord De Luca, you need to touch Tessa. Salazar will have his hands all over her. She needs to get used to that. It can be very disarming. And Tessa, one last tip. Get Salazar against a wall. It will put you in control."

Finally, I practiced the entire routine. A coquettish strut, a girlish giggle. Leading Emilio through a doorway as if I were taking Salazar to a room. Shutting the door and facing him with a suggestive smile, then pinioning him against the wall with a kiss while my hands slithered up his chest to remove his jacket and waistcoat. Emilio tried to follow Hannah's instructions and touch me, but he was far too polite, his hands hovering tentatively around my waist.

Salazar would never be such a gentleman. Bloodthirsty, cruel, and cunning, he'd see me as property he'd paid for. Kissing Emilio...kissing Nicholas...these men cared for me and would never hurt me. I was fooling myself if I thought a dance with Nicholas and a kiss with Emilio would prepare me for what Salazar had in store.

I tried to bury that thought as I started my act from the beginning again.

CHAPTER FORTY-TWO

THE EDGE OF THE world was before me. The curling waves of the ocean, their tips alight with amber sunrise, rose and fell beneath me like the heads of galloping horses. Directly overhead, the periwinkle sky still housed a spattering of stars, their light dwindling in the brightening sky. The wind kicked over the promontory, bringing with it the smell of all things green. Too long I had been wrapped up in the smell of blue—the sea and the sky. The sharp tang of grass and tree and living things filled me with vigor.

I fought to keep my hair from blowing in my face, constantly tucking it behind my ears. I thought about how it had been cut—something I didn't generally spare time for. I hadn't cared much about my hair the moment that Captain Black had sawed it away with his knife; I was far more concerned about keeping Nicholas alive. But in retrospect, now that both Nicholas and I were safe from him, I hated Captain Black for cutting my hair more than anything else he had done. Nicholas would have scoffed at my vanity if he knew.

I hugged my knees close to my chest, focusing on the rhythm of the waves breaking against the shore. It helped calm the nerves that had been choking me all night. Before the sun set upon this day, I would take on Salazar.

The sun broke above the horizon. I listened intently for a sizzle from the ocean, a habit from my childhood. My father had always told me that if I listened carefully at sunrise or sunset, I could hear the ocean sizzle as the fiery sun passed through it. It was a sailor's yarn, but I always listened for it anyway.

The sun flooded the promontory with golden light. I closed my eyes and lifted my face to it, willing its power to seep into my bones. I had done the same thing nearly every day that I had spent on Port Winslow. This place, at sunrise. I could see the world. I could be above the fear that held the walls of my world together like mortar.

I breathed in the sun and the smell of green, my heart calming a little. My thoughts drifted blankly as the sun climbed higher and its light changed from soft gold to blinding white. My moment was over. I slowly made my way back to the bordello, resolved to meet this day with the strength and grace of the sun.

Charlotte was standing outside the entrance, her scarlet-painted lips curled around a miniature cigar. Her eyes were rimmed with kohl and her silvery blond hair was an artfully disheveled pile on top of head. I felt the familiar pang of jealousy that I always felt when I saw her. Meg's story illuminated the bond Charlotte shared with Nicholas, but it didn't put me at ease.

"There you are," she said, as if disappointed by the sight of me. "Everyone's been in a fuss over you. Thought you'd turned tail."

"Just watching the sunrise," I murmured without looking at her.

She leaned over the railing, her bosom spilling out of her low cut dress. Her corset was half undone, I idly noted. I would need to dress like that tonight.

"I told them you had some pagan sunrise ritual and not to bother with you. They're all inside, forming a search party. Better hurry."

I walked past her but before I could enter the bordello, she grabbed my arm. "That Italian, he's your fiancé?" Her eyes lingered on my engagement ring. "You've done well for yourself. I don't know what he sees in you, but why should I care? Here's hoping that it finally lets Marks return to the man he was." She lifted her cigar in a mock toast.

I could no longer hold back. "You'd like that, wouldn't you? He's your precious knight, riding in on his glorious steed to save you from yourself, one night at a time."

Charlotte smirked. "Bitter, are you, that he spends his nights in Port Winslow with me? Did you think you were the only one?"

"He's never even touched you." I prayed that was the truth. I tucked my head down and barreled past her, embarrassed that her goading affected me so.

The tavern was empty—it was still too early for patrons. The imposing figure of Mother Ivy appeared in the doorway. I cast my eyes down, as though greeting someone of power.

"Tessa."

I curtsied where I stood.

"Your companions are looking for you."

"Where?" I asked, looking around the empty room.

"In the kitchen."

"Thank you," I mumbled, keeping my eyes down as I made my way to the kitchen.

My companions were huddled around the stove, talking and gesturing frantically. My entrance was not noticed. I cleared my throat. "Hello? Good morning."

Everyone whirled around to stare at me, their eyes a mix of relief and anger.

"Where have you been?" Meg asked angrily.

"I was watching the sunrise."

"You really should have told someone you were going out."

"I did not realize I was forbidden to leave," I snapped at her.

Skidmore glanced at me, pleading in his blue eyes. He didn't like tension, and the cattiness that had grown between Meg and I made him particularly uncomfortable. A pirate who hated conflict. I smiled again at Skidmore and let my indignation slip.

"I'm sorry," I said. "I suppose I should have mentioned something to someone. I did not realize my absence would cause such a fuss."

"You know how we worry," Skidmore said softly.

"I know. I'm sorry."

Nicholas shook his head. "I told you. Now that she's back, can we please eat?"

There was a worn, round table in a corner set with breakfast sausages, porridge, lobster, and hot, buttered bread. Combs of honey oozed in earthenware bowls. My mouth watered as I sat and reached for a plate.

Nicholas approached the chair next to me but Emilio shot him a pointed look. Nicholas pulled it out with a flourish. "For you, my lord."

Emilio took the seat and Nicholas seated himself on the other side of the baron.

Peering into my eyes, Emilio lowered his voice. "Are you all right?"

"Yes, of course."

"If you have changed your mind—"

I silenced him with a look. "I have not. I simply went outside to enjoy the sunrise."

Nicholas cleared his throat. "If your lover's spat is over, I would like to go over today's events."

I noticed Skidmore give Nicholas the same look he had given me a moment before. It worked its magic and Nicholas softened. "We believe Salazar will be here either late afternoon or early evening. I'll watch for his arrival. Skidmore, don your disguise immediately and stay in the tavern at all times. Tessa, be dressed and ready by noon, just to be safe. Do you have all you need?"

I nodded, thinking of the costume Hannah and Meg had scrounged up for me.

"Quin and De Luca, when you finish breakfast, go to the market and restock the ship. We need tar, thread, a dozen barrels of water, rum, molasses, and pepper along with fresh food. We sail for St. Kitts as soon as this is done. I don't want any delays on our return. By noon, I want you all armed and in position. Skidmore, you know where you're to sit. De Luca, Quin, you're upstairs and out of sight. He probably won't be here until after dark, but be ready for action at midday, understand?"

"Where will you be?" I asked. "Upstairs with Emilio and Meg?"

Nicholas exchanged a heavy look with Skidmore. I expected Nicholas to offer me an explanation, but it was Skidmore who said, "It's too dangerous here for the captain. Salazar is out for blood with him. He'll bring the ketch into the harbor, ready our escape."

"Oh." I had spent enough time convincing Nicholas that I would not need his protection that I should have been convinced myself. I shouldn't have felt so unsettled about Nicholas being away from the fray.

As the others went their separate ways when the meal ended, Emilio pulled me aside. "I am proud of you, Tessa."

"Really?"

"Imagine the stories we will bring back with us to the Italian Court. My bride: the woman who stopped a war. Do you feel ready?"

I nodded but my throat was dry.

"It's not too late—"

"Please, Emilio, I need you to believe in me."

His smile was tight and a little apologetic. "You are the girl who freed a man from the gallows. Who survived pirate captivity and marooning. Who stole the heart of an Italian baron who swore it would never happen. You don't need my belief. You are quite unsinkable on your own." He pressed his lips to my temple.

"Thank you. I needed that," I lied. Knowing that I was going to break his heart as soon as we returned made every moment of affection excruciating.

I slipped the diamond ring off my finger and held it out for him.

He took it with a certain sacredness I felt guilty for not sharing. "I'll keep it safe for you until you're ready to have it back."

I feigned a smile, trying my hardest to hide the cold truth that was certainly lurking in my eyes.

CHAPTER FORTY-THREE

I WAS READY. THAT'S what I told myself as I looked into the mirror. The girl staring back at me was pretty with chocolate-colored eyes ringed with kohl, ruby lips, and dark hair shining from a thin layer of rose-scented oil. The peacock blue dress was Charlotte's. I was surprised she'd allowed me to borrow it. She had even helped dress me, lacing my stays tighter and tighter to make my figure acceptable. The result was both impressive and embarrassing. She had unlaced the top of my bodice to reveal scandalous amounts of cleavage. I would have never thought it possible for me to appear buxom. I was wrong. But looking beyond the showy costume, the girl in the mirror told another story. Her eyes were wide and wild. Her teeth kept worrying her lips. Her hands were clenched to keep them from shaking.

I thanked Hannah and Charlotte for their help and ventured into the tavern area of the bordello. It was midday and a few patrons had trickled in for lunch, but on the whole, it was quite empty. A man approached me and I had to remind myself not to slink away. I wasn't Tessa Monroe anymore, but a lady of the night who would greedily welcome such attention.

The man was short and covered in matted black hair. His blue eyes twinkled happily. I thought I sensed a friendly smile under his flowing mustache but I couldn't be sure.

"Marks asked to see ya when you be ready," the man said.

"Skidmore?" I chuckled. "I didn't recognize you!"

"Good! Then Salazar won't either."

I glanced around, expecting to see Nicholas somewhere.

"He ain't here. He's on a hill out back, keeping an eye on Salazar's ship."

I swallowed hard. "Will you show me to him?"

Skidmore offered an arm and led me out the back door. A well-worn pathway led away from the town and into the jungle thicket, a canopy of green nests closing in over our heads. The earth gave way softly with each step.

I carefully stepped over a rotted tree trunk that bisected the jungle trail. "What are you going to do after this mission? Go back to your wife and girls?"

"I will take a leave with them, indeed, but I know this won't be the end of things. Marks needs me. I'm first mate. I've pledged my life to 'im and I'll sail with that scungy bastard 'til I die." He flushed a red so deep it was almost purple. "Pardon my tongue. I forgot myself."

I couldn't help the affection I felt for Skidmore. I pulled him to a stop and kissed him on the cheek.

"What was that fer?" His complexion threatened to turn puce.

We slowly began walking again and I nestled close to him, resting my head on his shoulder. "You give me hope. Hope for him. Can I ask you something?"

"Aye, miss. Anything ye like."

"Do you think Nicholas knows how to love?"

Skidmore's look was one of shock, but a knowing smile stole across his lips. "Aye. He does."

"But you said…when we talked about his mum…"

"I never said he did not know how to love. Only that he was scared of it. Love comes as naturally to him as it does anyone else."

I looked down at the hem of my skirt. It was already collecting a ring of muck at its edge. Charlotte wouldn't be pleased. "How can you know that?"

Skidmore responded confidently. "Because he loves me."

My heart settled into the truth of it. Nicholas and Skidmore were brothers. Family forged not by blood but by destiny—by love.

"He loves, Miss Monroe. He loves in a way that terrifies him, I think. The question you should be askin' is not if he knows how to love but if'n he knows to recognize it in himself."

We finished our slow ascent up the hill and found Nicholas sitting at its crest, an elbow propped on his knee and a spyglass in his hand. He was staring at the sea as though he'd never seen it before, watching it stretch out in an undulating dance and spilling over the edge of the world. His beauty was breathtaking, the lines of his face and the wave of his hair. I envied the breeze that caressed him. His face was drawn, his eyes distant, focusing on neither sky nor sea. There was sadness in his eyes. Something that haunted him. Something that made me think of the nightmares he never spoke of. I felt I had trespassed into a private room of his heart.

"Marks," Skidmore said, breaking the spell without hesitation. I blushed, still feeling as though I had witnessed something I was not meant to see.

Nicholas startled. He offered a nod of welcome to Skidmore. Then he saw me. He stiffened and his eyes traversed over me from head to toe, his lips parting. There was no denying my costume was effective. I stepped back instinctively and crossed my hands over my bosom.

Standing up, Nicholas pried his eyes away from me as if it were a chore. He held a brief conversation with Skidmore that was lost on the wind to me, then Skidmore left with a slight nod in my direction.

And then we were alone. I felt myself shrinking backwards even more, painfully aware of my state of undress, my painted face, my ladylike charms so fully on display. This was not me.

Nicholas eyed me steadily, a strange combination of amusement and concern on his face. He didn't say anything about my attire and I was endlessly grateful. Skidmore hadn't either. Both must have known that even a well-intended compliment would have made me uncomfortable. He pointed towards the ocean where several white sails spotted the expanse of blue. "Salazar's ship is near."

My voice trembled. "How much time do we have?"

Nicholas pressed the spyglass to his eye again. With his attention directed elsewhere, I let my eyes linger on him. He was dressed for battle. Over his red cotton shirt, he wore a stitched leather vest. His baldric was heavy with weapons and his belt hung on his hips, cockeyed from the weight of his cutlass. He wore fitted breeches and knee-high black boots that looked new. Colorful sashes tied around his waist blew in the breeze like banners of victory.

"An hour 'til he's in the harbor. And at least another hour until he's settled enough to seek low companionship at the bordello." He put the spyglass aside. "I thought you might like to train in the meantime."

I shook my head.

"The more prepared you are, the more at ease you'll be."

"I need to prepare here." I touched my head. "I need to take my mind away from it all. I am nearly mad."

"Are you, now?"

"Would it be terrible to admit how frightened I am?"

"Yes. Because then I would stop you from carrying through with this foolish plan."

I smiled pathetically. "I was lying. I am not nauseous with worry. I am not more terrified than I have ever been in my entire life. I am not cursing my impetuous mouth for insisting on this risky bid."

Nicholas took a deep breath and looked at me with a soul-searing gaze.

I cut him off before he could say anything. "Yes, I do."

He blinked in confusion. "What?"

"You were going to say that I didn't have to do this. Everyone's been saying that."

"Well, you don't. If you're scared, you do not have to set foot in that bordello ever again. We'll sail away right now."

"Being scared is not the same as being unwilling." I hugged myself to fend off the chill that ran down my spine. My words made me sound much braver than I felt.

We stood facing each other. I was close enough to touch him, to wrap my arms around him.

"Let's make sure you can access your weapon in that getup." Without hesitation, he pressed his hands against my hips and felt for the dagger under my skirt.

"Excuse me!" I slapped his hands away. "That is not very gentlemanly!"

He gave a crooked smile and put his hands back on my hips. "You should know by now that I am no gentleman." He slid his hand into the pocket of my skirt and felt for the hilt of the knife. Hannah had helped me cut a slit into the bottom of the pocket for access. He struggled to remove the knife. "Can you get it? I can't manage. Maybe it's my angle."

I put my hand in my pocket and fished the knife out, though not smoothly.

He shook his head. "You need better access."

"I need a bigger opening." I handed him the knife and pulled out the pocket. Not caring to pop open the seam like Hannah had, Nicholas roughly cut through the fabric, obliterating the entire bottom of the pocket. I cringed.

"Favorite dress?"

I shrugged. "It's Charlotte's. She hates me anyway."

"She fancies me." He said the words as if they were a meaningless fact. "Tell her I did it. Try again." He passed the knife back to me. I put it back in its sheath and extracted it again, much easier this time.

He nodded, satisfied. "You're set to go on your merry way."

I took a deep breath and forced myself to smile. "It will be all right."

Nicholas's smile looked as strained as mine felt. "Remember, Skidmore will be in the tavern with you the entire time. De Luca and Quin will be right upstairs. If and when you need intervention, scream. There are four of you against just one. You will be fine."

"I know. I shall see you later, then. Hopefully with a Declaration of War in my hands."

"Before you go…" Nicholas produced something from his pocket. "Will you wear this again?" I recognized the golden chain winking in his hand.

I nodded and he carefully fastened the clasp behind my neck, his fingers tracing the line of the chain over my collarbone.

"Perhaps this will offer you the protection I can't provide." He looked as though he had more to say. I waited for a moment, but no words came.

My fingers curled around the cross. "Thank you." I moved to go.

He grabbed my arm and pulled me into a hug, my head nesting perfectly under his chin. He was tender and strong and soft and powerful. "Be safe. Your captain orders it."

He released me, and looked at me longingly as I started down the path, dread evident on his face. Clutching the crucifix, I walked back to the bordello as battle ready as I would ever be.

CHAPTER FORTY-FOUR

A NIGHT OF DEBAUCHERY was in full swing.

Port Winslow was a small town with no presiding European government—a pirate haven designed for illegal trade and illicit hungers. It existed for nights like this. Pirates poured into the taverns and inns, eager to overindulge in pastimes that could not be found at sea. Each pirate ship was a gold mine for proprietors like Mother Ivy and nearly all of Salazar's crew members had found their way to the bordello. I watched as pirate after pirate checked his weapons at the door and settled at a table with a tankard of ale to drink and a wench to tickle.

I stood with Charlotte at the bar and tried to settle into the chaos, my eyes sweeping across the boorish crowd, wondering which man was Salazar. Sailors were a filthy lot. Pirates were worse. They had the same stooped posture, rotten teeth, and leathery skin as any mariner, but also boasted unseemly manners and gut-twisting disfigurements from their bloody professions. I hadn't even bothered to ask Nicholas what Salazar looked like. I'd be kissing a man without a nose for all I knew.

"Have a drink. You'll feel more relaxed." Charlotte offered me a beverage in a tin cup.

I shook my head. "No, thank you."

Charlotte shrugged and downed the drink herself. My eyes swept up her black satin gown and perfectly coiffed hair. She settled on a barstool with the smoothness of warm butter. I was a jitter of nerves, ready to fracture with any amount of pressure. I tried to copy Charlotte's languid movements, hoping I looked natural.

The bordello erupted with joyous cheering. I turned to see two men enter the bordello, garnering slaps on the back and jubilant "huzzahs!" as they checked their weapons at the door and joined the celebration. Through the noise, I heard the name Salazar.

Both men were tall and young with dashing good looks not often seen among the swill of the sea. Angular noses, smooth tawny skin, and shrewd dark eyes. Their faces looked similar; they must be brothers. The taller of the two had a scar that split his top lip in half. His head had been shaved bald and when he turned to the side, I could see that he was missing an ear. I could only see the lower half of his arms, but they were covered with rows of parallel cuts. Some were smooth and glossy with ancient scar tissue, some were red and angry, still healing, and a few were still fresh with scabs and blood.

Skidmore made his way to me. "Those are the Salazar brothers. Captain Mateus Salazar is the younger of the two. The shorter."

I couldn't look away from the lines of scars on the elder brother's arms. "His arms…"

"That is Diogo Salazar. He marks his killing. Some say he carves a line in one arm for every woman he kills and a line in the other arm for each child."

"Child?" Both arms were hideously scarred. My stomach twisted.

"He used to mark his chest for every man he killed, but he ran out of space. See the pouch around his neck?"

A worn leather pouch hung about his neck on a leather cord. I noticed the skin behind it was a web of white scar tissue.

"I see it."

"They say now he keeps a tooth from every man he kills. They say the ghosts of the dead follow him wherever he goes. They say he doesn't mind the company of the dead. He's a minion of hell himself."

I shuddered, glad my business was not with this monster but with the fairer captain. But I knew that sometimes the fairest things were the most deceptive. I narrowed my eyes as I took in Mateus. He was a might shorter than his brother with brown hair that had been kissed by the sun and an easy smile. Men flocked to him, as eager for his approval as they were wary of Diogo's murderous stares.

"Tell me about Mateus."

"Where Diogo is brute, Mateus is brains. King of Pirates, he calls himself. Fancies himself as some kind of champion of our lot. He has a way of snaring men into dark fates."

"Do other pirates love him? Do they see him as their king?"

"Strange lot, we pirates. We live outside the law and condemn governments who would have us starve, yet someone proclaims himself their king and they uphold him. We who vote in captains and vote 'em out the same. I don't like it. Not one bit. The sea is no place for kings."

Mother Ivy shot me a beckoning glance and I took that as my cue to finally begin my charade. Clutching the cross that dangled at my chest, I said a silent prayer and sauntered towards Mother Ivy and the Salazar brothers.

"Captain Salazar, I would like you to meet Nora." Mother Ivy gestured towards me. "She appeals to those with singular tastes."

Captain Salazar slapped his brother on the back. "Just for you, Diogo."

My palms began to sweat. I needed to be alone with Salazar—Mateus Salazar. Not his brother.

I didn't like the way Diogo stared at me, as if he could bend me to his will with only eye contact. "Little brother, the best is for you," he finally said.

"Indeed, Captain Salazar," Mother Ivy cooed, "only the best for the captain."

I curtsied deeply before the captain. *"Boa noite*, Captain," I greeted him in his native Portuguese as I looked up at him through my lashes. He was surprisingly handsome.

A boyish smile played on Captain Salazar's lips as he shook his head. "I've too much to do in too little time." He exchanged a look with his brother.

"Such as what? You take no time for yourself, Mateus. It is time you celebrate. I will remain here. Ensure everything is in order."

Mateus Salazar looked as though he might decline again. I had to do something. I had to be alone with him. I was about to say something very forward to him when Liam scampered by, then screeched to a halt on his heels, his big brown eyes staring at me in wonder.

My breath hitched. Liam should not have been out here. Not in the middle of the mission, not with all these dangerous men around.

"Tessa, you look so pretty." Liam said, beaming.

"Tessa?" Diogo Salazar repeated, still staring at me. He made me want to peel my skin off just so he couldn't stare at it anymore.

Liam's eyes widened. "Nora," he quickly corrected, taking a step back. "I didn't recognize you, Nora." He mouthed the word *sorry* to me, then he vanished into the crowds.

Mateus Salazar looked amused as he glanced from Liam to Mother Ivy to me. Diogo's eyes darkened with mistrust. Mother Ivy offered an explanation without the slightest sign of fluster. "My son has revealed all our secrets. This is our newest employee, Tessa. The girls often prefer an alias. I hope you aren't offended that I selected a maiden for you. She is inexperienced but I thought you might appreciate her beauty. A true English rose. If you prefer, I can summon one of my more experienced employees. Hannah, perhaps."

Mateus leaned in close to his brother, speaking in Portuguese so I could not understand what he said. Diogo's response was curt and his suspicious eyes flicked to me. I waited an eternity, an outsider, not understanding what they were saying. Whether Mateus refused me again or whether he took me back to a room—I dreaded my fate.

Mateus turned to Mother Ivy. "I would like to dance with Tessa."

Mother Ivy smiled knowingly. "Not Nora?"

"Not Nora."

Diogo whispered something harsh, his voice rising as his brother waved him away.

Mateus offered me his hand. "Join me."

Through my gloves, I could feel the roughness of his hands, calluses as coarse as coral. We reached a spot of open floor near a pair of musicians—one playing a lively fiddle and the other a concertina—and Mateus Salazar, the self-styled King of Pirates, bowed before me and we began our dance. I choked the terror back and reminded myself to breathe.

I'd expected Mateus Salazar to be a standard sea dog— weatherworn and raunchy with a face full of half-rotted teeth. He was comely, with his large, dark eyes; he was intelligent; and he was polite.

I felt my stiff posture relaxing into the rhythm of the music. I spun gracefully, casting shy looks at my partner.

"You come from high breeding," he noted.

I was unsure how to answer him, so I remained silent.

"That's rare in a place like this. Why are you here?"

I did not need to invent a story. "My ship sank on the crossing from England. I was the only survivor."

"A cruel turn of fate," Captain Salazar spoke in my ear. He smelled like expensive tobacco. "You're too pretty a girl to be in a place like this. Too *pure* a girl. It's not too late for you, you know."

Even he was warning me away. I could walk away from him now, walk out of the bordello, and no one would blame me ever. I looked at Mateus Salazar's chest. Somewhere in the folds of his jacket or waistcoat or trousers was the Declaration of War. I was within inches of it. No one had come this close to winning this victory—not Nicholas with his strategies or Emilio with his wealth.

"I must feed myself," I said stoically.

"A girl as pretty as you ought to have no trouble finding a husband to care for her. At the very least, you could become a paramour to the most powerful man in the Spanish Main. A queen to the King of Pirates." He spun me around, then cinched me close to his body, giving me a smile that was as devilish as it was handsome.

I looked down, hoping Captain Salazar would not see the disgust etched on my features. I scrambled to find something to say. I had practiced all the motions I needed to retrieve the declaration, but this war of words rattled me.

"You f-flatter me, Captain—or should I say, Y-your Grace?" I said, tripping over my words. I took a deep breath, but was left wanting. The corset didn't allow it. "For now allow me to take the King of Pirates to one of the back rooms."

"So bold yet so nervous." His smile was kind.

I closed my eyes briefly. "I am sure I am quite off-putting."

"On the contrary, *Senhorita* Tessa, you are quite enchanting. I want you all to myself. Would you like a glass of wine?"

"Please," I lied.

With a snap of his fingers, two fluted glasses of burgundy liquid were on a tray before us. He handed one to me and took the other for himself. He excused himself and spoke to Mother Ivy, pressing several coins into her hand. She gestured for him to take me to the predetermined room.

The shame that hit me caught me off guard. Everything was going according to plan—*my* plan—but I never expected to feel so dirty at the sight of a handful of coins meant to pay for my virtue.

Salazar spoke briefly to his brother before leading me down the hall. I felt Skidmore's eyes on us as we disappeared from view. The room we were to use was only a fraction smaller than my cabin on the *Freedom*. A large bed with a sagging mattress and stained coverlet took up the bulk of the room. Beside it was a small table with a lantern and washbasin on top and a chair tucked underneath it. I shut the door behind me very deliberately, noting the amused twinkle in Mateus's eyes. I placed my glass of wine on the table, then reached for Mateus's.

"Are you finished with this?"

He let me take the glass and watched me with fascination as I set it next to mine on the table, then removed my gloves slowly, pulling each finger loose then wriggling my hand out. I laid my gloves by the wineglasses then turned my full attention to him. "This is all new to me."

"Take your time."

"First, I should kiss you." I sauntered to him, grateful he wasn't disfigured with scars, and wrapped my arms around his neck. I lifted my face towards his and with a smile, the young mercenary bent towards me. I could taste him before our lips even met. His breath was a cloud of tobacco, booze, and rot, the wine adding a cloying sweet scent to it all. The stubble on his chin scraped against my face, each bristly hair like a splinter. Our lips met. And then our tongues. He was hungry and pressed against me. I stepped back, scared. I didn't want to do this. All I had to do was scream or pound on the door or walk away. Nicholas wouldn't think less of me.

Mateus was oblivious of my revulsion—oblivious or indifferent. "And what next, *Senhorita* Tessa?"

His clothing was more complicated than I had expected. I felt as if I were staring at a puzzle I had never seen before. I could do this. I *had* to. "Then…then…I should take your jacket." To get to his jacket, I had to remove crisscrossing leather baldrics from his chest. It was easy to see where he wore a half-dozen blades. I was again grateful for Mother Ivy's policy of no weapons.

My fingers shook as I unbuckled the straps. Each fell to the ground with a bright, metallic *clink*. The jacket was next, long and heavy with golden embroidery and engraved whale-bone buttons. I slid my hands over his chest, feeling for the crinkle of paper in the layers underneath. I pushed the jacket off his shoulders and laid it over the back of the chair. The pockets rustled with the sound of coins and possibly paper. I couldn't be sure.

"Then do we kiss again?" asked Mateus.

"Yes."

He pulled me to him and his hungry lips pushed mine apart. His hands clutched my shoulders. He steered me towards the bed and gently pushed me on to the mattress.

"No, no," I muttered. "Too soon for that."

"Is it, now?" His fingers traced my jaw.

"You must behave." I grabbed his finger and nipped at it, drawing out a salacious grin. I stood up and let my hands wander to the wide leather belt around his waist. It was decorated with silver disks and bits of sea glass. Hooks and brackets and buckles attached a myriad of items to it—a tarnished silver flask, a coin purse, a spyglass, a compass, and various small containers that might hold gunpowder or tobacco. The belt fastened in the back and I had to peek under his arm to figure out how to remove it. I gently placed it on the bed. I blinked up at him through my lashes, allowing my lips to part slightly, a trick of seduction that Hannah had taught me. His eyes widened and I knew I had his attention. Keeping eye contact with him, I removed the striped scarf tied around his waist.

Next, my hands danced down his chest, my fingers undoing each button of his waistcoat. I slipped that off him as well and placed it on with the jacket on the back of the chair. When I turned around, Mateus had removed his shirt and stood bare-chested before me. His skin was a patchwork of scars.

"*Venha cá.*" He beckoned me to him.

I hesitated, trying to play coy, and he grabbed me by my shoulders and pinned me against the door, his lips devouring me. His hands traced the bodice of my dress. I cringed at his touch. My breathing was erratic and shallow—I hoped he thought it was from passion. I was trapped with no way out. I began to panic.

My hand slid through the folds in my skirt, finding the hilt of the knife. My eyes fluttered shut. Could I really kill this man? Would I carve a scar on my arm like a badge of honor? I knew then that no matter what happened, I wasn't a killer. My fingers uncurled from the hilt. I would never use that thing. It was as useful to me as a spoon.

I tried to remember what Hannah taught me—stay in control.

I kissed Salazar back, hard. I pressed against him and, as he had done before with me, I guided him to the bed and pushed him on it. I helped him remove his boots and stockings so he was barefoot and wearing only his roughspun wool breeches. He lay back with a laugh and pulled me on top of him. As I leaned over him, my necklace—Nicholas's necklace—swung across his face.

"I'm sorry," I giggled. "One moment." I sat back and lifted the chain over my head. I crossed from the table as if I were going to place it there, but slipped it into my pocket. With my body blocking Mateus's view of the table, I knocked the lantern on the floor. The glass panels shattered at my feet and the room plunged into darkness.

"Oh no!" I cried.

"Are you all right?" he asked.

Under the cover of darkness, I grabbed the jacket and waistcoat I had draped across the back of the chair, but the garments had gotten tangled in the chair slats. "I'm so sorry," I gushed. "I told you I was nervous. Yes, I'm all right. You?"

I could hear him rising from the bed. I tugged desperately on the clothes. The chair fell over but the clothing came loose.

"There's glass everywhere," I said. "Don't move."

"I can help you clean it up."

"No!" I said, too quickly. I fell to my knees and fumbled

with the clothing "No. You are barefoot. I'll fetch a broom from Mother Ivy and another lantern." I heard the crinkle of paper and blindly felt for the pockets.

Mateus reached for me, his hand finding my arm and pulling me to him on the edge of the bed. I squirreled the clothes behind my back. "There's no need to worry about the glass now, Tessa Nora." He pulled me closer to him. "We shall clean it up later." His hand stroked me.

I tried not to recoil as his hand traced the lines of my corset. He could not see my grimace in the dark. "It could be dangerous. What if we were to end up on the floor?"

Salazar guffawed. "You minx! I cannot argue with that."

"I'll return in just a moment." I sprang up and left the room, hiding the clothes with my body.

As soon as the door shut behind me, I sagged against it, closing my eyes and letting go of a cleansing sigh. If the declaration was to be found, I had it in my arms now.

I opened my eyes, ready to disappear into the night forever, only to see the mutilated face of Diogo Salazar staring down at me.

CHAPTER FORTY-FIVE

DIOGO SALAZAR LOOKED FROM my frightened face to the lump of clothing in my arms and back to my face again. His eyes held no mercy.

Fighting the urge to scream for Skidmore, I tried to step passed Diogo. "Pardon me." He blocked my way.

I nearly shrunk beneath his scorching glare. "Give me one reason I shouldn't kill you for stealing." He extracted a thin stiletto blade and pointed it at me. He wasn't supposed to have any weapons. Why was I surprised? Why would I think Mother Ivy's policy would prevent pirates from breaking the rules? I suddenly wondered what weapons Mateus was hiding.

I stared at the blade and stammered, "I accidentally shattered the lantern. There is glass in these clothes. I was going to shake them out and get a broom for the floor."

Over Diogo's shoulder I could see Skidmore. My mind eased only a little. If only I could tell him that Diogo was armed.

Diogo's eyes were slits of hatred. Something changed in them. They flickered infinitesimally and his mouth curled into a sneer. "I know you. You're no whore. You're the Monroe girl."

I blinked rapidly, shocked that he knew me. I flashed a desperate look at Skidmore. He signaled with his hand and crept closer. My eyes went back to Diogo, and I recognized him. I had seen him once before. He was the man who had stolen the Declaration of War from my father's study the night of the masquerade ball.

He knew what I was after.

My mouth worked frantically but nothing came out. Diogo raised a fist. I flinched, thinking he meant to strike me, but instead he pounded on the door. I looked around wildly wondering what I should do. Would Mateus kill me or would it be Diogo? Would I be a fresh red slash on his right arm?

There was the sound of a muffled thump and Diogo's eyes glazed over, then he toppled towards me. I quickly stepped back and Diogo crashed to the floor. Skidmore was standing there, a pistol glinting in each hand. He had used the butt of one to knock out Diogo and the other was pointed at Diogo's chest. I didn't have any time to react before Emilio and Nicholas—*Nicholas*—rushed towards me. What was he doing here? Diogo could regain consciousness at any second and see him. Mateus could open the door and see him. The three men bent over and grabbed the unconscious Diogo and began dragging him away.

I rushed alongside Nicholas. "He knocked on the door. Mateus is going to appear any second. What do we do?"

Nicholas swore and dropped the arm he was carrying. "I'll get you out of this."

"He can't see you here," I whispered fiercely. "Just tell me what to do."

Skidmore and Emilio disappeared around a bend in the hallway just as the door to Mateus's room cracked open.

Nicholas quickly whispered at me, "You do not know me," and then vanished into the shadows of the hallway.

I should have walked away when I had the chance. My hands were soaked with sweat and my blood hammered through my body, making me feel nauseous. Before I could warn Nicholas away again, Mateus appeared in the doorway. He was pulling on his shirt haphazardly. His eyes fell on my face first, then he noticed the wad of clothing I held. His face darkened.

"Sorry about that," I stammered, trying to sound cheery. "I tripped and banged against the door."

"What are you doing with my clothing?"

"They have glass in them," I blurted. I happened to notice a glinting shard of glass on top of the clothing. I picked it up and held it out to him before flicking it onto the floor. "I'll shake them out for you and fetch the broom."

His eyes swept up and down the hallway. "Have you seen my brother? He's supposed to be nearby."

"I didn't see anyone."

Mateus looked skeptical. Or perhaps annoyed. I willed my heart rate to slow down. I summoned a flirtatious smile and wagged a finger at him. "Now don't you go anywhere. I will be right back."

He ran a hand through his tousled hair and gave me a half smile. "I quite like you, Tessa or Nora or whoever you are. You're not jaded like other girls."

I kept smiling though I wasn't sure how to react. I thought through every movement I made, turning away from him and slowly walking down the hallway, one foot in front of the other, quelling my instincts to run as far as I could away from this man.

"Wait." Mateus caught up to me just as the hallway turned towards the open area of the tavern. "Let me get my effects out my pockets before you shake them all over the place."

I was rocked with defeat. But before Mateus could take the clothes from me, Nicholas breezed in front of us. Charlotte was on his arm and he appeared to be engrossed in whatever she was saying, though I knew his senses were all attuned to where I stood now.

Relief washed over me at the same time my stomach plummeted. I knew I would be safe now—but at what cost?

"Marks?" Mateus pushed passed me. "Marks?"

Nicholas turned and looked at Salazar. My heart shuddered. I clutched the bundle of clothes in my arms tighter to muffle the sound of my thundering heart. I saw Salazar reach to his side, an instinct to draw a pistol or sword that wasn't there. I had never been more grateful to Mother Ivy's policy of no weapons. I remembered Diogo's stiletto. I didn't think Mateus had any weapons hidden on him, but he might. Certainly some of his crew in the bordello tonight would be hiding blades or flintlocks. If Salazar chose to attack, Nicholas would not come away from a fight easily.

With a swat on her behind, Nicholas dismissed Charlotte. She squealed and scampered away and Nicholas turned towards Salazar. "I thought I saw that brother of yours but he was uglier than I remembered."

"You saw Diogo?"

"Aye, a moment ago." Nicholas looked around the room. "Probably off takin' a piss or something." Nicholas turned back to Mateus, feigning nerves. "I suppose I owe you an explanation."

"You owe me a might bit more than that," Salazar responded, his hand curling into a fist.

Nicholas looked at me with disdain. "Carry on, sweetheart, we've some business to discuss."

I uprooted myself from the ground. He was giving me a perfect excuse to escape, and I couldn't waste it. I slipped past Salazar before he could remember to check his pockets and headed into the din of the main room. Walking away without looking back, not knowing what Salazar would do to Nicholas, was the hardest thing I had ever done.

"Hurry back," Mateus called after me. "Don't leave me alone with this mangy cuss."

I furrowed my brow as I dashed into the kitchen, thinking that Captain Salazar seemed genuinely fond of my company. If he truly did, it was only to my advantage—and Nicholas's. Salazar certainly wouldn't attack Nicholas if I were standing right there. I dumped the clothes on a broad wooden chopping table and sorted through pockets, ignoring the scullery maid who looked at me in surprise. I found what I was looking for in the inside breast pocket of Salazar's jacket—a trifolded piece of paper signed by King George himself. The triumph I expected to feel never came. I quickly tucked the declaration down my bodice, then ripped a paper out of Mother Ivy's ledger, folded it to the same size, and slipped it into the same pocket.

I asked the scullery maid for a broom, then marched out into the tavern. Mateus and Nicholas were sitting at a square table. Mateus saw me immediately and stood.

I risked a glance at Nicholas as I approached, taking care to keep my face blank of any emotion. His eyes flashed with censure, his lips a thin line. He had meant for me to escape to the ship. Did he not understand I had returned for his own safety?

Mateus took the clothes out of my grasp, shrugging on his waistcoat and then his jacket. I held my breath as he patted his breast pocket. The paper crinkled. The sound was enough to satisfy him and he pulled out a chair for me. "Join us for a drink, *Senhorita* Tessa Nora."

I nodded compliantly and propped the broom against the table before sitting down. I let my knees buckle as I collapsed into the chair next to the Pirate King. He summoned a barmaid to bring me a tankard of beer. The metal was cool against my bottom lip, the beer inside watery. I pretended not to see the look of surprise that crossed Nicholas's face as I drained the last drop.

Mateus responded to Nicholas's incredulous look. "It's her first night on the job."

"You don't say," Nicholas muttered.

"I think I intimidate her," Mateus said with a pleased smile as he pushed his tankard in front of me. Then he swung his attention back to Nicholas. "Though, I must not intimidate you. You mock me with your defiance."

I shrank in on myself, suddenly doubting that Salazar would hold his violence just because I was beside him.

Nicholas unfastened his velvet coin purse from his belt and slid it across the table, the coins inside clacking together as Mateus clamped his hand down on it. "That's everything. Paid in full. With a few extra pieces of eight for my tardiness."

Mateus opened the purse and spilled its contents. My eyes widened at the cascade of gold and silver coins that poured to the table. Mateus looked at the money then swung his arm across the table top, sending coins flying in all directions. I flinched as one hit me on the nose. "You insult me." His words were ice.

Pirates and prostitutes alike fell to the floor, collecting the coins as fast as they could. I saw Liam dart by, small silver disks sticking out of his fist.

"That is more than the agreed price."

"You broke your oath. You're paying thirty days late so you'll be paying me thirty-times the original debt."

Nicholas gaped. "That's usury."

Salazar snorted a cold, dark laugh. "No, boy, 'tis piracy."

Nicholas's face was impassive, but his tone was icy when he asked, "When is your deadline?"

Salazar signaled to one of his men. The summoned pirate walked to our table, pulled a pistol from his oversized jacket and handed it to Salazar. Salazar dismissed his man and casually held the weapon, its barrel aimed at Nicholas. I gasped, my hands flying to my mouth.

"Does this scare you?" he asked me, laughing. He dangled the pistol by its trigger guard.

I scrunched my eyes tightly for a moment, and took a deep breath. "I thought you meant to use it."

"Not tonight. In fact, I'm not even sure how it got in here. As far as I understand, this place does not allow weapons. Strange." He set the pistol down and pushed it in front of me like an offering. "You best keep track of this." He turned back to Nicholas, but nodded at me. "This one has put me in a good mood. I'll give you until the end of the year."

"Impossible," stated Nicholas, his face composed. "I would need five years. Three, maybe."

I shrank against my chair, willing myself smaller, looking from the Pirate King to the pistol to my captain. The amount of money they were discussing was atrocious. Nicholas was right, it was impossible, even if the timeline were to be expanded.

"Who issued you a Letter of Marque?" Salazar asked, his tone changing into something more carefree.

Nicholas stiffened, despite Salazar's affable demeanor, and I knew he sensed a new danger.

When Nicholas didn't answer, Salazar continued, his tone still warm and pleasant. "Don't act so surprised that I know about it. As a king, it is my duty to know the business of my subjects."

"You are not my king."

"Governor Abner issued it. And his puppy Monroe. Do you make berth in Christophe Harbor between raids?"

Nicholas was still. Silent and still.

Salazar leaned forward with his hands on the table. All trace of friendliness was now gone, replaced by naked menace. His voice was like a razor blade. "You have an income. You have a ship. *My* bloody ship, to be precise. And what do I have? Nothing. You'll pay me my debt before the year ends or I'll take payment myself."

The threat made me tremble, but Nicholas remained steady. "You want your damn boat back?"

Salazar frowned and shook his head. "I care not for that hulk of driftwood. What I want is for my subjects to obey me. And to do that, they must fear me. That is something you lack, but you are not worthless. What I will do to you will strike fear into others. Somebody in St. Kitts means something to you. You're there more than you let on. It won't take long for my hounds to sniff 'em out."

I didn't think my heart could race any faster. The room was spinning and I felt dizzy. This wasn't supposed to be happening. I was supposed to get the declaration and slip away. I was a target now. Mateus didn't know it, but Nicholas did. Nicholas had always known it.

Salazar ranted on, spittle dripping from his lips. "I'll raze the entire bloody island on the off chance it'll scratch your pride and put a wrinkle in your day. I'll torture and kill everyone that means anything to you…and anyone that means anything to the people you care about. Got a best mate? I'll flay 'im alive. A bastard child? I'll drown 'im in the sea. Got a girl you fancy? I'll make her my whore and think of you as I take her. If there's so much as a puppy that wags its tail at you, I'll have its innards with my bloody tea. And it won't be until then that I'll even consider taking your head. So you either pay me the three hundred thousand by the end of the year or I'll wring payment from you bit by bloody bit."

Nicholas remained composed but the blood was gone from his face, leaving him looking like the ghost Salazar threatened to make him. His nostrils twitched. "You'll get your money." Underneath his stillness, he was fuming. Fuming and furious and browbeaten.

"Although, if you happened to come to me, begging, and bent your knee and bowed your head in fealty, I might take mercy and wash your debt away with your blood." Salazar offered, a smirk spreading across his face.

Very slowly, Nicholas repeated himself. "I said you'll get your damn money."

I shivered. Nicholas looked at me pointedly, then turned his attention back to Salazar. "Tell your hussy to wait for you elsewhere. I have a matter to discuss with you that's sensitive."

Salazar smiled kindly at me as if he had not just been talking about eating the entrails of fluffy animals. "Miss Nora Tessa is no milksop. You can speak freely in front of her."

Nicholas pulled his mouth into a tight smile. "I do not worry of offending the whore's ears so much as I worry about who she might repeat our conversation to."

My guts knotted when I heard him call me a whore. I knew it was just an act, but it still stung.

"Tsk, tsk. You are such a jaded thing for one so bright and young. And you really shouldn't call her a whore."

"Is that not what she is?"

Salazar eyed me with interest, his gaze sweeping from my chest to my face and to my eyes. I had to use every drop of my willpower not to slap his face. "Not yet. Maybe not ever. I've asked her to come away with me."

He had meant it. He had really meant it. And this pirate—like all pirates—would take what he wanted. I'd be his mistress, his queen. It did not matter what he called it, I would be his slave.

Nicholas glared haughtily at Salazar. "All the more reason to keep this between us. *Dismiss her*."

After a brief stare down, Salazar shrugged then kissed my hand. "Go back to the room. I'll join you in a moment."

"Yes, sir," I nodded. I could feel Nicholas's eyes on me the entire time, willing me to understand that I was meant to flee.

When I was certain Salazar wasn't looking, I snuck out through the scullery. As soon as I was outside, I bent over, bracing myself on my knees and gasped. I wasn't sure if I was retching or crying or catching my breath. An icy hand grabbed my wrist and I screamed, swinging around with a ready punch.

"It's me!" hissed Meg as she ducked under my swing. "Are you all right?"

"That man!" I sobbed. "It was awful! That man was awful!"

"Let's go."

"Nicholas is still in there!"

"I have my orders. Let's go."

She pulled me along behind her through the cobblestoned streets of Port Winslow down to the docks. The *Freedom* was anchored in the small harbor. It had been moved earlier for a quick escape—its bow was already pointed towards the open sea. Meg led me to a jollyboat and began untethering it.

"Get in."

"But Nicholas—"

Meg pushed me bodily into the boat, then shoved it into the water. "There's another jollyboat for him there. He'll be along when he can." She jogged with the boat until the water reached the thighs of her breeches, then jumped in with me.

"That man is a maniac! He means to kill Nicholas."

"Nicky's dealt with him before," Meg dipped an oar in the water.

It was twenty agonizing minutes before we reached the *Freedom*, positioned against the wind and ready to sail. I stared at the shore the entire time, hoping to see signs of Nicholas. The moon was weak and didn't offer me much light.

Emilio helped me onto the ship. "Are you all right? Did he hurt you?"

"I'm fine," I muttered. I noticed a lump at the base of the mainmast. The lump moved.

"Is that…?"

"Diogo Salazar," confirmed Emilio.

"Merciful Lord," I gasped, staring wide-eyed at the unconscious figure, "why do you have him? Mateus still has Nicholas! He'll never let him go when he discovers we have his brother!"

"He won't discover that for a long time."

I rushed to the man tied to the mast and fumbled with his ropes. "We have to release him."

Emilio pulled me back. "Diogo recognized you, Tessa. He will lead a war back to St. Kitts if he tells his brother who you are."

I trembled, thinking of Salazar's soulless eyes and cruel smile. "Do you know what he will do when he learns we killed his brother? Because I do." My hands were burning from the chafe of the ropes. The sting was nothing of what would come to us all.

"No one is going to kill him. He's too valuable. We'll take him back to St. Kitts. He may be able to tell us more about his brother's plans. If he refuses to cooperate, your father can at least ransom him."

Skidmore's voice came down from the rigging where he was letting the sails loose. "Did you get the declaration?"

I felt for the paper hidden in my bodice. "Yes. Yes, I did," I said, though my reply held no triumph. That paper meant nothing if Nicholas didn't return.

I balled my hands to push back the sting of the rope burns walked to the stern of the ship where I could keep vigil. The wind snapped my dress. Shivering, I laced my bodice up to offer more warmth. Energy surged through me, a thrill of success at getting the declaration overshadowed by my worry for Nicholas. I was shaking, bouncing, unable to hold still. I rooted myself down, placing my hands on the wooden caprail and splaying my fingers over the cedar, channeling the spirit of the wood and the sea and all their strength into me and willing it into Nicholas.

My heart fractured. I needed Nicholas. I needed to tell him I loved him. That I forgave him. That I was his forever no matter what. Why did it take this tortuous moment for me to see that?

I raised my eyes to the stars above, the stars that had seen us through so many struggles before. *Dear God, please let him come back to me.*

A shadow moved on the shore. I held my breath. Yes, a shadow, darting quickly between the buildings. "Do you see that?" My voice was weak but the wind carried my words so that Emilio, Meg, and Skidmore joined me at the stern.

The shadow got into the jollyboat and rowed towards us. I didn't breathe easily until I could see the moonlight reflecting off of Nicholas's face.

"Aweigh the anchor!" Nicholas called as he climbed the rope ladder up the side of the hull.

Grasping his wrist, Skidmore hauled Nicholas onto the deck and into a hug, each clapping the other on the back and insulting one another's part in the mission. I stood dumbfounded at their giddy boyishness. We were all doomed.

Nicholas ran his hand through his hair and turned to me. "You all right?" He was breathless.

I nodded and offered him the paper. He let out whoop and swung me around, my feet flying through the air. "Hang the British navy, luv, you just thwarted a war!"

His enthusiasm was contagious and I found myself laughing wildly as he set me down, more from hysteria than from joy. I stared at the declaration in wonder as the rest of the crew hoisted the jollyboat and raised the anchor.

The sails ballooned against the dark sky and the ship made its way towards open water, the surface of the ocean gleaming like black obsidian in the dark.

Skidmore passed bottles of wine to everyone. Nicholas raised his high. "A toast to us all! From this day forward, may legends tell of how four gormless sea dogs and one bullheaded lass saved the western world with only a pair of pistols and a pair of breasts!"

My jaw dropped with shock and I instantly covered my bosom with my hands.

Meg drank from her wine. "To Skidmore's pistols and Tessa's breasts!"

"Here, here!" Skidmore saluted.

Even Emilio piped in. "I'll drink to that!"

Try as I might, I couldn't suppress the smile that broke through my embarrassment. I clinked my bottle against Nicholas's, quietly adding, "You're not getting nearly enough credit for your part."

He shrugged as if he didn't care, and I knew that he truly didn't. Skidmore produced his flute and filled the night air with dancing music and we celebrated as only pirates could.

CHAPTER FORTY-SIX

IT WAS LATE. VERY late. The moon, having buried itself behind a gauzy layer of clouds, cast an ethereal glow on the now quiet deck of the *Freedom*. The subdued voices of Nicholas and Skidmore drifted down from the rigging where they were harnessing the wind. Meg had tripped down the hatch and fallen into a drunken sleep in the foyer over an hour ago. Emilio had vanished a little more gracefully. Diogo Salazar had regained consciousness. He alternated between spouting off insults and silently seething, no doubt plotting his revenge.

My blood was still buzzing with the events of the day. I sat quietly at the stern, hoping the night would calm me.

The men descended from the yardarms above, soaring down the lines like spiders on a web. They alighted on the deck in turn. Nicholas spoke to Salazar, his tone brassy, though I couldn't make out the words. He crouched down and patted Diogo on the cheek; Diogo spit in his face. Nicholas laughed and went to the helm while Skidmore bid the captain a goodnight and disappeared down the hatch.

I approached Nicholas. "Did Skidmore go to bed?"

He looked up from his books, startled. "You're still awake?"

"I'm still a bit rattled," I admitted. It was the wrong thing to say. Regret flared in Nicholas's eyes. I changed the subject.

"You shouldn't harass him like that," I said, glancing at our captive. "Not when he's tied up and defenseless."

"That is not a defenseless man."

"I know," I said, remembering how Nicholas made me swear to wear a weapon at all times now that Diogo was on board.

"I hear you!" Diogo hollered from across the deck. "Maggots. Traitors. You're right to be scared of me, you sod. I'll have my revenge. Tenfold. I'll have your woman, Captain. I'll have your manhood. And then I'll have your head."

Nicholas glared at Diogo with exasperation but did not bother to respond. "Let's go to the galley. Maybe some tea will settle your nerves." He led me to the hatch, his hand on the small of my back. "Start the brew. I'll see if that berk needs to relieve himself."

I lit two lanterns, the sharp smell of the flint mingling with the fragrance of the tea. I had finished pouring the tea when Nicholas entered the galley.

He looked at me for a long time. "I haven't had the chance yet to ask you. Are you truly all right?"

I held my arms out to my sides. "Not a scratch on me."

"What about other wounds? The kind that can't be seen. What happened in there?"

I placed the steaming tin mugs on the table and took a chair, gesturing for Nicholas to sit across from me. As I relayed the story, I could see two personalities warring in Nicholas—the warrior and the protector. One was pleased with the night's events; the other was disgusted.

"What happened on your side of the door?" I asked, my fingers cocooned around the hot tin mug. "Why were you even in the bordello? You were supposed to stay aboard the ketch."

"You know me. I can't let a chance for glory pass me by." He shrugged and gave me an apologetic half smile. "Charlotte let me know as soon as you had gone in. We all came downstairs ready for anything. I would have liked to have been just outside the door but that brother was standing guard with no intention of leaving."

"What happened after I left?"

"More discussion about payment. I made a few promises I don't intend to keep. Then he went to go find you and I left as fast as I could."

"I can't believe he didn't accept your money."

He rubbed the back of his neck. "I should have expected as much. He's deranged. He's violent. He's unpredictable."

"This is all my fault. I botched everything. You shouldn't have had to show yourself to him."

"Tessa. No. You were brilliant tonight. Bloody brilliant. You didn't have a single misstep. It's not your fault that Diogo was standing outside the cabin. You navigated both of the Salazars beautifully and you probably saved my life."

"It's my fault you have to pay him an impossible sum of money now."

"Hey, Tess, look at me." He placed his hand on my wrist. "I made a choice to enter into a deal with that man. And I made the choice not to pay him. It's my debt to settle. I will not let you blame yourself."

No amount of reassurance would penetrate the guilt I felt. I didn't want to burden Nicholas with it, so I changed the subject. "I still can't believe we did it."

He played with his mug. "I've never been so scared in my life. Never. There were so many ways for things to go wrong. So many ways you…I've never been so scared."

"Never? Not even with the mutiny or the church in Curaçao or all the other times you have crossed blades with someone who meant to kill you?"

He smiled sadly. "While it's true that I find myself petrified whenever you're concerned, the answer is no. Nothing has ever scared me as much as tonight."

"And yet you still let me do it."

He shrugged.

"Because it was sound strategy," I stated, hoping to validate him.

The look he gave me seemed to question my intelligence. "No. It wasn't."

"Then why?"

Quiet settled over us as Nicholas looked into his empty cup as if the answers might be hiding in his tea leaves. "You wouldn't've been happy if I had forbidden you from doing what you felt you needed to do. I care about how you feel. Very much. The decision may have been terrifying, but it wasn't a hard decision. There was no other choice to make. Your happiness is worth more than my suffering."

Looking at Nicholas, I was transported to the first time I saw him in the galley of the *Banshee*, sitting at a rough, wooden table by lantern light, just like now, my breath having vanished from my lungs at the sight of him.

Those same feelings stirred deep inside me. My blood sang through my veins with a concoction of wine and words and hope. The scent of fire behind me mingled with the scent of the sea that Nicholas carried with him. I was hypnotized by the way the firelight caressed his face, the way the shadows danced in the hollow beneath his cheekbones.

I blinked and looked away, overwhelmed.

Nicholas stood. "Are you finished?" He picked up our mugs and walked to the basin.

I followed him and when he turned around and faced me, I stated with conviction, "Yes."

"Yes?" he repeated with confusion. "Yes, you're finished?"

"No." I shook my head. "Well, yes, I am finished with the tea, but no, that's not what I what I meant."

His lips quirked up in half a smile. "Is your corset laced too tight?"

"Probably," I responded dryly, my hand absentmindedly going to my cinched waist. I steeled my nerves for what I was about to say. I looked at his face, really looked at him. I saw past his brilliant grey eyes shining with intelligence, the soft lips so ready to smile, and saw the soul behind his beauty—the soul that had suffered more than he would ever admit. I could see a young boy finding his dead mother and trying not to care that his world had shattered. I saw that boy begging for food scraps. I saw a scared stowaway captured by pirates, too proud to properly mourn the loss of his freedom, the loss of his mother, the loss of his innocence. A man who hid behind arrogance and achievement as if they were armor. Seeing him—all of him—made what I had to say that much easier.

"On this very spot you asked me if I still loved you. I never answered you. Yes."

"Oh." His mouth fell open. Seconds ticked away. "You seemed quite clear before when..." he trailed off.

"I was hurt. Afraid of being hurt worse. I still am. But I don't care anymore. I can't let another moment go by without telling you what you should already know. I love you. I am meant to be by your side. The stars know it. They have brought us together time after time, seen us through impossible situations. From the moment you lit the lantern in the galley of the *Banshee*, all I have wanted was to be something to you that no one has ever been before." I could no longer stand the distance between us. I crossed to him and placed my hands on either side of his face. "You're that person for me. I love you. You are my destiny and I am yours. I shall never let you doubt it again."

Closing his eyes, Nicholas sank into my touch. When his eyes opened again, they were blazing. "I thought I'd lost you."

"I am never lost to you. Never."

I raised my chin, my lips brushing his, my heart pounding with anticipation. He pulled back and left my kiss unmet.

"You belong to another," he explained, his voice faltering.

"No," I whispered. "I belong to you."

I raised my lips to his again but, still, Nicholas denied me.

I hooked my fingers around his baldric and tugged him to me. "Kiss me," I demanded.

Nicholas laughed, a playful gleam returning to his eyes. "Only a fool would refuse you, but we both know I am just that. I'll not be kissing you again until we are back at St. Kitts and things are properly settled with De Luca."

"Those sound like the words of a gentleman. And I have it on good authority that you are no gentleman. I cannot believe you'd make me wait."

Nicholas smiled softly and wrapped me in an embrace. Against my hair he murmured, "We are written in the stars, luv. There is time for us yet."

CHAPTER FORTY-SEVEN

I WAS STILL GROGGY but I could no longer sleep. My night had been fitful, my dreams filled with the sounds of gunshots, of Salazar's dark eyes, and of Nicholas's sweet touch.

In the last day my heart had experienced everything from pure terror to the flights of love. It couldn't take much more. A quiet day was in order. A quiet week at that. We'd be back to St. Kitts by then. I'd explain things to Emilio. I'd be free to love Nicholas without reservation—and he'd feel no guilt about loving me back.

A glance out the porthole revealed a scarlet sunrise. Despite its beauty, there was something disquieting about it. I much preferred the soft glows of amber and ivory to welcome the day. I quietly donned a lavender dress, taking care not to wake Meg, and splashed my face at the basin. The briskness of the water drove away sleep's lingering ghosts. I combed my hair, noting how it grazed my collarbones. It was growing.

I slipped out of the cabin and quietly closed the door behind me. Skidmore emerged from the lower hatch, his breeches rolled up to his knees. His feet glistened with water.

"Pumping the bilge?" I asked. I had only done the task once. Aside from the exhausting nature of the work, the water was putrid and smelly. It was a dreadful chore.

"It'll be a good day for a bath."

"I'll fill the tub after breakfast. Are you pumping alone? Do you want some help?"

He waved off my offer. "De Luca is with me."

I walked into the galley and Skidmore followed me. "Did you need something?" I asked.

"A flask of grog to quench our thirst."

"Let me get it for you." I found a flask and began to fill it. "Skidmore?"

He grunted and stepped a little closer to me.

"The red sky. Does it mean something? Isn't there a saying about a red sky being an omen of ill things?"

"Red sky at night—a sailor's delight. Red sky at morning—sailors take warning."

I nodded. "Yes, that's the one. Is there any truth to it? Or is it only whimsy?"

"Storms move eastward. When the sun is low in the sky, say at sunrise or sunset, it lights up the edges of water in the sky. If'n you see red in the morning, it means the storm is on its way. Red at night…well, the storm's already beyond you."

I cast a glance at the crimson glow outside. "You think we'll have a storm today?"

"A strong rain, leastways."

Skidmore took the flask from me. Before he left, he paused, and said, "I don't know if this sounds wrong, but I'm right proud of you for last night, Miss Monroe."

I thought on that for a moment and decided that nothing sounded better. Skidmore proud of me. I stood a little taller. "Thank you. And thank you for being there last night. You saved my life."

He nodded and shuffled to go out the door, but he didn't. There was a hesitation to his movements as if there were more to be said.

"What is it?" I prompted.

He looked away, a flush of pink stealing across his

cheeks. "Just wanted to say that I'm glad yer here, one of us now. A pirate."

"A pirate! How do you figure that?"

"You stole and plundered without a Letter of Marque. That makes you a criminal. And a damn fine one at that."

I beamed. I never thought I would relish being called a pirate.

"I used to worry about Marks. Not anymore."

Before I could ask him what exactly he meant, Skidmore vanished, leaving me smiling to myself. I placed a dish of hash on the stovetop and decided to see if the prisoner wanted to eat. To be safe, I slipped into my cabin and slung my weapons belt around my waist, the dagger Nicholas gave me resting at my left hip.

I approached Diogo with a plate of freshly sliced apples and cheese. He was struggling, fruitlessly trying to pull his legs up underneath himself. He would bend his knees, dig his boots into the deck and lift himself an inch or so off the deck, only to drop back on his rump. How miserable to have been lashed to a giant tree overnight. He probably longed for the luxury of a brig.

"My legs cramped up," he explained. "I was trying to stand. Could you...damn."

"I won't untie you."

Diogo shook his head, a sheen of sweat glistening on his brow. "I just want to stand up."

"Is there enough slack in the ropes?"

"I think so." He lifted himself up again, but couldn't get his feet underneath the weight of his body. "My legs are too cramped."

I set the plate down. "What if I helped lift you?" I hesitantly hooked my hands under his armpits and lifted. His feet scrambled and finally he stood.

He breathed out heavily, satisfaction on his face.

"Better?" I asked, dropping my hands from him.

He grunted out his thanks.

I held an apple slice to his deformed lips. He ate it silently, his eyes sweeping all around. Then he spoke. "I am a patient man. So is my brother. Tell your captain he'll live in fear for a very long time. And then, he'll live in pain."

I pressed my lips together. "I won't deliver any messages to the captain."

"Yes," Diogo said, a dark smile on his lips, "I think you will." His right hand snapped out and clamped around my neck, clenching, crushing. I dropped the plate and tried to scream, but I had no air. I heard, or rather *felt*, the sinews in my neck popping in protest. Diogo's other hand caught my right wrist, crushing it in a powerful grip.

A tingling sensation cascaded down my face. I could feel the tension of trapped blood behind my skin. I couldn't breathe. A vignette of colorful spots clouded my vision around the edges. My mouth worked, frantically trying to suck in air. I had only moments—seconds—to reclaim my life. I kicked and lobbed punches with my left arm. His grip on my neck grew tighter.

I remembered the dagger on my hip. My right arm was cemented in Diogo's grip. I'd have to fight left-handed and I'd have to use the reverse grip, but I could bury the point of the dagger into his neck.

I awkwardly unsheathed the dagger—my fingers barely had the strength to grip it. With all the fading power I had left, I raised the dagger high and brought it down hard.

Diogo saw the blade and pulled away from it, but he wasn't quick enough. The edge of the dagger opened up his face from his eyebrow to his chin.

He instantly let go of me, exhaling a curse.

The momentum of the slash propelled my arm behind me, past my hip. Instead of swinging into air like it should have, the knife met resistance right behind me and sunk into something soft. Soft and warm.

I turned to see what my knife had found.

Skidmore stood half a foot behind me.

My knife was buried to the hilt just above his left leg.

Time froze. I saw everything, heard everything. Skidmore looked curiously at the knife embedded in his groin. The cutlass he carried slipped from his hand and fell to the deck with a tinny crash. My heartbeat thundered in my ears. I sucked in a breath of air, the sudden rush of oxygen nearly drowning me. Salazar lunged forward and collected the cutlass. A flash of motion rushed by me, barreling into Salazar. It was Emilio. Before they hit the deck in a scraping thud, Emilio cried for the captain.

I felt as if a hundred years passed in a single second.

I pried my fingers off the handle of the dagger. Hardly any time had passed at all, yet my hand was coated with a glove of blood. My mouth dropped open in horror, my eyes wide with disbelief as I looked into Skidmore's face. His blue eyes were dark as sapphires in his too-pale face. His mouth hung open like mine, forming around an unheard scream.

"Captain!" Emilio screamed again, the panic in his voice piercing the muted morning.

Words, pleas, and prayers flowed from me, though I can't say if any of them escaped my lips. Skidmore looked at his wound, looked back at me, his eyes glossy with fear. He staggered back a step then slipped in the large puddle of his own blood, falling down hard, his head hitting the deck with a sickening crack.

I lunged after him, falling on my knees next to him, my hands frantic and helpless. Should I pull out the dagger? Should I cradle his head?

Emilio was still shouting, though I knew not what he said. Rough hands shoved me aside. Nicholas bent over Skidmore and saw the dagger buried in his groin. Horror washed over his face.

Screams and curses flowed from the fray behind us. Nicholas glanced over his shoulder. I followed his gaze. Emilio had been knocked to the ground. Diogo towered over him, Skidmore's cutlass poised for a killing blow. Meg was running towards him with an axe in her hand.

Nicholas grabbed my hands and flattened them against Skidmore's wound. "Push," he commanded. My hands shook as blood squirted through my fingers. "Harder!" Nicholas yelled. "Don't move the knife." He scrambled to help Emilio, screaming at me one last time to push harder.

I rose to my knees and pressed my entire weight into my hands, willing the blood to stay inside.

Skidmore lay still, staring into the sky, his eyes blinking rapidly in the pink morning light. He was not trembling or panicked, not like me. I looked at my hands, scarlet and slippery, and leaned harder into the wound. No matter what I did, red fountains erupted between my fingers. My face was covered with the spray of it. I could taste the metallic tang of it on my tongue.

Nicholas rushed back to us and crouched across from me, his eyes wild. He pressed one hand down on top of mine, his weight more than doubling the pressure I could provide. Surely this would be enough. Together, we could stop the flow of blood. With his other hand, Nicholas cupped the back of Skidmore's neck and looked into those glassy but still blinking eyes.

A garbled cry ripped from Nicholas. He looked at the wound again, covered by our bloody hands. And then he looked at me, his eyes shining with a dreadful emotion I had never seen before.

"Get back," he said, his voice muffled and low.

"I can help," I cried, still pressing on Skidmore's leg with all my might.

"Get back!" Nicholas yelled, taking his hand off mine long enough to tear me from Skidmore. He scooped Skidmore onto his lap and cradled his head in the crook of his arm while resuming pressure on the wound with his other hand.

Thunder boomed overhead and the sky shifted.

I cowered on my hands and knees, watching each harrowing moment unfold before me. Nicholas was in a frenzy, his chest heaving as he held Skidmore close to him. He pushed against the flow of blood, still unable to stymie it. He pulled the dagger out and tossed it in my direction. It skittered along the deck, coming to rest between my hands. My tears fell on the bloody blade.

Nicholas flattened the butt of his palm against the wound but the blood still flowed, not in fountains anymore but with a steady rush. Skidmore's chest barely rose and fell, his eyes jerking in their sockets. Nicholas abandoned the wound and cradled Skidmore in both arms, rocking him back and forth. Nicholas's mouth was moving, I could hear his voice, but whether he issued words of comfort or commands to survive, I'll never know. Skidmore's mouth moved. The men looked into each others' eyes for a moment, and then Nicholas did something I wouldn't have thought possible. He smiled. It was a tragic sort of expression, but it seemed to quell the fear that had been gripping Skidmore. Nicholas caressed Skidmore's face, smearing blood across his marble-white skin, and pressed his cheek to Skidmore's forehead.

Nicholas held Skidmore like that long after he stilled.

The image before me seared itself in my mind. It was strangely beautiful, the graceful lines of Nicholas's bowed head, his arms entwined around his first mate, the first raindrops of the impending storm falling on them.

"NO!" I screamed. Before I could throw myself at them, Emilio's arms snaked around me, holding me back like a harness.

I clamped my eyes and sagged against Emilio's grip on me, certain the scene would erase when I looked again. It was all a bad dream, a mistake. The universe would right itself.

A deep breath later, I opened my eyes. Nothing had changed. Skidmore's body was still, no matter how strongly

I willed it to take a breath. Nicholas cried to the sky now, rain running down his face, the sounds coming from him barely human.

I dared a glance at Diogo. He was lashed to the mast again. His face was bloody and his eye was swelling, but there was a sneer on his lips.

A quiet fury unfurled within me at the sight of Salazar's smile. Not a righteous and galvanizing sort of fury. Something darker. Something calculated. I stilled myself and Emilio loosened his grip on me. Slowly, my fingers curled around the blood-smeared handle of the knife before me. I stood, hiding the weapon in the folds of my skirt. I walked to the captive, aware of Emilio rising up to follow me.

Silent sobs rattled me as I stood face to face with our captive. I cared not that he was too valuable to die. I cared not that he was bound and defenseless. I cared not that his brother would undoubtedly avenge any harm that came to him.

Diogo's smirk grew into a contemptuous grin, his eyes dancing at the sight of me, thrilled by the chaos he had caused. I stood before him, broken and splattered in blood—a newly-minted killer. I was an inadvertent killer, true, but it didn't change the fact that I had just taken a life. Time to be deliberate about it.

He laughed at me, about to say something. I had not the patience to hear it. I plunged the dagger into his stomach. Diogo gasped, his eyes bulging with shock. I leaned in close, slowly burying the knife as deep as it would go, and just as Nicholas had taught me, I flicked my wrist and twisted the blade, never taking my eyes off Diogo Salazar's face, watching his features contort with mortal horror. Emilio was on me, shouting at me, trying to pull me away. I twisted harder, then made a horizontal yank through his belly. I pulled the dagger out and let it clatter to the deck. I walked away, pushing past Emilio, ignoring the wide-eyed stare of Nicholas, and disappeared down the ladder.

The reflection in the porthole glass that met me at the

bottom of the ladder looked like it had just escaped from a slaughterhouse. A mask of drying blood covered half my face. Crusty tendrils of hair hung in my eyes. My lavender dress was covered in a wet, red pinafore. The smell of the blood was sharp and metallic. Its flavor weighed on my tongue. My arms were coated with it and only a few patches of my own peachy skin were visible through the gore, each looking like small islands in a scarlet sea.

One thought suddenly broke through my stupor—breakfast was still on the stove. I found myself in the galley without remembering having walked there. Using a rag, I pulled the smoking dish of burned hash into the basin. The blood was drying on my hands, and it fell off my skin in rust-colored flakes into the burned breakfast.

People always talked about blood being red. And so it was when it flowed out of a person. But within moments it decayed into oranges and browns. Did Skidmore know his blood would be so orange?

I dumped the pitcher of water over my hands and scrubbed my knuckles, trying to wash away the blood. There wasn't enough water. Our ship was floating on a vast sea and yet I didn't have enough water to get the blood off my hands! I tossed the empty pitcher aside and went to the lowest compartment of the ship.

A foot of bilge sloshed over the floorboards. I sank into it, immersing my arms and face in its filth. The water swirled around me, taking on an orange stain. I scrubbed my hands, my arms, my face. Tears fell from my face, a sacrifice of my pain to purify the water I bathed in. I washed away the sight of death on me, but I couldn't escape the smell of it. The smell of copper, steel, and fresh cut apples.

CHAPTER FORTY-EIGHT

DIOGO SALAZAR WAS GIVEN a villain's burial, his body weighted and tossed overboard without formality. Skidmore was buried in St. Vincent. It was the nearest port and we found a priest to offer him a proper Christian service. The night before the burial, I watched as Nicholas slowly shaved Skidmore's chin and dressed him in clothes much nicer than I had ever seen him wear. When I asked why we weren't returning his body to his wife and children, Nicholas explained that there wasn't time before the rot began. It seemed wrong to bury him far from any who loved him. But everything about his death was wrong.

Nicholas used Skidmore's golden earrings to pay the cost of his burial. I was appalled that his valuables wouldn't be returned to his kin until Meg explained that one of the reasons sailors often wore valuable jewelry was for such a purpose— they often died away from home. The service was simple. I expected Nicholas to say something as our captain and Skidmore's closest friend, but he was silent throughout it all. It sickened me to watch the soft mud being scooped on to Skidmore's casket. It was my fault he was dead. I had killed him. I had no right to stand among his mourners and pay my respects. I left before the others and returned to the ship.

When I wasn't in the galley, I stayed in the cabin. Meg never brought up the incident, but often inquired about my health.

Emilio reached for me—physically and emotionally—but I withdrew every time. His eyes were a sea of sadness, big, black, and utterly at a loss of how to help me.

Every morning I awoke genuinely surprised that I hadn't been killed in my sleep. Surely Nicholas had every right to order me dead. I should have been marooned, hanged, or at least caged like the criminal I was. I had killed his dearest friend, the one person on earth he had dared to love.

Nearly a week of icy numbness passed when a knock sounded on my cabin door. It was late and I was lying in bed, doing all in my power to avoid sleep and the nightmares that came with it. A flame flickered in one of the sconces on the bulkhead. I couldn't stand the dark.

Before I could dismiss the knock, the door opened. Emilio.

"Are you awake?" He invited himself in and sat on the edge of the bed. I kept still. Perhaps he would think me asleep.

I heard him set something on the table beside the bed. "I brought your ring back to you."

I inhaled sharply. Never had I imagined Emilio still harboring intentions to marry me.

"*Per favore,*" Emilio begged, "I am your fiancé. Talk to me."

I rolled on to my back and looked up at him. "I cannot marry you, Emilio."

I was prepared for shock, anger, sadness, begging… something. He showed no such emotion. He smiled sadly and placed a tender hand on my cheek. "Of course."

He did not believe me. "I mean it. The engagement is off." The words I had dreaded saying for weeks came easier than I imagined. They were freeing. I wished I had said them sooner.

"I understand, *carissima*. Consider the wedding postponed."

"Not postponed—cancelled. Forever. You think it is because of Skidmore, but it's not. I cannot marry you. I never could."

Still, there was nothing in Emilio's eyes but pity. "*Sì,* it's cancelled. Whatever you wish."

"Would you please leave me, now?"

Emilio let out a mournful sound. "Please do not send me away. Suffer me to comfort you."

I turned away from my former fiancé, pretending to settle into bed, knowing full well I would not sleep. "I am tired, my lord. Please go."

He left.

I exhaled slowly, a tremble drumming through me. My future was finally severed from Emilio's. Why couldn't I have done it when it mattered?

On the other side of my cabin door, I overheard Emilio's voice. "She refuses comfort. She broke our engagement."

"She will kill herself with this self-loathing." The voice belonged to Meg.

"How I wish she would talk to me. Talk to *somebody*," Emilio said.

"She won't talk to me either. If anyone were to reach her in her sorrow, it might be the captain, but I am reluctant to ask that of him," Meg said.

Why would Nicholas want to comfort the woman who murdered Skidmore? I thought in a silent response.

"Ask what of me?"

Nicholas.

There was an awkward pause, then Emilio answered. "It's Tessa. Her grief consumes her. We thought perhaps you could speak to her."

"Why would she want to speak with me?"

"Please, Nicky, you know why."

"She will refuse me as well," said Nicholas.

Would I? A pang of hope stabbed me—I never knew hope to be so painful. My necessary exile from Nicholas had been as wrenching as my guilt. But I had no right to talk to him, let alone accept comfort from him. He was the one who deserved comfort. I deserved misery. I deserved hell.

"Please, Captain. Try."

I heard a deep exhale of breath. "I need your permission to be alone with your fiancée in her cabin," Nicholas said.

"Anything you need," Emilio agreed.

"Mind the helm. Don't interrupt us."

The door creaked. Nicholas stepped inside then closed the door behind him. I steeled my nerves. I didn't know if he would echo the hollow words that Meg or Emilio offered — that Skidmore's death wasn't really my fault — or if he would take the chance to call me a murderer to my face and damn my soul.

I felt Nicholas lay next to me. He was so still for so long that I thought he might have fallen asleep until he said, "The nights will get easier."

His first words to me since the incident surprised me. I rolled on to my back and looked at him. He was staring at the ceiling.

"The nightmares never go away, but you get used to them. You'll be able to sleep again. In the dark, even."

He knew.

I followed Nicholas's gaze to the ceiling, wondering if all the answers were there.

After another minute of silence, Nicholas said something else unexpected. "I was fifteen."

His cryptic comment worked. I was too intrigued to let it slip away.

"You were fifteen…when what?" I asked.

"When I killed someone for the first time."

I stiffened. I did not know how to have this conversation. Not with Nicholas. "I can't talk about this."

"I just want you to listen. I know a bit of what you're going through because I have walked the same path. I am the only one here who has an inkling."

I vaguely wondered about Meg's experience as a pirate, but I was too apathetic to ask.

It was as if Nicholas read my mind. "Meg has never killed outside of combat. It's different."

I lay there, staring at the ceiling, concentrating on my breathing to maintain its evenness. Every fear I had worked so hard to push away for the past few days was now surfacing.

Nicholas continued his story. "I was fifteen. I had been aboard the *Banshee* for several months, but I had avoided bloodshed. There was a lad named John, though we called him Jack. An unfortunate looking fellow who was bullied somethin' fierce by the other pirates. He was a couple of years older than me, but he was fragile in body and spirit. He'd been an outcast all his life. Run out of his village. Even though he abhorred violence, he knew that pirates accepted everyone—he thought he would find a home there. Not so. They treated him with cruelty. He was kind to me, though. We became friends.

"We had just chased down a prize ship. Our captain demanded that John kill the defeated captain. A man on his knees, already surrendered. John would be keelhauled if he didn't follow the order. It was a spiteful thing to ask of him. I knew a kill like this would stain his soul in a way he couldn't come back from. I didn't want that for my friend. The jeers and taunts from our shipmates grew. John stood there. Shaking. There were tears in his eyes. I was so angry that the pirates would break this boy in such a way. I snatched the sword from John's hands and ran the defeated captain through."

I gasped.

His voice grew quiet. "I killed a man on his knees."

I could perfectly picture the cruel group of pirates led by a sinister man like Captain Black. I could see a small, tormented boy shaking with fear. And then Nicholas grabbing the sword and killing a defenseless man in front of him with a single thrust. I shuddered.

"That moment changed me. There was no going back to what I was before." He rolled onto his side and propped himself up on his elbow. It was the first time our eyes had met since Skidmore's death.

My tears turned to open sobs. I was a killer. Like the captain that wanted a bullied boy to kill a helpless man. Like Nicholas who had done it. I thought of Captain Black and Wrack and Beck and Mendoza and all the scores of other pirates I had ever met. Each one of them had a first kill. Each one had to look at the blood of another man on their blade. Each had an innocence that was lost in that moment. Like starving Nicholas or the boy John who surely stepped into his role as a pirate just as Nicholas had. Pirates were not just overgrown boys or drunken monsters with swords as I may have thought at one time. I knew better now, for I was a pirate myself. Skidmore had said so. We were damaged beyond imagination, all of us, seeking solace and survival where we could.

I reached for Nicholas and in an instant his arms were around me. I buried my face in his chest, ugly cries pouring out of me. "I'm so sorry. I'm so sorry," I sobbed over and over again.

"Hush." Nicholas stroked my hair. "Hush now."

"I didn't mean it. It was an accident, but that doesn't matter. He's dead and it was my hand and my knife and I *killed* him, Nicholas, I killed him." I couldn't stop the words that poured from me. "He's gone forever and so are you. And so am I. Everything that mattered is gone, and no matter how hard I pushed, the blood kept coming. It was on my hands, Nicholas. It was on my face. In my *mouth*. The blood is inside me and I can't get it out and everything that mattered is dead."

"Tell me, Tessa. Tell me," whispered Nicholas.

"He smiled, Nicholas. He smiled and I couldn't stomach it. He had no right to smile. He had no right to breathe, so I took it from him. I did it calmly so Emilio wouldn't stop me. I did it swiftly before you could do it yourself, because I knew you would." I remembered the feeling of my knife sliding into his belly. I choked on a sob. "I had never felt such a pure emotion, ever. Pure hatred. I *enjoyed* it. God above forgive me, I enjoyed it."

I broke apart, convulsing, terrified of what I had become. The tears poured out of me and the words too. I wished I could have held them back, kept them dark and hidden where no one would ever know, where I could pretend they didn't exist, but they gushed from me like the blood had gushed from Skidmore. "It only lasted a minute, but it was glorious. And then I hated myself. I am stained and broken and ruined forever. I'm a killer, Nicholas. I killed two men in five minutes' time. I look down and see blood on my hands all the time. I feel it spraying on my face. I can't get it out of my mouth. I close my eyes and their faces haunt me. Your face haunts me, too. When I try to sleep I see your eyes full of dread. Your face, stricken with the inevitable. I can't stand it. I can't close my eyes. I can't sleep. I can't look at you. I can't look at myself. I wish I could just die. I can't live with what I've done. You ought to kill me. I can't do this! I can't do this. I can't. I can't. I can't." My words dissolved into sobs. Nicholas held me tenderly, stroking my hair, stroking my cheek, like our first night together in the galley when I sobbed into his chest. What a naïve girl I was then. I knew so little of loss and heartbreak.

After a long while of crying, Nicholas sat up and pulled me with him. He grabbed my shoulders and peered into my eyes. "You have to stop this. You'll make yourself mad. Don't ever wish yourself dead. Do you hear me? Ever."

I looked away.

Nicholas grabbed my chin and forced me to look into his fervent grey eyes. "What happened to Skidmore was an accident. No one blames you. I don't blame you. It was terrible and we are all upset over it, but *no one blames you*. What you did to that bastard was justified. If you hadn't killed him, I would have. He deserved to die. I can tell you two dozen stories of him raping and murdering innocent people. He was not a good man. Does that make the guilt easier? No, probably not. But it's the truth.

"Tessa, you will never be the same again. You will scream into the night. You will hate yourself. You will hate everyone who knows this about you. You will see yourself as a monster. A murderer."

Tears streamed down my cheeks.

Nicholas continued, his gaze penetrating my hysterics. "And someday…things will change. The nightmares will become dreams. The dark will no longer torment you. You'll get past it. You'll hate yourself even more for that. But it will happen."

His words spoke of hope, but I couldn't feel it. "What if I never do?"

"You will," he reassured me. "It has nothing to do with you or what you have done. It's simply a fact of time, a gift from time. Moments pass. Slowly at first. And then days pass. And then months. And then years. The world moves on and you'll move with it, whether you want to or not."

"I don't deserve to!"

"It doesn't matter. You will. Look at me. Did I deserve to move on from my past? You know as well as anyone what I have done. Yet, you found something in me worth redeeming. You pushed me towards a second chance. A third, a fourth, a hundredth chance. We don't move on because we deserve to. We do it because it is part of being human."

I met his gaze without resistance now and Nicholas released his grip on my chin. My lip quivered but the tears had stopped. I had finally run out.

"I can't go back to who I was," I stated flatly.

Nicholas shook his head. "Never."

"I don't know what to do."

Nicholas grabbed my hand without breaking our stare. "You'll create a new you."

CHAPTER FORTY-NINE

I WAS EXHAUSTED AFTER Nicholas left, but I felt different. Not renewed, never renewed, but not as full of poison and bile. I felt as though a torrent of water had surged through me and flushed away everything in my brain and heart. It hadn't left me clean…it left me empty. It was better than before.

I fought sleep, but I succumbed. I dreamed of Skidmore's dying eyes and Nicholas's frantic eyes, and when I tried to run away, I was running through a puddle of blood that grew bigger and bigger until I was swimming in it, then drowning in it. The only thing I found to grasp to keep my head above the blood was Diogo Salazar's rotting, waterlogged body.

It was the least horrific dream I'd had since the night of the murders.

The next morning I awoke alone in the bed. By the strength of the light coming in the portholes, I knew it was early. I washed and dressed, disregarding the lavender dress stiff with dried blood at the bottom of my trunk. I didn't know why I kept it. I needed to burn it.

Hushed voices came from the galley. I stood outside the door and eavesdropped. They were talking about me.

"…back to her old routines, she'll be herself again," I heard Emilio say.

"A few days back at Amerscott won't change a thing. It could even make it worse." The voice belonged to Nicholas.

"Worse?"

"Something like this alters a person. The pressure to return to who she was before can be quite damaging. Give her time. Give her space."

"Is that what she asked for?" Emilio asked.

"It's what she needs," Nicholas replied.

"What did she say to you?"

"She cried."

There was a long pause. "She cried?" Emilio's voice was disbelieving. He was wounded I had cried to Nicholas after I had refused him. I should have felt ashamed, but the capacity for that emotion was gone.

"Did she say anything?"

Nicholas exhaled. "Of course she did, but it's not my business to tell you."

Emilio's voice was stern. "I have a right to know. She's my fiancée."

"Perhaps you should reevaluate that," snapped Nicholas.

I was done listening to their bickering. I entered the galley. At another time I might have been mollified by the guilty surprise on their faces, but I felt no satisfaction. I barely felt anything at all.

Emilio crossed to me and kissed my cheek. I pulled back slightly. "Good news. St. Kitts is on the horizon. We'll be home tomorrow."

I swallowed and nodded. Part of me was so ready to be off this blasted ship, away from the horrors of this voyage, away from the bloodstain at middeck that had not yet faded. But back at St. Kitts I would face a new set of horrors. I'd face my father's wrath over the broken engagement and I would face the nightmares alone. I didn't think I could do it.

I looked at my captain. Though his head was down, he was peering up at me through his black lashes, an ineffable sadness in his eyes.

"Tomorrow," I repeated. My voice was hollow.

Emilio hovered around me. "Imagine the reception. Returning in victory. I'm sure there will be a magnificent celebration before the week's out."

I nodded at Emilio, forcing my lips to curl into a half-convincing smile.

Emilio turned to Nicholas. "You'll be hailed a hero." It was almost painful to see how hard Emilio was trying to infuse the room with a bit of delight.

"Take the praises for me, mate. I'll not be staying."

My eyes snapped to Nicholas. He wouldn't look at me.

"Surely you can stay a few nights," Emilio prodded.

Nicholas shook his head, finally risking a glance in my direction. "I'll be setting sail before the day is out."

The air seemed to grow thicker. I knew Nicholas would return to sea. He was under my father's management and Salazar was still a threat. Yet knowing he wouldn't even stay one night made me fear that once he set sail again, he would be gone forever.

Nicholas grabbed a piece of hardtack and left the galley, his eyes on the ground.

I could barely bring myself to look at Emilio when I said, "I wanted to return this to you." I held out the engagement ring.

He took a step back, as if the ring were a weapon. "Tessa, you can't."

I stared at the ring, the vibrant emeralds, the flashing diamond, the smooth gold stamped with the De Luca crest. It was by far the most beautiful, valuable thing I had ever worn. "This was a symbol of a promise. I broke that promise. You deserve your ring back."

His eyes were sadder than I ever imagined they would be. "It's not my ring."

"I can't keep it. Not after—"

"It was a gift. A birthday present. It's yours to do with as you wish, even if that is throwing it in the ocean. You've wounded me enough already. Do not give it back to me."

I escaped to the deck, the ring still gripped in my palm, a lump forming in my throat.

Meg was scouring the boards. I greeted her indifferently then meandered to the stern of the ship and draped my arms over the caprail. I held the ring in my fingers. If I let go, it would be gone forever. Emilio said I could do as much. I slipped the jewel into my pocket.

The ocean glinted with the salmon-colored sunrise. I would miss this. The colors at sea. Three hundred different shades of blue. Argent clouds. Watercolor skies.

Trying to stay too busy to think, I found a holystone and fell to my knees next to Meg, scrubbing away the brownish stain that had once belonged in Skidmore's veins.

Dinner was a disparate event. Emilio and Meg tried to drum up enthusiasm for tomorrow's debarkation while Nicholas and I sat in individual pools of silence. My eyes strayed to the empty chair at the table. I pushed my plate away. I could no longer pretend to eat.

Not long after dinner, Meg found me organizing the storage room. "It's going to be odd tomorrow, isn't it?" The yellow glow of the lantern she held made her hair shimmer like a net of gold. "You'll be Miss Monroe again and I'll be drawing baths and sweeping floors."

I frowned. "I thought you'd be staying here."

Sorrow passed over Meg's pretty features. "The captain doesn't want me to stay, even if I wanted to, which I am not sure I do."

Not knowing what else to say to her, I turned my attention back to the jars of food and crates of supplies. Meg stood in awkward silence for a time. Then she said, "It's late. I'm turning in."

I nodded without bothering to look at her.

"Oh. Nicky's in the galley. He wants to see to you before you go to bed."

Everything inside me twisted. I had expected he would vanish from St. Kitts again as he had after accepting the Letter of Marque. I didn't think I could bear a formal farewell.

I waited a half hour before going into the galley, hoping, perhaps, that Nicholas would be gone. He was still there. A few lanterns blazed from hooks on the low ceiling, illuminating what he was doing. Skidmore's duffel bag and all its contents were spread across the table. I stopped short and a high-pitched noise sounded at the back of my throat.

Nicholas looked up, his eyes brimming with sympathy. "Come in."

I managed to take a single step forward.

Nicholas lifted something off the table, his hands encircling the object. He closed the distance between us and handed it to me. It was Skidmore's flute. "You should have this."

My head slowly shook from side to side. "I can't."

"He'd want you to have it."

I stared at the flute in my hands. It was nicked and battered, the blonde wood faded and dull. "It should go to his wife."

Nicholas nodded slowly, considering my words, and gestured to the display on the table. "Aside from a few mementos for me, everything else goes to her. He adored you. He'd want you to have something. Take what reminds you of him best."

My eyes skimmed the table without really focusing. The stacks of clothing and piles of trinkets were bits of a shattered vase that would never be put back together. All that was left of him. I didn't deserve anything, but in truth, I wanted something. I closed my hands tightly around the flute, claiming it.

Nicholas noticed and turned back to the table. He set aside Skidmore's baldric and hat for himself and packed the rest of the items neatly into the duffel.

"You didn't eat much at supper. Are you hungry?" he asked as he finished clearing the table.

"I am constantly hungry yet when I try to eat..." I shrugged.

"Me too."

My fingers rubbed the smooth wood of the flute. I wondered if I could ever stand to hear its music again. I walked to the nearest porthole and stared out. Twilight swept across the sky in a depressing arc of indigo. Fat clouds billowed over the horizon, giving the feeling that the sky was closing in on itself. It was a good night for mourning.

"Why won't you stay?" I asked, my gaze still fixed on the gloomy seascape.

"I have obligations," he said quietly.

"Your obligations can wait a few days. I've told Lord De Luca that I cannot marry him." I turned and looked at him. "I am all yours now."

His shoulders slumped and his face pulled down, lines forming at his mouth. I had hoped for more excitement.

"I mean, if you'll have me," I added quietly to blunt the sting of the rejection I could clearly see on his face. "I understand if you don't want me. After what I did, I don't blame —"

"Shh!" Nicholas rushed to me and grabbed my shoulders. "Don't ever think that. I want you. I want you more than I have ever wanted anything. And that is exactly why I have to go. Because if I do not appease Salazar, he will find what I love and destroy it. He'll destroy you."

"But there's no way you'll be able to pay him back in time. You should stay off the water. Stay in St. Kitts."

He shook his head. "He knows I'll be there."

"Then we'll go somewhere else!" I cried. "We'll run away. We'll hide together."

"I cannot hide from that man!" he shouted.

"Hang your pride, Nicholas. If hiding is what will keep us alive and together —"

"This isn't about pride!" he erupted. Despite his anger, there was something sharp and vulnerable in his tone. Something that sounded desperate. "It's about keeping you safe! Don't you understand that? Salazar knows of my connection to St. Kitts. It won't be long until he knows about you. He'll go after you—"

"You'll protect me."

He scoffed. "While I appreciate your faith in me, I cannot protect you from what he will do. He will cause you any pain he can simply because he knows your pain will hurt me more than anything else. He'll attack St. Kitts. He'll burn Amerscott down. He'll kill Mr. Dean. Miss Maisley. De Luca. Your father. Those are the things I must protect you from. And I cannot do that if I am in hiding with you."

"So you'll leave and he'll come after me anyway. I'm no safer without you." There was a tragic look on his face. He knew that already—he knew I was not safe with or without him—not as long as Salazar was alive. A quiet fear crept into my stomach. "When you say you're leaving tomorrow, where are you going?" The expression on his face told me everything, but I needed to hear the words. "Nicholas, where are you going? What are you going to do?"

"I have to go to Salazar."

My throat was dry. "But he'll kill you." The words were barely more than a whisper.

"Maybe."

"He said if you came to him and bent your knee and bowed your head, he'd show mercy and give you a swift death. Is that what you're after?"

He looked at me with a terrifying conviction. He placed his hand on my face, his thumb skimming my cheekbone. "My death will protect you. I'd die a thousand deaths to keep you safe."

"No!" I tore his hand away from my face. "You can't just give yourself up for slaughter!"

He frowned. "You know me better than that. I mean to kill him before he kills me."

"His men…his crew…you'll need a fleet to survive this. My father could send the navy with you. Your victory would be certain."

Nicholas smiled tightly and gave a sympathetic nod. He had already dismissed the idea. It was like talking to a wall. "Declaration or no, Salazar is hell-bent on stirring up a war and I think he will start at St. Kitts. You will need your navy right where it is."

Fragmented thoughts raced through my mind. I grasped at them, desperately trying to piece together some kind of coherent, infallible argument. "He gave you until the end of the year to settle your debt. You have three months to come up with something else. This doesn't have to be decided today.""This is the only way I can guarantee your safety." He was calm. Resigned. It made me furious. "I've crossed him. And by now he must suspect me in his brother's disappearance. He'll want more penance from me than an exorbitant amount of money. I cannot count on him to keep the deadline. He'll do something unthinkable. If I go to him quickly, confidently, it might temper his suspicions about Diogo's disappearance."

I closed my eyes. I felt like I was running in a labyrinth and every avenue was a dead end.

Nicholas touched my face again. "It's the only chance I have of protecting you. My reasons for intercepting that bastard are entirely selfish, but I might even derail a war. So why not give it a go?" He gave me a boyish smile.

His quip had no effect on me. I shook my head slowly, refusing to believe the inevitable. "Your life is not yours to throw away!" I cried. "Part of you belongs to me."

Nicholas smiled sadly. "Nor is it mine to keep. You gave me a glimpse at a different life. It was beautiful and I have loved every moment of it. But it never was mine. My life has always been forfeit, Tessa, ever since I became a pirate. But you've given it a purpose. At least now I've found some honor in my life, and if I die, there will be honor in that too. Because I'll be dying to save you."

I closed my eyes and bit down hard on my lip to keep it from trembling.

"Tessa?" he asked softly. I looked into his face. His eyes were wide and gleaming, his lips softly parted. The warrior's conviction from moments before was gone and now he was simply a boy who looked as scared as I felt. "It's our last night. I can't help but feel we should pass it together. Will you stay with me?"

I nodded. "I don't want to sleep. If I only have you until sunrise, I don't want to waste a minute of it."

"We'll get some blankets and huddle together on the deck. We won't sleep."

"What about the others?"

Nicholas glanced at the doorway. "I've issued an all night in. No watches tonight. Quin and De Luca are already asleep. I'll furl the sails and drop the anchor. The night is ours."

He squeezed my hand. The touch was like a healing tonic and I needed more of it. I sank against his chest and wrapped my arms around him. His body welcomed mine, his arms sliding up my back and his chin resting on my head.

"Let's go," he murmured and I felt the warmth of his breath against my hair.

CHAPTER FIFTY

THE NIGHT CAST A spell on us. Cocooned under the low hanging clouds, we lay on the deck, tucked together in a tangle of blankets and limbs, the ocean rocking us gently. My head rested on Nicholas's chest. One of his hands was interlocked with mine. His other hand traced circles on my back. The universe had granted our troubled hearts a respite, if only for this night. Like all enchantments, it was temporary. It would be broken with the dawn.

Grief engulfed me. I had barely gotten my Nicholas back—first from the misunderstanding with Emilio and then from the sorrows of Skidmore's tragic death—and he was as good as gone again. I pushed those thoughts away and focused on the moment. The feel of his breath on my cheek. The sound of his voice. The warmth of his touch.

The conversation between us flitted like a butterfly, landing lightly on one topic before quietly dissipating and drifting to another. I tried not to notice the march of the moon across the sky. The clouds shielded me from that reality as best they could, but the truth was there: the night was diminishing.

I shivered and Nicholas tucked a blanket tighter around me.

"What's on your mind?" he asked.

"The sunrise is coming soon," I answered. "I wish there were a way to stop it."

"There's a Greek legend about a god who drives the sun across the sky in a chariot. It would be more than welcome if he were a bit late for his watch today."

The moon approached the far side of the sky and changed from a silvery, white slice to a buttery shade of yellow. The sky was still dark. The sun had not encroached on us yet, but I knew it soon would. Every breath brought sunrise closer. Every breath was a labor.

"Nicholas?" I asked hesitantly.

"Mmm?"

"Why won't you stay? Just for a few days? Two or three days won't matter at all."

He was quiet for a long time. Finally, he answered me. "If I stay one day, I'll stay a thousand."

"I know," I whispered, the air in my lungs feeling as heavy as salt water.

Nicholas ran his fingers down my back. "I need to tell you something."

"Hmm?" I murmured.

His fingers stopped moving and he was still. "I love you."

They were the words I had longed to hear, words I worried he would never—could never—say. A month ago—even a mere week ago—those words would have made my heart soar. Those words should have changed everything, but they changed nothing. And for him to say them on this night, just hours before our permanent parting, was a rare form of torture. A finishing blow to my already riven heart.

He looked deeply in to my eyes and his fingers traced the lines of my lips. He looked like a man in love. "I used to think that love equaled possession. Belonging to someone. Having them belong to you. A ring. A promise. A vow. I was wrong. Love is a crucible. The heat of it burns you away until there is nothing left of the individual. What survives reforms into a devotion so pure it cannot be sullied by greed or jealousy or lust or any other by-product of possession. I love you and it has transformed me. It has changed the way that blood flows through me. I would call it a fatal condition but I know it will last beyond even death."

If love wasn't transformative in its own right, his words were. Looking into his burning grey eyes and listening to the most beautiful, most tragic confession of love I had ever imagined, I felt my soul entwining with his, reshaping itself, never to be the same again.

"Oh, Nicholas." I laid a hand on his cheek. He felt feverish but it was only because I was so cold. "I love you, too. It's the most intense, real thing I've ever felt. And it's killing me."

He stared at me with searching eyes. I could see their color better now—striations of blue and slate in the soft grey—and I knew the sky was lightening. "I did not want my words to hurt you. But I need you to know that I will never stop loving you and I will always do what is best for you. It's from this place of eternal devotion that I say this to you now," he closed his eyes briefly as if he were gathering strength, then stared at me with burning conviction, "I want you to marry De Luca."

I opened my mouth to protest, but he placed a finger over my lips.

"He is a good man and he will take care of you always. You need to move on from this ill-fated interlude with me and reclaim your life."

I pulled his hand away from my mouth. "No. This is not some ill-fated interlude. You said it yourself—we are written in the stars."

His face was taut with agony. "Then we must defy destiny." Soft fingers brushed away my tears. "If you love me, you'll do this for me. You'll make the happiest life possible for yourself."

"No," I cried, pulling away from him and burying my face

in my hands. "No. Why would you even ask that of me? You talk as if our parting is permanent."

"Tessa. I think it is."

"No! It isn't! You'll kill Salazar and you'll be back. I will wait for you."

"Tessa," he said my name again as if it were some kind of protective ward, "you can't wait for me. I'll be months just trying to find Salazar. He'll have an army around him that I'll have to get through. If he doesn't kill me on the spot, he'll keep me as a slave. And only then will I be close enough to kill him. If I'm successful, his men will retaliate against me. Chances of my survival are minuscule. I will not have you waste your life waiting forever for a dead man."

"That choice is mine to make, not yours."

"Don't be angry, Tessa. I know it's too much to think about it right now. But in a few months when you're lonely, when you fully feel my absence, consider the wisdom of my request. Don't be lonely. De Luca loves you. He'll provide for you. I know you get along with him. Your father admires him. So do I."

"I cannot do it, Nicholas. I am in love with *you*!"

"And I you. Nothing will change how we feel about each other, not even your marriage to him. Find peace and stability and a shred of comfort. I'm begging you. It's a dying man's wish and it's in your power to give it to me."

I lifted my hand to his face. My fingers trembled as I gently caressed the planes of his cheek. "I have too many dreams for us and I just can't walk away from them."

Nicholas looked at the sky. A patchwork of starlight shone through the drifting clouds. "Remember our first night on the ketch and we talked about our mothers and how they were immortalized in the stars? I had dreams of us, too, Tessa. Dreams that should have had the chance to live and breathe and become memories. A lifetime's worth. You're right—they are too precious to simply discard. Tonight is our last night on the ketch. Let's immortalize them in the same fashion."

He looked at me expectantly, but I was unsure what he wanted me to say.

"Tell me one of your dreams," he whispered. "One of those memories that will never be."

I took an unsteady breath. "Walking through Basseterre with you. Tomorrow."

He nodded his head once and pointed out a star. "That star is for that memory."

How simple a wish that was. Nothing bombastic. Just the hope of Nicholas in my life for one more day. But that hope was gone now. It had been taken from my heart and hung on a star a thousand miles out of reach.

"Tell me another one," said Nicholas.

My jaw was clenched to control the shaking in my voice. I shook my head.

He took a turn. "I always thought I would teach you to shoot my flintlock. I can only imagine how entertaining that would be. In the end, you'd be an impressive shot. That memory goes there, with that star." He pointed out another pinprick of light. "Go again, Tessa. The stars are waitin'."

I swallowed hard. "Finally cooking something for you that you liked."

He laughed. "Well done! It goes with that star there. How about our first fight? I suppose we've already been there." He gestured broadly. "We're both stubborn. We'll say this quadrant of the sky is reserved for a lifetime of quarrels. And this quadrant," he made another sweeping gesture in the other direction, "is for each time we reconcile."

Tears spilled out of my eyes and silently trickled down my face. I didn't bother to wipe them away.

"It's your turn now," he said.

I shook my head. I couldn't do this. It didn't matter how romantic this was, the finality of it all was too tragic.

Nicholas continued without me. "That star there, that's me taking you to Barbados to show you where I was born. And that star...see it? It's me going to your father and hopefully surviving with all my limbs intact as I tell him how I feel about you. That star below it is a bouquet of wildflowers on a day you're feelin' down."

Tears blurred my vision. I couldn't keep up with him as he ticked off stars and pretend memories of the life we would never have.

"Oh look—Venus." He pointed to a very bright star shining through the clouds. "Brightest star in the night sky. Especially bright at twilight and dawn. The ancients thought they were separate stars. Called them the evening star and the morning star. It deserves somethin' special. Venus gets the memory of standing across from you in a church and making you my wife."

Sobs broke free and my hands covered my face. Nicholas held me tighter but he didn't stop. His voice was soft. "Building you a house. The nightly routines that would become second nature. You carrying my child. Arguing about names. Building him a cradle. We need half the universe alone for all our kisses—a kiss every morning, a kiss every night, so many kisses between. That star there, for you waking up in my bed for the first time. And this star for the mundane things I want so badly with you—going to the mercantile on a Saturday for flour and fabric."

"Stop," I whispered, barely able to form my lips around the word.

He turned his face to mine. "There aren't enough stars in the sky for this."

"No more," I said, sobbing. "I can't bear it."

He pulled me to his chest and rubbed my back. "I'm so sorry."

I lay like that until I noticed the sky lightening. There was no brightness to it yet, but stars began to wink away and the sky turned from black to inky blue.

I turned my tear-soaked face up to Nicholas. "I want something of you before morning comes."

"Tell me."

"I want you to kiss me."

His expression grew anxious. "Tess...it will only make sunrise harder."

"No. No, it won't make it any harder than it already is. Take one of those kisses from the stars and give it to me now. Give me a real memory."

Nicholas sat up and pulled me with him, our legs stretching out in opposite directions. He looked at me fervently, reverently, and stroked my cheek with his knuckles. He moved his hands behind my head and released my hair from its pins. Messy tendrils fell around my face and brushed against my cheeks like sheets of satin. He tucked a lock of hair behind my ear then traced the line of my jaw with a single finger, and lifted my chin up. He sighed, an aching sound of pleasure mixed with pain. Then with his fingers in my hair, his thumbs on my face, he gently guided me into his kiss.

His lips moved slowly against mine, their steady heat melting me, blurring the edges of my existence until I became part of him. I wanted more. I wanted him to consume me. I grabbed the front of his shirt in a fist and pulled him hard towards me, yearning, desperate, and frantic. Nicholas placed a hand over mine, his touch calming me, silently telling me to let go. This was not that kind of kiss. I released his shirt and surrendered my expectations, slowly entwining my fingers in his hair and letting him lead me in his quiet fervor.

This was not a kiss of barely contained desire like so many of our other encounters. It was a kiss of worship. A kiss of sorrow. This...this was a goodbye kiss. There was such tenderness in the way Nicholas held my face, as though I was something precious—something too fragile and too priceless to handle with anything but the most delicate touch. Like lace that might turn to dust in a hard wind. My throat tightened and tears welled behind my closed eyelids. I blotted out thoughts of the coming day, thoughts of even the next five minutes, and existed only in this kiss.

Nicholas expertly brushed my tears away and pressed his mouth harder into mine like the pressure of his lips would somehow stop the flow of the tears, the way the pressure on Skidmore was supposed to stop the flow of his blood.

I tried to memorize everything about Nicholas. The smell of salt and wind and endless summer. The stray tendrils of his hair as they glanced across at my cheekbones. The pillowy softness of his lips. The way he could make my skin bloom with just the brush of his fingertips.

And when the kiss was ended, I stared at him with my emotions bared, water shimmering in my eyes and simply said, "I love you."

A smear of gold stained the eastern sky, a harbinger of day. I stood up and walked to the starboard railing and stared in grim acceptance as light broke on the horizon and sent a spattering of sparkles across the waves. The sight should have been beautiful. I hated it. Nicholas's arms wrapped silently around me. I turned in to his embrace, my head tucked under his chin, and memorized the shape of his body, the sound of his heart.

"What happens now?" I asked.

"I will hold you until the sun crests over the water. Then I'll sound the bell." His voice was measured. "You will go to the galley and make breakfast. We'll raise anchor and navigate into the harbor." He pointed to a green island looming in front of the ship. I hadn't realized we were so close. "And then," his voice caught, "you'll walk up the deck with Lord De Luca, that damn ring on your finger. You will get in a carriage and you will go to where you belong."

"And you?"

He didn't answer.

Our hearts beat against each other for those last few moments. The smudge of light on the horizon flooded the sky with its fire, turning the clouds above us into a canopy of flame. The morning star lingered long after the other stars had vanished, but it held no power against the dawn, finally fading away. The sun lifted itself from its sleeping chambers, a perfect orange orb above the water. Nicholas let go of me, and I was instantly cold. I stared straight ahead and clutched the caprail. My knuckles were white.

The bell rang.

The End

Photograph by Jason Miller www.millcreekphoto.net.

Born and raised in Idaho Falls, Idaho, Lara is the youngest of five children. She had to be pretty dramatic to get any attention whatsoever. She has since learned to channel her theatrics into writing.

At age seventeen, Lara's poetry and a short story was published in an anthology of teen writers. Lara has since utilized her writing skills as a technical writer and creative copywriter.

Lara holds a degree in psychology from the University of Idaho. She lives with her husband, two daughters, and four pets in southeast Idaho. She hates Oreos and loves brownies.

She is the author of the young adult historical adventures *Oceanswept* and *Undertow* and is currently working on the final installment of the trilogy. To learn more about Lara and her books, visit larahays.com or follow her on at Facebook.com/ LaraHaysAuthor.

Printed in Great Britain
by Amazon

47396897R00262